COURAGE

COURAGE

A Novel

The Eventing Series
BOOK THREE

NATALIE KELLER REINERT

FLATIRON
BOOKS
NEW YORK

COURAGE. Copyright © 2017, 2025 by Natalie Keller Reinert. All rights reserved. Printed in the United States of America. For information, address Flatiron Books, 120 Broadway, New York, NY 10271.

www.flatironbooks.com

Designed by Gabriel Guma

Library of Congress Cataloging-in-Publication Data

Names: Reinert, Natalie Keller, author.
Title: Courage : a novel / Natalie Keller Reinert.
Description: First Flatiron Books edition. | New York : Flatiron Books, 2025. | Series: The eventing series ; book 3
Identifiers: LCCN 2024043193 | ISBN 9781250387752 (trade paperback) | ISBN 9781250387769 (ebook)
Subjects: LCGFT: Romance fiction. | Sports fiction. | Novels.
Classification: LCC PS3618.E564548 C68 2025 | DDC 813/.6— dc23/eng/20240916
LC record available at https://lccn.loc.gov/2024043193

Our books may be purchased in bulk for promotional, educational, or business use. Please contact your local bookseller or the Macmillan Corporate and Premium Sales Department at 1-800-221-7945, extension 5442, or by email at MacmillanSpecialMarkets@macmillan.com.

Originally self-published in 2017 by Natalie Keller Reinert

First Flatiron Books Edition: 2025

10 9 8 7 6 5 4 3 2 1

COURAGE

1

THE BAY FILLY eyeballed me, her dark iris small against her bright white sclera, her expression nervous.

"I agree," I told her sympathetically. "I think this is a terrible idea. But here we are."

There was every chance I was going to get hurt this morning. Would it at least make the blogs? I could see the headlines now: *Jules Thornton, professional three-day event rider, injured in training track accident. Reports are the rising star was just trying to keep her head above water, both financially and emotionally. The racing stable head trainer was heard to say, "That girl has no business getting on racehorses, but we're short-handed this morning so leg her up."*

Except no one seemed to be planning to give me a leg up. I was alone with a small, wild-eyed Thoroughbred filly, and I had no idea what to do next.

Down the barn aisle, there was a bang of hooves against wood and a harsh shout. I was jolted out of my imagined obituary as neglected hinges shrieked a few feet away, and suddenly there was a clatter of horseshoes on hard ground before another young horse appeared, prancing nervously outside the stall where the filly and I lurked. Balanced on the horse's tiny exercise saddle was a short, sharp-faced man, glaring through the stall bars at me.

"What're you waitin' for? Let's get goin'!" His Appalachian accent was a full-on banjo, plucking a new string with every syllable. I could barely understand him, but that didn't matter; it was easy to tell what he wanted: me in the saddle and caught up with him in the next thirty seconds. He kicked his horse on and the wide-eyed little Thoroughbred beneath him jumped forward, flimsily shod hooves sliding on the asphalt barn aisle. "Hurry up!" he shouted as they disappeared from view. "We goin'!"

I looked at the stirrup dangling in the vicinity of my left ear and wondered how on earth he expected me to mount up. I wasn't used to the little exercise saddle, and I was pretty sure most exercise riders got a leg up from grooms. But something told me this ramshackle shed wasn't your typical racing barn. Maybe I'd never ridden a racehorse before, but I'd seen where they lived, and none of the training barns I'd seen before looked like this place.

I was getting the distinct feeling I'd chosen my first gallop-girl position very poorly.

Down the aisle, an unseen groom—presumably the one who had tacked up this filly and left her for me to find—switched on the radio.

"It's six A.M., time to rise and shine, Ocala! We're rocking on the wind with all the classic hits you love!"

If I needed the impetus to find a way onto this horse and out of this barn, the end of the commercial break on Ocala's six-song classic rock station was it. I'd heard about as much of their limited playlist as I could handle—WIND was the soundtrack of every feed store, farm supply depot, and gas station in town. North Central Florida seemed to have a serious Pink Floyd problem.

"Okay, little girl," I told the filly. "I'm gonna lengthen this stirrup and get on you, so no freaking out on me, got it? You're getting plenty of warning."

The filly shook her fuzzy black forelock out of her eyes and gazed anxiously through the stall bars, hoping to see her work mate waiting for her. When she realized he really had left the barn without her, she whinnied plaintively and started turning a circle in her stall. I went with her, pulling down the left stirrup as she wheeled. The moment she stopped, I hiked up my leg, stuck my boot in the stirrup, and mounted.

Well, almost mounted. The tiny exercise saddle, lacking a tree, didn't exactly stay put on her back. Instead, it slid halfway around the filly's barrel the moment my weight hit the iron, landing my right foot back on the ground where it had started. I nearly laughed, but the filly didn't see the joke. She snorted and kicked at the saddle with her near hind hoof, narrowly missing my thigh. I danced out of her way just in time, the smile wiped off my face. I felt my temper rising, along with a dangerous desire to march right out of this barn and go straight home to my own horses and my own saddles, which stayed put when I mounted up.

But that wasn't an option.

The filly and I regarded each other for a moment. She blew out her breath in a ruffling horse sigh.

I sighed in return. "Come on, mama. Can we just go outside and play racehorse?"

While I struggled to get the saddle back in place and girthed up more tightly, I heard the banjo voice cussing me out from somewhere outside the barn, wondering what was taking the new girl so long.

This guy is going to be my coworker, I thought grimly. *This is my life now.*

I wished I could just go home. Take my hard hat and my whip, my safety vest and my coffee mug, and get back in my truck for Briar Hill.

I'd slip through the front door of the low-slung stucco house, walk down the hallway lined with photos of Pete's grandfather eventing around the world, and creep back into bed, where I'd pull the covers up tight and try not to wake Pete.

We'd steal an extra hour in the luxury of cotton sheets, and I wouldn't have to feel nervous and sick about being in someone else's barn, riding someone else's horses, trying to make someone else happy, when I had no idea what I was doing.

No chance of that, though. Life had changed, yet again, just when I thought everything was coming together. Pete wasn't even home, and if he had been, he wouldn't have wanted my company.

I'd returned to Briar Hill in late August from a summer apprenticeship at a show barn near Orlando, ready to slip back into my old life. No—ready to be better at it. I had all sorts of lofty goals. I would be a better partner for Pete, who'd taken me in when my farm was destroyed by a hurricane over a year ago, and who then became the one thing I swore I'd never have: an equestrian boyfriend. I was determined to be a better trainer for my horses and for my clients, who deserved a rider who truly dedicated herself to three-day eventing, even if that meant riding a lot more dressage than she liked.

Why stop there? I'd decided I would be a better person in general: less harsh-toned and thin-skinned, more caring and mellow. I'd spent the summer learning to swallow my pride and accept that I wasn't always the best, that I had more to learn. That lesson went far beyond riding.

Naturally, the moment I had a self-improvement plan firmly in place, the earth tilted.

Briar Hill, the farm we loved, might not be our home for much longer. For years, Pete had lived with the reality that his grandmother planned on selling the farm where his grandfather had raised champion event horses. She couldn't let go of her bitter hatred of the sport that claimed her husband's life, and before Pete could prove to her that she would be saving his life, not destroying it, if he was allowed to keep the farm, she'd died. Her death had come suddenly, leaving Pete in shock.

Even if I wasn't already terrified of losing my home twice in less than two years, I still would have been terrible at comforting him. Sympathy wasn't something I'd been offered much in life, and unfortunately, in my case it appeared to be a learned behavior. I barely knew how to offer anything more than a few stuttered words, most of which were incoherent gibberish, when I was in the presence of any extreme emotions. Pete's tears rendered me speechless.

There was also the awful fact that Pete didn't particularly want my comfort.

Maybe that was for the best, since I wasn't exactly the world's best hugger, but I didn't like the reason.

Yes, I'd threatened all summer to give up the apprenticeship and come home, which would have cost us the sponsorship we badly needed to keep the farm running. Sure, that had been shitty of me. But I *hadn't* come home early, and we *had* the sponsorship, and still, Pete wasn't ready to forgive me.

He watched me warily, and when I made one of my signature big, bold proclamations about our glorious future, his smile was twisted. He was waiting for me to get bored or mad or both, and leave. In my more annoyed moments, I considered giving him what he wanted. But then that would have been giving in, and Jules Thornton never, ever gave in.

Anyway, things weren't all terrible.

Sometimes he forgot he was still determined to be angry with me.

Sometimes he looked at me with a twinkle in his eye and quirked that damn eyebrow of his, and I thought he'd forgiven me. I thought we'd go back to the way things had been. I'd tease him, and he'd tease me back, and everything would be fine.

But it always went back to this new, wary Pete in the end, the Pete who thought I'd been untrustworthy. I stuck around for the old Pete; I reasoned no one could stay mad about such a slight mistake forever. And also, of course, I had nowhere to go. I lived at Briar Hill Farm and, more importantly, so did all my horses.

Leaving was out of the question, even if I'd wanted to give up on him, so all I could do was to try and fix our problems. And that meant lots of hard work. Fortunately, I was good at working. I'd been working since I was ten. That was fourteen years of non-stop hard physical labor. If I couldn't be nice, at least I could be industrious.

Lucky for me, that was exactly what we needed: the ability to keep noses firmly pressed to grindstones. We were going to try and keep the farm, but that meant money: money for attorneys, and also for insurance premiums and taxes and a hundred other bills that had previously bypassed our mailbox. Who knew Pete's grandmother had been paying for so much? Pete had told me that he was hanging on by the skin of his teeth, but the size of the farm had always dazzled me a bit. I could never have guessed how much a property like this actually cost in upkeep. Life, I was beginning to understand, would remain a struggle even if we managed to stop the sale of the farm. This was mildly disappointing but not altogether surprising.

Either way, here I was, in someone else's barn yet again. *Just like summer,* I told myself, *just like working for Grace.* I knew that wasn't true, though. This time, I was in way over my head.

I gazed at the filly and she gazed back, the tension in her muscles clearly showing in the dim glow of the stall's bare lightbulb.

"I *have* to get on you," I said. "So, you need to chill the hell out and let me get up."

Her ears flicked.

"Need a hand?" I turned as a groom slipped into the stall, and, without giving me any judgmental looks or anything, he grabbed the saddle's billets and tightened the girth strap a few more notches. The filly grunted.

"Sometime they get the swelling," he explained, shoving the girth up another hole. The filly staggered a little as he threw his weight into the job. "The hematoma, you know? But you put it up all the way anyway. They gonna get tough after a few time, and you don't lose the saddle while you galloping."

That sounded like a fair tradeoff on a morning straight out of hell. I would feel bad if the filly got a hematoma under her elbow, but I'd feel worse with her hooves slapping against my face when the saddle slid under her belly midstride.

I nodded and smiled to show my appreciation.

The groom grinned at me companionably. He was a young guy, Latino, wearing a blue Gators shirt and a flat-billed Brooklyn Nets cap, the holographic sticker still shining on the brim. He looked like he'd be perfectly at home on a city street, instead of standing in the stall of an Ocala racehorse training barn, holding the reins of a green racehorse-to-be. "I get you up there," he assured me. "You watch this."

He held the stirrup away from the filly's side until the stirrup leather was taut, then slapped the strap against the saddle a few times. The filly's ears swiveled in alarm and she shifted, standing up straight and tall. Her spine hollowed.

A horse with a high head couldn't hold a hump in her back, couldn't throw a buck as soon as a rider mounted. Well, would you look at that. Just past six in the morning and I'd already learned a clever new trick.

The groom cupped his hands, the universal symbol for a leg up. I breathed a sigh of relief and put my left knee in his palms. "One—two—three!" I pushed off the ground with my right foot as he pushed my knee up, and just like that, I was on top of the bay filly at last, nudging my feet into the short stirrups while she circled the stall impatiently, shuffling her hooves through the dirty straw.

"Make 'em longer," the groom instructed, taking the filly's reins and pulling her up to an uneven halt. She flung up her head and clicked her teeth together, but he ignored her with the aplomb of a racetracker, an easygoing attitude that came from either innocence or experience, I couldn't decide which. "You know the saying? The longer you ride, the longer you ride."

That didn't sound like any saying I'd ever heard. I looked at my knees, bent close to the pommel of the exercise saddle. I certainly looked like a jockey.

"Really? I thought I was supposed to keep them short in this saddle."

"Nah, mami. Only for breezing. And you ain't gonna breeze this baby. She just going for a gallop. So make 'em long and keep your feet in front of you, okay? You got this."

I lengthened the stirrups until they were closer to my regular jumping length, banging just above my ankle bone when I let my legs hang loose. The groom nodded. "Jus' hang on and follow Billy Joe," he advised. "You be fine. No problem."

I poked my boots back in the irons, and realized they didn't have any tread. No rubber pads, or even a thick wrapping of latex to give me some grip. "No stirrup pads?" I raised my eyebrows at the groom. "Seriously?"

He shrugged and turned away, opening the door as wide as it would go. "You be fine," he repeated. "Remember you duck you head on the way out."

The filly made a beeline for the open door, and I fumbled with the fat racing reins, hastily tying a knot in the impossibly long stretch of nylon between the rubber and the buckle.

I have my doubts, I thought. *I have my doubts.*

There was a bundle of nerves in my stomach, and I briefly considered leaping off and leaving the wide-eyed filly with this guy. He could explain how the fancy English-riding girl got nerves and couldn't hack it as an exercise rider. He and Billy Joe could laugh about how those eventing girls acted so tough but didn't even have the balls to take a horse around a racetrack. It was fine. I didn't mind at all. The alternative, which was rapidly appearing to be my imminent death, seemed a pretty high price to pay for my reputation, and I wasn't as concerned about the way others saw me as I used to be.

Still, the other, other alternative was not having enough money to keep a roof over my horses' heads, to say nothing of my own. I had a barnful of horses at home. Them, plus the constant specter of Pete's distrust, made my mind up for me. He was waiting for me to cop out. Proving him wrong was the most important job I had right now, if only because he was annoying me.

I shoved my feet home as far as they'd go in the slippery stirrups and guided the filly through the door, swaying dangerously in the unfamiliar flat saddle, remembering at the last second the groom's warning to duck as we went through the door.

The filly's long-striding walk tipped me gently from side to side. The exercise saddle felt strange, disorienting. How could sitting on a horse's back, arguably the one thing I was best at in the world, feel alien to me now? The saddle reminded me of a bareback pad, with less cushioning. With no steel tree between us, I could feel the filly's spine; with no leather flap under my leg, I could feel her ribs, the sleek lines of her muscle, the fluttering of her heart. Or maybe I was just imagining all of it.

"What took you so long? My God! Women!" Billy Joe cackled at me and turned his colt down the hillside path beyond the barn with a jerk of the reins. I winced and nudged my own filly, who suddenly seemed to have left her gas pedal in the barn, to follow.

Ocala was putting on her autumnal best this morning, and it should have been perfect for an early ride, with the fog winding through the trees, and a touch of coolness to the humid morning air that gave away we were in September. The hill we rode down was studded with live oaks, their branches stretching over the path like the arms of giants, limbs dripping with curlicued ribbons of Spanish moss, nearly reaching the ground in places. There was no better way to experience a fall sunrise in Ocala than on horseback; this countryside had been designed for horses, from the limestone seeping its bone-building calcium into the water and grass, to the gently rolling hills perfect for growing strong young horses.

Ocala might have every sort of discipline and breed roaming its hills now, but the town had first been discovered by Thoroughbred owners, and racing was its horsey heart. I should have been thrilled to be out here, finally seeking out the holiest ground of my adopted home, but the truth was, I was scared.

Jules Thornton, three-day eventer, was scared of a ride. It didn't sound right to me, either.

But I'd never ridden a racehorse—it was that simple. I'd taken ex-racehorses and trained them to do other jobs: eventing, dressage, jumpers. That was a matter of getting inside their heads and understanding their past.

Racehorses came with a history that made them razor-sharp, horses on the edge of leaping or bolting or rearing at the slightest provocation. I brought them back to earth, taught them to take life a little more slowly, explained the art of relaxation. I was very experienced at teaching a horse not to be a racehorse. It was going in the other direction that was new.

Pete said exercising racehorses was simple for any rider with a good seat, steady hands, and nerves of steel; technically, I had all of those, or I wouldn't be able to pilot horses around Intermediate level event courses, with logs and ditches and banks designed to scare the breeches off the bravest of equestrians.

Simple work, and good money, too: right now I was getting paid twenty-five bucks to take this filly down to the training track, take her for a gallop in a circle, and then ride her back to the barn to hand her off to the groom. Add in that we were riding at six in the morning, before I would even think of riding my crew back at home, and it was a good source of extra income that really only disrupted my sleeping patterns, not my actual workday.

The sloping path ended at the rickety wooden fence of a training track, its oval disappearing into the fog. The wooden railing was raw and new; the sand footing was pocked with a few days' worth of hoof marks, and speckled with weeds. It wasn't the kind of ground I'd usually gallop a horse over. The filly pranced beneath me; she knew what was up. Billy Joe pointed at a flimsy-looking red-and-white-striped pole, its crooked white cap just visible through the thick fog.

"Okay, Miss English, we trot up to that pole, and then we turn around, stand 'em up for a sec, and then we gallop back to here. You got it?"

Seemed simple enough. I didn't know what "stand them up" meant, but I figured I could follow along. I nodded at Billy Joe, gathering up the thick reins again, gripping them just past the knot I'd tied into them. By now, Billy Joe was already trotting away, which annoyed my filly very much. She took off at a fast clip after his colt, who was already doing some serious Standardbred action on the weedy sand of the training oval, trotting with an extension that would've made a dressage queen drool.

I sighed, letting the filly pull against my hands. "Catch up if you want." I wasn't exactly going to ask her to soften her mouth and accept the bit, after all. The only thing we needed this morning was a measure of speed. Manners were just a bonus. I posted like a D-Level Pony Clubber, balancing against the filly's mouth, lever-aging against the knot in the reins.

She rewarded me with an impressive plow horse impression, digging her head down and dragging me into a faster and faster stride as Billy Joe's colt went skimming ahead of us. I soon gave up attempting a ladylike rising trot and imitated his position: I planted my hands on the filly's withers and lifted my backside into the air, a sort of awful two-point position. My heels dropped obediently and my lower leg slid ahead of the girth once my weight was on the stirrups instead of the saddle, and suddenly that "longer you ride, longer you ride" line made sense. Now I had too much leg in front of me to get thrown forward if she did something stupid, like stop dead or drop her head to buck. I felt secure for the first time since I'd slid into the exercise saddle.

The lack of tread on the stirrup iron was still worrisome, though. My boot's grip on the stirrup was tenuous, sliding back and forth a little if the filly took a misstep on the hillocks of sand. With such uneven footing, the chances she'd take a hard stumble and throw me right over her head seemed decent.

My apprehension rose as the striped pole loomed before us. A quick trot was one thing, but galloping was going to be a whole other story.

Billy Joe had already pulled up and turned his colt around, and I did the same, the filly tossing her head and gaping her mouth against the bit. I pulled her up next to his horse, as if we were fin-ishing a hunter under saddle class and lining up for the judge. He tossed me a gap-toothed grin. "You ready, Miss English?"

"I'm ready," I said, with all the false confidence I could muster. "I'm Jules, by the way." There'd been no introductions this morning. I'd driven into the barn driveway at five thirty, found a hard-faced woman in the first barn who said she was the owner and gave me directions to the training barn down the drive, where the groom took me completely in stride, as if new faces were a normal thing around this farm.

Probably not a good sign, I thought in retrospect.

"Billy Joe," he returned, still grinning. "Joey and Jules."

"Joey and Jules," I repeated weakly, praying this wasn't going to become a thing.

"Okay, then, Julesy, let's gallop!" He picked up his reins and kicked his horse into a trot, and then a canter, and then—they were gone, streaking away from us, literally leaving my filly and me in a trail of dust. Hadn't this guy ever heard of a warm-up?

The filly danced anxiously, half rearing.

"Oh, fuck me," I muttered, and kicked the filly after them.

She was fast, but Billy Joe's horse had the lead and the fear of God in him, so we didn't even begin to close the gap already opened between us. I was pretty sure there was more to training a racehorse than just galloping them full tilt around a track, but I had bigger problems: slipping and sliding on the bare metal of my stirrups. I tried to press my weight onto my hands and my knees, but I felt myself slowly failing as my muscles, unaccustomed to this position and this saddle, tried to revert to more familiar poses.

I knew I was going to lose my stirrups; now it was just a question of what would happen when I did. I couldn't pull this horse up, obviously. I needed this job. Horses would always need to eat—there was no getting around that. If I pulled up, I'd get fired, and in a few days, I'd have hungry horses waiting on a feed delivery that didn't come. There was no job security in galloping racehorses, you just showed up, rode, and got paid . . . or you didn't.

I could feel my right stirrup making its way to the tip of my boot—I was standing on the edge—and then it was gone. My knee gripped the tiny saddle instinctively, and I had to drop the left stirrup as well, or I'd have been so off-balance I'd have gone over the side. Stirrup-free, I sat down on the exercise saddle.

At least I had a tight seat, no matter what kind of tack I was sitting in. As the filly galloped on, head high and mane streaming, spurred on by the loose stirrups banging around her shoulders, I realized Pete had been right: a good seat and strong nerves really were all I needed. I knew how to stay on a horse. I'd stay on this one.

It was a cheering thought. I immediately felt much better about the entire morning, even though things probably looked pretty dire. We were going to finish this gallop, even if it was ugly, and how was that for proof I could do this job?

We came up to the red-and-white pole, where Billy Joe had reined back his horse, and I bounced the filly down to a fast jog, then a walk. I grinned at Billy Joe. At least I hadn't died. I should get brownie points for that.

"What the hell happened, English? You ride with no stirrups?" Billy Joe did not look nearly as impressed with me as I thought he should. I noticed he'd already stopped using my name, too. So much for Joey and Jules.

"They didn't have any tread," I explained. "If you have latex in the tack room, I can wrap them real quick before the next horse."

Billy Joe looked at me like I had suggested we tack up the gators in the barn pond next. Then he wordlessly turned his colt back toward the gap in the railing, leaving me to follow.

We rode back to the barn in silence, the horses huffing and blowing, while I tried to figure out who was wrong here. I used to use latex wrap on my cross-country saddle's stirrups before

Rockwell Brothers sent me fancy safety stirrups. It was totally normal. Laurie, my old trainer from my riding-school days, had said eventers learned that trick from racing people. Did she make that up?

Nope, I thought. I wasn't the one who was wrong. Something about this place was just *off*. That scruffy little training barn with only six horses in it. The groom who showed me a horse to ride without even asking who the hell I was. The way we just galloped flat-out around the track, no attempt to rate or teach the horses anything.

I untacked the blowing filly in her stall and hesitated in the doorway, looking for the groom, but he'd gone missing. I looked at the horse regretfully; she was hot as hell and I couldn't leave her there that way. I led her back out and took her for a few turns around the shed row, the way I'd seen racing grooms cool hot horses when I'd visited training barns to look at sport horse prospects.

I passed Billy Joe standing in the tack room doorway, sipping coffee, pretending not to stare at my ass in my tight jeans. I had no idea where his horse was. He didn't say anything to me. Another reason I hadn't wanted to work at a racing barn: too many men. Pete said if anyone could handle rude men, it was me, but I didn't feel up to challenging the patriarchy this early in the morning.

After the fourth walk around the shed row, the groom appeared and took the filly without apology. I looked for Billy Joe, but the tack room was empty. I found him in another stall, where he'd gone to tack up his next ride.

"Who do I ride next?" I asked through the bars, and he snorted.

"You don't have another horse." He laughed. "Boss saw you ride. She was up the hill. Said you scared her. They'll write you a check for your ride in the office up at the main barn."

The hard-faced barn owner took a cigarette out of her mouth long enough to tell me thanks for riding, and good luck. Then she wrote me a check for twenty-five bucks and handed it over without a smile. She'd written *barn supplies* on the memo line. "So there's no taxes," she explained, but I knew that—that's what everyone in Ocala put on their paychecks. "Good luck," she said again.

"Same to you," I said, and I meant it, even if she'd called my riding scary. This place needed all the luck it could get.

With the fog burning off and early-morning sunlight pouring through the oak trees, daytime was spotlighting the flaws that hadn't been visible when I'd arrived in the predawn darkness. The entire place had a rotting feel: the fences were coming down, the weeds were taking over the driveway, the barn aisle was deeply rutted and smelled faintly of cow. The stalls were mismatched, as if they'd been made of found wood and abandoned panels. It wasn't exactly the kind of place where I could take a glamour shot for my Instagram feed, showing off my cute new Rockwell Brothers skullcap with navy-blue silk and gray faux-fur pom-pom (although I'd definitely have to do that later—I was behind on my sponsored content).

"You said you event, right?" The barn owner looked as if she was trying to place me, but I knew I'd never laid eyes on her before. She was the hard-bitten varietal of horsewoman—a permanent frown carved into a face bronzed from a lifetime in the sun, and bone-thin in a way that made you think more of mineral deficiencies and rough living than Instagram models and kale shakes.

"Yeah." I slipped the check into my back pocket. "I'm a professional event rider."

"You know a Lucy Knapp? I gotta horse for her to pick up, but she won't take my calls."

"No," I said. "But there's a lot of eventers here. It's hard to know everyone."

She nodded. "Same with racing." She peered at me. "You want a horse?"

"Is he sound?" I asked, automatically interested, even though I knew I shouldn't take anything off this farm.

She shrugged her thin shoulders.

"I can't take another horse right now anyway."

"Yeah, you and me both." She laughed. No hard feelings, I guessed.

"You know anyone else hiring?" I figured it was worth a shot, even if she thought I couldn't ride. "Your neighbors, maybe?" There were farms on either side of this place. Both of them looked much nicer from the road, which I now realized meant I should have tried one of them out first.

She coughed out a laugh. "You go next door, don't tell 'em Mary Archer sent you. That's all I can tell you."

She turned, still chuckling, and walked off down the dirt aisle, which I guessed meant she was done with me. *Okay then, Mary Archer,* I thought.

Thanks for the opposite of an endorsement.

Back in my truck, I looked at the check and sighed. All that, and I got a paycheck that wouldn't even cover a bag of grain. The clock told me I had more time: two more hours until I needed to get back and ride my own little crew. I wished Lacey was back at the barn, waiting for me; I needed to tell someone about this hell of a morning, and Pete wasn't a good audience right now.

I looked to the left, looked to the right: farms on either side of me, each with their own training tracks, each with their own barns full of horses. The beautiful thing about Ocala was there was always another farm. It would take years to work my way through all of them. I could turn left, or I could turn right. Made no difference.

I turned right, drove a few hundred feet, then made another right at the next driveway. At least this one was classy, I thought, driving through arching black gates like the ones back at Briar Hill. Maybe their stirrups would actually have some tread on them. Or at least a roll of latex.

2

I HAD ALREADY been home for half an hour when Pete came inside, saw me sitting on the couch in bare feet and a clean shirt, and shook his head ever so slightly, as if he wasn't surprised.

I felt a rush of blood warm my cheeks. "I just got home a little bit ago," I snapped. "I rode one horse. No one else needed riders today. I'm having a cup of coffee and I'm going to ride my crew afterward. So you can lay off the dirty looks."

"I didn't *say* anything," he retorted, ready for a fight.

"It was just the way you looked—" I heard my own voice in my ears. *Is this how you're going to fix things?* I shut my mouth, swallowed, bit my tongue a few times. "Fine. There's fresh coffee in the pot. You look like you had a hard morning."

Pete dropped his hard hat on the kitchen table and wiped sweat from his forehead. He'd worn the hat inside, which meant he'd been driving around Ocala with a riding helmet on, like he was piloting a golf cart at a horse show.

Anywhere else that would get some strange looks, but it was common enough around here.

He ran a hand through his dark chestnut hair, roughing up the helmet head. "I rode six at Plum Meadow," he said.

"Six! And you're already back? That's a full day's work." I was impressed despite myself.

"It was just babies. We mostly trotted around a big pasture. It wasn't too bad, like trail riding with a few more spooks than usual."

Nine o'clock in the morning, and Pete had already ridden six horses to my one.

I considered different ways to spin my own debut into the working world. The more prosperous-looking farm I'd tried after leaving Ms. Archer's fabulous No-Name Acres had turned me away, as had the next two up the road. I tried a new road after that, thinking I needed a change of scenery. But there were no takers.

"I rode one, and that was all they had for me," I fibbed, not wanting to admit I'd been sent on my way. "Everyone wanted experienced riders for their older horses, and they kept saying they didn't have babies yet." I wasn't sure what that line had meant, but Pete seemed to have stumbled onto a farm that already had these mythical babies.

"I even tried Windsong Arabians," I added dolefully, to express just how wide I'd cast my net. The idea of riding short-backed, short-legged Arabian racehorses had been even less appealing than regular ones. *Way* too much agility in those close-coupled little bodies, like trying to ride a coiled spring with a mind of its own. "They said to try them next month, when they have horses coming back from up north. Are you destroying that bread on purpose?"

Pete was slathering peanut butter onto wheat bread fresh from the fridge, shredding the surface in the process. He flashed me a wry grin. "Too hungry to wait for the toaster. You want some?"

"I'm good." No need to tell him I'd had plenty of time for breakfast. We both knew that driving around the winding roads of Ocala looking for work all morning could end only one way: fast-food wrappers and regret.

"I'm going to take a couple more boxes to the barn this morning, if you want a ride."

I winced, and it wasn't just from the McMuffin congealing in my stomach. I didn't want to be reminded just now, after a morning of failure and twenty-five dollars (nineteen if you subtracted breakfast), of the impending move. I still couldn't believe it was really happening. The past few weeks had been so hectic, everything moving so fast and yet not moving at all.

Here's a hard lesson you only learn at the worst moment in your life: when people die, someone still has to pay their bills. After a quick, confusing consultation with a lawyer recommended by Pete's friend Amanda (the Hunter Princess, my brain always added automatically), we'd found ourselves looking at bills we'd never seen before, with no idea how we'd ever pay them.

Worse, we didn't know if they were worth paying.

"Your agreement with your grandmother was purely verbal," the attorney had told Pete, her expression regretful, as if she was rooting for us but there wasn't much she could do. "There's nothing here stating that if you win some competition, you win the farm, too."

"It was making the US Equestrian Team," I interjected, hot-tempered on his behalf, "and he is very close to being invited to a team training—"

"Still not here," the attorney continued, "and so the bulk of the estate very clearly goes to her former college. And that includes the farm." She pushed her short black hair behind her ears. "If you don't want it to go to the college, well . . ." She spread her hands, inviting us to speculate.

"A *college* with classes in Pearl Necklace Wearing 101 and Table-Setting for Society," I muttered. "I'm sure they really need a horse farm."

Pete shot a look at me before saying, "This is all dated five years ago. My grandmother made this deal with me three years ago. She gave me a timetable to make the equestrian team and she'd leave me the farm. I still have another year."

"But you didn't make that deal with her will," the attorney said. "Are you asking me if you can contest it?"

"I am."

"Anything's possible," the attorney agreed, adjusting her tortoiseshell glasses. Her look of sympathy disappeared, replaced by a more steely television-lawyer glare. "But I have to tell you, nothing's free."

Yes. We were learning that.

For a moment, the cold room fell silent. Pete looked at his hands. I tried to imagine a life outside Ocala. Making the best of things was my specialty. I could fix this. I had ten ideas already.

First: we could leave and start over somewhere cheaper. We could rent a barn way out past Morriston or go up toward Gainesville, spreading our search to Chiefland or High Springs if we really couldn't find anything down here in our budget, and all that would change would be that the drive to horse shows and the feed store would be a little longer. The grass might not be as green and the oaks couldn't possibly be as magnificent and the neighbors would probably raise cows instead of horses, but we'd still have space to ride and train, and wasn't that all we needed?

I'd lost my farm already. I knew the drill. I wasn't even surprised to see this particular train coming at me again. The only way to avoid heartache in this business was to get the hell out of it.

I looked at Pete's face, saw the hurt there, and I knew it wasn't as simple for him. This was a blow he hadn't been prepared for. The end of the life he'd seen for himself. My dream was eventing, pure and simple, but *his* dream was wrapped up in the farm where his grandfather had galloped. His dream was Briar Hill.

I touched his hand, cold from the air-conditioning or maybe from shock, and told him we would keep the farm, no matter what. His fingers closed around mine, gripping so tightly I bit my lip and turned away. But I didn't pull free, despite the pain. I let him hold on to me. It was the least I could do.

The attorney pushed her glasses up on her nose and gazed at us with the accumulated wisdom of many years of college. Pete and I had none; we were outwitted, out-gamed. We accepted the terms the real world laid out for us. It would cost us; luckily, she knew how to make money.

With her guidance, things changed so quickly, we could scarcely keep up. The attorney made suggestions, real estate agents were called, and within a few days, a winter lease for the house and training barn was signed and delivered. We needed someone who could pay our bills for us, with a minimum of disruption to our business, they all explained. Someone who could get us through the woods while the legal drama played out, and beyond that, until we could be self-sustaining with our business.

One change after another was outlined in head-spinning rapidity: Pete and I would move into the guesthouse. Pete's horses would join mine in the annex barn. The tenants would take over the training barn and the house; they were jumper people from Virginia, trying to decide where they wanted to build their million-dollar dream farm in Ocala. They didn't have the problems we had, like wondering how to pay for their horses' next load of hay, and I was trying really, really hard not to hate them before they even arrived.

The Virginian jumpers weren't coming until mid-October, still a month away, so we had plenty of time to pack up the house. We set aside an hour each day, and this was the only moment in our busy days that went slowly: placing the little artifacts of Pete's grandparents' life into boxes we thought we might never open again. We approached the task cautiously, wrapped up breakables with slow fingers, and backed away when emotions ran too high.

There was time, we agreed. A little bit every day, and we'd finish right on schedule.

Maybe that made things worse, the way we were dragging this process out.

Maybe we should have just left everything alone and waited for the inevitable estate sale. Would it have mattered so much if Mr. and Mrs. Virginia lived among the things we'd thought of as *ours,* when the odds were we'd lose them anyway?

But it gave us a little fake power to take away our treasures and hide them. On the day the Blixden family attorney produced the signed lease, Pete took down the photos of his grandfather that decorated the house. From every wall, that great horseman had looked down at us, leaping through history on storied horses who changed the sport forever. Their absence showed in the unfaded squares on the beige walls, and changed the very atmosphere of the house. It was as if a god had been exorcised from his temple. Now there were only plaster walls, and carpeted floors, and water-stained ceilings, like any other middle-aged Florida house that has seen a few hurricanes pass by.

Pete put the framed pictures into a rubber storage bin he'd emptied of spare saddle pads, set it tenderly beside him on the golf cart, and drove it out to the annex barn, where my horses had lived in quiet isolation since we'd moved here last autumn, under similarly stormy skies. He tucked the bin into a spare stall and wrapped it with a tarp.

What are you packing today?" I asked Pete now, taking my own mental inventory. Most of the personal items were gone. The house was a collection of furniture now. We would have to leave them our bed, along with the antique bedroom furniture, and sleep on the double bed that my former working student, Lacey, had left behind when she moved back to Pennsylvania a few weeks ago. Thank goodness she'd taken the massive plush horse collection that shared the bed with her.

"The tack trunk," Pete said. "I hate to move it out of the AC, but . . ."

I nodded. But he didn't want anyone to see it. I knew.

I'd never even seen inside the tack trunk that sat in the corner of Pete's office, but I knew it was an antique. The gleaming wood exterior had the rich glow of mahogany, and the dancing horses inlaid on its lid were fine art in themselves. I'd only seen them a few times; Pete kept a plaid rug over the trunk to protect it from dust.

"Do you need help lifting it?" I asked. I had no idea what was inside. A saddle? Gold bullion? Nepalese treasures? It might be the Ark of the Covenant, for all Pete's reverence.

Pete shook his head. "It's light," he said. "You know what? I'll do it later, if you don't have anything to take down. We can walk to the barn. We could use a few quiet minutes before we get back to work."

I looked at the lines of exhaustion on Pete's face and wondered if moving out was really the worst part of this limbo period. Galloping racehorses in the morning had been his idea, but I had no doubt he'd work himself to the point of a breakdown. And then what would happen? I'd have to take care of him. But I wasn't sure Pete was ready for me to be in charge.

He sensed my eyes on his face and looked up at me. He smiled. A real smile, too, that reached right up to his blue eyes.

I felt a surge of love for him. I'd take care of him, whether he wanted me to or not. I'd be tough for him.

I reached out and touched his cheek, sliding my fingers across the rough reddish stubble of a day-old beard. My lips parted, I felt my heartbeat rising.

His hand caught mine and his own calloused fingers stroked my wrist.

Though his touch was gentle, I could feel the purpose in it. He was stopping me.

"A *quiet* walk, I said." He chuckled ruefully. At least there was a hint of regret in his tone. He *wanted* to stay here with me. Didn't he? Or maybe he really did just want to get to work.

"It's this late already," I pointed out, though the moment had come and gone in a matter of seconds.

"And so we really need to get going," he insisted.

He held on to my hand, though, all the way to the barn.

It felt like a start.

3

"IT SEEMS TO me you could have at least googled the place."

Becky was throwing manure into a wheelbarrow with practiced efficiency, the kind of tosses that didn't even require looking. She'd been mucking stalls, first for me and then for Pete, for years now. At twenty-three, Becky had decided to make barn management her life's work, rather than training horses, and I couldn't help but respect someone who chose the dirty work over the glory.

"Half the farms out here don't have websites," I defended myself. "Or the internet."

"If they can't even afford a satellite internet connection, do you really want to get on their horses? Class counts with racehorses. Don't get on cheap ones."

That was a very solid point. Becky was entirely too good at putting me in my place. I pulled aside her full wheelbarrow and replaced it with an empty one; she went on hurling manure and wet bedding without a pause in stride.

Tuesdays and Thursdays, Becky did all the barn chores, morning and evening. It would be funny to have her working for me again. Technically, she was Pete's groom. But once Pete moved his horses down to my barn, we'd be working as a team. There would be no more Pete's horses and Jules's horses. There were just the Briar Hill horses.

In a way, that was a win out of all this loss. It put me on more solid ground with Pete. If we were business partners, he was less likely to decide he couldn't deal with me anymore. I couldn't forget what he'd said to me a few weeks ago, in Orlando—that he couldn't trust me now.

I'd been so conflicted by that, I'd actually called my mom for advice.

"Don't act like you have the high ground here," my mother told me, supportive as ever. "You finally drove him crazy. But he's giving you a chance to prove you're human under all that ambition."

So I asked Lacey what she thought.

"I mean, he'd have to be kinda nuts to want to be with you, right?" Lacey said. "I guess there's no telling what he'll do next."

Dr. Em, my faithful vet, who had once tried to set me up with Pete, put things a little more gently. "Everything is terrible for Pete right now. So just be really, really nice to him. Nice, and reliable." She paused and considered me, one finger on her pointed chin. "Those things aren't really your strong suit, I know. But try."

That was the plan, then.

So our relationship had nearly taken a spill. Now we were cantering stride-for-stride again, perhaps not as close together as we'd been, perhaps eyeing one another suspiciously from time to time, but still committed to making it to the finish line together.

An outcome that wasn't going to happen if I didn't find a way to pull my own weight around here and make some damn cash.

I made my way back to the present with a shake of my head.

Becky lifted her eyebrows at me. "You're losing it, Jules."

"I'm freaking out here," I argued. "I need horses to ride. More to the point, I need someone to pay me to ride their horses."

"So go ride horses. Ocala is nothing but horses who need riding. You've always said that."

"This is different. The big farms don't *want* me on their horses. I'm nobody to them."

"Well, that makes sense. You have no racing experience."

"Right?" Finally, Becky was seeing reason. If only Pete was so astute.

"It's a shame that galloping horses is so different from one discipline to the next," Becky added silkily. "You could never learn it."

I narrowed my eyes at her. "Okay then, what do you want me to do?"

"Dump these water buckets?"

"I already know you're smarter than me, Becky. You've proven that over and over. Stop rubbing it in and tell me what I should do."

Becky actually stopped mucking the stall. Her mocking little smile fell from her face and she gaped at me. "Jules Thornton . . . are you *sick*? Do you have a fever? Come let me feel your forehead."

"Stop it—"

"I'm dead serious. If Pete ever heard you say anything like that, he'd probably call an ambulance."

"Move over and let me get the water buckets. I'm done with you." I snatched at the snaps on the buckets, wrenching them from their screw eyes on the wall. I wasn't going to humble myself in front of someone and then get teased for it.

Becky caught me by the arm as I tried to escape, dirty water splashing from the half-empty buckets. "I'm sorry. Really. That's just not like you. And it's not true. I'm not smarter than you. We just think differently." She paused, and her mocking smile crept back. "*Really* differently."

"Okay!"

"Now I'm serious. I promise. Here's how to get a riding job. You have to present yourself as a catch. Stop showing up and asking if you can ride and apologizing for being new to race-horses. Walk in like you own the place and announce that you're an upper-level event rider looking for extra galloping time, and their farm looks like the kind of place with quality horses you'd like to ride. Show off your skills and compliment them on their lovely horses, don't act like you're some novice rider just because you've never galloped on a track. Lord knows you can ride any horse, any time, any saddle." She dropped her hand from my elbow as if she'd just realized she was touching me, but there was no malice in her gesture; Becky just wasn't into touching people. Or into people, in general. I could respect that. "Be Jules, you know? You're a tough girl. You can hold your own out there. Acting humble isn't your style."

I nodded. That much was true.

"And under no circumstances do you go to any barns that don't have websites. Or that look like they have meth labs in their tack rooms. Be picky. Their horses will only be as crazy as they are."

"Got it. Websites yes, meth labs no."

"Thanks for dumping those water buckets for me." Becky disappeared back into the stall.

I stepped from dark to light, out of the barn's shade and into the sun's glare, and tossed the water in two shimmering arcs into the frail grass alongside the driveway. It splashed and puddled on the summer-saturated ground.

I turned back to look at the barn, feeling that sense of futility that crept over me on rough days, when the comforting routine turned into something darker.

Look at what we were doing with our days! Trying to make money to pay for horses, riding horses to make money, making money to pay for horses . . . so the snake eats its tail and Jules gets up every morning to do the same routine over and over.

I tried to shake it off; usually just a glance at my horses eating or napping peacefully would remind me they were reason enough—there was nothing deeper, this was all simply about being with horses. I felt uncharacteristically delicate and blue this morning, though. I supposed Pete's rebuff had caught me by surprise, and made everything seem a little more uncertain.

Forget it. Focus on the future, I told myself. *Forget right now. Right now sucks.*

And it wasn't all bad. The morning light was glistening through the shady live oaks, casting dappled shadows on the old barn. For a moment, the annex barn looked more than respectable; it looked like a damned nice place to keep horses. I pulled out my phone and snapped a few pictures, picked out the best one, and posted it to my Instagram. *Hot and sunny with a chance of eventing,* I captioned it, and tagged Rockwell Brothers as our sponsor. Sure, the pics were supposed to have Rockwell riding gear in them, but sometimes it was okay to just enjoy the atmosphere.

I scrolled through my feed once I'd posted the picture, seeing what all my contemporaries were up to. Like me, most of the Floridian eventers were just emerging from their summer caves, although there were some riders already having a fabulous competition season up north, or in Europe. The *Eventing Chicks* blog was posting updates from events in Virginia and Kentucky; they'd be back in Florida soon enough. The show calendar was picking up here already. Pete and I had backed off on the September events, too overwhelmed by life to consider competing, too, but we had to get busy or we'd fall behind.

On cue, the next photo in my feed was from Hope Glen Farm, a horse jumping into a water complex. *Don't forget! Hope Glen Horse Trials and Three-Day Event will offer unrecognized three-day event divisions for Novice and Training level this year! This is the perfect opportunity to prep for those big winter goals.*

They weren't kidding. Pete and I had been discussing the Hope Glen event since we got back to Briar Hill—it seemed like the one time he was happy and animated about the future. Taking our less experienced horses through the added complexities of the three-day event format, from the morning inspection trot-up in front of judges, to the challenging cross-country course, would test their confidence and coping abilities before we moved them up a level.

So the plan was that in three months, at Hope Glen, we'd take our most competitive horses out for a grand finale in their current divisions. That meant Mickey would go in the Novice three-day event division, before moving up to Training level in January. Pete would run his dapple-gray gelding Barsuk in the Training level three-day, before taking him Preliminary. In the upper levels, recognized by the FEI, I'd run Dynamo at Intermediate and Pete would run Regina at Advanced. It was early in her career to try the mare at an Advanced three-day event, but Pete figured the summer of cross-country training in England had her as ready as she'd ever be—and he needed the horse to move up to get a shot at the equestrian team invitation, in case the legal challenge came down to his living up to his grandmother's expectation.

Would it? Who could say? The legal system was its own strange world.

I stared at my phone. The Hope Glen post stared back at me. Twelve weeks felt so soon, and yet an eternity when I considered how much might happen between now and then. We could lose it all. We could win. I could come off a racehorse and break my neck.

Stay focused, Jules.

Get to Hope Glen, and get the horses around safely, and bring home a ribbon to make the sponsors and the owners happy, and go into the new year trailing clouds of glory: that was the plan.

Simple enough, right?

I was still standing in the sun, working my way through my internal pep talk, when Pete came riding up the driveway, his feet hanging alongside the empty stirrups.

He was on his silly black-and-white Thoroughbred-draft cross, Rorschach. The gelding eyeballed me as he came closer, rounding his neck and shoulders away from me as if I was a panther waiting to leap up and devour him.

"You're an idiot," I told Rorschach.

He blew a hot, loud breath at me.

"Be nice to my horse," Pete said.

"I don't think he speaks English."

"I think Amanda has a buyer for him, anyway." Pete jumped down from the saddle, his boots lifting two puffs of dust from the driveway. "Looks like rain," he added. "You want to get on a horse with me so I can finish my crowd before it storms? Barsuk and Mayfair need a hack. I'll help you with your guys this afternoon if you need it."

Of course I wanted to. I would never turn down a ride with Pete. I turned into the barn with him, a hand on Rorschach's drooping reins. "Is she going to get your price?" I asked.

Based on his trot, his jump, and his overall amiability, Amanda the Hunter Princess had been marketing Rorschach to her well-heeled clients as a big eq horse. Equitation horses had to jump quietly so that their riders could sit quietly in the saddle, taking every fence as if they were posing for a riding catalog cover. It sounded like a fate even worse than dressage, and that's really saying something, because at least in equitation you got to jump. Equitation was so boring, as far as I could tell, that riders literally bought splashy-colored horses just so they could stand out to the judges. Like, they couldn't even be told apart from one another if they didn't ride a paint or a chestnut with four white socks and a blaze.

At least, that was how I interpreted things. It might be possible I was just biased against anything from the hunter/jumper world, because that's where Amanda came from, and Amanda annoyed me.

Gorgeous, twig-thin, Daddy's money, and a decent riding seat: Amanda the Hunter Princess was not my favorite person. Too pretty, too put together. Horsewomen should be messier. Our paths never would have overlapped, but she happened to be good at turning the occasional unenthusiastic Thoroughbred into a hunter or show jumper. When Pete got an off-track Thoroughbred whose life's calling was neither racing nor eventing, he called Amanda. They were like double retirees. Way Off-Track Thoroughbreds. The farther they got from eventing, the more expensive they got, which was both hilarious and sad, and a good reminder I had chosen the wrong sport to make a living in.

Pete was adamantly pro-Amanda. "She'll get the price," he said. "She knows we need the money. Anyway, if the client screws her around with a lowball offer, she'll take a hit in commission, so she's got incentive to make this work. She's probably quoting them ten thousand bucks over what I'm asking, just to be on the safe side."

"That much? Seems a little dishonest."

"That's her cut," Pete said. "She won't charge me commission."

I wondered what Amanda really saw in Rorschach, a horse with more flash than brains. I looked at a horse's legs and their leaps and their expressions and the tilt of their shoulders and croups, always searching for the horse with the most heart and turning away from the beauties with empty heads, but it seemed like those beauties went for more money than the rough-and-readies with the hearts of gold.

"Well, if she really gets him sold, that'll be a big help," I said, shrugging away all those deep thoughts. What counted was getting paid. Not who paid us.

Pete had already moved Barsuk and Rorschach to this barn, staggering the task over the weeks just like packing up the house, so Becky came out to untack him while we went down to get Barsuk. The small horse looked at me through the stall bars and fluttered his black-skinned nostrils at me, the white star that lit up his pale gray face shining at me from the dim recesses of his box. I remembered the potential client Amanda had sent me at the beginning of the summer, who told me my barn was too dark and insisted horses could only thrive with bright sunlight flooding their stalls. Barsuk's stall was the most shadowy one in the entire barn, because a massive live oak trunk nearly blocked his entire window, but the cloud-colored little horse didn't seem to mind. He was always bright-eyed, always ready to say hello or have some carrots or pull at my ponytail or go for a hack.

"Hey sweet thing," I cooed, putting my lips to the gap in the bars and planting a kiss on his soft nose. "Today's the day Pete gives you to me and we run away together."

"Oh, now you want him?" Pete grumbled.

"I do," I said. Barsuk pushed his lips against my nose. His muzzle was silken-smooth. "He loves me."

"Go get Mickey," Pete said. "Stop stealing my horse."

4

WHEN WE RODE over the cross-country field, I felt the implications of leaving this farm the most deeply. If we lost this cross-country course, I would never have its equal in my backyard again. I'd never seen such a magnificent course on private property, and I'd paid hundreds of dollars to compete on lesser versions. Riding anywhere else after this would be like moving from the Four Seasons to a Motel 6.

We'd been talking about opening it up for schooling sessions. Charging fifty dollars a head would be a big help with the legal fees that were sure to mount as we tried to claim the farm as our own. The insurance we'd have to buy first was a big obstacle, though. It would take months, maybe years, to make back the money. We needed something better than two or three horses coming in once or twice a week.

"I wonder if we could hold an event here," I mused out loud. That would be hundreds of horses. Did events make any money?

Pete looked at me, an eyebrow arched in surprise. "I was just wondering the same thing."

I laughed, tickled that we'd had the same idea. "Should we do it?"

"Well, we can't right now."

My smile faded. I was ready to daydream, not get a lecture from Practical Pete.

"If we can build up a little money in savings, maybe we can try in the spring," he went on. "But I can't take any time away from riding to plan an event. Neither of us can."

I nodded reluctantly. We wouldn't be able to in spring, either. We'd be competing, selling horses, turning them over as quick as we could. Oh, well. I took out my phone and told Pete to smile for a selfie. Team Briar Hill had to post pics for their supper, and Mickey and Barsuk always looked cute together: two grays out for a stroll.

Photos snapped, we trotted on over the green Ocala hills, our reins slack and our horses prick-eared, while dark clouds built in the west and thunder began to roll over the countryside. I loved the way the white tops of the clouds rode over their black underbellies and brought out the green of the hills, but somehow, all that beauty wasn't enough for me today. I looked across the land and the barns and saw only the astronomical cost of keeping it.

As we rode, I only wondered if Pete was thinking the same bleak thought I was: we were digging ourselves deeper and deeper into a hole we couldn't climb out of. Hanging on to Briar Hill Farm felt like a fool's errand to me. Maybe I'd just never loved anything enough to go bankrupt for it. Or maybe losing my farm just made it impossible to see a piece of land as anything but a temporary place to graze my horses and lay my head. When I looked over at Pete, I saw the fatigue dragging down the edges of his mouth.

"Let's canter," I suggested. Nothing cheered a person up like a canter.

"Sure," he said.

We shortened our reins and lifted out of the saddle into half seats, letting the horses stretch out beneath us. We thudded down the hill toward the beginning of the course, which was close to the training barn and arenas. I could see the newly empty stalls in the distance, their doors hanging open and waiting for the horses from Virginia, and I felt a hollow sadness rise up and take over even the joy of a good gallop. Despite all my good sense about leaving this money pit behind, I didn't want things to change.

Or to end.

I glanced over at Pete, his horse a few feet to my left, and was startled out of my misery by his bizarre posture: he was bent at the waist, his hands resting on his horse's withers. It wasn't a safe cross-country gallop position at all; if Barsuk tripped, and tripped hard enough, Pete would go right over his horse's pretty head. A safety seat was just slightly behind the horse's motion, hands independent of the neck, shoulders back and weight in the stirrups, prepared for the worst.

He felt my gaze and looked over at me. "What?"

"What are you *doing*?" I couldn't disguise my confusion. That wasn't how he rode.

"Practicing my galloping position." He stood up in the stirrups and then eased back into a proper seat. Barsuk flicked his ears at Pete's change in balance. "Stretching out my muscles for work tomorrow morning. I got sore today."

"You actually ride like that?"

"Haven't you ever seen a jockey ride, Jules?" Pete sounded impatient. His attitude flowed into Barsuk, who flung up his head and promptly tripped over his own forehooves. Pete, back in his safety seat, didn't move an inch. *Some luck,* I thought.

"Hunched over on the neck? Sure. But you're not doing that."

"No, like when they're exercising?"

I thought about it. Outside of occasionally driving past training tracks when a group of horses was galloping around, no, I hadn't seen anyone exercise a racehorse. I definitely hadn't seen how Billy rode; he'd been too far ahead of me and I'd been too busy trying to keep my ass in the saddle.

"Nope," I said. "This is a thing?"

"Of course it's a thing, it's how you do it."

I bit my lip. How many times had I said I didn't know how to exercise racehorses? I don't know, a *million*?

Pete managed to look dumbfounded. "It's really basic, Jules. I'm surprised you didn't pick it up this morning."

Oh no he did not. "Really? You're really surprised, because it's really basic?" My voice hit a high pitch that sent Mickey scuttling forward, and I reined him back, keeping him alongside the equally alarmed Barsuk. "Ask me how my morning went, Pete! Ask me where I rode! Ask me what happened, what the people were like, what the horse was like, what the tack was like! Because you didn't, you know that? You didn't ask me anything but how many I rode. You don't even know what happened."

"Hey, now." Pete pulled up Barsuk, who danced in a tight pirouette, his hindquarters bunched with nerves. "Stop and tell me."

I kept riding. Mickey balked and I pushed him on with my calves. "I don't want to talk about it. I'm trying to forget it."

"Wait up, Jules." His voice was edged with steel now; he was pissed off.

Good. Let him be pissed. Let him be as angry as I was.

Pussyfooting around Pete, what had I been thinking? I was strong with outrage now. I let Mickey canter away from the two of them.

"I could have died this morning and you just would've been sad I didn't bring home another twenty bucks for the Save Pete's Farm Fund," I shouted over my shoulder.

Barsuk whinnied plaintively, and Mickey planted his hooves in the grass, whirled around and neighed back. "Call yourself an event horse," I snapped at him, and he rolled his dark eye at me as Pete and Barsuk trotted up to join us.

Pete was standing in the stirrups, not even bothering to post. His face was set in hard lines. "What the hell happened this morning?"

I could spill the whole story right now, the way I had to Becky, and he could sympathize and say he was sorry, and I could apologize for shouting, and we could go on with our day. I could, but I didn't want to. I wanted to be angry, because it felt better than being so fucking sad.

"I made a bad choice and ended up at a shit barn," I said tightly, grinding out the words through thin lips. "I'll be more discriminating tomorrow. And I'll ride like a jockey, if that's what it takes."

He gazed at me, measuring me up. "Do you want me to show you how to ride in that seat?" His tone was almost conciliatory, as if he'd decided to let Jules have her little fit.

"Nope. I'll figure it out myself." I thought: *Should've asked me before you told me to set my alarm for five o'clock and go get on racehorses for your farm's sake.*

"Oh. Well, let me just tell you—you press down your hands on the withers like you do in the gallop lanes on cross-country, but then you almost stand in the stirrups and—"

"I'm not riding like that," I interrupted him. "So you can stop." I turned Mickey in a circle and started back toward the training barn. Time to find some shade, anyway. Sweat was greasing Mickey's reins and dripping from beneath his bridle. The humidity was getting to him, and to me, too. I pulled up my shirt and rubbed the sweat from my face.

Pete let Barsuk walk alongside Mickey. "It's the way it's *done*," Pete argued, not ready to quit yet. "You're not going to be the style police out there and start telling everyone to get their heels down, I hope."

"No, I'm going to tell them to get their shoulders back and stop leaning on their horse's neck like a second grader," I retorted. What a stupid conversation.

As if I'd talk to anyone there. Wherever "there" was. The mythical training track where I'd magically be riding tomorrow morning. As if tomorrow would be so different from today.

"There are good reasons for this riding position, just like there are reasons for everything else we do."

"Well, I don't *know* them, do I, Pete?" I burst out. "I don't know anything about racing. I'm not you. I event. That's all I know. That's all I *want* to know."

I glanced at him sideways as we rode, warily cataloging his rigid jaw and narrowed eyes, wondering when I was going to push him too far, wondering what I was going to do then.

I didn't know.

I didn't want to think about it. And at the same time, I was just a little curious. It wasn't that I *wanted* to bomb this relationship. But neither of us were having fun anymore. So, what came next? Did he get over it first, or did I?

He turned away from me and pushed Barsuk on, riding with a rigid seat and back. The horse didn't like it; his head was up and he gaped his mouth at the bit, white foam flying from the corners of his lips. I watched him move away from me, Barsuk's strides quickening under his insistent push. My hands tightened on Mickey's reins, then loosened again as he pulled back; he wasn't used to a clumsy rider. He was used to perfection. I let him open up his stride to catch up with Barsuk. I was suddenly consumed with the need to say something. Right or wrong, it didn't matter—anything was better than silence.

Then Mickey snorted at a dragonfly zipping through the air. I saw it as a blur and turned my head away from Pete to see what it was, and that's when I saw the big storm that had been creeping up behind us, its fluffy white shelf cloud stretched like a bright ribbon on a dark gown ballooning across the hillsides. The sunlight on the green pastures made the gleaming clouds all the brighter against their own dark backdrop, and I felt a sharp, unwanted tug of love for Briar Hill, for Ocala, for this corner of Florida I'd worked so hard to call my home.

Then lightning flicked like a striking snake from behind that gleaming white shelf cloud.

"Time to go home," I called, as the first rumble of thunder echoed my words.

Pete's head swiveled and I saw his eyebrows go up. Both of them, not just the one this time. "Oh, shit. How did we miss that?"

We were arguing instead of paying attention. "Go to my barn," I said. "It's quicker if we cut down the barn lane." I turned Mickey toward the gate by the training barn. Just a few hundred feet away, a hop out of the saddle to open and close the gate, mount up again, and then a five-minute walk down to the annex barn . . . and we'd *just* beat the storm. If we were quick.

"We might have time to turn around and go back the way we came," Pete suggested, but then a sharp growl of thunder, markedly louder than the one before, changed his mind. He nudged Barsuk to follow Mickey's lead, which he did eagerly. Barsuk wasn't a big fan of getting wet.

Mickey tugged at the reins as we neared the gate, anxious to get home. I wasn't letting him move quickly enough, distracted by the beautiful landscape ahead of us: the way the training barn and arenas gleamed golden in the September sun, the way the paddocks were lit emerald green under a blue sky studded with white cotton-ball clouds. If I turned my head the opposite way and looked behind us, it looked like the end of the world was sweeping across the sky, but directly ahead everything still looked like an oil painting of a perfect day, and I thought that was both one of the reasons I loved Florida so much, and a fitting metaphor for my life.

"Look at this place," I said to Pete. "Incredible. Can you believe how gorgeous it is right before a storm? Does that mean something?"

Pete loosened his reins and looked around, and Barsuk took the opportunity to look around as well. If I hadn't been so busy encouraging Deep Thoughts in Pete, he might have noticed that Barsuk was fixated on the training barn where he'd lived until a few days ago. After a moment, Pete hopped down from the saddle to open the gate for us, leaving Barsuk to stand. Lots of horses knew the command "stand"—it was helpful when you were putting up poles during a jumping session. Barsuk was no exception.

But this time, Barsuk decided the storm was a little too close.

"Whoa!" Pete shouted. I swiveled in the saddle, just in time to see Barsuk jogging contentedly toward the training barn. "Barsuk, come on!"

I glanced back at the storm cloud, which by the looks of things was threatening to swallow up the neighboring farm and obliterate the landscape with endless darkness. "Pete," I said, "I think we're going to get wet."

What I meant was that Pete was going to get wet. I still had a horse. Barsuk was going home lickety-split.

"I'll follow him across the field," Pete decided, and took off at a jog after his horse.

"I guess we'll take the road," I told Mickey.

The sun had been fully swallowed up by the time we got to the barn. The training barn was a very Florida-friendly stable, built for hot climates. The stalls opened onto the wraparound aisles, with a single chest-high railing to contain the occasional loose horse. Usually there would be a dozen or more horses leaning over the grills of their stall doors, but today there were only a handful. They looked out and whinnied at Mickey.

Halfway down a row of newly empty stalls, I found Barsuk. He was circling anxiously in the stall he'd called his own until a few days ago, looking for his water bucket, his hay pile, his bedding, anything familiar besides the bare wooden walls, their panels streaked with tooth marks and kick marks from the generations of horses who had lived here before him. I dismounted from Mickey and kept my hands on his reins while I stepped into the stall. Barsuk came to meet me as I stepped over the doorsill and pushed his charcoal-colored nose against my chest, huffing a deep breath of relief (I imagined) at the sight of me. I could tell this hadn't gone the way he'd expected at all.

"I know, buddy," I told him, slipping my right hand around the reins while my left hand explored his forehead, the white star between his eyes, the dark fall of forelock from between his black-tipped ears. "No one likes change, especially not like this."

A shadow passed between the watery storm-light and the three of us—Pete had arrived. I handed over the reins. "Let's go—this storm isn't waiting around," I told him.

Behind him, a wicked snake of lightning darted from the cloud and struck at the not-so-distant tree line, where a glade of oak trees marked the far corner of our property. I was still blinking from the dazzle of electric light when the thunder exploded around us like a bomb. Mickey jumped back, nearly tearing the reins from my hand, and Barsuk leaped up in the air, his ears pinned and his eyes wide, before performing something very close to a capriole. There was no way we were getting back to the annex barn, even if it was just five minutes away.

"Stay inside!" I shouted, probably unnecessarily, because Pete was already backing Barsuk into his stall. I tugged Mickey into the neighboring stall.

"You are staying right here," I told my horse, slipping off his bridle and running up the stirrups of my saddle. I backed out and closed the stall grill. He pushed his head over, watching me. "And I am going in the tack room."

Pete appeared in the shed row, bridle in hand, apparently with the same idea as me.

Lightning flooded the barn with light as he grinned. "To the tack room, my dear?"

The rain was marching toward the barn in a solid white sheet as we hurried down the barn aisle, running clumsily in our tall boots, the reins of the bridles slapping around our thighs. I might've giggled, despite it all—there was something so mischievous and summer-camp about it all.

The tack room wasn't completely packed up; there were still some rubber storage bins full of extra wraps, and some trash bags stuffed with horse blankets.

I claimed one of those for a throne and sagged into it like a queen in retreat. Pete left the door open and we watched the lightning illuminate the barn's central breezeway. The rain roared on the metal roof, too loud for casual conversation.

"Big one," Pete remarked—or shouted—after a while. Our phones chose that moment to buzz and we both pulled them out, observed the weather warning, and nodded our heads in agreement. You better believe there was a severe thunderstorm warning.

"I wish we'd made it back to my barn," I said. There were probably puddles in the western-facing stalls; it would have been nice to have closed their shutters. Becky might have gotten to it, I supposed.

"You don't want to be marooned with me during a dangerous storm, babe?"

I looked at Pete, sitting there grinning at me. Nice to see him smiling, but how long would it last? I was tired of the mood swings. *No,* I thought. *I don't want to be marooned with you at all, not until you're over whatever this is.* Waiting out a storm with him was different from working with him, plotting the horses' competition schedules, going over the barn finances, listening to the attorney drone about hours and fees and motions and statements. We had nothing to do here but wait, and the intimacy was too forced. We weren't ready to do nothing together. We needed tasks and chores, or we'd be cornered into thinking about all the words between us.

Now Pete was looking at me like he'd never said any of it, like the past few weeks had never happened.

I was annoyed.

"Not really," I answered stiffly. "I'd rather be getting some work done."

Pete lifted an eyebrow at me. "So you'd rather work than relax with me?"

"You know me," I said with a shrug. "Workaholic."

He frowned, making me wonder if I'd lost a chance at a moment with the real Pete.

Thunder roared through the barn like an airplane was crashing down around us and I shivered, ducking a little despite myself. The sound wasn't like a hurricane—that was more moan and creak than crash and boom—but I couldn't shake the memory of the last time I'd waited out a huge storm in a tack room. The roof wasn't going to peel off, I reminded myself, and the storm wasn't going to plunge in and threaten to blow me away—that was another time, that was all in the past. I put my hands between my knees and pressed them tightly together, breathing deeply.

Then Pete was at my side, nudging close to me on my bag of horse rugs, the plastic crinkling beneath us. His arm was around me and I leaned into him immediately, without meaning to, forgetting I was angry. He'd been there that night, the night of the hurricane, and he was here today, and my brain put those two things together and decided it meant *safety*. The flood of adrenaline started to seep away from my trembling fingertips. It was okay. Pete was here.

He could turn away from me again in a few minutes, he could decide he was still angry with me after all, and I'd let him, I'd trade it for a few minutes of his comforting closeness. I felt his mouth against my hair, my neck, close to my lips . . . *I must taste like salt,* I thought fleetingly.

There was a flash of lightning and the tack room lights promptly went out.

All the better, I thought, and turned my lips to Pete's.

A n hour later, we rode our horses home to my barn in the dripping gloom left over from the clouds. Pete had a lazy smile on his face; I had a tense jaw and a nervous tic above my left eye. Apparently what was emotional turmoil for me was a pleasant afternoon for Pete.

Becky was gone until the evening, and Pete's (now part-time) barn manager, Ramon, was in the barn dumping lunch grain, something both Barsuk and Mickey were highly interested in. They danced impatiently in the doorway as we dismounted, tugging at our grip on their reins while Ramon pushed the wheelbarrow full of buckets down the shadowy aisle. He nodded at the horses. "Those two cool enough to eat?"

"They're fine," I said. "Dump their feed and we'll untack them."

I started stripping Mickey's tack in the aisle so he could go right in and eat, and Pete followed suit, humming a little as his fingers flew through the buckles.

"So tonight, Becky's here. We could go to dinner, if you want," he said casually. I was touched—money was tight and going to town for dinner was a special treat. It was also a bit of an ordeal, unfortunately, if we were going to get up at five in the morning to ride racehorses. I looked at my wide-faced sports watch, the one I timed gallop sets and cross-country rides with, and did a little mental math—waiting for the horses to digest lunch, riding the rest of my horses, getting back to the house, showers, driving to town, ordering, waiting . . . "I won't be done until seven, with this rain delay."

"So, Cinderella?"

"So then we won't get home until almost eleven, and if you want me up in the morning to go find a galloping job . . ."

Pete was silent. Something told me I'd just punctured his chipper mood.

Well, I couldn't help being the realistic one. If he needed me on the road at five looking for work, then I needed more than four or five hours of sleep.

"Is that okay, Pete?"

"Okay," he said shortly.

"*Okay*, Pete?" I snapped.

"It's *fine*," he retorted, walking Barsuk into his stall. The horse danced beside him, completely thrilled at the prospect of lunch.

I'll bet that's exactly the response Pete wanted out of me when he suggested dinner, I thought. Sometimes it seemed like he was just looking for a reason to fight with me, as if he had to prove to himself, again and again, that he was mad at me—long after he was really over it.

5

THE NEXT MORNING I was in my truck at 5:05, at least an hour before the sun, with a mug of hot coffee and a determined set to my jaw. Last night I had done my research as Becky had instructed, googling the names of several large farms in the area to get an idea of how many horses in training they might have and the likelihood they'd need riders, and I had mentally rehearsed the speech I'd present at the gate. Today I was a professional, not a confused horse girl in need of some spare cash.

I looked at my hard hat and my safety vest and my cross-country whip, which was actually a racing whip, spread out like talismans on the passenger seat beside me. It was probably time to perform a little ritual to the racing gods, who were presumably a different pantheon from the eventing gods, but I didn't know any horse-racing witchcraft. I rearranged the items on the seat, finally pointing the whip toward the dashboard, as if it was an arrow leading us—me, the truck, maybe Pete by extension—into our un-certain future.

I turned on the truck and waved to Pete, who was walking out to his own truck, his whip in hand, his vest on his shoulder, his hat on his head. He smiled and gave me a thumbs-up. He wasn't mad at me about dinner anymore; he'd gotten over that on the walk back to the house when I reminded him we had a frozen pizza. His mood had lightened so much, I wondered if the whole tantrum was just a result of his inner teenager craving a pizza.

Perfectly understandable.

Pete turned on his truck, his high beams shattering the dark morning, and drove away. All I could do now was follow.

I flipped on the radio and hit the gas and there I was, a journey-man exercise rider, setting out for the day's horses with the BBC World Service solemnly reporting on the state of the world. Not that I was a huge fan of the news, but I was afraid music would put me right back to sleep.

I turned right at the end of the drive, heading deeper into Red-dick and the massive training farms that spread out north of Briar Hill. More and more farms were sprouting cross-country courses and dressage areas where once only training tracks and broodmare barns had held sway, but there were still plenty of thriving Thor-oughbred farms here, ones that had waited out the recession and survived the hurricane. You could say only the strongest survived, but that really wasn't true here; in the horse business, anything could happen. People could get lucky with one big sale and use the cash to patch the roof and buy new mares, or they could have bot-tomless bank accounts and just pour money on their problems un-til the fires went out. It wasn't about being strong, sometimes—it was about being lucky and being rich, which was one of the things I hated about the horse business.

A reporter with an unpronounceable Irish name was explaining far more than I'd ever need to know about the latest European crisis as I pulled into the first farm I'd marked on my list. Another truck had just turned into the driveway, heading past the darkened farm office on the way to a bright line of lights in the distance that could only be the training barn. The sight of it, so close, made my stomach sink to my boots. I was going to have to get out of the truck and walk into a barn full of people I didn't know, ask for the person in charge, so obviously looking for work in all the wrong places, and I didn't think my heart could handle the stress. I'd never been a particularly socially anxious person, but I didn't seek out opportunities to embarrass myself, either. I wasn't someone who could cold-call strangers. Above all, I was scared to death of racetrack people. Any sensible person would be. They chose to live this way, riding in the dark, on half-broke horses.

I let the taillights in front of me dwindle to tiny red stars before I gunned the engine to follow. At least let the person get out of their truck and go into the barn before I arrived. At least let me not have to follow some confident, employed person into their place of work if I had to go hat literally in hand, begging for a job from strangers.

This was what I'd skipped, I realized, back when I'd gotten my college fund from my grandfather and found it was just enough to buy my own little farm west of Ocala. If I'd gone the normal ambitious-horse-girl route, I'd have been floating from barn to barn for several years now. This would be my lifestyle. Maybe I *had* been lucky, and I hadn't even known it.

I parked under an oak tree, its branches blocking out the stars, and looked over my steering wheel at the barn. It was a hive of activity. The first horses were already being led out, riders up. Through the open grills of stall doors I could see horses standing tied, grooms knocking off the dirt and shavings of the night, putting on saddles and bridles in preparation for more riders. I could be one of those riders, I thought, if I just had enough guts to get out of the truck and ask.

I thought about Pete and the lost look in his eyes when we were talking about the future. I thought about his fleeting good humor yesterday; I thought about how happy we'd been back in the spring, before the summer came and tore things apart; then I clambered out of the truck and marched across the gravel parking lot, determined to make something good happen.

The barn foreman was writing names on a whiteboard. He was easy to identify as foreman because his clothes were clean, and he wasn't wearing chaps or a safety vest, just jeans and a collared shirt with the farm name stitched across the chest. He looked down at me from a comfortable six foot five, scratched at his woolly mustache, and wrinkled his brow. "You got experience?"

"I'm an event rider." I stood up as tall as I could, which seemed a little counterproductive for someone seeking a job riding racehorses, but I wasn't trying to be an actual jockey and this man's towering height was intimidating, even if his middle-aged face was already settling into grandfatherly lines. "I train upper-level event horses. I'm competing at the Intermediate level. Galloping strong horses is what I do for a living. Mostly Thoroughbreds, too," I added. "I'm used to them."

He crossed his arms, the uncapped dry erase marker lending a chemical undertone to the scents of hay and shavings in the barn. "I've had some good event riders," he conceded. "You guys are not scared. Even when you should be."

I started to smile.

"But," he went on, holding up a hand, "I need experienced exercise riders for my older horses. You come back in a month, when I'm starting babies, we can use you then."

I made myself continue to smile. "You tell me what to do out there, I'll do it. I can ride these horses." Becky told me to be confident. Becky said to sell myself. Becky was always right. It was the single most annoying thing about her.

His smile grew more patronizing. "I don't doubt it. But I'm not training new riders this morning. Come on back. I'll be starting babies mid-October."

I left. What else could I do? More riders were coming into the barn, looking at the whiteboard for their horses, buckling on their hard hats to get ready for their morning's work. I walked out of the barn under their curious glances, knowing what they were thinking: another starry-eyed horse girl, thinking racehorses were just like show ponies, gonna get hurt out there before she learned better.

I wasn't that girl, but I wasn't ready to be the girl who proved them wrong, either.

The next farm on my list was back by good old No-Name Acres, the junkyard I'd ridden at yesterday morning. They were neighbors, actually—so if I'd turned left instead of right after leaving that barn, I'd have gone to see someone who was hiring riders, not someone who told me to come back next month, like all the others.

I shook my head as I passed the dark entrance to yesterday's worksite. Mary Archer, telling me not to mention her name. Who said things like that? Why couldn't horse people just be normal for once?

Anyway, last night I'd found this farm through an ad in the local Thoroughbred newsletter, *Wire to Wire,* saying they were
looking for exercise riders, and while I didn't doubt they'd have
plenty of other applicants, something in their website had given
me hope: their trainer was a woman, and a fairly young-looking
woman at that. In the divide between horse sports and horse racing, I thought the gender line was the most interesting of all: most
of the trainers and riders and clients in horse showing were women,
while most of the trainers and riders and clients in horse racing were
men. I had private ideas about how that might relate to the treatment
of horses, or an overall necessity of patience in the years-long attempt
to produce a fully developed and athletic sport horse, as opposed
to the *run-run-faster-faster* mentality of training racehorses, but I
didn't have any actual proof, and so I thought it might be interesting
to actually see a woman in the sport. Maybe we weren't so different
after all. Or maybe she was a lunatic, like Mary Archer, and my entire theory was way off course. I'd have to wait and see.

"Cotswold Farm, please don't be crazy-cakes," I muttered,
turning into the drive. The arched gates were closed, which meant
either they didn't like visitors, or they were extra vigilant about the
potential for loose horses. I popped open the truck door and leaned
down to the call box.

A tired-sounding woman answered after the electronic ringing
had gone on for so long, I'd nearly given up hope. "Cotswold Farm,
how can I help you, please have coffee."

"Um—" I bit back a giggle. "You had an ad? I came to see if
you needed a rider this morning?"

"Oh. Uh . . . let me do a headcount."

I heard her counting aloud. When she got to six, I interrupted.
"I have an extra mug of coffee in the truck."

The woman burst into laughter. "Oh, seriously? Get yourself down here. I dropped my coffee pot *again* and I'm dying. Straight past the house. The road ends at the training barn. Come into the tack room. I'm Alex."

The call box clicked and the line was dead. I was still staring at it, jaw hanging open, when the gate motor began to hum and the black steel bars slowly opened for me.

I was in.

The truck's headlights lit up black-board fencing lined with wire mesh as the driveway curved sinuously around live oaks and gentle hills. At a turnoff I looked left and saw a barn perched above me on a hilltop, lights shining through the stall windows. By its design, a center-aisle barn like my own, I figured it was for brood-mares or yearlings. She'd said to drive straight to the end of the road, so on I went, until the training barn revealed itself.

"Oh, shit," I muttered. It was a big barn, bigger than the last one, and that had been a nice stable in its own right. Just like Pete's barn, two wings stretched out from a center square that housed the tack room, feed room, and office, and around its brightly lit shed rows I could see the shadows of horses walking. The approach ran between a patchwork pattern of small paddocks; off to one side, I could see a round pen, and to the other, a tree-lined path with a few streetlights reaching over their branches. The symmetry was perfect, striking a chord within me. In our hearts, equestrians are always striving for a perfect order. Cotswold Farm had it.

I parked along a row of trucks, slipped on my vest and hat, stuck my whip down my right half chap, and grabbed the coffee mugs. Time to do this.

Taking deep breaths, I walked through the central aisle and looked to my left—feed room—and to my right—tack room—and there in the tack room a slim blond woman who looked only a few years older than me was leaning on the green-painted metal door, tapping her fingers on the cream cinder blocks behind her. She was wearing skinny jeans and a kelly-green polo shirt, brown half chaps and jodhpur boots. She looked like a hunter princess, with less bling . . . no, scratch that. She looked like me, with more confidence.

"Please say that mug in your hand is for me," she said, tilting her head tragically. "My horse for a coffee."

"This one is mine," I said daringly. "But *this* one is for you." I took out my spare travel mug from behind my back, thanking the eventing gods—the racing gods?—I'd thought to put an extra in the truck this morning, in case the drive to find work stretched beyond the first coffee's powers.

Alex pushed off from the wall and took the tumbler I offered her, grinning at the event horses leaping around its sides. "We're best friends now. What's your name?"

"I'm Jules. Jules Thornton. I'm an event rider—"

"I've definitely heard your name before," Alex interrupted, sipping at the coffee. "Mmm . . . black? You're my hero. I can't even tell you—" Horseshoes rang on the cement of the center aisle and Alex turned, waving the tumbler in the air. "I have coffee, Alexander, this girl saved the day . . ."

The man in the Western saddle lifted his pale eyebrows at Alex, and then let his gaze travel to me. He was older than she was, but muscular and comfortable on a horse. He didn't wear a helmet, and his gold hair was lighter than his skin, as if he'd spent decades out in the sun. "You've saved the day for all of us," he told me. His accent was English, his tone was ironic. "No one wants to deal with Alex after she's broken another coffeemaker."

"Does this mean I don't have to go to Starbucks?" A baby-faced rider poked his head out of the tack room; he was wearing a green-covered helmet and safety vest, and there was a tiny exercise saddle over one arm. "Alex, say you forgive me."

"I'll never forgive you," Alex declared, waving her hand like a bored duchess. "But you don't have to go to Starbucks."

"He didn't even break it this time," Alexander observed. "This was all you."

"Diego is my scapegoat," Alex announced solemnly. "He will always take the blame. Those are the rules."

Diego nodded.

The man on the track pony sighed and rolled his eyes.

I watched this little comedy routine play out and decided I really needed these crazy people to hire me. "There's more where that came from, you know," I said, as if I was describing a cache of coke and pearls in the back of my truck. "I can make all your coffee dreams come true."

Alex burst into laughter. "I love you. Did I say that already? Alexander, Diego, meet my best friend Jules, the famous event rider."

"I don't think I'm *famous*," I started to stammer, before I realized she was just messing with me. I blushed.

"So you need a riding job?" Alex went on. "We need someone for the babies. There's always more babies than we meant to have. I think we're addicted to them. Or do you gallop? Can you breeze?"

I had only the vaguest idea of what a breeze entailed: it meant going very very fast, but that was as far as my knowledge went. I went for the low-hanging fruit, as it seemed safest and less likely to kill me. "I can gallop, but I haven't breezed. I can learn. But I can definitely do babies." Every other foreman and trainer had told me to come back for a job riding babies; therefore, I concluded, I could ride babies.

"Have you ridden yearlings before?" That was Alexander, who settled back in his Western saddle, watching me carefully.

Wait, what? Yearlings? I bit back my surprise. I couldn't even imagine riding a yearling. Was that what everyone meant when they said "babies" all this time?

I'd been thinking they meant two-year-olds. I'd thought Pete had meant two-year-olds, too. No one had mentioned *yearlings*. "I've started young horses before," I said cautiously. "I can start a horse under saddle and get them going."

"They're pretty easy," Alex assured me. "If you've started an older horse, you can definitely do a yearling. You just have to be gentle and patient."

"And be ready for them to spook," Diego added. "They spook at everything."

Great. "I can ride a spook," I asserted, pushing the falls I'd taken over the summer out of my mind.

"Oh, I'm not worried about you. I've seen you jumping. You're bold." Alex laughed, and I wondered where on earth she'd seen me. In person? On a blog? I had sworn off horse blogs after I'd run into trouble with a teenage blogger over the summer, but not looking at them certainly didn't mean I had stopped appearing in them. In fact, there was no chance *Eventing Chicks* wouldn't jump on our galloping gigs with glee once someone tipped them off. "In the *Chronicle*," Alex added, seeing my confused look. "Last week? Congrats on the sponsorship."

Our subscription to *The Chronicle of the Horse* had been allowed to expire because we couldn't afford to renew. It had been a real wrench to throw away that "Final Notice—Subscription Ending!" envelope. Losing the *Chronicle* had felt like losing a piece of our professional credibility. Everyone read it to see what everyone else was up to. "Thank you," I said faintly. "I didn't know it was out there."

"Just a little news blurb that you and your partner—sorry, don't know what your situation is—are competing this season with the Rockwell Brothers brand. That's great! Love their stuff. I keep looking at their close-contact models and wondering if I should just pull the trigger and buy a new one."

"They're amazing saddles," I said. "They're sending me a custom dressage saddle *someday*, no idea when though, and I'm hoping for a cross-country one next. Hopefully I don't grow old and die waiting for it." I'd almost given up hope of ever seeing it, even though I knew custom saddles took forever.

"Oh, a custom saddle," Alex sighed. "Yes, please. Alexander? What do you think? Custom saddle, yes?"

"Decide what you want to do with Tiger and then buy the right saddle for the job," Alexander intoned with an air of great patience, and Alex turned and stuck her tongue out at him.

"I'll do whatever I want," she said naughtily.

"Could you want to get to work?" His voice was pained.

"I guess so." Alex turned back to me. "I feel caffeinated and delightful. Let's get you on a horse! We have a couple just in from Keeneland, and some of ours will be coming in from the field in the next couple weeks. We're going to be neck-deep in yearlings before too long. I swear, we have a bunny farm, not a horse farm."

Twenty minutes later, I was wondering why we didn't *only* ride babies, and then just turn out older horses to watch in pastures for the rest of their lives. Because damned if this wasn't delightful.

And I was getting paid to do it.

The yearlings were all in the neighborhood of eighteen months old, and they came in all shapes and sizes. Some were slight and still looked like babies; Alex put the smallest, most jockey-sized riders on their backs, and told them to take it easy out there. Some were nearly sixteen hands and filling out through the shoulders and hindquarters like grown horses already; Alex put the second tier of riders, the ex-jocks who were filling out themselves, on those horses, and told *them* to take it easy out there. The middle horses, the fifteen-hands or so, fairly middling-sized horses, she matched with riders like me. Average-height, average-weight, average-experience riders on average-sized youngsters.

"Take it easy out there," she told me, as I joined the line of horses and riders parading around the shed row, and then she went back to the center aisle and mounted up on her pony.

We strolled twice around the shed row, the yearlings shying at the buckets and wraps hanging from the outer rail. I was on a solid chestnut colt with a white blaze; his leather neck strap read COTS-WOLD RAMBLER—DEVIL MAY CARE, and I sincerely hoped he was not going to live up to his dam's somewhat portentous name. But he seemed like a solid young citizen; his spooks were more like exaggerated double-takes, and his forelock, too long and thick to really belong on a horse his size, drifted over his offside eye every time he bowed himself away from the railing on his right. "I'm calling you Chandler," I decided.

Alex heard me and laughed. "Could he *be* any more adorable?"

Chandler snorted, his forelock drifting over his rolling eye as he glanced back at me.

That was the other cute thing the yearlings did: they physically turned and looked at their riders, often in astonishment. When I mounted Chandler (I was dedicated to calling him that now), he turned to look at me so quickly his entire body followed his head and he found himself turning in circles without any clear idea of how to stop himself. I drew up the outside rein and helped him come to a halt, then leaned down and rubbed his neck. He turned his head again, more cautiously this time, and nosed at my foot. Then he very slowly and methodically opened his jaws and placed his teeth on the tip of my boot. Tenderly at first, and then with increasing pressure. I gave him a nudge with my other boot and he darted forward, letting go of my boot just in time to run into the wall. Then, embarrassed, he turned and looked at me again.

They had no idea what to do about anything. Run into the wall? Stop and ask for help. Run into the tail of the horse in front of them? Stop and ask for help. I rode three different yearlings and each one had a different personality, but the underlying attitude among all of them seemed to be of puppies: they were dying to please, but they still had a lot of wiggling to do.

Then the fourth yearling happened.

After each ride, we took our saddles and bridles to the next horse on our list, knocked off the shavings, and tacked up the horse ourselves. I paused at the whiteboard and checked the grid: my next horse was in stall twelve. From the moment I entered stall twelve, I knew I was in for it. A plain chestnut filly lurked in the corner, watching me with pricked ears. When I came inside, those ears flipped to the side, and her head went up. I took it as a warning. She was checking her surroundings and deciding if she should flee or fight.

I wasn't really up for a fight, and chasing a baby around a stall sounded pretty terrible, too, so I pretended I was going to catch her in a pasture and trained my eyes on her shoulder, as if I wasn't at all interested in slipping my fingers around the strap of her halter.

It worked, of course; she wasn't old enough to know my tricks yet. But she still reacted badly when she felt my hand close around the halter's noseband, darting backward and nearly pulling free. I managed to stabilize her with a lot of quiet talking, and I clipped her to the tie hanging from the wall with more than my usual share of nerves.

Typically I wouldn't tie up a horse so hyped and ready to run; I had too many experiences of a horse pulling back against the tie and fighting it when they were worked up. I'd seen them flip over, I'd seen them hit their heads, I'd seen things go very, very wrong. But I was alone, everyone else was isolated in their own stall, doing their own work, and I was just going to have to wing it with the tools I was given.

Fortunately, she settled against the wall. I got the saddle on, and the bridle, and when a groom was passing, I called out for a leg up.

FUN SUPREME—LOUISA DOLL was going to make for a fun racehorse name someday, but at the moment she was just a little deer underneath me, all bones and nerves. She was a bright-red-coated thing, with a gold shimmer in the sunlight, just like the colt I'd ridden first, but where he'd been solid and interested in his surroundings and pretty fun to ride, she was delicate and frightened and completely nerve-racking to ride. I wasn't sure who was going to fall to pieces first, her or me. By the time we danced out of the shed row, jigging sideways and startling at particularly alarming rocks that glared up at her from the gravel horse path, I was sweating and ready to call it quits.

Unfortunately, we still had a long ride ahead of us: we were heading out to the big pasture behind the training barn, where we'd be riding along the fence line like a group of kids on a field trip to a Western trail barn. We rode in single file, noses to tails, with the fence on one side to keep our wiggly babies moving forward instead of sideways (most of the time). Their legs rattled the lush late-summer grass and their heads dipped suddenly for occasional nibbles. With only the thin exercise saddle between me and the horse, I felt like I was riding bareback.

Louisa clearly did not care for the great outdoors. She shied at the rocks, she shied at the trees, she planted her hooves and simply would not go through the gate, although I was pretty sure she'd been turned out in pastures before in her life (like, say, last night). The other yearlings moseyed through the gateway and stood on the other side, staring in prick-eared astonishment, while she balked and threw her head and danced from side to side and basically acted like a fool.

I was nudging her with a gradually more emphatic series of heels to her ribs, but it was dawning on me that, as a horse who had only been ridden maybe three or four times before in a round pen, she had no idea what that meant. I was a person who was inexplicably sitting on her back and thumping her sides, and all she wanted me to know was the damn gate was scaring her.

I dropped the pressure and loosened my reins, and she mouthed the eggbutt snaffle for a moment before turning her head and looking at me with wide-eyed appeal.

Diego grinned. "That's a 'help me' face all right," he said. "Hey Alex! We need a tow."

Alex laughed and came around the crowd of yearlings, who were all watching Louisa's show with keen interest, and snapped a lead rope onto her halter. Now I knew why we left them on under the light nylon bridles. Louisa snuggled close to Alex's ride, a quiet bay Thoroughbred with a been-there-done-that attitude, and only resisted a little when the pair of them led us through the gate and into the pasture.

"Thanks," I said as we joined the others and started to walk along the fence, headed toward the distant tree line where the property ended. Louisa crowded Alex's horse but the track pony didn't so much as pin his ears. She felt completely different now, more like the others I'd ridden that morning, as if she needed a big brother to give her confidence. I felt bad I hadn't been able to offer her a similar level of reassurance.

"Some of them need a little extra help," Alex said, smiling down at the filly, who was currently rubbing her ears against Alex's boot. "But we're in no hurry around here. That's one reason we start in September. A half hour of trail riding in September is a lot easier than taking them straight onto the training track in December."

"What happens between now and then? We just ride them in the pastures?"

That sounded pretty incredible. If all I had to do for the next two months was get up early and take these well-bred babies on trail rides, I'd landed on my feet for sure.

"Oh no, lots more. The most mature ones will start jogging and galloping on the track after a while. The others will get turned out for some growing time. Everyone gets their own curriculum." Alex grinned at me. "We're basically a very exclusive private school."

Louisa jigged at a butterfly and curved her body against Alex's pony again, pressing my leg into his ribs. I gave her a nudge without thinking and she popped out again, moving sideways for a few strides. "Hey," I said. "She moved off my leg!"

"She'll figure it out," Alex said. "They all figure it out if you just give them a little time."

I thought about Alex's words all the way home. Time, to me, had always felt like a luxury I couldn't afford. I was always racing to catch up, breathless for fear I was too late, my class finished before I had started.

It was a dangerous game to play with horses, though. Horses, as Alex reminded me, required all the time in the world. And then some.

"I have to learn to slow down," I said out loud. The trees and fences and grazing horses flashed by, too quickly. Everything was moving too quickly. I put my foot down on the brake and slowed the truck to a respectable, law-abiding rate of speed. Another truck roared past me, driver glaring at me, even though the center lines were double solid. I took a long breath, and then another. "Slow. Down."

It seemed impossible, I thought, driving up the barn lane, the shadows dancing beneath its canopy of live oaks, but maybe riding for Alex could teach me to relax and slow down. Wouldn't that be a funny lesson to bring home from a racing stable?

Lacey texted while I was parking the truck at the house. *It's snowing.*

I stared at the text. *No way,* I finally replied. *Pics?*

OK it's not snowing just wanted you to feel jealous.

I snorted. *Snow will not make me feel jealous I promise you.*

I slept until nine this morning.

OK that makes me jealous.

Thought so.

I could practically see her grinning face. I sighed. I missed Lacey so much.

I really needed her right now.

6

RIDING DYNAMO FELT completely strange after a morning on yearlings. The saddle was too big, the stirrups too long, and the horse was definitely too tall and broad. I found myself missing the comfortable chair-seat I'd settled into as I'd grown accustomed to the exercise saddles—definitely a no-no in any of my actual riding disciplines—with my lower legs slung comfortably in front of me instead of tucked back decorously. Plus, I could swear Dynamo had grown several hands during my brief absence. "Did you turn into a draft horse while I was gone, buddy?" I asked.

He flicked back his red ears to listen to me, then flicked them forward to focus on the road ahead. We were walking up the gravel road to the dressage arena, the midmorning sun filtering through the oak trees and dappling the puddles in the driveway with dancing light. The air was dripping with humidity, and I imagined yesterday's pools of rainwater evaporating into the air, lifting up in muggy spirals around us, preparing to condense into clouds and storm their way back down in the noisy hours after lunch, when thunder drowned out the barn radio. Ah, summer. In late September, the season began to feel endless.

"Almost fall," I sang tunelessly, rubbing my gloved hand on Dynamo's sweat-slick neck. "Almost fall, cool days ahead."

Well, in about two months.

I settled back in my black dressage saddle and dropped my stirrups a hole on either side, trying to find the freedom I'd felt in the tiny exercise saddle. Maybe I should get one for myself. The lack of any padding between me and my horse had been incredibly revealing. A horse couldn't pull many tricks on a rider with so much sensitivity.

I tried to imagine what would happen if I attempted a dressage test in an exercise saddle at an event. Was there actually a stipulation about what sort of saddle was allowed in competition? I'd never thought of riding a dressage test in anything but a dressage saddle, so I couldn't think what the rulebook said on the matter.

"At X, working jog," I joked to Dynamo. "Between C and K, pick up a gallop." It was funny, and a little addictive, the way the racehorse people said "jog" and "gallop," instead of "trot" and "canter."

The dressage arena came into view as we turned a bend in the road. There was Pete, trotting Regina on a long rein. The regal liver chestnut mare pushed her nose toward the neat clay furrows, her trot a long, easy swing. Pete, his legs steady, his hands still, his back straight, did not seem to suffer any lasting effects from riding in an exercise saddle. Well, he was more used to it than me. He'd galloped at training farms before, and it was always easier to switch between disciplines once you had your muscles trained to sit one way in one saddle, and another way in another saddle. The principle was the same with dressage and jumping saddles; I remembered the first time I'd sat in a dressage saddle—it had been like I'd been picked up from my comfortable jumping saddle and deposited into another dimension, where nothing made sense.

Pete brought his mare down to a walk as I rode into the arena. "How was the morning?" he called, patting Regina on the neck.

"It was good." I walked Dynamo alongside Regina and she pinned her ears, snaking her neck out to nip at him. Dynamo sidestepped quickly and kept his distance, ears tilted back. He didn't understand mares. I didn't either. "Babies are smaller than I expected."

"It's nice riding, though," Pete said. "They're more surprised by us than anything, so they don't have big fights about how independent they are. I'd much rather start babies than get back into breezing. Maybe we'll be lucky and by the time they start real training, all this will be behind us."

I hazarded a glance over at the half-empty house, the home we were about to pass to strangers. "Let's hope."

It was going to hurt riding past the house every day, knowing someone else was living in our rooms. I wished the arenas weren't so close to the training barn and the house; I wished we could just stay at our end of the farm and not have to see the newcomers every day.

Pete was going on about upcoming shows, leaving the unpleasant reality behind in favor of more cheerful topics, like ride times and entries. I appreciated the effort, so I nodded along and smiled as he listed our schedule: "Beginning of October, there's a dressage show at Red Hook Farm we can go to, and then the week after that, we have Sun Valley for these two, plus Mickey, Jim Dear, Barsuk, and

Mayfair . . . maybe it will have cooled off by then." He looked up at the fluffy white clouds floating innocently overhead, pretending they weren't condensing into larger and more dangerous shapes by the second. "And dried off a little, too. Mayfair doesn't like wet footing at all. Such a princess."

Regina shook her long head. I imagined the look of disdain she'd give pretty little Mayfair, a young Thoroughbred mare who was still going Novice. *You think* you're *the princess?* she'd snort. *I'm the princess, and I eat mud for dessert.*

Regina felt herself every bit as royal as her name, the grande dame of Briar Hill Farm, or wherever she was going to live in six months. As a champion mare about to attempt her first three-day event, a cut above the Advanced level horse trials she had competed at earlier this spring, Regina knew her worth and wasn't afraid to flaunt it in front of every horse who came near her. Pete said she thought she'd been adopted by the royal family while they'd been training in England this summer, and now she wanted everyone to call her "Your Highness."

"And what about you?" Pete asked. "Are you ready to show off your new dressage skills?"

I shrugged, as if I hadn't just spent the entire summer becoming a dressage queen. "Do you really think I'm better?" I asked, faux-humble, fishing for a compliment.

"Are you kidding? After three months in dressage boot camp, you better be." Pete laughed, but it was a hollow sound.

I felt the coldness in his tone, and stiffened. "Well, you saw me at the dressage show. I have a nice ribbon and a signed test that says I'm pretty good at sandboxing now." I picked up Dynamo's reins and squeezed him past Pete and Regina, ignoring the mare's flashing eyes and pinned ears. "I'll take my crew to Red Hook," I called, not bothering to look back. "Email me the entry link."

D ynamo moved through the dressage arena with the grace I'd come to expect from him. He had never been a naturally good mover, but over the summer, Grace had helped me put together his pieces with more style than I'd been able to master on my own, and now he felt taller, stronger, and more capable in every way. His arched neck rippled with muscle as he floated across the arena's diagonal, flinging out his forelegs in a tremendously forward extended trot.

When I brought him down to a halt, placing an appreciative hand on his hot neck, Pete clapped his own hands together. "Bravo, my queen. Bravo."

I rubbed my hand up Dynamo's chestnut mane, giving him a caress without dropping the reins, and tossed Pete a careless smile that didn't reveal how pleased I was that he was watching. Dynamo *had* done beautifully; we deserved the attention. I didn't bother addressing the little feeling of unease in my chest about the level of submission I was asking for, and receiving, from Dynamo. Something about it didn't feel right—should an event horse, who had to make split-second decisions on the cross-country course without waiting for his rider's calculations, be giving in to his rider's will so completely in the dressage ring? Could he be an elegant machine in the dressage arena, and just a few hours later be a brave, independent jumper?

That's what Regina does, I reminded myself, glancing back over at the regal mare, her coat nearly black with sweat but her poise unchanged. Pete picked up her reins now and she collected herself immediately, arching her neck and holding the bit delicately in her mouth, her ears swept back to listen to his every murmured instruction. Regina was a dressage horse first and foremost, but she had never shown Pete the slightest hesitation on the cross-country course. She jumped everything with the same haughty precision she showed in the dressage arena.

Still, Dynamo wasn't the most well-proportioned horse. He'd always found warming up into a collected frame to be difficult. If moving in self-carriage was just easier for her, wouldn't that mean she required less submission to get the same results? Wouldn't that just mean Dynamo—

The sound of palm fronds rattling made Dynamo jump, shifting me out of my dressage philosophy session, and I turned to see a large horse van making its painstaking way along the narrow driveway, nearly taking out a few palm trees clustered near the house. It downshifted with a minor roar and turned along the dressage ring's edge, making for the training barn Pete had so recently vacated.

"Pete?" I called, but he was already pulling Regina up, hands tight on the reins, watching the truck's slow progression. From inside, there was a chorus of shrill whinnies, and I could see high heads and pricked ears cast as shadows on the truck's frosted windows. I nudged Dynamo alongside Regina, who was watching the affair with such absorbed disdain, she didn't even bother to make a face at Dynamo. "Pete, they're not supposed to be here yet, right? I thought we had another three weeks."

"Bastards," Pete muttered. "They think they can just show up and—" He put his heels to Regina's sides and the mare sprang forward, just as eager for battle as her rider was.

Dynamo pulled at the bit, anxious to follow her, and after a moment's hesitation I let him go. We cantered down the arena and right out the in-gate, in a breach of protocol we never allowed our horses.

The truck's side door was pulled up flush with the earthen loading dock by the time we reached it. A red-faced man in a white cowboy hat jumped down from the cab, brandishing a clipboard. "I got a load here from Virginia I need to drop off on the way to Tampa!" he shouted.

"Oh, and they just thought they could show up whenever—" I started indignantly, but Pete was already jumping from the saddle and throwing Regina's reins to me.

He strode up to the driver with his hands fisted. "I don't know who gave you this address, but it's private property and we aren't expecting any horses. You'll have to take them along."

Inside the trailer, hooves stomped and anxious voices whinnied. Dynamo lifted his head and sang out a lilting neigh in return. "Shush," I scolded him. "Don't make them more upset."

The driver handed over the clipboard and pointed to a paragraph. I was too far away to even squint at the letters, but Pete bent over it and after a few moments, I saw his shoulders sag.

"No, no, no," I scolded, kicking Dynamo forward and dragging Regina along, her ears pinned furiously. "We are *not* accepting these horses."

The driver looked up at me, pushing back his cowboy hat. "Well, lady, I sure ain't takin' them to Tampa with me."

"We'll take them," Pete interjected.

"Oh, I don't think so—"

"Jules," Pete said quietly. "We're taking them."

I felt an angry flush reddening my cheeks. My entire temperature was spiraling toward a fever, in fact. I was so furious I was dizzy. "They can't just dump their horses on us whenever they want!"

Pete held up a finger. "Please. A moment." He was so deadly calm he was starting to make me nervous. "I'm going to call Mr. Blixden and get this straightened out. But we can't leave them on a trailer heading two hours away with nowhere to unload. It's not their fault."

I hunched over and leaned against the pommel of the saddle. Of course I didn't want the horses to get stuck in some sort of never-ending trailer ride. I just didn't want them *here*. Not yet. We had contracts and agreements that were supposed to keep this awful rental agreement from getting too awful. Now they were sending their horses for us to take care of, three weeks early and without so much as an email? A telegram? Smoke signals?

Pete pulled his phone out of his back pocket and started dialing with angry punches of his finger. Ah, there was the outrage, simmering below his tidy surface. I felt a little better. Pete would handle this.

The truck driver crossed his arms, clearly annoyed. I decided against taking the opportunity to yell at him. This wasn't his war.

What with all the neighs echoing from inside the trailer, I could barely hear what Pete was saying into the phone. "Mr. Blixden, these are not the dates we agreed to at all *(neigh)* back to your farm for all I *(neigh)* of course not, that's not what I meant *(neigh)* well certainly but there's going to have to be new language *(neigh)* of course, we're in agreement *(neigh)* thank you, Mr. Blixden."

By the end of this one-sided conversation, the authoritative note had left Pete's tone and his chin had tipped toward the ground. He'd lost, I realized, as he slowly slipped the phone back into the slim pocket of his breeches. He'd been beaten, and we weren't just going to accept these horses, we were going to thank the Blixdens for sending them down early.

"Go ahead and unload them," Pete said wearily.

"I'll need help," the driver said. "You got a groom?"

A month ago we'd have had four grooms to offer. Becky, Lacey, Ramon, Mikey. Today, we had only Ramon, who worked mornings unless we paid him extra to stick around, and since it was noon, he was getting ready to leave for the day. Pete looked back at his showy training barn with a despairing expression. I read his thoughts: a trainer with a barn like this should at least have a groom on hand.

I could see his dignity falling in pieces around him, and it made my heart ache. I knew all about stops and stutters on the way to the top, but this one was crueler than most.

"I'll help," I offered. "Pete, why don't you take these two back to the barn so Ramon can start on them before he leaves? I'll get these guys in stalls with hay and water, then I'll hustle back down so we can ride our next two." I tried to emphasize that we had other horses, that we did have help, that we were on a tight schedule because we had so much business we could barely make it through the day. This truck driver wasn't anyone we knew, but he might run into other people who *did* know us, and they might all be talking about us by evening feeding time. Barn gossip was so seductive. And since it went online so quickly, it was also an easy way to poison a person's business.

I imagined *Eventing Chicks* finding out that we were operating on a shoestring just a month after our triumphant return from the Rockwell Brothers–sanctioned training sessions. Nope. We had to look put together and fabulous, not broke and panicked.

Pete shook his head at my offer. "We can both help. There's four horses here, and nothing's bedded or ready. Let's just take off our guys' bridles and stick them in stalls until we've got these horses settled in."

My gut twisted in knots as I rode Dynamo into the barn, Regina huffing at his side. I jumped down in the shed row and a few small sparrows flitted from the nearest stall. Had we been in here just yesterday, playing at being a couple again? The memory made the empty stalls even worse to deal with today. For a few fleeting moments, I'd remembered what *we* felt like.

I opened the stall's wire-grill door and let Dynamo walk in, the reins slipping through my fingers. When he circled around to face me, I ran up the saddle's stirrups and slipped off his bridle. He ducked his head to look for leftover grain in the empty corners while I closed the grill and took Regina to the next stall.

They both ignored me as I walked away, jaw tight to keep my chin from wobbling. It was time to bring in the tenant's horses.

They were elegant warmbloods, heavy of bone and yet light of foot, each one well-mannered and obedient. They walked around their new stalls with eyes wide and ears pricked, whinnying at regular intervals to make sure everyone was still accounted for, their shod hooves digging crazy patterns into the bare clay floors.

The truck driver left to finish his run to Tampa, his two remaining horses anxiously neighing as the trailer crept back down the driveway.

In the middle of all this noise, Pete and I were still pulling out bags of shavings from the storage room and dumping them in piles in the stalls, leaving the horses to spread them out on their own, and filling up the water buckets the driver had tossed out of the trailer before he left. "Who's going to feed them?" I asked, already knowing and dreading the answer.

Pete laughed shortly. "We are, obviously. We're being paid the normal day rate."

Well, that was something. I brushed shavings off my breeches and went to pull down some of the leftover hay bales from the little loft above the tack room.

I threw down the hay bales so they burst open on the concrete floor of the breezeway. It was satisfying, and it also did the work of shaking the flakes apart so I could check each one for mold. I glanced over to my right: the paddocks, the arenas, the house. It would be strange having someone else's horses in the barn so close to our house. I had always liked looking out the kitchen window and seeing familiar faces in the training barn: I loved Pete's horses as I loved my own, simply because they were his. Now when I went back to the house for lunch, I would look out the window and see four faces I didn't know peering over their stall grills, wondering where they were, and what had happened to all the humans. They'd be lonely in that barn, with no one around all day long, and we didn't even know if they were allowed turnout or not. Blixden had told Pete he'd have his barn manager email with all their usual care instructions. He hadn't said why he hadn't done that before, or why he hadn't told us the horses were coming, and Pete hadn't asked. We knew why.

Blixden wanted us to know he was in charge.

Oh, I wasn't an idiot. I knew all about intimidation—that was a tactic rich people were taught in rich-people kindergarten. Blixden probably wanted to buy the farm. Who wouldn't? Briar Hill was a jewel. The shed row–style training barn with its cool breezes, the comfortable house, the gorgeous pastures—in a countryside brimming with beautiful farms, Briar Hill was a standout.

I remembered when Blixden had first come to look at the property with his wife. The agent paraded them past in a golf cart while we were riding. Their eyes had been round and their heads swiveling, trying to take it all in.

I knew how they felt.

"Thanks for getting all this hay," Pete said, taking an armful himself. "I have to arrange a delivery on Blixden's account."

He sounded so defeated. I wondered what Blixden had said to him. I wished I'd answered the phone. I'd have told that bastard to call the feed store and get his accounts and deliveries settled himself.

But no. Pete was going to be courteous and hospitable until the bitter end. He wasn't going to risk offending our new tenant, just like he'd never dreamed of defying Rockwell Brothers' demands in exchange for our sponsorship. Pete was *such* a good boy. Maybe, I thought hopefully, this whole experience would teach him that good behavior was rarely rewarded.

In the meantime, I would pretend to be optimistic about his efforts.

"It's going to feel so good when this whole thing is sorted and we kick him out," I said.

Pete didn't even look at me, just threw hay over the stall grill into the closest occupied stall. "Well, this ride's over," he said, walking down the aisle to fetch Regina from her temporary stall. "No point in trying to salvage any of it. I'm going to head back. You coming?"

So, being the cheerleader wasn't going to work. I considered whether I really wanted to ride back with him while he was in such a mood. I cast around for an excuse and decided fitness was the answer. We hadn't done any galloping sets since we'd come back from Orlando, and the aerobic work would help Dynamo prep for his next event.

"In a few," I decided. "I'm going to take Dynamo out for a quick gallop over the grass."

He nodded and took Regina away without a look back.

7

THE GREEN SLOPES slid away in a pleasant blur beneath Dynamo's pounding hooves. Released from the tight control I'd required of him in the dressage ring, he lengthened his stride with obvious pleasure. The cross-country jumps dotting the field around us were inviting, or as inviting as piles of logs bolted together can be, but my stirrups were about four holes too long to do any serious jumping. I was just able to lift myself out of the saddle in a half seat, leaning slightly forward to give Dynamo the freedom he needed to extend his gallop.

That would have to do for today. I'd missed galloping so, so much.

A CANTER IS A CURE FOR EVERY EVIL: so saith the T-shirts and cross-stitch patterns and faux-driftwood signs on Etsy, so it must be true. If a canter cured evil, a gallop saved lives. Lord knew I needed this one. Pete's unhappiness was making me crazy.

Every time I turned a corner and saw his worried face, my

stomach did a slow, nauseating flip. Every time I looked over at him from across the couch, or across the kitchen table, or across the barn aisle, and saw a faraway look in his eyes, proof he was lost in racing thoughts, my fingernails clenched into my palms. He was sad. There were a hundred fancy words for it, but the bottom line was, Pete was sad, and I couldn't make him feel better. I *knew* I couldn't snap my fingers and insist he cheer up, and yet . . . I really wanted to try it.

Especially if he was going to be training out of my barn—and now, with the Blixden horses arriving three weeks early, I assumed the rest of Pete's horses would move down to the annex immediately, maybe even tonight. That meant all Pete, all the time. Now, I loved having him around during the workday. I even *wanted* him working out of my barn. Who could have predicted that? I'd always said I'd never date a man who knew anything about horses. To not only date one, but risk being second-guessed in my own barn?

Oh, hell no!

But it wasn't like that at all. We helped each other. We liked each other's company. And with Lacey gone, and Becky only around to help us a few days a week, pooling our responsibilities just made sense.

I glanced over my shoulder, to see if Pete had made it back to the annex barn yet. I saw his shape in the distance, walking alongside Regina. "We're going to come out on top," I said. "Just hang on, Pete."

Dynamo's long, steady strides brought us across the field and to the fence line, a black-painted four-board fence shaded with oak trees. I slowed him down to an easy canter, and then a walk, and we strolled along, looking over the neighbor's pastures. Their breeding farm was situated on lower land than ours, with flatter fields, and I could see right across the property to their training barn and track, at least half a mile away. Horses milled near the far pasture gates, looking for hay or grain or trouble. The sight of all those horses soothed me, knowing our neighbors were in the same business as us, knowing we shared the same worries. I loved living in an equestrian community.

A rumble from behind us caught my attention, and I swung around in the saddle to see a dark-bellied cloud, its upper stories spreading into a blinding white canopy high in the atmosphere, making its unhurried way toward us. There was a quick stab of lightning, so fast and faint it was like a wink, and another rumble. Another early storm, just like yesterday. September was proving to be quite the little bitch.

"Are you *kidding* me?" I grumbled, and turned Dynamo back up the hillside toward home. I glanced at my watch as he broke into a trot: eleven thirty. "Way too early for this shit," I told the cloud, now off to my right and sauntering closer, its gray undersides weeping rain. The lightning winked again, and the thunder rumbled so deeply the ground must have shaken beneath Dynamo's hooves.

Well, two could play at that game. I shook out the reins at Dynamo, nudging him back into a ground-covering gallop. I shifted myself into as close an approximation of a galloping seat as I could with my dressage saddle and long stirrups, bridging the reins across his hot neck and perching my weight above his withers. It was the same trick we used on cross-country courses to preserve energy on the long gallop lanes between the clusters of obstacles. We only needed collection and precision at the jumps. In between, we let our horses put their heads down and gallop the way they would in nature, with as little interference in their gait as possible.

Dynamo should have pressed his nose down, taking hold of

the bit and pulling against the reins. But he didn't. I waited, and gave him a few friendly nudges with my calves to encourage him to speed up and take control. He went on galloping strongly, but the long stride that should have brought us close to racing speed didn't come. He held the bit tenderly, instead of biting down on it. He arched his neck, instead of shoving it out in front of him.

I realized what was happening with a sickening certainty. *I told you so,* I thought, and I was talking to myself. I'd known all along that there was a real danger to teaching an event horse to perform dressage with an advanced level of collection, and here it was: when he was told to manage his own affairs, he was still waiting to be told what to do. Everything I'd read by the great old-timers crowded into my brain, all their stories about brave cross-country horses spoiled by too much dressage, all of them ending with "and the horse was never the same again."

The worry unfurled itself in my gut and added itself to the collection of anxieties there. The gallop that should have eroded all the morning's bad feelings just became a means to an end: enough to get us home before the storm, but no longer its own joyful creation, a moment in time when a sport horse could just be a horse, while I got to ride along.

It's only because you've been on those racehorses," Grace said crisply. "You're confusing yourself with too many disciplines and too many saddles."

I adjusted the hot phone against my cheek, wishing they made special Florida editions of iPhones that didn't feel like a car windshield that had been sitting in the sun all day. "But Grace, I've read about this. If a horse is *too* submissive they lose the edge that made them a good cross-country horse in the first place. And Dynamo's whole thing is that he's a good cross-country horse!"

"Now he's a good dressage horse, too," Grace insisted. "We spent all summer getting him there, if you'll recall. His 'whole thing' is that he's a well-rounded and well-trained event horse who can do all three phases well. And that's what you want."

I wondered why I'd ever called Grace in the first place. She was just as strong-willed and opinionated as I was, plus she was three times my age. If anyone out there was going to change her mind, it wasn't going to be me, her ex–working student with an authority problem. Still, I tried. "Something's going on. I know Dynamo's gallop inside and out. When I asked him to put his head down and run, he didn't do it. He stayed up in my hand, he stayed light, in a frame."

"Which is good training." Grace sighed.

"But now he's not galloping correctly," I repeated.

"So, teach him to."

"He already knew how to!" I nearly shouted with exasperation.

"Then teach him again." Grace paused and I heard voices in the background. "Jules? I have to go. Horse assignments gone wrong. This new working student doesn't have the same grasp of novice riding ability as you."

I winced on behalf of the new working student. "Okay, Grace. Bye."

The thunder was drawing away into the distance, leaving behind a humid and sparkling world, and Pete had gone off on another horse. I needed someone to talk to, and right away. Who knew about galloping?

Oh, right. I pulled up the newest number in my phone.

"Jules!" Alex trilled. "What's up?"

"Alex, I need ideas."

"I definitely know what you're talking about," Alex said thoughtfully, after listening to my half-hysterical description of how I broke my horse. "Except when I get this kind of thing, it's usually because a horse doesn't want to run."

"That can't be it, though. Dynamo loves to gallop."

"No . . . I think he's just confused. You told him to listen to every word you say, and so that's what he's doing. Waiting. Listening."

I started to pace the barn aisle. Dynamo watched me, ears pricked, leaning over his stall grill with a mouthful of timothy hay. Next to him, Mickey nosed through hay on the floor, his eyes flicking over to me as if to say, *Settle down, lady, you're making us nervous here.* "This is what I said would happen. No one listened to me. Win the dressage, they said. Win it at all costs. Well now I won't be able to make my cross-country time because my super-dressage horse is going to take the galloping lanes at a nice collected canter . . ."

I was so frustrated, I thought I might cry. And, I realized, I was babbling pretty incoherently to a person I'd only met this morning who was also my employer.

"I'm sorry," I said, taking a breath. "I really just meant to ask for your advice, not go off on you about it."

"No, no, it's fine." Alex brushed away my apology. "It's a big deal, I understand. I used to event, too. Not like, upper-level or anything, but . . . I get why it's important."

How interesting! I wondered if she'd been like me once, and gotten into galloping so much that she just decided to do racehorses, instead. Not enough jumping for me, though. "Do you have any ideas?" I asked hopefully.

"Not off the top of my head, but this seems like one of those things you have to feel, you know what I mean? So maybe while I'm riding it will come to me—"

"Come ride Dynamo," I said impulsively.

"Your upper-level horse? No, I can't do that. I'm not good enough, I'd mess him up."

"He's already messed up. I did that. And you're plenty good. I saw you gallop this morning. And you used to event? You're fine. Please. Come out sometime," I cajoled. "It'll be fun, and you can feel him and tell me what you think."

There was a pause. I heard a horse whinny in the background and imagined I could hear it across the few miles of fields between us. Then Alex laughed.

"Okay. Why not? Alexander will say it's good for me. He wants me to show my retiree, even if he acts all crotchety about it when I'm thinking about showing instead of working. Any time I sit in an English saddle, he takes it as a good sign."

I was giddy with sudden relief. Alex galloped horses every single day. She was a gallop professional. If anyone could figure out how to put the bold back in Dynamo's stride, it would be her.

8

PETE WAS OUT of bed and pulling on breeches—what else was new?—when I registered the sunlight streaming into the room and remembered: today was Monday.

Monday has ever been the unofficial International Day of Equestrian Rest, because horse shows happen over the weekend. It was our day off: no babies to ride, hence the extra two hours of sleep. Of course, we always managed to fill the day with little projects. Today, I had thought, we could probably spoil the fun of a day off by moving hay from the training barn down to the annex barn. The Blixden hay delivery had come, but we needed to get the rest of our supplies out of there before his grooms showed up and started feeding our hay.

But Pete was putting on the wrong clothes for a day filled with manual labor and grass stains.

"Those are your show breeches," I said. "You clearly need coffee."

Pete went on hopping around the room on one leg, halfway into his white Taileds. "I have to look good today," he grunted, yanking at the resisting fabric.

"For God's sake, you have to put them on like pantyhose. Are you new to this?" I sat him down on the bed and gathered up one leg of the breeches in my fist. "Do it right or you'll tear them. Why do you have to look good?"

Pete sulkily pulled on the breeches the way I showed him. We went through this every time with his Tailored Sportsmans, which were more fitted and less forgiving than his daily collection of schooling jodhpurs. Please don't ask me how he got ready for events and shows before I arrived on the scene. I don't want to consider the possible answers. "Amanda's coming over to take some video."

"Ugh, it's too early to talk about Amanda the Hunter Princess."

"It's too early to *argue* about her," he said pointedly.

"Who is she trying to sell? You don't have anyone besides Rorschach, and she already has video of him."

"She's selling me," Pete answered cryptically.

I gave him a dark look. If it was too early for Amanda-talk, it was definitely too early for vague nonsense. "You wanna get specific?"

He shrugged.

I watched him fumble with his new show belt, a Rockwell Brothers number with two brass circles for a buckle. It was awkward to put together at any time of day, but this morning he had serious butterfingers and the clasp didn't want to catch. He was moving so clumsily that I had to remark on it. "Dude, you're being very weird," I told him.

Pete sighed and took out a white show shirt.

"Nuh-uh," I said, shaking my head. "You're telling me what's up, right now. No one puts on white first thing in the morning. Even if you had a dressage test. What's going on? Are you going out to take video for Rockwell?"

In addition to posting pictures on our social media accounts at least three times a week with Rockwell tack, the company had decided to load us up with their autumn line of apparel as well, and asked us to model them in our posts whenever possible. Unfortunately, no one in their PR department considered that while the temperatures were dropping in most of the US, we were still dealing with the nineties every day in Florida. Our contact at the company had receded into embarrassed silence after the first few requests for "more Rockwell" in our Instagram feeds turned out to be very sweaty and red-faced versions of Team Briar Hill.

I was still waiting on my custom dressage saddle, and then they'd get an unboxing worth a few million views.

Pete avoided my gaze, reaching into the little cedar box where he kept his watches. "Not Rockwell. Amanda wants to send some business my way. She's going to put me on her website as an associate trainer."

"Wait . . . but wouldn't that make you a *hunter* trainer?" Pete wasn't a hunter rider. I didn't even think he could fake it to make a few bucks. His style was all wrong. He aimed for the most efficient trip between two jumps, not the most leisurely. He rode his courses in a very classy way, but he rode them *quickly*.

"No, no . . . jumpers. Amanda wants to stick to hunters and do less show jumping. But a lot of her clients do both. They have two hunters and a jumper, that kind of thing. So I'm going to try and take on a few of her jumpers."

"Like, their riding lessons?" That made sense . . . if he could fit it into his schedule. But he was already galloping in the morning and riding his horses in the afternoon. I didn't see where the extra hours would come from.

"And some training. A lot of them don't have time to ride during the week."

Like Grace, I thought, down in Orlando with her boarding stable that was nearly empty of people all day long, just her and Anna riding the clients' horses, prepping them to behave like good boys and girls during their owners' riding lessons on the weekends. Grace had said it was a failed model, though. It no longer paid the bills, and she'd had to diversify, moving into trail rides, kids' lessons, and anything else clever she could think of that no one else in the neighborhood had to offer.

Even if Ocala was still supporting this kind of business, Pete and Amanda didn't think they were going to be the only hunter/jumper game in a town overflowing with hunter/jumpers. Or even the best, I thought disloyally. Amanda won her share of ribbons and sold her share of big horses, but she wasn't even close to the top of the heap in this horsey town. Pete was a solid jumper and won the occasional mini prix on a Friday night, but he had no reputation in regular jumper classes. As an eventer, he was a big deal, though. Why give up that currency?

"I think you should stick to eventing," I said. "I'm sorry, but do jumper people even trust eventing people? They think we're insane for going cross-country."

"Amanda doesn't, obviously."

"Oh, *Amanda*. If *Amanda* thinks it's a good idea, who am I to question it?"

Pete tucked in his shirt. "We're not going to argue about Amanda. If you don't like her, steer clear of her while she's here. She's a business partner of mine and I intend to keep it that way."

I'm a business-slash-girlfriend partner of yours, do you intend to keep it that way? It was a stupid retort, so I didn't say it out loud. I just bit my lip and watched through narrowed eyes as he strode out of the room, deerskin show gloves in hand. Not the tough technical fabric he wore normally, but the elegant, more-pretty-than-functional gloves he saved for horse inspections at three-day events. After a few moments of silence, I heard the front door open and close. Well. He was going to the barn without me. I guess I'd really annoyed him this time.

Marcus padded into the bedroom, his hound-dog eyes looking perpetually concerned, and pulled himself onto the unmade bed with a flop of long ears and wag of long tail. I pulled at his silky brown ears. "Beagles are better than men," I told him, and planted a kiss on his head. "You don't expect us to share our barns with princesses wearing glittery hard hats." This was a problem with a shared barn I hadn't anticipated: there was no avoiding each other's guests and clients. No matter how much we might want to, for the sake of domestic tranquility.

Marcus suffered my attention for a few minutes, then lumbered back to his feet and made his way to his real target: my pillow. He settled onto it with a sigh, stretching out his freckled legs. I glared at him, but my glares had no effect on Marcus. Unlike my horses, who knew my different expressions and tailored their behavior accordingly, Marcus had absolutely no respect for me. I was expected to feed him, adore him, and let him sleep on my pillow on hot days when he didn't feel the need to join me at the barn. I was perfectly happy with this arrangement, except for the pillow part, but I let it slide because he was a beagle and beagles got whatever they wanted, or else they ate your shoes, your bras, and your bridles, in that order.

I took my time finishing my coffee; Ramon was feeding the horses this morning, a *definite* advantage to sharing the barn I hadn't enjoyed before Pete moved in. There was no rush. Monday morning was mine to savor.

In the spirit of laziness, I was still sitting at the kitchen table, idly flipping through the final issue of *Chronicle of the Horse* we'd be receiving for the foreseeable future, reading month-old show results I'd already memorized, when Amanda's glossy red Dodge truck went racing down the unpaved lane to my barn, leaving a golden spray of puddle-mud flying in its wake. I bit my lip and slapped down my coffee mug hard enough to splash the creamy magazine pages with black coffee. Did she think the barn lane was some kind of raceway? She was going to run over a squirrel, or worse, a barn cat, or God forbid, Marcus, and if anything happened to Marcus, I was going to murder her, whether Pete liked it or not.

I decided the best course of action was to march down to the barn and confront her. I left Marcus snoozing on my pillow, then reconsidered and maneuvered Pete's pillow so that it functioned as a drool receptacle, and *then* marched out into the humid morning, ready to wage war.

Amanda had pulled up haphazardly in front of the barn entrance, in blatant disregard for my rule that all vehicles park neatly and perpendicular to the buildings. I noted this infraction as I passed from the brilliant golden sunlight of Florida at eight o'clock in the morning and into the still-cool darkness of the barn's center aisle, and mentally added it to the list of Things I Dislike About

Amanda. I blinked, pausing for a moment by Dynamo's stall door to adjust my eyes to the dim barn, and ran my fingers through his chestnut forelock when he shoved his head over the grill to say hello.

Beyond the aisle, I could see Ramon, a dark shadow in the sunlight on the other side of the barn, loading up a hay cart with bales from the shipping container parked out back.

Stealthily, my footsteps masked by the roar of the box fans blowing into every stall, I made my way down the aisle, letting my gaze fall into every occupied stall as I went. A few horses moved to their doors to look at me as I passed, but most kept their noses firmly planted in their hay piles, their dedication to breakfast far outweighing any curiosity they might have about humans in the barn aisle. Some horses took the "you can't see me, I'm invisible" approach to life; if the trainer didn't spot them, could they really end up being ridden in the hot sun that morning?

Just outside the tack room door, I heard their voices. Pete's, low and urgent, too muffled to be understood. Amanda's less so. I was ready to burst in and give her hell, but my curiosity overcame my outrage, so I hung back for a moment, eavesdropping shamelessly.

It was my barn, after all. Or it had been.

Amanda's voice was cajoling; she was trying to get him to do something he didn't want to do. Something told me a pretty blonde who sold horses for as much as Amanda did was good at that. "Be honest with yourself for a moment, is this what you really want? Of course not. You're just doing it to keep the peace, you're just trying to be nice. And that's great, that's what people love about you, you're so *nice* and *likable* and who's like that in the horse business? Honestly. But listen to me, Pete, you have to think of yourself for once. Stop making decisions based on keeping someone else happy, okay?"

Pete's reply was a murmur, too low for me to hear. I leaned back against the cinder-block wall, digging my fingernails into its peeling latex paint, and tried not to panic. *This* is why you don't eavesdrop, I thought, *this* is why they always say it's a bad idea, you won't hear anything you want to hear; you'll only hear upsetting, life-changing, hurtful words.

But what the hell was she talking about now? Why could I only hear one side of this conversation, and not the important one, at that?

"If that's the way you feel, you should tell her."

Pete's voice rose with emotion, and I could hear him now. "I can't do that to her."

Her. He was talking about me. I started to inch away, creeping down the aisle to put physical distance between myself and this conversation.

"You're not going to help anyone by dragging this out." Amanda's voice sharpened. "Pete"—and when she spoke his name, I felt hatred bubble up in my throat—"Pete, you have to be honest, *now.* Or—"

From a stall away, a horse blowing hot breath against my neck, I could hear the hesitation.

"Or what?" He was done being quiet; he was angry. The horse, one of Pete's string, heard the upset in the air and backed away from me, retreating to the safety of his hay. "Or what, Amanda?"

"Or I'll do it," she said simply. "I'll tell her. She's probably in the barn right now."

I bolted.

9

WHEN THEY CAME out of the barn at last, blinking in the hot sunlight, I was strolling down the lane toward the barn, fingers slipped into the slim pockets of my corded breeches, face studiously nonchalant. There was no way to see the upset in my reddened cheeks or damp eyelashes; when a morning is eighty-five degrees with 90 percent humidity, there is a 100 percent chance of flushed skin and a dew of sweat. One advantage of Ocala: it is easy to hide your heartbreak behind your heatstroke.

Pete was still resplendently clean in his show-ring whites, which meant he hadn't yet touched a horse, despite coming to the barn nearly an hour before me.

Amanda was more casually dressed in houndstooth riding tights and a matching sleeveless shirt, all made from the kind of summer-friendly tech fabric I'd hoped Rockwell would send me, instead of the wind-resistant, waterproof gear currently languishing in my closet. Amanda didn't have to wear Walmart tank tops while waiting for a sponsor to find some samples left over from summer clearance. She just bought things for herself, when she wanted them. Amanda lived a life in which she could look at what she wanted and take it.

But she couldn't have Pete. For a trainer in her business, or for anything else, either. She'd have to go through me.

I tightened my jaw and felt my molars lock into position, grinding together like a horse clamping against a hard hand on the reins. Amanda saw my expression and her eyes widened a little. *That's right,* I thought. *Be afraid. I am very scary!*

I walked up to them and put my hand on Pete's arm, precisely where Amanda's had been, and smiled at her, a slow, wide, generous smile. "Amanda," I said, "I didn't know hunters got out of bed at all on Mondays. Shouldn't you be waiting for your butler to bring you a mimosa?"

Amanda giggled nervously. "Oh my God, Jules, I'm not rich just because I ride hunters."

"Of course not," I agreed. "You ride hunters because you're rich."

Beside me, Pete stiffened. He knew my moods and my attitudes better than I did half the time, another reason he shouldn't be whispering secrets in the tack room with any woman but me. I wondered if he knew I'd heard them; I wondered if he could see through my smirk.

"You ought to leave this guy alone on Mondays," I went on. "We poor eventing folk only get off once a week. We were going to celebrate our day of rest by moving hay bales."

"I know Monday's a good day for projects." Amanda smiled, running the back of her hand against her forehead as if to brush away a sea of sweat. "We were just going to take some video for my website, help you all out with some extra publicity."

"I don't see a horse," I observed. "You're just going to take some B-roll of Pete looking sexy in his show clothes?"

"Wouldn't you?" Amanda said teasingly, trying to cool off the moment. She gave Pete a questioning look, and I saw him nod at her slightly. The thought that they had private conversations in those glances made my skin burn with outrage. I could feel the redness creeping into my cheeks, prickling the tips of my ears, flushing right through my woodsy brown tan. Red was not a good look on me, which made me even more upset.

"Whatever you two are up to—and I don't think it's just a photo shoot to show off Pete's ass, because there are already entire Instagram accounts devoted to that purpose—why don't you just be honest with me?"

Honesty: the most dangerous request of all. Honesty meant being open with another person, something that had never ended well for me in the past, Before Pete. BP. And now? Whatever they were up to, if he made a mockery of the feelings I'd shared with him in the past year, I would never forgive him.

Pete opened his mouth to speak, hesitated, and looked at the ground. "Jules," he said hoarsely. "The thing is—we've been working so hard, with the racehorses, and everything, but I don't think . . . I don't think it's going to be enough." His voice trailed off.

Amanda decided to help out. "It's about the house," she offered tentatively. "The guesthouse."

The guesthouse where we were supposed to be moving in three weeks? "It would be tight for three," I said. "You'd better stay at your own house."

Amanda smiled. "Pete—tell her what's going on."

"Yes, Pete, tell me what's going on."

"We can't stay in the guesthouse," Pete blurted, his words running together. "We can't stay anywhere. Everything we've done . . . the extra work . . . renting the farm out . . . it hasn't been enough. We have to lease out the guesthouse, too, which leaves us . . . homeless, I guess. We're through, Jules. It's over." He licked his lips. "Wait. That's not what I meant."

I knew what he meant. This was about the farm.

Only the farm. Only our home. Only everything.

For a moment I felt its loss like Pete did, and then I shook it off. I wasn't going to get attached to one piece of land. "Okay," I said, putting my shoulders back. "We have to leave? What about the horses?"

"We can keep the barn. They don't want *this* barn. Not yet, anyway." He forced a smile and my heart twisted for him. "Blixden wants the guesthouse for his grooms. He'll pay more, but if he doesn't get it, he's backing out of the lease. I just found out a few minutes ago, while we were out here discussing the video," he finished lamely, and I didn't know if that was true, or if he'd just cried to Amanda because she was more sympathetic, or what. It didn't matter now.

We were stuck.

Blixden *couldn't* back out of the lease. He was our only hope to pay the insurance and the truck payments and the manure removal service and the hay man and the other thousand bills that had become our responsibility. He was our only hope should the attorneys come through for us and we actually had to pay the tax bill that came with inheritance. Without this deal, we were sunk, and that nasty old shark knew it.

Why couldn't anyone in the horse business just play nicely, just play fair, just one time?

I looked at the barn behind Pete's slumped shoulders, its peeling cream-colored paint gleaming defiantly bright despite its age. The sagging roof was still missing a few shingles from last year's hurricane, but otherwise it was a tough old barn, ready to stand up to another fifty years of Florida's shenanigans, the daily madness we called the local weather, the hurricanes and tornadoes and thunderstorms we and our horses needed shelter from. The barn wasn't desirable, but it got the job done.

I thought about it, weighed what I was about to say against the possibility they'd both think I was insane. But what the hell. *I've had worse ideas,* I decided.

"We can stay in the barn," I announced. Of course we could live in the barn. Of course that wouldn't push our delicate relationship past the point of repair. Of course it wasn't a terrible idea. Hey, we were horse people. If there were two things we needed to have a future, it was a barn and horses. No one ever said anything about needing a house. Houses were for regular people, with regular jobs and regular lives.

Amanda actually laughed. "You're so optimistic, Jules! That's what I love about you, you know? But you don't have to stay in the *barn.* I was telling Pete you all can come stay at my place. I was just telling him that he needs to convince you it's time to move! I have a studio apartment above my barn with no one in it right now. It's a little small, but hey—"

"Wait—we *could* stay in this barn, Jules," Pete interrupted. His eyes, locked on mine, suddenly came alive again. "We could stay in the tack room—we'll get a window air conditioner. We can move the feed and the extra tack trunks down to an empty stall, and I think there's an old carpet rolled up in one of the closets, we can put that down on the concrete floor, and—"

There was the Pete I knew! He was problem-solving, he was eager, he was back on his feet. It didn't even matter that we were discussing moving to the tack room, out of an entire house. What was important, right now, was that Pete looked like himself again for the first time since this whole battle for the farm began.

Amanda looked disappointed, as if she'd been counting on our company (or just Pete's company? Was I imagining how much she liked him?). "There's no shower," she pointed out. "There's only *kind of* a bathroom. It's not a great solution, is it?"

The little closet with a toilet and a spider problem wasn't the best bathroom in the world, admittedly. There was always the hose and cold showers, but the weather would be turning a little chilly for that in a few months. Damn. If there was one thing you couldn't live without on a Florida horse farm, it was a daily shower or three. Almost everything else in life was negotiable.

"There's no kitchen," Amanda went on. "Are you going to eat McDonald's every day? That's going to cost you."

"Well, we have a fridge and a coffee maker and a microwave out here already," I retorted, annoyed she was turning my brain wave into a childish fantasy. "That's practically a kitchen." I was firmly in the camp that believed that if a meal required turning on an oven, it was too much work. Pete was the chef in the relationship. I'd bet he had no idea what terrors I was capable of with a box of noodles, some canned goods, and a horseshoe box filled with assorted condiments swiped from fast-food joints.

"There's a shower *and* a kitchen in the horse trailer." Pete smiled at me, still riding high on problem-solving. "It would cost too much to leave it running all the time, or I'd say we should just move into the living quarters, but we can park it right outside the barn and turn on the generator when we need it."

"Genius," I breathed, delighted with the way everything was coming together. At last! How often did that happen? "We have everything we need right here. We ought to just move some jumps down here and not even bother with the riding arena."

Pete's smile turned a little grim. "It might come to that, if they keep playing hardball like this. Don't tempt fate."

Amanda was looking at us with disbelief. "Wait, so you're going to move into the tack room? Instead of a real apartment with, you know, plumbing?"

"Yes," I said firmly, because I would rather sleep in one of the stalls, complete with a horse for a roommate, than move to Amanda's farm and see her glittering white smile every day.

"Yes," Pete said gently, putting a hand on her shoulder (and I didn't even mind). "Because we have to show the world we can take care of ourselves. It's better for business. But you've been more than generous, Amanda. We really appreciate it." He glanced at me. "Don't we, Jules," he encouraged.

"We appreciate it very much," I parroted, but the smile I showed her was real.

I left them to make their video; if he thought he had the time for extra work in his day, let the man have his little daydream. I went down to the tack room to start imagining our new home, as excited as a kid building a blanket fort.

As soon as Pete agreed to the new lease terms, the truth came tumbling out: the grooms were already driving south from Virginia, hot on the tails of their horses. We could have stayed in the main house a little longer, but with the prospect of new neighbors who might be reporting back to the Blixdens on us, we decided to start moving to the annex barn over the next week.

And at first, it felt more like an adventure than a chore. We were kids playing a game. It was the first spontaneous and crazy thing we'd gotten to do in a long time. We were going to show the Blixden family how tough and tenacious we were . . . and how bad could it be, really? We spent most of our days in the barn anyway. Now, we'd just spend our nights there, too.

So, although we were leaving it for a while, I was able to wander around our pretty house with dry eyes, certain we'd be back soon. Once we got ourselves on our feet and figured out how to make the farm pay for itself, we'd get our house back. The place where everything had started for us would wait, putting up with the Northern tenants and their pushy ways, until we could return in triumph.

It wasn't hard to decide what to bring with us to our tack room studio. When we moved the feed cans and the tack trunks out, we were left with a square of concrete, twelve feet by twelve feet, in which to reimagine our non-working lives. The bed, obviously, would come. The dresser from Lacey's old bedroom in the guesthouse, which was smaller than the big antique model that had been Pete's grandfather's, wedged into a corner nicely. The extra rug, unrolled, had only minor stains from an incident involving a puppy at some point in the farm's history, and was exactly the color of a crystal-clear swimming pool, which was just what I wanted to see when I came in from a day of riding, drenched in sweat and dreaming of cool water and gentle breezes and a less sticky life.

We discovered that if we consolidated the bridles to a couple of hooks in one corner and removed the other racks, there was room for a bookshelf, so Pete's library of dressage, jumping, and veterinary manuals made their way down to the barn as well. I hopped onto the bed and gazed at the fat texts on the shelves while he finished sliding the last few titles into place. "It wouldn't feel like a home without books," I decided. "This makes the room. I had so many riding books at my old farm. They kept Marcus and me company when we lived alone."

"I've never seen you read a book," Pete said, amused.

I stuck out my tongue. "With training books you have diagrams and pictures."

He laughed and pulled out *Training the Three-Day-Event Horse and Rider* by James Wofford. Flipping through the well-thumbed pages, he paused at a diagram of a jumping course and tapped it. "I see your point. How many of these did you have?"

"Definitely that one. *Centered Riding.* Those vet books over there. And then I mostly had a ton of old riding manuals I got at thrift stores. Some of them were probably worth money as antiques." I missed my books. I learned a lot from them, even if I mainly stuck to reading the captions and not the walls of training text. I pictured the pages scattered around the old farm, white butterflies waving to me from fallen trees, tufts of pink insulation, jagged metal slashes of roofing.

Pete sighed. "A shame." He put away the Wofford book and gave me a kiss to apologize for bringing it up. It was fine, though. I was getting used to these seasons of loss and change. A person could get used to anything, I guessed.

"Should we take a picture of the shelf for the socials?" I asked.

Pete lifted an eyebrow. "Do we want the world to know we're living in a tack room?"

"We'll have to be careful with angles," I decided, and centered a Rockwell Brothers catalog in front of the Wofford book, before taking a picture. Then I opened Instagram.

A classic if you want to prep for a classic! The classic three-day might be a novelty now, but there's no master of eventing like Jimmy Wofford. Is this book on your tack room shelf?

The last thing we did before moving in was install the air conditioner. The tack room was dark once the AC filled the single window, but at least there was cold air. Barn Kitty approved the setup fairly quickly, after peering around the corner, seeing the furniture, and fluffing out her orange tabby fur until she was three times her normal size.

"She's a blowfish," Pete observed.

"Don't you dare call her Hootie," I warned, sensing where this conversation was heading. "Her name is Barn Kitty forever and ever. That's the best name a kitty can have."

Barn Kitty concluded a thorough examination of the room, decided the fluffy duvet and ice-cold air offered a massive improvement on her old pile-of-saddle-pads bed, and settled in for the evening. "You still have to mouse," I told her. "Don't think you're a house cat now."

Barn Kitty's predatory instincts won out once the sun went down, and she cheerfully peeled herself out of bed, ate her Meow Mix, and went out into the night to destroy any and all rodents in her path. The horses turned out for the night, Pete and I went down the aisle switching off the box fans, listening to silence take the place of daytime's humming white noise. When we met at the far end of the barn, all that was left was the grumbling and rattling of the air-conditioner unit in the distance. Pete took my hand and rubbed it, his callouses rough against mine, and I smiled at him in the dusk.

"We're going to make it," I said.

Beyond the oak trees, lightning flashed on and off like a store shutting down for the night. I heard a low, distant growl; the storm was miles away, flooding someone else's evening. But Pete still stared out at the humped shapes of the clouds, their topmost peaks taking on a cotton-candy pink from the last remnants of the sunset, as if he thought it might drift back our way.

I leaned against his shoulder, despite the heat, despite our sticky skin and its fine powder-coating of shavings, hay, and horsehair. He'd come around, just as soon as we spent the first night in our little studio. He'd see everything was going to be fine.

10

THE SMELL WAS what woke me up, the tangy acid scent of sparks and then the dingier smell of burning rubber, melting plastic. I flung back the sheet and kicked Pete on the way out of bed, leaping over him, scrambling toward the source. The little room was weirdly lit by the red light on the air conditioner, the light that meant something was wrong. Without thinking, I snatched at the heavy cord and wrenched it from the electric socket, stifling a scream at the show of silver sparks when the prongs left their holes. Then it was over: the machine shut off, the red light extinguished, the sparks disappeared, and I was left standing in the darkness, holding the end of a cord that could've given me a hell of a shock.

Pete shoved himself out of bed and flicked the light switch. The fluorescent light flickered fitfully to life over our heads, bathing us in a dull, half-awake glow. I blinked and stared at Pete as if his tired face held all the answers. "It smells like a tire fire," I said confusedly. I still wasn't sure what was happening, exactly. I was working on instinct: red means bad.

Pete pointed to the electric socket below the window. Fingers of black soot reached up the plastic housing. "It was almost a barn fire," he said, voice hoarse with sleep.

We took a moment to stare at each other. Suddenly, the clouds cleared from my brain and I was trembling, my fingers and toes prickling with horror. Our first night in the tack room, and we'd almost set the place on fire. Suddenly, the past week of carting down our things, laughingly setting up our new room so that we could move before the grooms showed up, seemed incredibly foolish. All that, and we hadn't had the electric socket in this old barn vetted for safety.

I took a few steadying breaths, which wasn't great because the room still smelled like burned plastic. "Thank God everyone's outside."

"We weren't outside," he pointed out, rubbing his forehead with both hands. "Marcus wasn't outside."

"We're not locked in." I flung open the tack room door to let in fresh air, and Marcus skedaddled into the dark barn aisle. "It could have been worse, obviously. We've got that going for us."

"Can you stop looking on the bright side?" Pete rubbed his head until his red-brown hair stood on end. "Now is not the time."

"Not dying is the perfect time to count your blessings," I retorted. I slapped at a whining sound near my ear.

Pete swung a hand, too. "What the hell do we do now? We can't live without air-conditioning. And the bugs are gonna eat us alive."

He was right, this was the wrong time to be optimistic. I slapped another mosquito. Everything was bad, and I might as well accept that. I picked up my phone to check the time. Only three o'clock in the morning; we had a few more hours to live through before we could get on with our day. "We could go back to the house and sleep on the sofa," I suggested. "I mean, it's still ours for another week. We have time to fix this place so it's livable and not . . . you know, a firetrap."

Pete looked at me. "Do you want to go back to the house?"

I thought about the blank spaces on the walls where his grandfather had once jumped in black-and-white glory. If we went back to the house tonight, it would be like going back to the night of the hurricane, seeing the ghost of my old double-wide trailer, before the hurricane took it, tore it up, and presented me on Pete's doorstep, nothing but a girl who used to have a farm once.

And I missed it still.

The farm, and the girl who didn't have to rely on *anyone*.

I didn't want to live through that loss again. I was tired of living through things.

I wanted Briar Hill for us, as it was, or I didn't want anything to do with this place. This half-and-half existence. This *tack room* I thought could be our home.

"No," I said to Pete. "I don't want to go back to the house." I knew someone had to stay strong, and it wasn't going to be Pete, he'd proved that.

Pete went out into the barn, leaving the door open so the light streamed into the dark aisle. I stayed behind, looking at the bed, at the books, at the remnants of normal life. When I heard some knocks and bangs, and the clang of metal against a stall bar, I knew what he was doing. Sure enough, a few moments later he walked back in with one of the big steel stand-up fans we were slowly replacing the old box fans with. He ran an extension cord through the door and shut the door gently against it. "The plugs in the barn aisle are heavy duty," he said. "No more fireworks tonight."

I sat back down on the bed as he flipped the fan on. Its comforting roar took over the little room.

"There'll still be a few mosquitoes," he warned, climbing under the sheet next to me. "But the moving air should keep away most of them."

"We'll live," I assured him. "We've got this."

He didn't say anything. I felt him beside me, his body still tense and ready for the next blow to come. I wanted to tell him there wasn't going to be another attack tonight, that we could sleep easy, that the worst was over.

But who could say?

As we sweated together under the thin cotton sheet, I felt myself slipping into the same worry that was clearly eating at Pete. What if we couldn't make this work? What the hell were we going to do next?

We woke up late.

Neither of us heard our alarms over the roaring fan, and although I'd thought we'd never get back to sleep after the temperature started to rise in the tack room, both of us fell into a deep unconsciousness at some point. I woke up when Barn Kitty, frustrated when the rising of the sun failed to coincide with breakfast in her bowl, finally managed to shove the tack room door open wide enough to slip inside. The door squeaked on its hinges and Kitty jumped onto my stomach, scaring me out of psychedelic heatstroke dreams.

Pete picked up his phone and cursed when he saw the time.

I picked up mine, shoving Kitty back to the floor, and did the same.

"Please tell me Amanda isn't coming today," I muttered. It was past eight o'clock. I hadn't slept this late without a doctor's note since summer vacation, seventh grade. The pre-horse life.

"She's not. But neither is Ramon. He's staying in Cedar Key with his cousins this week, remember? It's not a Becky day, either, so we have to do chores. And we *both* missed work. I'd been planning on feeding when I got back from work, but . . ."

I groaned. I'd honestly forgotten we both had jobs now. Or, we'd *had* jobs. Alex must be rethinking my employment right now.

"We'll deal with that after we feed."

I started pulling on shorts and a sports bra while Pete just shoved his bare feet into muck boots and marched outside wearing his boxers and T-shirt. *Good,* I thought, *he's going to get started right away.* And then I heard a door shut down the aisle and realized he had gone into the bathroom.

Naturally, I had a sudden and urgent need to go.

Well, I was a horse show girl, wasn't I? I ducked into the nearest stall, tucked myself into a corner, and had a quick pee. "Sorry, Rorschach," I muttered as I realized whose stall it was. I hadn't purposely picked one of Pete's stalls to pee in; just the closest one. "When a girl's gotta go . . ."

From the pastures, the horses heard us moving around in the barn and began neighing for breakfast. I heard hoofbeats pounding the ground as they started teasing each other and cantering in circles. Someone was going to get hurt, and it would probably be Mickey, since he was fairly low in pasture politics. I hustled to get breakfast feed thrown into the buckets; there were already hay piles in each stall waiting for them.

Fifteen minutes later, the barn was full of happy horse sounds, and I was sending a text message to Alex: *sorry didn't make it this morning, had a small fire last night, threw off whole day.*

Pete, ever more responsible than me, phoned his boss, but said much the same thing.

"At least we had a damn good excuse," I said hopefully when he came into the tack room. I was sitting on the bed, drinking coffee, not entirely unhappy with any scenario that put my bed and my coffeepot right next to my horses. We'd have an electrician out to fix the socket, and then we could live here happily for as long as necessary. "You can't exactly fire someone for having a fire."

"Really? Why don't you tell my former boss that." Pete poured himself a mug of coffee.

"You got fired?"

"Contract labor, baby. You show up and work, you get paid. You don't show up, you forfeit your job and they put someone else on your horses. Whoever drove in this morning looking for work got lucky."

"I don't think Alex will fire me. She seems pretty chill."

Pete sat down in my desk chair and said nothing, flipping through his schedule book as if I wasn't in the room.

My phone buzzed. I pulled up the message from Alex: *Oh shit girl you ok? No worries, alexander said you flaked out on us but he's just being a pill. Let me know if you need anything. Oh and let's schedule some time for me to come over and see your horse. Later ok?*

I smiled at the message. I liked my new boss, even if I didn't much care for having a job.

Amanda was in the barn by 9 A.M., having been alerted to our predicament, for whatever reason, by Pete. I was prepared to be standoffish and aloof with her, as usual, but she walked down the aisle flourishing greasy paper bags from the country market down the road, and when I saw she'd brought us egg-and-cheese sandwiches, there wasn't much she could do wrong in my eyes for at least the next thirty minutes.

"For the Homeless Eventers!" she announced, snapping open a bag and handing out paper-wrapped sandwiches.

Pete, less a hostage to his stomach than me, grimaced. "Be careful. If anyone hears you saying that, it'll stick."

"Who would hear me?" Amanda batted long lashes at him. "It's just us here."

There was hardly anyone in most barns, but gossip still managed to fill up the internet. If word hit *Eventing Chicks* that we were living in our tack room, I'd know exactly where the story came from.

When we didn't have help, we always made sure morning chores were literally just dumping feed and bringing the horses in. Everything was done the night before: stalls were mucked, water buckets filled, hay piles replenished. For lack of anything else to do while the horses ate, I had raked the aisle clean of hoof prints, simply because I loved the way it looked, and now I watched in annoyance and Pete and Amanda wandered aimlessly down the aisle, setting their boots into the pristine furrows and generally ruining my zen. They were talking about a student of Amanda's who had beautiful form but no bravery, and what Pete could do to improve her show jumping.

"If her horse is safe and it's all in her head, we can bring her out here to jump some cross-country fences. She'll learn to feel comfortable moving forward over jumps."

"That sounds good," Amanda agreed happily. "Let's set that up! Thank you!"

"But if her form is so good," Pete went on, "why doesn't she just stick to hunters? I know she's not being judged, but if she's staying out of her horse's way, and if she's comfortable with the slower pace . . ."

"Oh, her horse is a jumper." Amanda shrugged. "He's a stellar jumper. He'll take her places if she can keep up with him. And if not, I'll show him."

I crumpled up the wax paper from my dearly departed sandwich. I'd heard this line before. I waited for Pete to ask the next question. I'd already learned the answer while I was working for Grace.

"Why did she buy a jumper if—"

"Because he's an amazing horse!" Amanda interrupted, laughing. "She's lucky to have him. I got him from Germany and he's just the most athletic thing you've ever met. Watch—you're going to be so jealous. If I show him at HITS this winter, he'll sell for a fortune after a couple Grand Prix wins."

Go on, Pete, tell her what you think of that kind of trainer, I urged silently. I propped myself up against the frame of the tack room door, Barn Kitty weaving in and out of my legs, and watched him. Pete hated over-horsing riders just to make a few bucks . . . and so did I, even if it was a standard industry procedure.

Again, there were reasons we'd always be broke. But at least we'd be happy.

Well, sometimes we'd be happy, I amended to myself.

Maybe.

It did take a lot of money to be happy in the horse world.

Pete was standing outside of Rorschach's stall, and the white-faced gelding leaned out to nudge him in the arm, stretching lips begging for his sandwich.

Pete absently tore off a bite of bread and handed it to him. The horse nodded his head up and down as he chewed, spitting bits of soggy bread through the air.

"How did she end up with a jumper type if she isn't comfortable doing the division?" he asked after a while. "Did she just fall in love with the wrong horse?"

Amanda hesitated, and I could tell she realized Pete was questioning her motives in selling a student a horse which that student couldn't ride and didn't want to ride. She could tell, and she was embarrassed. I wondered why she kept trying to make this work with him, why she'd want to partner with a man who was steered by a different compass than she was, and then I remembered the way Grace wanted to go into business with me, even though part of her business plan was placing expensive horses with clients who would always need her assistance to go on riding them. Pete was the stand-up guy she needed to make new clients comfortable, I realized. She wanted his reputation to save hers. Poor, noble, horses-first Pete.

"You know how it is," Amanda said at last. "Girls just fall in love with the wrong horses all the time, don't they?" She looked back at me, hoping for support.

I pulled out my phone and flicked through my Instagram, more to keep my mouth shut than anything. She wasn't getting any help from me.

While Amanda tried to talk her way out of Pete's disapproval, I skimmed photos, noticing how they were basically the same three photos over and over: girls hugging their horses, girls jumping their horses, girls cantering their horses. It was occasionally broken up by some selfies. I followed more than a thousand accounts and they all seemed to be fourteen-year-old girls who did nothing but ride and spend a lot of time constructing #ROOTD pics—that would be Riding Outfit of the Day, to civilians. They were all so put together, so elegant, like Amanda was right now, and I knew my photos were just as ridiculous, when right now felt more normal than anything on this feed. I was bone-tired, drenched in sweat, wearing raggedy clothes and tasting the harsh taste of acrid smoke in the back of my throat. This was farm life. This was what no one was sharing. Last week, Pete said it was all fake and I'd smirked, but right now, I just wanted one person to understand what we were going through.

I angled the phone to capture my messy state, grinned wickedly at my own reflection, and clicked the button.

I wrote the caption, then read it over again, nodding to myself.

#ROOTD: *Why wear your best breeches when you can sling sweet feed in style with a pair of ripped cut-offs and the latest ironic tank top from Goodwill? Today I'm wearing denim so decimated it's practically falling off my hips—maybe because I've been riding horses in them since I was a sophomore—and rockin' a faded purple tank with a hilarious Manatee County Arts Council Fun Run logo on the front. What could that mean? Who knows? What if it used to be blue? I can't tell! This is #barnfashion, girls. This is what #horsewomen wear. Welcome to reality.*

It was a long caption, sure, but I thought it had a certain flair.

I read through the text, smiling, while Amanda went on tinkling her laugh at Pete, explaining all the ways she was going to make him rich. On the second read-through I knew I couldn't post it just like this—Rockwell would kill me. I added:

As if I'd waste my #RockwellBros designs on stall-cleaning duty. Check back with me later and I'll give you a real #ROOTD from in the saddle.

That was better.

11

"HONESTLY, ALEX, I have real problems. I don't even care that Pete is working at Amanda's farm this afternoon. They can flounce around at her fancy barn all day, and I'll still be here holding down the fort, making sure we have everything we need to keep going. Amanda isn't offering him any suggestions for keeping on living at the farm. I am. And that's what he wants."

Alex nodded absently, her eyes trained on the rippling chestnut of Dynamo's mane as she walked him around the dressage arena. I was standing in the center of their circle, as if I was giving her a riding lesson, but I wasn't saying anything constructive. I hated teaching—I never seemed to know what to *do,* and I didn't have the time or forethought to put together comprehensive lesson plans, which meant any lesson I taught usually just devolved into me shouting something over and over (usually "Leg!") and the student getting angry and shouting back ("I *am* using leg!") and then never coming back again. This was more like hanging out with a friend, and since Lacey had left, "hanging out" wasn't something I was doing very often these days. I was just a tiny bit thankful Pete had decided we had to be working men and women of the world, since it gave me Alex as a friend.

"So, you're not worried about Amanda being hot and Pete working with her, is what you're telling me?" Alex smirked. "Just to be sure."

"Not worried," I said. "Not even a little."

"Okay, good. Because for a minute, it sounded like you were worried and overcompensating—"

"Nope," I said. "Not me."

Alex nodded. "You know, the trouble is, there just aren't enough straight guys to go around in this game. Amanda probably isn't a threat at all, but just because she's female, you—"

"I'm sorry," I interrupted, "did you not hear me say I wasn't worried?"

Alex grinned. "Fine. Join me on the dark side. I've given up worrying about Alexander. I'd like to see some other woman put up with his shit the way I do."

"That's the basis of a healthy relationship," I decided. "True love is probably just two people who are really good at dealing with the other person's shit."

"Yup. He's Mr. Bossypants and I just ignore him as much as possible. He's not going to change at this stage in the game. What does yours do?"

"Pete?" I thought about it. What *did* Pete do that annoyed me? "It's just some quality that he has. He's very . . . I don't know . . . tidy? And good-looking. Not that I wish he wasn't," I clarified, as Alex burst out laughing, doubling over Dynamo's neck, "just . . . he's so cool and stylish without even trying. He looks good in dirty jeans and a sweaty polo shirt. Any time a camera finds me, I always look like I was just missing for a week in the jungle."

The Instagram photo from two days ago was very popular, though, so maybe people preferred my jungle look.

"Oh, that is *very* annoying," Alex agreed, hiccupping back her laughter. "I completely agree."

"He's really nice, too . . ."

"That's enough." Alex picked up her reins again, grinning at me as she straightened in the saddle. "I'll only give you so much. Too gorgeous is one thing—but too nice? You're on your own. Tell me about this pony of yours now, before we gallop away."

I looked over Dynamo, my big horse, the one I'd sunk all my hopes into for years, as he walked agreeably enough under Alex's light seat. Dynamo was the one who had gotten me this far, from a paddock in a suburban boarding barn where I worked off lessons and board instead of doing my homework, to one of the most beautiful eventing barns in Ocala, competing at Intermediate and preparing for the deep dive into Advanced. It was kind of amazing, because he didn't necessarily look the part of a modern event horse.

Red chestnut with a squarish sort of build, sturdy legs with lots of bone, and a big beautiful hind end—Dynamo was not a natural dressage horse, and dressage was where eventing as a sport was trending. But where his legs and spine were not long, they were at least in good proportion, and so with proper riding and cues, he was able to come together to produce a nice swinging trot and a beautiful rocking-horse canter, and to use those powerful hind-quarters as an engine for big movement.

I thought about how to put it all into words. "He's built to run down on his forehand a little, as you can tell," I began, and Alex nodded. "It takes a lot of leg and seat to put him together in a frame. Once you do, he'll hold the bit and stick with you for as long as you keep your leg on him."

It felt inadequate, to describe my life's work as "down on the forehand," and "takes a lot of leg," but there we were.

"I don't know if I would have enough leg to really put him together," Alex admitted. "But that's why I'm in your jumping saddle. I find that even when I'm riding my retired guy Tiger regularly, it's hard for me to get my lower leg on. I ride with all my contact through my thigh, you know? I guess that's where my muscles are from galloping."

"You can still get nice gaits out of him with your leg up there. He'll collect for you. I can't stand jumping a horse with a flat back, so even with short stirrups I can leg him up into collection pretty easily."

"Gotcha. I totally agree . . . I don't know how people stand a horse with its nose sticking out. Okay, and so he's doing all this dressage like a fancy warmblood and then . . . what, he won't gallop on his forehand anymore?"

"Exactly. He's staying in my hand the whole time, when I want him to reach down on the bit and take a hold."

Alex grinned. "Oh, okay. I know this problem."

I nearly fell over with relief. "You *do*?"

"Definitely. Babies do this. Remember, we have to teach them to take a hold, too."

"So what do I do about it?"

"Let me ride him a little and then I'll see if I can explain it. I'm no riding instructor."

"You can't be any worse than me." I retreated to the shade of the oaks along the arena fence while Alex warmed up Dynamo, slowly getting used to his gaits and his personality.

It was nice to see someone else ride Dynamo, if only so I could admire him.

The summer of dressage had given him a new, muscular topline that made him almost unrecognizable from the horse he'd been six months ago, and he truly bore no resemblance at all to the half-starved wreck I'd bought from an auction all those years ago. When I was in high school, Dynamo was my rock, and I was his. Since life had progressed without getting much easier, we were still holding tight to each other in a way I knew would be nearly impossible to replicate with another horse. Dynamo and I were soulmates, if you believe in that sort of thing, and it made me worry even more about his progress. We were almost to the highest levels of the sport, but he was moving into his teen years.

There was a clock running somewhere behind the scenes, ticking away as he grew older, and if we ran out of time before he'd truly lived up to his potential as a top competitor, I'd always feel as if I'd failed him and failed our partnership. There would be other horses, but would there ever be another Dynamo?

I figured we all had horses like this—Pete clearly had a special connection with Regina, and she had come at the right time in his career, when he needed a horse to really make a splash and climb up the levels rapidly. Regina was naturally more standoffish, being a mare with a pretty high opinion of herself, but with Pete she showed her softer side, behaving almost motherly with him, in the way she tucked her neck around him and lipped at his pockets and the fringe of hair spilling over his collar. She was a queen with everyone else, horse and man—"Don't Touch Me or I I'll Kill You" was her royal motto. I respected that; Regina kind of reminded me of *me*, now that I thought about it. Of course, she was elegant and

I was . . . an overgrown barn rat. But the personality quirks were pretty similar, and we both loved the same guy.

I was so wrapped up in watching Dynamo move, I didn't hear the feet crunching on the gravel driveway until they were right next to me. Arms appeared next to mine, crossed over the dark arena fence, and I jumped, spooking like a silly filly.

"Sorry," Carl Rockwell said. "Didn't mean to scare you."

Carl Rockwell would've scared me even if I had been given six months' notice of his arrival, but I managed to pull myself together, laugh awkwardly, and stick out a sweaty hand for him to shake. Rockwell's hand was cool and smooth, probably from the perfectly engineered air-conditioning in his Mercedes, which I could see behind us, parked up near the house. I swallowed a grimace, hoping he didn't expect to be invited inside. He didn't know about our current situation, and if I took him into the house, with its bare walls and empty shelves, he'd have questions for sure. Why did we need sponsors, anyway? This guy freaked me out more than an owner.

When I finally managed to greet him, my voice was high and nervous. "How are you, Mr. Rockwell? What brings you to the farm?"

Rockwell stretched his thin lips in a smile. I suspected he was more comfortable in the VIP seating at indoor show-jumping competitions, cocktail in hand, making business deals, than tramping around farms and hanging out by dressage rings. Still, he knew about horses. "I came up to see your progress since last June. And Pete's, of course. I haven't seen either of you ride since you went on your training camps."

Then why didn't you come to my dressage show? I thought impatiently. I'd ridden like a star at the show *he'd* made me compete in against my wishes, and he hadn't even come to watch. My God,

Pete had come to see me. We'd basically been one fight away from breaking up completely, but he'd been there. "Well, it's nice to see you," I lied, putting on the Nice Jules act I'd been working on all year. "Pete's down at the barn. I'm not sure who he's riding first."

Rockwell looked around the farm, and pointedly let his gaze stop on the training barn, where the Virginia horses were leaning over their stall doors and pulling at hay nets Ramon had strung up for them. The other stalls were plainly empty. "Where are Pete's horses?"

"Oh, we just moved them—"

"This is what you meant, right, Jules?" Alex thundered by on the rail, standing in her stirrups and bent at the waist, cantering Dynamo like one of the seasoned exercise riders on her training track. She turned her head back as Dynamo progressed up the arena, his back round and his neck bent in a tight U-shape. "He's all bound up in himself!" she shouted. "Totally confused!"

Rockwell looked at the horse, and then at me. His eyebrows went up toward his endless forehead. "Is that your upper-level horse?"

The one you're investing thousands of dollars in for me to compete with your tack and your riding clothes, you mean? "Yes, that's Dynamo."

"And what exactly is going on? I assumed after three months at Seabreeze the two of you would have worked through any of your problems."

"Oh, we worked through our old problems," I said. "We just came home with a fresh new one."

He stared at me coldly, as if he'd known all along taking me in the deal with Pete was a massive mistake.

I felt a rush of anger rising up and I turned away and leaned back over the rail, my jaw set tight to hold back all the things I wanted to say.

I needed Pete right now. Pete would have reminded me to be nice. Pete would have reminded me that we couldn't do this without some financial backing, and a good sponsor for the million pieces of tack and equipment and therapeutic gear like magnetic blankets and deep-freezing ice boots and kinetic tape and whatever new kind of crazy flavor-of-the-month miracle product came out next.

But Pete wasn't here, was he? Pete was off at Amanda's farm, teaching hunters to be jumpers . . . or jumpers to be hunters, I couldn't remember which.

I watched Dynamo gallop with his mouth tenderly clutching the bit, his ears flopping lazily, while Alex stood in her stirrups and bridged her reins and waited for him to put his head down and take control the way he used to. Pete wasn't here and my horse wasn't right and this guy had showed up at just the wrong moment.

I opened my mouth to tell him he'd fucked up my good horse royally, and I didn't appreciate him showing up here uninvited, anyway. We were trainers, and we had schedules, and we couldn't just be entertaining him whenever he felt like driving up from Tampa in his fancy-ass car with his fancy-ass suit and his fancy-ass shiny shoes and—

I closed my mouth, because that *was* why Pete wasn't here by my side—moments like this, when I lost my sense of the greater good and just pleased myself, when I went for the cheap score and the good feeling I had for a few moments afterward, when I saw the gaping mouth and the shocked eyes of my quarry, and I knew I'd shot my arrow and hit my target right in the chest.

If I ruined things with Rockwell now, Pete would never forgive me. For real this time.

I took a deep breath, and put on my best Pete impression. I would be the Wise Trainer. I would be the Teller of Tales. I would Indulge My Investors. These were all Pete's personas, and they worked.

"You've heard of the long format versus short format debate in eventing, right? The long endurance phase in a three-day event, the classic version of the sport, or just a cross-country course, instead. The new version."

Rockwell nodded. "I can't say I ever had a real investment in either side. Short format won."

"Exactly, so the debate doesn't matter in real life anymore. That's what we train for. But what short-format eventing really means is the dressage phase has become overemphasized—at least, to me and a lot of other riders, it's overemphasized—while the cross-country course has gotten a lot more tricky and technical because, let's face it, without endurance to knock horses out of their place after dressage, everyone would go clear. But the thing is, they have to be amazingly submissive and obedient in dressage, then think for themselves in these tight cross-country combinations. They have to be brave and smart and take care of themselves, the day after they're told they have to listen to every move their rider makes. See how those two things can cancel each other out?"

Carl nodded, but he looked impatient. This had all been hashed out long before.

"Okay," I said. "So what I have right now is a horse who is brave as hell, but he's done so much dressage work, which emphasizes *submission,* that now he doesn't think he's allowed to be in charge. As a rider, we can just change the saddle and bridle and say, today we're riding cross-country so everything should look and feel different. But it isn't that simple for the horse."

I paused for a breath and looked out at Dynamo, who was still cantering in a perfect, unwanted frame. Alex had wisely taken him away when she'd seen the look on the suited guy's face, but there was no doubt she was trying to get Dynamo to take hold of the bit, and he just wasn't doing it.

Rockwell was looking, too. His face grew a little more pale as he understood the gravity of the situation. "Are you able to fix this?"

Scared now, aren't ya? "Of course we can," I said with a bravado I didn't feel. "I'm an event horse trainer. She's a racehorse trainer. Fixing horses is what we do."

Just saying the words aloud made me feel better. One thing I'd noticed about this profession (and maybe it was true of any profession): if at any point I felt overfaced and like no one respected me, I just said out loud, "I'm a trainer," and that simple reminder, an easy affirmation, was all I needed to straighten my shoulders and stick up my chin again. *I'm a trainer, bitch, how about you?*

"So you're on track for the three-day event at Hope Glen, correct?"

"Of course." As soon as my horse remembered how to gallop at a cross-country fence, we'd be just fine for Hope Glen. We had two more months.

No problem.

"That's good," Rockwell said, regaining some of his color. "Because I have something for you that you'll want to break in before then." He turned and started back toward his car, and I hotfooted it after him. Was this the saddle? At last? If it was, I totally forgave him for showing up uninvited and intimidating me into an apology.

From the cool, leather-scented back seat of the Mercedes,

Rockwell retrieved a cloth-covered bundle in exactly the shape I was hoping for. Even clad in its royal-blue cover, the Rockwell logo stamped all over the canvas in silver, I could see the long flaps, the high point of the cantle. I wouldn't mind dressage training nearly as much with that beauty, made just for me. I might even like it.

He pulled back the cover and let me gaze upon it in silent delight.

Butter-soft leather and sleek padding, a gleaming black beauty to bring out the dressage queen within, with my name stamped on a brass plate on the cantle, declaring to the world: *Juliet Thornton.*

"Oh," I said, seeing the nameplate.

"A problem?"

"I just . . . no . . ." I wasn't ready to hand back my dream saddle for a flaw like that. "It's fine." But I felt a little curdle of disappointment. My name was Jules. The last person to routinely call me Juliet had been my high school principal, and it wasn't because she admired me. I had an uneasy feeling that if the gossips caught sight of this nameplate while I was at an event, they'd start calling me Juliet in a mocking tone, and I'd never shake it.

"Good," he said. "We're ready to take your cross-country saddle measurements next."

I bit back a squeal. Custom cross-country saddle, to go with custom dressage saddle! He could put "Juliet" on all of them. The nameplate was not a big deal. I just needed to get a little screwdriver and remove it before anyone saw it—

"Whoa! What is *that*?" A shadow appeared at my side and the afternoon sun promptly hid behind the clouds.

Amanda. What was she doing here? And Pete was right behind her? They were supposed to be teaching all afternoon.

"Wait, is your name really Juliet? That's so cute! Hi, I'm

Amanda Cunningham, you must be Carl Rockwell? A pleasure! So exciting to meet you! I ride in a Rockwell Symphony . . . yes, it's my favorite! Hunters, mostly, yes—"

Amanda took control of the conversation with ease, her slight frame slipping between myself and Carl, and I took a few steps back, the dressage saddle still nestled in my arms like a newborn.

Pete raised his eyebrows at my armful of leather. "What's that, now?"

"My life's work," I informed him, hugging the saddle. "My hopes and my dreams. In this saddle, I shall finally win the dressage and kick everyone's asses to kingdom come."

"Hold it up and let me look at that beauty."

I obliged. Pete studied the shapely lines of the saddle; jealously, I hoped, although his was probably coming too. His eyes fell on the nameplate, and he quirked his eyebrow at me.

"Apparently I had to go back to my birth name in order to fulfill my destiny," I said dryly. "It's a common problem for warrior princesses."

"Well, it seems like a fair trade." He switched his gaze over to Amanda, who was still gushing about Lord knows what to Carl. "What's going on with *them*?"

"I think Amanda wants a deal, too." I rolled my eyes. "I should be pissed at her, except I don't want to talk to him anyway, and she plainly loves to talk to anyone."

"Anyone with money." Pete laughed. "But don't worry, she doesn't need his. She can buy her own saddles. She just wants to own the room. It's her way, she doesn't mean anything by it."

I opened my mouth, a hundred snarky responses on my tongue, and then stopped myself.

I will not fight with Pete. I will not fight with Pete. I turned on my heel and began to march toward the arena gate, instead. This was probably only marginally better than hurling insults at him, but I didn't have a lot of patience to work with. I was doing the best I could with the materials I'd been given.

At least Alex was pulling up Dynamo, which gave me an excuse for walking away besides my own bad temper. She saw me coming and waved, and I promptly shoved the Petemanda problem right out of my mind.

"What do you think? Can we fix him?"

Alex smiled and rubbed her hand along Dynamo's sweat-soaked red neck.

"He'll be fine. Let's cool him out and talk about what you're going to do next. I have ideas."

12

"SO THE FUNNY thing is," Alex said, deftly running up the stirrups of my battered old dressage saddle (goodbye, old boy) while Dynamo stood quietly in the barn aisle's crossties, "I'm teaching the opposite thing to my off-track horse. I keep mentioning Tiger, right? He's one of my old racers that I retired last year, and I'm training him to . . . I don't know, to jump, to event maybe, right?"

She pulled off the saddle, dragging along the pad and the girth without unbuckling it from the other side. I cringed inwardly, since my first riding instructor had essentially beaten that little shortcut out of me in my very first riding lesson, but Alex just caught the girth with her free hand before it hit the ground and wrapped it around the saddle, tucking the loose end under the stirrup iron. It was all so efficient I wondered why I wasn't using the same trick. It was kind of crazy how many multipart everyday tasks had been reduced to one quick motion in the racing industry.

"Anyway, I usually send my retirees who aren't going to the

breeding shed to this trainer Lucy, out in Williston? And she was going to take Tiger but then she couldn't, a tornado hit her barn, yada yada yada, we've all had Florida fuck up our plans before, right?"

I thought of the hurricane blowing my farm to bits and nodded. Florida was kind of a bitch. And my old farm was very close to Williston. "I think I remember that tornado."

I picked up Dynamo's lead rope and unsnapped the crossties.

Alex followed us out to the wash rack. "So Lucy can't take Tiger, I'm stuck with him, I'm freaking out, and she says to me, if I have any trouble, there's this trainer named Jules Thornton who's good with off-track horses. And then I was looking at *Eventing Chicks*—"

I stopped unreeling the hose and stared at her. "What did they have to say?"

"It was a list of top riders to watch for fall," she said.

"Oh." Well, that was fine, then.

"So I saw your name there. And then you showed up at my *gate*? And now here we are. Isn't that crazy? I love things like that. I love the horse world." She took the hose from me and sprayed Dynamo, who leaned into the cool water.

"I love Ocala," I agreed. "Even when they're gossiping about me. You know what I mean."

"Totally. Wait until you get into the racing world. All gossips. Anyway, with Tiger, I have the opposite problem. He's leaning into the bit like a freight train and sometimes I'm not sure I'm doing enough to get him off the forehand. I was with a trainer for a while last year, but the farm was kind of bananas and we ended up coming home." Alex paused to shake a kink out of the hose, and I took the opportunity to interject some Jules-wisdom, courtesy of Grace and every other trainer in the world.

"The answer is always more leg."

Alex laughed. "I know, right? But like I said earlier, I don't ride with a lot of leg when I'm galloping, so sometimes I'm just searching for the feel and nothing feels right. I need some lessons on a horse who knows what he's doing, I think." She grinned at me. "You interested in teaching me?"

At this point I would probably do just about anything for a dollar, even teach. And Alex was so nice to be around, so alive and so enthusiastic about the horses, I didn't even stop to think about numbers and schedules and how much I might be able to make out of this. I just knew I wanted to have her around, and I wanted to be the one to help her out. For *friendship,* not for money. "Of course, I would love to!" I exclaimed, and I meant it.

Alex flung up her arms and water cascaded through the air. Dynamo gave her some side-eye for interrupting his shower, but she was too excited to notice—excited about riding with *me,* wasn't that one for the books? "I'm sure reminding some crazy gallop girl to sit up in a dressage saddle isn't high on your list of priorities, but whenever you can squeeze me in, I'll make it worth your time. And as for this guy . . ." She shut off the water and reached for a sweat scraper. "I'll lend you an exercise saddle and give you a little coaching on how to gallop in it, since you're only jogging babies at my farm. You can even trailer over and use the track if you want to. Alexander won't mind, and it would be super useful for what I have in mind."

I watched her slide the plastic sweat scraper across Dynamo's muscled back, the water slipping from his coat and flying through the air, catching the sunlight like golden beads. I imagined galloping him like a racehorse and immediately felt goose bumps prickling my bare arms. To gallop this glorious powerhouse on a groomed track, letting him soar in full flight with nothing in front of him? Dynamo might be past the first blush of youth, but he was well-conditioned and strong as hell. This would be an adventure. "So what's your plan for the track?"

"This guy needs galloping lessons. He raced before, right? He'll know what to do when he gets out there. So if you're just perched on him like an exercise rider, give him a little time for muscle memory to kick in. Then he'll start to push down on the bit. I think if you alternate between dressage tack and racing tack, and ride really radically different in each of them, he'll start learning how to make that distinction between what you want in dressage and what you want when you're galloping cross-country. Horses remember actions as scenarios, I think. They replay old behavior when they're confronted with similar conditions."

Pete had said something similar once, right before he scared the life out of Mickey and me. He'd been right, too. He'd fixed Mickey.

Alex put down the scraper and took hold of Dynamo's tail in both hands. I raised my eyebrows: What the hell was she doing? In two quick motions, she shook the end of his red tail through the air, shaking the water out of it.

"Whoa," I said appreciatively. "I've never seen that before."

"Handy, right? I never saw it before I got into the racing business, either. They make a science out of getting the horse as dry as possible before he goes back in his stall. Even towel off his fetlocks. It's because at the track they spend so much time standing in straw or shavings and it dries out their heels something awful."

"That's a shame," I said, momentarily distracted from all the good things about to happen. "I keep my guys out as much as possible."

"I do too. I trailer to the races whenever I can. But anyway." Alex shrugged, because some things were out of our hands and we both knew it. "Tomorrow morning you're coming to ride with us, right? Still my new star exercise rider?"

I tried to muster some enthusiasm. For all that I really liked Alex, 5 A.M. was 5 A.M. "Yes, ma'am!" I replied brightly, pretending I wasn't dreading my alarm already.

"Perfect. I'll ride out with you and give you some help with the saddle and finding your position. Then I'll send a spare home with you." She ran her fingers along Dynamo's lips and he wiggled them on her palm. "I'm guessing you ride him in a plain snaffle, right? Not a gag?"

"Oh, no," I said. "No gag bits."

"Perfect. Some of those big bicycle-chain bits you see on cross-country would tear up his mouth if we tried this. I swear, some riders get so worried about how to stop, I guess they forget how important it is to help your horse go."

Alex went on in that vein for a while, as we took Dynamo in, put him away, and pulled out Mickey so I could get on with my riding. I wished she'd just hang out all day. With Lacey gone, the barn could feel pretty lonesome. Having Pete around alleviated things a little bit, but sometimes the strained atmosphere around us made it easier to just be alone. Alex didn't know our personal problems, but she seemed to sense something was going on when Pete came in, silently tacked up a horse, and rode out, all in under fifteen minutes. Amanda was nowhere to be seen.

"Isn't it annoying having Pete in your barn?" she asked while I was kneeling next to Mickey, a pile of polo wraps beside me. "I get so annoyed at Alexander. He's always second-guessing me. And undermining me. And telling me I'm wrong. That's the same thing, right? He's such a pain, I get flustered just thinking about it."

I was startled into laughter. "I mean . . . that's why I always said I'd never date a trainer. I didn't want to at all. But it was like falling in slow-motion . . . we weren't and then we were. I guess Pete and I just kind of happened."

"And are you still happening?"

My hand slipped and the polo wrap sagged. I shook it out and began to wind the fleece up again. "We're still happening," I said slowly.

"Sorry, too much for the first date. I can be bad about that. Boundaries."

"No, it's fine." I focused on the polo, on Mickey's gray-flecked white leg in front of me. "It's fine," I said again. I couldn't think of anything else to say.

Then Alex was on her knees next to me, taking the polo wrap from my hands and deftly slipping it around Mickey's leg. She was unbelievably fast, her fingers flicking the wrap into place with perfect, symmetrical layers.

The Velcro crackled into place at exactly the right spot, around the cannon bone and directly beneath the knee joint, and for a moment I forgot that I was struggling with stupid man-problems and just gaped at the wonder of that polo-wrapping job.

"You should do YouTube videos," I breathed.

"Like, tutorials?"

"No, just set to classical music. Like meditation videos."

Alex laughed and helped me to my feet. She put her hands on my shoulders and looked into my eyes. Her eyes were light blue, her eyelashes sun-bleached to the same color as her tan skin. I thought we probably looked a lot alike, but at this moment I could tell she was older than me. Maybe *much* older than me, mentally. Which is why what she said next was so funny.

"Boys are stupid," Alex said seriously. "But the right one is worth all the stupid."

I burst out laughing and after a moment of twitching cheek muscles, so did Alex. "Seriously!" she protested through her bubbling laugh. "I mean it!"

"Save it for the YouTube channel. You're gonna be a star."

Alex took a few breaths and recovered her chill. "In all seriousness, really," she said, picking up a wrap and heading over to bless Mickey's other foreleg with her magical wrapping skills, "if you ever need to talk about sharing a barn with your perfectionist boyfriend, I am definitely your girl."

"I *wish* it was just that he's a perfectionist," I said.

"Well, whatever it is."

"It's commitment."

"His?"

"Mine."

She patted the Velcro on the second wrap, which was just as gorgeous as the first one. "Well, stay or go, but don't drag it out. There's plenty of barns for rent out there."

"It's stay," I said quickly. "But he doesn't always seem to believe me. And he's stressed, so he assumes the worst about everything right now."

Alex nodded. "Oh, girl. I understand that." She put her fingers up to Mickey's muzzle and let the mouthy horse lip at them. "Just stick him out, then."

She waved goodbye from her truck as I mounted on Mickey

and started toward the arena. I was already feeling excited about riding with her in the morning.

Even if it was going to be ungodly early.

I managed to get through riding Mickey without having to engage with Amanda, who was in the jumping arena, taking photos of Pete like his personal paparazzo as he took Regina around a four-foot course. The mare had her game face on, cantering around the fences with her neck arched and her tail lifted, and I knew even if Amanda had the photography skills of a toddler, those pictures were going to look fantastic. Whichever pics made it to his Instagram feed were going to make Rockwell very happy.

I wished someone felt like doing a photo shoot with *me*. Most of my photos were screenshots, with a big watermark right across my face or my horse's chest. Mickey pictures were the exception, since his owners had the money to buy the prints. I had a lengthy wish list of old Dynamo photos, wasting away on event photographers' servers, waiting for me to click buy.

Mickey was still a little grouchy about how much time we spent in the sandbox these days, but he was young and this was understandable. I rewarded him with a stroll in the cross-country field. The jumpers in the training barn whinnied as we walked past, reminding me that in a couple more weeks, this barn would be full of someone else's horses. Why was this year turning out so awful?

"All we need now is a hurricane," I told Mickey. He flicked his black-tipped ears back to me, then forward again, carefully watching the green pasture ahead in case of boogeymen or horse-eating plastic bags. "Another storm would be just about par for the course, the way things have been going."

A sandhill crane stalked over the ridge in front of us, nearly five feet's worth of gray bird with his red-capped head cocked, looking for some bugs, and Mickey stopped short, lifting his head in astonishment. The crane sauntered off toward a clump of sabal palms, never once glancing in our direction.

I gathered up my reins and pushed Mickey forward, his neck lifting in front of me in total giraffe mode. I could remember being a kid and this kind of situation sending me flying off the handle, out of balance and easily dislodged by a single hard spook. Now I rode through silly moments like this without a second thought, laughing at my horse, reminding him if I wasn't scared, there was nothing to be afraid of.

In some ways, I guessed, it really was good to be an adult. There were bigger things to be afraid of, but at least we didn't have to worry about the little things quite so much anymore. It seemed to even out.

A shadow passed over the hillside as Mickey recovered from his crane encounter, and I took an appraising look at the sky. Late September and the rest of the country was gazing back at summer with nostalgia, but in Florida the sky was still hazy with humidity and dotted with cotton-ball clouds slowly swelling their way toward storm status. "Let's head home," I told Mickey, nudging his hooves in the direction of the back gate by the annex barn.

Two more horses to ride, maybe a nap while it rained, and then evening feed, turnout, and stall cleaning. I'd hang out with Pete and tell him jokes and make him laugh and remind him he loved having me around and I wasn't going anywhere. I'd show him that even when things were a mess, I was still here to support and love him. He'd catch on sooner or later. Honestly, it didn't sound like the worst way to spend a day. It sounded pretty great. My life might be a roller coaster right now, but when I just focused on the routine, it was a damn pleasure.

O f course, things didn't go as planned. As soon as Mickey was put away, a storm rolled in.

I went into the tack room, leaving the door open behind me. The rain was pouring down in streams against the tack room window, rattling against the otherwise-silent air conditioner. I fiddled with some pictures I'd taken while riding, trying to find one that showed off Mickey's Rockwell Competitor bridle, when Pete came storming in, his mood as black as the clouds outside. He was ready for a fight.

"Well, Rockwell called me on the carpet while you were with Alex, and he isn't happy," he began, starting to slam the tack room door behind him, before he remembered our air-conditioning situation and opened it again. A fly buzzed in and started circling the ceiling fan chain. He looked up at it instead of me, watching the bug whirl in deranged circles. "He doesn't want word to get out that we're sleeping in the barn, or the trailer, or wherever. He said to keep it close and not let clients into the barn. Amanda is canceling those clients who were coming to look at Rorschach. I don't know what's going to happen."

"That's ridiculous. What's wrong with sleeping in the barn? Also, he's a total coward for not saying it to me." From my desk chair, I propped my bare feet up on the bed, and Marcus sighed contentedly from my pillow. Besides everything being covered with sand and the lack of climate control, living in the barn seemed pretty smart.

"It looks bad, Jules. He didn't sign us to his team because we were poor and he wanted to give us money and make our lives better. He signed us, in part, because of Briar Hill. Because we look *good*. Why do you think he made you get that Instagram account and take riding selfies every day? To show off. How can we show off if we're living in a barn?"

"Well, he's an asshole," I said dismissively. I hated those stupid riding selfies, but I'd do much worse for a new saddle. I glanced over at the Rockwell dressage saddle, swathed in its elegant blue cover. *Oh yeah, baby, I see you there, looking all sexy.* Tomorrow I'd take some pictures of it on Dynamo and Mickey. "Anyway, what's he going to do about it? We signed a contract. We fulfilled our end of it. We continue to fulfill it. Nowhere in the contract does it say *must live in house.*"

"Any contract is breakable," Pete growled. He threw himself down on the bed, the only available place to sit, and glared at me as if my sitting in the desk chair was a personal attack on his masculinity.

"He can't handle the bad press," I said, imagining what the gossip mill would do if the industry's leading brand dumped their ambassadors because they were too broke to live in their own house. "Can you imagine what the blogs would do? They'd boycott the brand. Even the Eventing Chicks would stand up for me."

Pete huffed, but I allowed it. He didn't have the same experience with the ruthless faceless armies on the internet that I did. I figured Alex would agree with me, too—I'd done a little research on that girl and *oof*—they'd nearly eaten her alive not too long ago with some kind of abandoned horse scandal. A former racehorse that had been born at her farm had been found wandering the Everglades on his own, and animal rights activists made Alex their target, even though she'd never owned the horse. The internet rabble could be crazy. Alex and I had more in common than I'd realized. Meanwhile, Pete had his own hashtag.

"The internet wouldn't stand for it if anything happened to Sweet Pete," I reminded him.

He gave me another dark look; I wasn't supposed to use his hashtag out loud, as I knew perfectly well. Then he leaned back on the bed. Marcus looked up from my pillow, sighed, and put his head back down, long beagle ears streaming across the pillowcase. "I'm guessing Rockwell has ads on that *Eventing Chicks* website."

"Of course they do, and every other big horse blog. They're stuck with us as long as you look pretty and I look bitchy. People will root for you and hate on me. We're like the perfect power couple."

"How powerful are we, really, when we live in a barn?"

"Blame it on me, they'll *love* that." I wasn't even bitter about it. Why not exploit the eventing world's drama-loving little hearts? If the people wanted a soap opera, Jules Thornton could give them a soap opera.

"You can't use a bad attitude as some sort of publicity stunt," Pete argued.

"Why not? I'm starting to think it's a good plan. Before, people called me a diva, and I fought it. Now I embrace it, and I get followers on my Instagram." I pulled out my phone and looked at the last post I'd shared, a pic of Dynamo snoozing in the crossties after Alex's ride. Hashtags: #SleepyPony #DynamicDuo #Dynamo4Prez #EventingDiva.

After two hours, the post had 564 likes and a smattering of comments ranging from *I luv u Dynamo* to *id be tired to* if *I was Jules thorntons horse.*

I considered this a win.

"You're taking 'embrace the hate' a little too literally."

"Shut up." I sighed, going back to my calendar. This conversation wasn't going anywhere. Like most of our conversations these days, it was just a lot of head-butting.

"I'm not going to shut up, Jules, we have to take this seriously."

I slammed my pen down on the desk and spun back around to face him. "Pete, for fuck's sake, we are controlling the narrative on this one, not him. We have his money. I'm not sure our lives are better because of it, but we get his money and we get his tack, so he can just shut it. Our job is to ride horses and win events. Anything else is none of his goddamn business."

Pete's eyebrows came crashing together and I whirled the chair back to the desk. I glared at the calendar. I was supposed to be filling in the days I would be trailering Dynamo down the road to Cotswold Farm for gallop schools, but now the dates were blurring together. Damn Pete for bringing this up right now!

I *knew* our lives weren't better because of the contract. They were a mess.

Summer had killed us, it was that simple. It had brought out all the worst in me and I'd flung it all at Pete, and now the distance between us was palpable, like an icy wall we could just peer through if we squinted.

We'd done all this for money, that was the sad thing. We'd done it to stay alive in the game, but at the end of the day, all any of that meant was we'd done it for money.

Pete got up again and walked around the little room restlessly. I gritted my teeth and tried to ignore him, but it was like ignoring a pacing tiger while it was trying to decide if it wanted to eat me or not. I waited for him to continue his argument, but after a while he just said, "It's almost done raining. Do you want to finish riding?"

I'd planned to ride Jim Dear next. His debut at Training level was almost here, so he couldn't really get an extra day off right now. "I'd like to jump Jim over some gymnastics if the ring isn't too wet."

Pete had his hand on the door, halfway into the barn. "I'll just go and set some up real quick."

"Oh!" The worst part of jumping gymnastics was setup, hauling the heavy standards and poles into place. "Thank you—"

But he was already gone.

13

AFTER A NIGHT of actual sleep on the horse trailer's thin mattress, the generator running and the air conditioner blowing sweet cool air against our cheeks all night, the dual chirping of our alarms at five wasn't the tearjerker it might have been. We slithered down from the loft bed in the gooseneck and pulled on our riding clothes: jeans and polos, paddock boots and half chaps. Pete went into the barn to make coffee and leave me the little bathroom in the trailer, which was statistically less likely to contain any large and startling spiders when I flipped the light on. I paused in the trailer once I was put together for the morning, anxious to enjoy a few more minutes of air-conditioning before the humid morning hit me, and decided to post to Instagram.

I couldn't help it. Rockwell got tagged in the posts sharing beautiful sunsets at the farm, and #betweentheears pics I took from the saddle—all the inspirational, dream-life type pictures. But being brutally honest was kind of my thing. I brought up the alarm clock on my phone and screenshotted the various alarms: 4:50, 4:55, 5:00. Then I posted *that* to Instagram. Caption: *#equestrianproblems.*

The picture had twenty-seven likes and six comments from British teens who were already up and studying their phones during class by the time I had filled my travel mug with coffee, received a stiff kiss from a half-asleep Pete, and clambered into my truck, feeling with one hand to make sure my vest and hard hat were on the seat where I'd put them the night before. Marcus watched me dolefully from the barn aisle, sitting in the pool of orange light from the streetlamp hanging above the barn entrance. He wanted me to appreciate how lonesome he was, but we both knew he was heading straight back to bed the second we left—I'd left the tack room door open and Pete's pillow tugged into prominence above mine. Anyway, it was Becky's morning to feed, so she'd be down shortly and he'd have some company and probably a few bites of breakfast sandwich.

Pete's truck was a pair of red taillights in the distance; they turned down the county road in the opposite direction while I headed north, through the heart of Ocala's most voluptuous hills. I didn't know where he was heading this morning, since Plum Hill had cut him loose for missing work yesterday morning, but he had more racing connections than I had. There were always more horses to ride in Ocala, he was always saying. Let him put it to the test.

At Cotswold Farm, Alex was running around the training barn already, the big open shed rows blazing with light against the dark sky. Horses were rooting around in feed pans for the last few bites of sweet feed, and grooms were setting out fat foam saddle pads and slips of green cotton towels in front of stalls. Alexander was in the office, looking at a training calendar; I ducked out of the doorway before he saw me. I hadn't really spoken to him yet, but he made me nervous. There was a lot of quiet confidence in that man.

The board was already set for the morning: rider names down the left side, with horse names jotted in for each set. I slipped into the tack room, narrowly avoiding a groom rushing out with a pile of saddles over his arm, and put down my coffee mug on a table already crowded with other travel cups.

Alex poked her head in. "Good morning, sunshine!" She kept doing this because she knew I hated it, and I respected her so much for that. "Ready to ride? I have a nice lineup for you today."

Another groom raced in, threw three exercise saddles over his arm, and dashed out again.

"This barn is quite a machine," I said. "It's been a week and I still can't figure out what everyone is doing. I think I'd be a bad tour guide."

"That's because you spend most of your time out on the track," she said. "But I get it. I was an eventing girl brand-new to a training barn once, too. *This* barn, as a matter of fact. And now I'm in charge of it. That alone ought to tell you it's not that complicated."

"But I can never figure out why racing feels so different from every other horse sport," I said. "Like, it's *just horses*. I can walk into any other barn and fake it, but racing is like . . . it's like a secret, isn't it?"

"It really is," Alex agreed. "I guess it's because everyone is really trying to make money. We're passionate about horses, but whereas in eventing you can get owners who just want to be part of the game, or want to fund deserving riders or something else totally generous like that, most of our owners are trying to make money. That's why they're here. We have owners who don't even like horses. Well, that's going too far," she amended. "We have owners who don't know a thing about horses and aren't really interested besides when they can take clients to the owner's box to show off. So it makes everything that much more competitive between barns, and so . . . it gets secretive."

"That makes sense," I agreed, but I didn't know if I'd want to work that way. It sounded exhausting. I found it tiring enough trying to keep philanthropic owners who were just rooting for me to succeed with their project pony. Imagine having some businessman breathing down my neck for results every day. *Like Carl Rockwell?* a little voice chirped in my ear.

I pushed away the thought with the more cheerful mental image of my gorgeous new saddle, and paid close attention as Alex went through the morning routine: checking the whiteboard to see which horses I'd be riding, tacking them up, waiting for a leg up, walking the shed row with the other riders for a few "turns" before we headed out to the back pasture.

"We'll jog and gallop a little in the pasture for a couple weeks yet. Just like you did on Sunday: we ride single file, sticking to the fence lines, so you have walls to bump into and keep them straight. They're all really good babies. I can't imagine anyone doing anything worse than a few crowhops."

She looked down the aisle where sweet feed–studded noses were starting to appear, bright-eyed small Thoroughbreds looking out at the world, ready to get going with their day. At the end of the shed row, the dark sky spread out behind their profiles, stars still in full control. No sign of sunrise, but these little pistols were begging to get busy.

Their racehorse work ethic was already on full display.

The other riders had all arrived by now. The group was mostly men, although a middle-aged woman with deeply grooved lines in her weathered face was mixed in with the boys, listening to them gossip over coffee mugs. I didn't try to join their conversation. After nodding good morning, I went down the aisle and slipped into my first horse's stall.

A few minutes later we were tacked and ready. A friendly groom came by, gave me an easy leg up, and walked my horse around the stall while I found my stirrups and knotted my reins.

This morning, I started on a little chestnut filly I hadn't met before. Her face was marked with a white stripe that ended crookedly over her right nostril, giving her a lopsided appearance. She wore a neck strap with her dam's name in scratched brass letters: LOVELY LILY. Next to her mother's name were two numbers, which stood for last year—her foaling year. Probably there was already a new little Lovely Lily out there. The only way to tell them apart in the records was by year. That would change when they were older, and had registered names of their own. To say nothing of racing records.

She was a slight filly, but sturdy. It was amazing to find an eighteen-month-old horse could feel so steady, completely unconcerned by my weight on her back or my hands on her mouth, and when we walked out into the shed row to join the rest of the horses in the set, she lifted her head and pricked her ears. That was it . . . her entire reaction was of polite interest. She was like most of the others I'd ridden here at Cotswold Farm.

I considered the way any one of my event horses would have come bouncing out of the stall, ready for mayhem, if they were allowed to go out with six other horses at once, and decided maybe riding yearlings was far better than riding "mature" Thoroughbreds of six or seven or eight, who seemed to have bourbon for brains. I was really starting to fall for these babies.

After a few turns around the shed row, we headed out, following Alex on a tall bay colt with a white ring around his eye. The colt had attitude, and I watched how she handled him. As soon as we stepped out of the barn, he began to pull on her, jogging instead of walking, and she sat upright with her lower legs in front of her and her heels down, letting her body absorb his pull while she kept her hands as flexible as she could. She was such a sympathetic rider, I wondered why she'd given up eventing. She could clearly have gone far with such a strong seat and those light hands. Maybe, I realized, those had come from the racehorses.

One by one we walked sedately through the open pasture gate behind the barn, and turned along the dark line of the fence, marching over the dusky hills in a reassuringly straight line. All of the riders, myself included, took a hold of their nylon neck straps, threading their ring fingers through them along with the reins, and Alex called out, "Let's jog!" Every little horse's ears pricked and eyes widened as the lead baby bounced into a springing, long-striding trot.

I already felt like an old pro at riding the babies—they were green but willing, curious about their surroundings, happy to bump into one another and take comfort in their comrades.

This is nothing like I expected," I told Alex a couple hours later from my perch on an overturned bucket. We were eating tacos, their corn tortillas tearing in jagged lines, spilling crumbling white cheese and a green snowfall of shredded cilantro onto the barn aisle. The battered minivan with a Mexican flag hanging in one window had pulled up just as we were taking the tack off our last set of horses, and everyone had gleefully chorused *"Taco Lady!"*

I couldn't say no to tacos, even if nine o'clock in the morning seemed really early for Mexican food, and I was glad I hadn't—these little monsters were outstanding.

"The beginning's the best," Alex admitted. "They get older, you know. And fitter. The grown horses can be real assholes." She took a swig of neon-orange Mexican soda, the first thing I'd seen her drink besides coffee. I felt a slight concern for her hydration levels. "Next week we'll add some actual work: pas de deux in a way," she said. "Some drill-team type stuff where we're working in pairs. Then in a month, we'll be moving to the track. But the beginning, just jogging around the pastures . . . it's probably the nicest part of the year for me, besides vacation. Everything just slows down for a month or so."

"Vacation, though? What's that?" I grinned.

Alex gave me a serious look over her orange soda. "It's something we kind of insist on now. You should consider it. We work hard. Getting away together for a little while is the nicest thing we can do for ourselves."

I nodded noncommittally and went back to my taco. Vacations, what a nice idea! Like unicorns and a dressage score in the twenties and a credit score in the seven hundreds! Pete *was* always hinting he'd like to go on a trip with me, away from the horses and the endless grind. Or, he used to. I'd always laughed at him. The hints hadn't come in a while now.

But maybe I should've taken him more seriously. Maybe if we had done something together that wasn't working ourselves to death, we'd have been better prepared for all the drama in our lives now. Had we ever had fun together, if you counted fun as something more than splurging on dinner at Chili's during an event weekend? Not really. I was never up for anything that might take me away from work. That probably said a lot right there about the way I'd taken him for granted.

That probably said everything.

I crumpled up my napkin and wondered why I felt the need to devastate myself emotionally before most people had started their workday.

"Welp, that's all the babies," Alex announced when we were done with tacos and the riders were starting to stand up, stretch, and head outside for a smoke. "I have a couple older horses to send out and then we're done for the day. You want to watch?"

I guessed I wasn't allowed on the older horses, if I was being invited to stay as a guest. That was fine, because I had my own crew to get back to and get riding, and the sun was starting to sizzle. "I better go. It's getting late."

"You're bringing Dynamo over tomorrow, right?"

"At one," I confirmed. Midday would be awfully hot for a gallop, but so would any part of the day, and if it rained in the midafternoon, we'd be stuck with a muddy track. Sloppy footing wouldn't exactly be ideal for his first time galloping on the training track, especially since I had no idea what kind of horse I'd have under me. He might go completely rogue and take off like he was three years old and it was race day again. I was excited to find out what that would feel like.

"I'll ride out on Parker with you and show you the ropes. Plus, if he gets silly because it's his first time back on the track, you'll have a hand."

I smiled at the thought I might need some help controlling Dynamo. "Thanks," I said. "And then we'll take a look at Tiger? We haven't set a time for that yet."

Her face lit up, telling me for sure that Tiger was her favorite child. "Definitely! I'm excited to see what you think of him."

"I'm sure I can't tell you anything you don't already know," I cautioned her.

Alex burst out laughing. "Jules! Don't be so modest! You're an eventing star, you know that, right?"

"I wouldn't say star . . ."

"You're right," Alex chortled, picking up the bucket she'd been sitting on. "Last week's *Chronicle* called you a 'rising star.' That's completely different."

I blushed. "I don't get the *Chronicle*," I said sheepishly.

"I'll bring it down from the house for you tomorrow."

I basked in Alex's words as I drove out of Cotswold, slowly steering along the curving barn lane. I turned onto the county highway and drove past the endless black-board fences. A little gang of weanlings, the first of the year, galloped along their fence line as I passed the next farm, their steps bold and their heads held high.

Next year's crop of yearlings, I thought. *Thanks, Alex, now I'm thinking like a racetracker!*

Alex just had a way of wearing her knowledge like cool confidence, instead of showing it off like me. Alex gave the impression she didn't worry about what the people around her thought—she *knew* she was the boss, and through her self-awareness, everyone around her knew as well.

I wondered if I could ever reach that level of confidence. I wondered what she'd gone through to attain it. I knew things like that didn't come easily to people like us. While I didn't know Alex's history, something told me she'd had to fight to reach this point in her career, just as I had been fighting. The difference was, she seemed to be past fighting.

I was envious.

I'd been struggling and fighting and trying to wave my hands over everyone else's heads for so long, being a pushy know-it-all had become my nature, my reputation, my calling card. Pete said it had to go, and up until this fall he'd pushed me to be better, be nicer, hold my tongue when I thought I should criticize, and say nice things when I thought I should just march away. Lacey had encouraged me, too. We'd all looked at my attitude, at that chip on my shoulder, at my inability to take advice, as some sort of group project.

Then the summer happened.

Then Lacey moved back to Pennsylvania.

Then Pete backed away from me.

I'd lost my cheerleaders and my coaches.

But I'd managed to make friends and take orders from Alex anyway, without them.

So maybe I was improving after all.

I turned into the drive at Briar Hill and drove straight to the annex barn, without letting my gaze slide wistfully over the house where we no longer lived.

Pete's truck was out front, and I went into the barn ready to tell him all about my day: I was learning to ride the babies, Alex and I were collaborating on our horse problems. Things were going pretty well, actually!

The aisle was dark after the glaring morning sunlight, and I had passed three stalls, Mickey whinnying hello, before I saw Pete.

The tack room door was open, and the plastic bin where I stored my bandages and wound-care supplies was leaning crazily on the concrete sill, half in and half out. There were festoons of gauze decorating the sandy aisle, and they led straight to Pete, kneeling beside Regina, spools of white wrapping around her off foreleg. I took in Regina's distress before his—her half-lowered head, her white-rimmed eyes, her flaring nostrils.

Pete looked up at me with wild eyes, and his voice was so thin and desperate my heart seemed to stop in my chest. "I'm afraid if I take my hand away she'll bleed to death. Please call the vet, and tell them to hurry."

14

IT'S HARD TO dial a phone when your fingers are numb.

Dr. Em was in the middle of a lameness exam, her intern informed me. Could she call me back?

Did she not hear the desperation in my voice?

"I have an FEI eventing mare who is about to hemorrhage and die," I hissed, quickly putting distance between myself and Pete so he wouldn't hear me. I didn't know what was under that gauze he was pressing on her lower leg, but Pete never freaked out like this, so something bad was happening. "I need Dr. Jackson. I need anyone who's gone to vet school. Have you gone to vet school?"

"Um?" I heard the indecision in the intern's voice. She was new. She didn't know how to tactfully interrupt her vet's prescheduled exam and let her know they needed to get into the truck as quickly as possible before her crazy client had a heart attack. "Let me talk to her. Hang on, okay?"

There was a scrabbling noise as the phone was carried across a few yards of grass and driveway to wherever the lameness exam was taking place. I pictured the peaceful scene, the solemn ritual of the trotting horse and the kneeling vet, everyone carefully watching the horse's hooves track up underneath him. The tranquil farm stretched its green arms around them, going about its morning with perfect harmony, the way I had imagined the rest of my morning would go. There's nothing quite like a horse for turning your day upside down.

"Jules," Pete called. "Is she coming?"

"She's coming," I lied, because of course she was coming, it was just a matter of getting the final confirmation she was in the truck, putting on her seat belt, turning the key, getting onto the highway.

"How far away is she?"

"I don't know." She could be anywhere. She tried to stick to Reddick, but what if someone had called her to the outskirts of Ocala? What if she was in Williston, or Citra, or one of the other center-less farm villages that made up Marion County's horse country? She'd call back to the practice and have them send someone else out, I reasoned. The practice was only fifteen minutes away, and there was always at least one vet truck parked outside when I passed. Someone was close. Someone would come. Someone would save us. "Pete—what did she do?"

"She caught her leg in the wire fence," he said tonelessly, and I could tell immediately he blamed himself. "I left her there for one second while I ran into the tack room for my phone . . ."

Our fences were either four-board or diamond-mesh wire, stretched tight underneath a top board. The diamond mesh was too tight and tiny for a horse to stick a hoof through, even a foal, which was why it was so prevalent on the breeding farms—it kept out coyotes and kept in babies—but we had one little section, just a few dozen feet, at the back of the annex barn, where the fence was the wider square mesh. We'd had to replace a section when a tree limb fell in a storm back in spring, and we hadn't had any diamond mesh on hand, and no money to buy the expensive rolls. We'd settled for regular wire, reasoning we'd replace it with safer fence just as soon as we could. After all, horses lived all over Ocala with regular wire fencing, and they managed just fine. Hell, horses lived with barbed wire, not that we'd ever take such a risk, and they managed just fine.

Apparently our horses did not manage just fine, which should surprise no one.

"I looped her lead rope around the fence line; I was just getting ready to work her." Pete's voice cracked and his face fell, as if he couldn't bear to look at me. "She's so talented, Jules, she's so fucking talented, she could do anything, and I've ruined her—"

"Jules?" Dr. Em was on the phone. I jumped, then bounced away from Pete again. I didn't want him to hear anything.

"Yes!"

"What's going on?"

"Regina cut herself bad on wire. There's a lot of blood, she's sliced something wide open."

"Oh, sweet Jesus, Regina? Leg, chest, face . . . ?"

"Near foreleg. Looks like . . . fetlock, maybe heel? Pete has gauze and pressure on it. I just got here, I missed it."

"There's a vein back there. Fine. You're fine. I'll be there in ten. Don't change anything."

Dr. Em clicked off.

I put the phone in my jeans pocket and lurched back over to Pete. I was suddenly aware I was horribly thirsty and he probably was, too. "I'm going to get us some waters," I said. "Unless you want to trade places. Do you need to stand up?"

"No," he muttered. "No, I'm staying right here."

"Okay."

I tipped a water bottle to his lips when he wouldn't take it from me, and I stood vigil there beside him, while Regina huffed miserably and Pete stared down at the reddening gauze beneath his fingers, his face a picture of guilt.

There was no use telling him it wasn't his fault. He was so far gone I didn't think he'd hear me. I could tell I was seeing Pete at his absolute lowest, after weeks of lows, after a summer of exhaustion and upheaval, and I honestly didn't know what to do.

Just stay in charge, I thought.

I was a woman of action, and if I thought I could have moved him aside, I would have thrown myself to my knees and dug under that gauze to see just what Regina had done to herself. I wasn't a person to throw money at a vet if I thought I could handle it myself. At my old farm I'd prided myself on how rarely I actually needed a vet to visit, but that wasn't the right thing, either. You didn't futz around with an Advanced level event horse with a major international sponsor. You called the vet.

If I couldn't play vet, I could at least play girlfriend, right? I looked at my shell-shocked boyfriend, who had been weathering one storm after another for the past month, and my heart broke for him. He didn't deserve this.

I got down on my knees next to Pete and wrapped my arm around his shoulders, and tipped my hot cheek against his shoulder, and I whispered, "She's going to be fine, she's going to be fine, she's going to be fine."

Hours later, Pete and I stood an arm's length apart in the clinic's sparkling barn aisle and stared through the stall bars at Regina, huddled miserably in the corner of her box. Everything was brighter and whiter and cleaner than a real barn, as if it had just been built and opened this morning. As if it was a display model of a barn, not a real place with real horses kicking the walls and spilling their feeds and messing up their shavings. Nothing felt real right now.

Regina was a tall mare, but she seemed small now, with the coiled IV cord springing from her neck to a contraption in the high ceiling, and her foreleg bandaged from hoof to mid-forearm. Her muscles still rippled beneath her dark chestnut coat when she moved even slightly, shifting weight from one hind leg to the other, but the formidable presence that was Regina, Advanced Mare, Queen Bee of Briar Hill, had diminished to something delicate and frightened.

It felt like a lifetime had passed since I'd come home and found the bloody scene in the barn aisle. We'd watched the vet assistants in their hospital scrubs slip the IV beneath the taut skin of Regina's neck, her fox-colored coat patchy with sweat, watched them guide her into the operating theater. We didn't watch what happened inside; I led Pete away instead, and we sat on the front porch of the vet clinic and looked down the sloping pasture out front, where a few late foals were playing beside their dams. I held Pete's hand for the first time in what felt like months, but was more likely days, taking this chance, at least, to crawl across some of the gaping space between us.

"We're so fucked," Pete said after a while. He said it matter-of-factly, the way you'd say it was a sunny day, or Barsuk had sprung another shoe. As if being completely fucked was an everyday occurrence.

I supposed it probably was.

"Not yet," I said instead. "Accidents happen. She'll recover, and you have other horses. We won't lose Rockwell over this." I knew losing Rockwell was really what stood between us and the abyss.

"I don't have another horse ready for Advanced."

"That's okay . . ."

"It's *not* okay." Pete took his hand away, ran it through his copper-colored hair. He needed a haircut, I thought absently. "Jules, my contract looks different than yours."

"What do you mean?"

Pete looked at his boots. He was dressed for riding, buff breeches and half chaps and paddock boots. There were a few drops of blood dried on the fabric clutching his thighs. I put my hand over them. His muscles were tense beneath my touch.

"What do you mean?"

His voice was a husky whisper. "I *have* to ride Advanced in the next year. It's part of the deal."

The porch and the foals and my hand on his thigh were all whirling, tilting, and I closed my eyes to ward off the dizzy spell. It was hardly enough. I wondered how much money they were giving him. I wondered how much we were depending on it to get through winter and the expense of show season.

Probably just enough. Probably completely.

"We'll figure it out," I announced, louder than I meant to, so loud the mares looked up from their grazing and the foals paused in their roughhousing. As soon as I said it, I felt better. I wanted the determination, I wanted the commitment, I wanted the fight. I wanted something worth fighting for. Sometimes eventing life felt a little pointless; yes we loved it, yes it made us feel alive, but was that all we were doing, chasing the feeling of being alive?

But it *was* our lives, for better or for worse; eventing was who we were, and when I looked at Pete I knew he had become an indelible part of that. My eventing had turned into *our* eventing. My life had turned into *our* life. It had taken his doubts to prove that to me. It was taking his heartbreak to show me what filled my own heart.

"Where will I find a horse ready to go Advanced?" He gave me a watery smile, and I just squeezed his hand and smiled back, because even though I couldn't say the words yet, I knew what the eventing gods were asking of me, and I knew I would give them whatever sacrifice they required to keep our life intact. Advanced level horses didn't grow on trees, and people didn't hand them out like party favors. In a town where good horses were always up for grabs, Pete was asking for a unicorn. You had to really, truly care about a person to lend them your Advanced ride.

You had to love them more than yourself.

I thought about it while we sat a few minutes more, the foals giving up their games and throwing themselves to the lush green grass, exhausted, desperate for naps, and the mares going on grazing as if nothing serious enough to drag them away from grass could ever touch them in their comfortable little paddock. I thought about it while we waited, until a whey-faced vet put her head out the front door and said Regina was back in her stall and standing upright.

I thought about it while we watched Pete's big horse hobble around her hospital room.

"She'll have to be wrapped up tight for months," the vet tech said. "The wire cut right through the coronary band, and the skin higher up needs to close up cleanly or scar tissue will give us a hard time later."

"I know," Pete said. "I saw it."

Regina put her head down and sniffed disconsolately at the pine shavings of her stall, their woodsy scent almost drowning out the hospital odors of Betadine and Lysol, and I took Pete's arm. "Let's go home and ride our horses," I told him.

"I don't want to leave her."

"She's going to be here for at least a week." I was the adult right now. "She's in good hands. Let the professionals do their job and let us go do ours."

15

WHEN WE GOT home, the clouds were covering the sun, and the late-September heat was dropping to a more comfortable temperature. It was the kind of afternoon that reminded me of being a kid, sneaking in a quick gallop around the pasture while the air smelled of rain and the yellowy light streaming around the cloud tops made every-thing spooky and dangerous. Thunder growled through the humid air, and the tree frogs around the pond at the bottom of the pasture were starting to sing their rain song.

It was simply gorgeous out, I thought, with one of those breath-less catches of love for Florida that struck me from time to time. It was like nowhere else in the world.

Pete wasn't feeling it. "We're not going to have time to ride."

"Let's be quick," I urged. "You never know, it might go around us. And we have this nice shade and breeze." I wasn't about to give up this moment of perfect weather. I opened the tack room door, and Barn Kitty ran in, ready for some air-conditioning. Marcus looked at her from the bed, warning her it was off-limits to kitties when King Beagle was in town, and then thumped his tail on the bed to welcome us home.

I darted over and gave him a big hug. "How long have you been on my pillow?" I asked. "Don't you know you should be on Pete's?" Marcus rolled over and showed me his belly, inviting me to an extended love-the-puppy session, but I pushed off from the bed. He gazed at me, his expression one of deep betrayal, but I couldn't stay. The eerie light and grumbling sky outside were calling to something deep within me.

First, though, I had to get Pete on a horse. Everything was better from the back of a horse. He'd feel less despondent once he was in the saddle, where he belonged. "I'm going to ride Mickey," I said. "And you . . ." I paused. The words were on the tip of my tongue, but I still felt hesitant to say them. It was going to be so final. It was going to be so real.

"I'll ride Barsuk, I guess," Pete said with a little shrug. "He's the next thing I have to an Advanced horse. I can call Rockwell and try to work this thing out—"

"You'll ride Dynamo," I blurted, the words all a rush, all smashed together, before I lost the courage to say them.

Pete stopped, his hand inches from where Barsuk's black bridle was hanging from its peg. He looked at me for a long moment, and I saw something like admiration in his face. I saw something like awe. "No," he said softly, shaking his head resolutely. "But my God, Jules, that's a sweet offer."

I bit down on the inside of my cheek, took a deep breath, and squared my shoulders. "It's not a sweet offer, Pete. It's the right thing to do."

"I could never take your ride from you—"

"You're not taking my ride. I'm giving you my ride so we can continue with the farm. If you have to have an Advanced horse, well . . . maybe he's not competing at Advanced yet, sure—"

"Not yet," Pete said quietly. "But you can do anything with him. *You*. Are you sure about this?"

Of course I wasn't. Dynamo was my heart. But if we wanted a fighting chance, Dynamo was the only one available. And anyway, if Dynamo was my heart-horse, who better to ride him than Pete?

"I'm sure," I replied firmly, and smiled to cement the lie in place.

Pete moved his hand over one hook to the right, and wrapped his fingers around Dynamo's bridle, the old chestnut leather and brass buckles gleaming dully in the storm-filtered light streaming through the window. He held it there for a moment, making up his mind.

Then, with the bridle clutched in one hand, he crossed the room in two long strides and put his other hand on the nape of my neck, under the frizz of my ponytail, tilting my face up to his. My fingers tingled and my lips parted, and I met his eyes. The guarded look was gone for the first time in months; he was looking at me the way he used to, hungrily, and with admiration. The way he'd looked at me when he'd been chasing me around Ocala, waylaying me at every event, while everyone else in town avoided me like the bad news I was.

"I know what this is, Jules," he murmured, his voice rasping. "What this means. And . . . I just can't . . ."

But I didn't know what he couldn't do, or say, because he kissed me instead, with one hand holding my horse's bridle and one hand on my neck, and the strange feeling of symbolism stayed with me for a long time afterward.

We rode side by side up the driveway, Dynamo and Mickey enjoying the unexpected pairing up. They pressed their noses together and whispered secrets, Dynamo always getting annoyed first and showing Mickey his teeth, nipping at him so Mickey would shy away and I'd have to straighten him out again.

Dynamo had gotten tougher with the strength he'd gained in the summer dressage sessions. He used to be all about peace and love, but now he didn't back away from a fight, and I'd seen him push horses around for fun once or twice. The transformation was fascinating, although I wasn't sure if it was from confidence or all that compressed energy from his collection and submission during training.

I let them play. There was a cool wind whipping across the farm from the rumbling storms to the west and the sun was buried under a high veil of clouds, and Pete was looking down at Dynamo with the veneration my good red horse deserved, and everything was going to be fine.

Everything was going to be *fine*.

I kept telling myself it would all be fine, because to repeat something is to make it come true. It's like a wish—believe in it with all your heart and it comes true. That's what the movies said, anyway, and wasn't my life dramatic enough to be a movie?

I didn't allow myself to be *too* disheartened at how easily Pete rode Dynamo in the dressage arena; after all, I'd spent the entire summer turning Dynamo into the Ultimate Dressage Machine, and the horse who had always been so hard to put together in a frame was certainly ready to kill it in an Advanced level test now. I probably could have tortured both of us and stuck with dressage, put on dress boots and tails, and gone on to Prix St. Georges, but who wanted to spend that much time in a sandbox trying to look pretty?

Life was still about galloping, when you came right down to it. I remembered my date with Alex the next afternoon, and wondered if it would make more sense for Pete to be the one to gallop Dynamo on the Cotswold Farm track. Probably.

I sighed and took my eyes off Dynamo, performing an animated extended trot across the diagonal, and decided to concentrate harder on my up-and-comer. "Can we do some shoulders-in without destroying the fence line?" I asked Mickey, picking up my reins.

Mickey mouthed the bit and arched his neck, giving me his best fake collection until I pushed my leg on and gave his rib cage a tickle with my little spurs. Then he shifted dramatically, lifting his back and bringing his hindquarters underneath himself.

I smiled as his body rose to meet my seat and his front end grew light, springing up before me. It was nice to know beyond a doubt that all the awful dressage this summer had truly been worth it. Mickey felt like a million bucks.

We edged into a shoulders-in along the rail, his spine curving neatly to move his forelegs into a track to the left of his hind legs, yet still moving forward on a straight line. I glanced down at his head, turned in toward the center of the ring, and saw a gob of white foam drip from his mouth onto his gray forelegs.

Dressage queen for a day, I thought proudly. *Tomorrow we're jumping.*

Still, as nicely as Mickey was going, it was hard to ignore Dynamo with another rider on his back. I kept sneaking glances, afraid Pete was pushing him too hard. Pete was such a dressage devotee, and Dynamo was moving so well, I could see him spending a full hour putting my horse through his paces. That would be too much. Dynamo was into his teens; he wasn't a spring chicken like Regina.

But of course Pete knew what he was doing. He kept Dynamo in a frame for precisely twenty minutes, then dropped the contact, letting Dynamo stretch his neck and drop his nose toward the ground. I suspected him of setting a timer.

Mickey was already tired from his lateral work, and happy to walk alongside Dynamo again. "What do you think?" I asked Pete, peering at him from beneath my hard hat. "How was he?"

Pete wiped sweat from his brow with the back of his glove. He smiled at me. "You have a very nice horse here."

Well, I knew *that*. "Can you take him Advanced?"

"He can do Intermediate at Hope Glen like you planned, run a few horse trials at Advanced in the winter, and we can qualify him for a spring three-day at Advanced." Pete ran his hand along Dynamo's short red mane, feeling the hard muscle bulging along his crest. "He's stronger than he was last spring, and probably a half hand taller from lifting his back. I don't think he'll have any trouble with the little stretch in fences."

"Will that be enough? To make Rockwell happy?"

"Yes. The Advanced three-day stipulation was to make it within twelve months. So we have a little wiggle room. Not enough to buy a new horse, obviously . . ." We both snorted. Buying a horse ready to go Advanced in two months would be require nothing less than winning the lottery.

"They don't have any crazy requirements beyond that, do they? They don't expect you to do a four-star, do they?" Four-star and five-star three-day events were for horses at their peak of performance, and getting them into one like the Kentucky Three-Day Event in April, or the Maryland Five-Star in October, would be like prepping a horse for the Kentucky Derby—a lot of luck was at play for years in advance, along with the sheer hard work and gobs of talent necessary to run around a course at that level. No rational person would require a sponsored rider to get a horse there in a certain amount of time . . . but rational people were few and far between in the horse world.

Pete shook his head. "Nope. There's no way I could've agreed to that. I don't even plan on prepping Regina for Kentucky next spring. I mean . . . I didn't." He fell silent.

"She'll be back," I said.

Pete shrugged as if it didn't matter, as if it wasn't tearing him apart inside. He was good at that. "We'll see." He dropped his eyes to Dynamo's curving neck and once more ran his hand along my horse's shining mane.

I watched his face; I could see the admiration and the possession there, and a tiny clutch of fear seized up in my stomach. I wondered what would happen if Regina didn't make it back to competition next year; if the coronary band and tendon sheath she'd damaged in the wire fence didn't heal properly. She'd make a very pretty broodmare and she'd make lovely athletic babies, but where would that leave Pete? Mounted on Dynamo for the foreseeable future. Barsuk would be running at Preliminary this winter; it would take another year or two to get him to Advanced, barring the very normal risk of injury and downtime.

I let Mickey slip the reins through my fingers and buried my hands in his salt-and-pepper mane, the better to hide their sudden shaking, as I wondered if I'd lost the horse I'd planned to conquer the world with.

16

MY LITTLE WORLD went wild when I shared the news about Dynamo.

Alex said I was an amazing girlfriend and team member to let Pete have the ride on my big horse, and she'd probably do it for Alexander but she wouldn't be nice about it. Lacey cried over the phone and said she couldn't believe what a wonderful person I was, which made me grit my teeth. Becky nodded coolly and said it was the logical thing to do, but I saw her tidy eyebrows go up just a little and I knew I'd surprised her. Carl Rockwell didn't talk to me about it, but he told Pete he thought it was a wise decision and he was glad the two of us were working so well as partners. Grace told me to be careful about giving up too much and letting Pete have the upper hand in all things, be it relationship or riding. My mother texted back that it was very sweet and she hadn't really expected me to ever do anything so generous for a boyfriend, or maybe have a boyfriend at all, but I was always surprising her. Ramon didn't say anything, because all Ramon cared about was getting the horses fed and the stalls mucked. What we did with them, whether we sorted cows or jumped hay bales, was entirely our problem.

I wished more people were like Ramon.

Training didn't wait for my emotions to get back in line. Pete and I drove over to Cotswold together for Dynamo's first gallop over the training track, Dynamo in the trailer alone. Alex promised me one of her track ponies to ride so I could gallop around the track with them. I was cautiously excited to see Dynamo run, but a knot of misery had settled into permanent residence somewhere in the back of my throat, and every time I looked at my horse I felt an un-Jules-like desire to burst into tears. I was going through serious seller's remorse, coupled uncomfortably with the knowledge that I'd done the right thing.

Pete, on the other hand, seemed more optimistic than he'd been in months.

He looked over at me now as we neared Cotswold's gates and smiled, an open and honest smile like the ones he'd given me back in the spring, before everything had gone so wrong. I smiled back without parting my lips, a sweet smile, I hoped, a gently loving smile. I didn't have a big, confident *the future is happening!* grin for him just now.

I was afraid I'd take everything back to square one if I told him how much this was hurting me, so I just had to wait it out. Eventually, I'd get over seeing Dynamo perform for someone else. Eventually, I'd get used to seeing Pete take him over fences and riding him down the center line. Eventually, I'd even start to enjoy it, because I loved them both so much.

It was just going to take some time, and some serious pretending.

I patted Pete's knee and looked out the window, watching my own reflection as the endless fences of Cotswold Farm rolled past.

Alex had two horses tacked up and waiting in the training barn's center aisle when we pulled up. She waved and ran over to the grassy loading dock at the far end of the barn, gesturing for Pete to follow. He pulled the trailer alongside the dock and I hopped out to open the side door and unload Dynamo. Alex put her hand on my shoulder as I ran up alongside her. "You okay?" she asked.

I looked at her sympathetic face and my facade nearly crumbled, but I nodded instead of sobbing. I was tougher than that. "It's the right thing to do," I said, or tried to say. The lump in my throat made my voice a painful whisper instead. "We're a team. He needs the Advanced ride right now. I don't."

Alex looked at me with something like wonder. "I couldn't do it," she said solemnly. "You're a damn hero."

I gave her a watery smile and turned to unlatch the side door. Dynamo nickered from within the trailer, and a few horses in the neighborhood whinnied back. As I led him into the shed row, I noticed most of the training barn stalls were empty. "Where is everyone?"

"Out," Alex said. "Everyone gets kicked out after lunch and they stay out until morning. I don't believe in keeping horses cooped up in stalls."

I liked her more and more every day.

I held Dynamo in the shed row while Pete tacked up. The horse turned his chestnut head back and forth, twisting to try and take everything in, his eyes big and his ears pricked.

Alex chuckled. "Something tells me he's been in a training barn before. This should be a pretty fun show out on the track."

Pete grinned and pulled down the stirrups, ready to mount.

"Since I've never galloped this horse before, it should be fun either way."

I bit my lip and pretended to smile. "Are we going to look at Tiger afterward?"

Alex's face fell. "I wish we could. But Alexander needs me to deal with the farrier in the broodmare barn after we're done. The broodmare manager went home sick. We will, though, soon."

"Deal," I agreed. I wondered how often the pressing needs of such a massive farm took her away from riding her project horse.

We went out to the track, three across, me on a petite Quarter mare named Betsy, Alex on a sturdy Thoroughbred gelding named Parker, and Pete on a dancing Dynamo between us. The gravel horse path was lined with palms and live oaks, and the spreading branches of the oaks gave a welcome shade from the slanting rays of the sun. In their shadows, I could feel the approach of autumn through the summery heat. The light was more yellow than it had been a few weeks ago, and the humidity had dropped. Only a few fluffy clouds lazed across the sky, offering little promise of afternoon rain. The absence of big boiling rain clouds just made any time spent in the sun that much hotter. All of us, horses and people, were soaked with sweat by the time we reached the training track.

Despite the heat, I felt a thrill of excitement as our horses stepped through the gap in the shining white rail, Betsy's hooves sinking into the neatly furrowed footing. I'd never been on a race-track before, and a training track like this definitely counted as the real thing. This wasn't the weedy, forlorn oval cut out of pasture I'd ridden at next door. Cotswold's track was the real deal. The banked curves of the turns shimmered in both directions, beckoning, calling out for speed. This was a cathedral for worshipping the sheer athletic ability of the horse to *run*. I wondered why it had taken me so long to get out here, and then I realized Alex had probably felt the same way when she'd come to Ocala. So much so that she'd abandoned eventing and just stayed here, where she could devote herself to the intoxicating sensation of speed.

Dynamo was twisting from side to side, dancing between our two quiet ponies. Pete, looking like a jockey in short stirrups, was already standing up, his hands resting on Dynamo's withers, letting the horse mouth the bit. "Look at this," he said, laughing. "He's already digging into the bit. Nice call, Alex. This is exactly what he needed."

Alex grinned. "So you wanna take him alone, or do you want an escort?"

Dynamo snorted and humped his back, nearly crowhopping as he pulled against the bit. He was like a youngster again. I remembered him being silly like this when we first started eventing, years ago. We were one of the scariest pairs in the warm-up ring before Novice cross-country, as I recalled. Now Dynamo had his baby face on again, ready to kick up his heels and go without worrying about any obstacles in his way. He was all Thoroughbred right now. The dressage horse had been left behind, somewhere on the walk over to the track.

"Better go with an escort this time," Pete said with a grin. "You have a strap?"

I didn't even know what they were talking about now. I kept Betsy off to one side, feeling left out while the grown-ups talked shop.

Alex produced a long leather strap and leaned over, threading it through the ring of Dynamo's loose-ring snaffle. She kept a tight hold of both ends, making a neat little lead between the two of them that she could safely drop if necessary.

Well, that's clever, I thought.

"Let's start with an easy jog the wrong way, to the backstretch, and then we'll turn them and gallop once around," she suggested. "He fit enough for that?"

"Oh yeah, Jules has him fit enough to run a race," Pete said. "Let's do it."

I kicked Betsy after them as they took off at a rapid trot, heading off to the left to circle the track clockwise, the opposite direction I'd been expecting.

Belatedly, I realized we'd turn around to canter the right way, the racing way.

That was what Alex meant by the "wrong way." How was there so much racing lingo I didn't know? How was there an entire horse sport right on my doorstep that I knew nothing about?

I felt silly, trotting after them like a little sister. *Hey, guys, wait for me!* But when I really didn't know what they were doing next, it seemed like the safest answer. Betsy didn't care. She just trotted, ears swiveling lazily, not sure why she was out in the middle of the day but not too bothered either way.

Be like Betsy, I kept telling myself as the workout unfolded, as the white fences flashed by and we found ourselves on the far side, turning around for a gallop. *Be like Betsy,* I told myself, as I watched Pete perch over Dynamo's withers as if he was going to post in the Derby, and my horse's red tail flared out behind him like a flame. *Be like Betsy,* I reminded myself, as he whooped with exhilaration when Dynamo picked up speed of his own accord going into the last turn, the horse clearly remembering his racing days and not finding the memory unpleasant. *Be like Betsy,* I chided myself, as I wiped a tear away from my eye and blamed the wind in my face, and Betsy pulled up to a relieved halt, chewing at her bit, as soon as Parker managed to convince Dynamo to come back down to a trot.

Betsy knew best.

17

I HAD TOLD myself life would be easier when the electrician had fixed the air conditioner, and for the most part, I was right. Our routine felt more settled and normal when we weren't running back and forth between the barn and the trailer, and the constant roar of the generator was switched off. I liked the hum of the window unit; it felt comforting and plucky, like there was always someone in the barn working to make sure I had a nice place to retreat to when the sun grew too hot.

Pete and I were used to living close together, so the loss of space in the house didn't hurt us too much. After a few initial power struggles regarding the use of the single desk chair, I moved a few saddle racks into an open stall and wedged in a love seat from the guesthouse. With somewhere to sit beside the bed, we piled together in the slowly lengthening evenings, Marcus at our feet, and watched television with the scent of leather and hay in our noses. Things really weren't that bad.

We went to Red Hook Farm's dressage show on the first Saturday afternoon in October, and I watched Pete ride Dynamo with an otherworldly grace that made my throat tighten. I drank a half bottle of lemon-flavored water to try and open it up again, and forced myself to keep watching as the pair flitted through the transitions, floated through the circles, and danced through the lateral work.

I even smiled at Pete as he rode out of the arena, reins slack on my horse's sweaty red neck, and his face fairly glowed at me from beneath his flashy new Rockwell SelectShield helmet, which cost about six times as much as Dynamo had when I'd pulled him from the Georgia auction all those years ago. Once again, I felt the strange mixture of joy and resentment I was starting to think was just a more mature version of love.

I slipped into Mickey's stall while Pete rode over to visit with some friends, and he turned from his hay net to give me a friendly nudge with his green-stained nose. "Thank you for the alfalfa kiss," I told him, rubbing his ears. "I needed that right about now."

I pulled at Mickey's tuft of white forelock and stroked his neck beneath the fall of mane, watching the way it darkened from white at his ears to near black at his withers. His dapples were steadily fading, so quickly I could almost watch the gray disappearing from his coat, as if he was in a hurry to grow up and appear a staid, mature, near-white horse. "You're a wannabe Lipizzaner," I whispered. "But let's skip the airs above the ground, okay?"

Mickey went back to his hay, leaving me unceremoniously. I couldn't blame him. There was half a flake of alfalfa mixed in with his timothy, and he was meticulously pulling out every green-leafed strand he could find. That was serious business. I settled down into the clean shavings in the corner and watched him eat.

"You're my big horse now," I told him. "Are you ready to step into Dynamo's horseshoes?"

Mickey realized I was still in his stall and took a step over to investigate my new position on the floor. He nuzzled at me, and ran his lips through my hair the same way Dynamo always did, pulling at loose strands as they escaped my scruffy ponytail, and I felt goose bumps rise on my forearms even as he turned back to his hay net once more, sighing contentedly.

Partners. That's what we were. Partners.

And we had the dressage test of a lifetime later that day, Mickey prancing through his paces like an Olympian, and when we came out of the arena there was a smattering of applause from the tiny collection of trainers, on-deck riders, and horse show moms who had gathered around the ring to half watch the tests, half look at their phones. The day was almost cool, so people were willing to hang around more, risk a little sun on their necks, and it felt like a big audience. Preparation for the crowds to come, I thought.

I leaned low over his braided mane and wrapped my arms around his neck in a bear hug, heedless of the gray hairs that would decorate my black dressage coat. "You were a star," I told him. "I don't deserve you."

Pete, waiting by the in-gate, overheard me. "Are you feeling all right?"

"What?" I sat up unsteadily, letting Mickey plow forward under a slack rein. "Of course I am. Why? Did something look funny? Did I slouch?"

"No, you looked amazing." Pete grinned. "But 'I don't deserve you' isn't something I ever thought I'd hear you say."

I don't deserve you, I nearly said, looking down at him, but then I noticed all over again how neat and trim he was in his unstained polo shirt and shining white breeches while the rest of us humans were dripping with sweat and streaked with dirt. Could he not be normal? Must he always be so perfect and gorgeous? He was obnoxious on so many levels. I totally deserved that in a man.

So instead of getting romantic, I just grinned back and said, "You're right. I was wrong to say it. We all get exactly who we deserve."

He quirked his eyebrow at me and I leaned over to give him a kiss, and a few of the more attentive members of the audience around us clapped again, to be cute or ironic or to tell us to get a room, I didn't know which and I didn't much care. Things were getting back to normal, I told myself, as if with these few signs—affection from Pete, a solid dressage test from my young horse—our foundering ship had righted itself.

The good feelings were short-lived. On the following Tuesday, Mr. Blixden arrived at last. The handful of horses he'd sent early had been with us for so long they were practically family, but adding in more horses, not to mention humans, was going to be a shakeup to the rhythm we'd found for ourselves.

I came back from Alex's farm early the morning Blixden was expected; we were short on work that day, as she'd given some of the babies a week off.

"They're growing," she had explained, pointing to their butt-high little silhouettes as they grazed in the paddocks next to the training barn. "I like to give them a little time to get used to their bodies when they have a growth spurt like that."

I was still feeling giddy on the way home, because she'd let me gallop an older racehorse who knew her job, and it was just about the coolest thing I'd ever done—all I wanted to do was tell Pete. I'd forgotten about the significance of the date. Then I drove up the barn lane and was jolted back to reality so quickly, it was sickening.

It was only about eight o'clock, but the moving van had already pulled up in front of the house, and there were a couple of young guys in shorts—their shirts discarded in the morning's humidity—hauling a huge sofa down the ramp. I stared at the sofa, hardly able to believe something so awful was going into our cozy little house. It was white. White *leather*. What kind of horseman had a white leather sofa? Sit down on it with your dirty breeches after a day of riding, and it would be trashed.

The moving guys stared back, their eyes popping with the sofa's weight, and after a few seconds of mutual glaring, I snapped back to reality and left them to their labors. I had horses to ride.

Pete came back from his own racehorses while I was tacking up Mickey, holding up a white paper bag with something he'd bought to counteract my temper. "I brought you a bagel. Cinnamon raisin with cream cheese."

I wiped my hands on my breeches and reached for the bag. "Gimme, and then tell me the bad news afterward."

Pete complied. Mickey watched longingly as I unwrapped the bagel and took a huge bite. He leaned on the crossties and fluttered his nostrils, like a girl batting her lashes. I ignored him. "Go on," I said around the mouthful.

"There's nothing new," he said. "You already saw the van. They're putting what's left of our living room and bedroom stuff in the garage, by the way. So, they didn't want our furnishings. I am a little insulted."

"The insults began when they dumped horses on us. I was kind of hoping it would get better." Even as the words left my mouth, I knew I was being ridiculous. Of course things were going to get worse. Now they would be here with their horses and their trainers. There would be spats about the use of the riding rings and the cross-country course. We'd be sharing our space with them every single day. It was going to be a disaster. Even if we didn't have constant fights, which I expected, we'd still be giving up whole chunks of the life we loved every single day. What had we been thinking? We should have just moved out last month and given up this whole crazy plan. Instead, we were tearing our life down inch by painful inch. I looked down the barn aisle at the rolling land out back.

"Can we build a ring down here?"

It was a ridiculous suggestion—there wasn't any money—but Pete apparently took me seriously, which made me even more nervous, because it meant he was expecting the same problems I was. "I thought about it, but I don't see any place flat enough to do it without major excavation. We *could* go down to the bottom of the gelding pasture. There's a big flat space down there. We could just start riding there if they get too annoying at the arena."

We walked out to the pasture fence, leaving Mickey watching us owlishly from the crossties, and gazed down the slope. There was a flat space down there, a little larger than a dressage arena, flanked on one side by a small pond. I thought of the furrowed arena with its clay footing. We were giving up a state-of-the-art training center to ride in a pasture? "I can't believe it's come to this," I said, shaking my head. "I really thought things would be different."

"So did I," Pete agreed, but his voice was low and taut, and I was reminded he was a bigger loser than I was in all this. He'd lost his grandmother, the one person he'd wanted to believe in him, the one person he'd wanted to see him succeed. It had been a blow to his self-esteem in addition to the natural grief of loss. I hadn't lost anyone, and no one believed in me but Pete, so it was hard for me to connect with this kind of grief.

If he lost the farm, though, we'd be on equal footing.

Because I already knew about that sort of loss. And if he would just let me, I'd coach him through it.

With riding finished by early afternoon, we retreated to the cool of the tack room. The horses had been uniformly difficult, fascinated by the moving van and activity at the nearby house, and I was ready to play hooky for the rest of the day. Sure, manes needed pulled, leather needed cleaned, buckets needed scrubbed, but for just a few hours, I was going to pretend nothing was on the agenda.

So now Pete was sending in entries, typing away at his laptop on my desk, and I was lying in bed trying not to fall asleep. Well, I was telling myself I wasn't falling asleep, as my head kept nodding onto my chest.

Lacey was texting me some nonsense about someone she'd met in Pennsylvania who swore she was an animal communicator and told Lacey she could feel Dynamo's vibrations "from afar" and knew Dynamo was sitting on a big win. I started to text her back that "sitting on a win" was something racetrack people like Alex said, not something eventers said, but it turned out even that effort was too much for me right now and I just typed *thanx good news* back, as if she wasn't in the running for most ridiculous human ever. (Right alongside the animal communicator, who hadn't even charged for this important insight into my horse's brain.)

My eyes closed and Marcus sighed against my cheek, squishing a little closer to me on my pillow. Marcus was a merciless seller of naps. They were his currency. *Cuddle with me,* his little beagle body suggested, stretching across the sheets. *Sleep is the best.*

Sleep *was* the best, and I wasn't getting enough of it. Just a little nap . . .

"Hey Jules, how old is Dynamo, anyway?"

My eyes snapped open. I turned my head on the pillow just as Pete spun around on the office chair. His face grew contrite.

"Oh damn, were you asleep?"

"It's fine, I need to get up . . . things to do . . ." I struggled upward, Marcus protesting with sorrowful eyes.

"You look like you could use a nap. Take the rest of the afternoon off."

"Ha, take the afternoon off, you're cute," I said, as if I hadn't been planning just that. "You should be a comedian."

"You can take a few hours to relax. What's the panic? We don't have any shows for . . ." Pete consulted the calendar hanging on the back of the door. "A week."

"Where is it again?"

"Sun Valley Horse Trials."

I groaned. "I'm supposed to ride Dynamo in that."

"I emailed them. They're changing the entry to my name."

"Oh." It dawned on me why he needed Dynamo's foaling year. "Are you entering him in something new?"

"Just Sunshine State three weeks before Hope Glen," Pete said.

"Oh. To prep for the three-day event." It stung.

Pete nodded. "And I'll take Dynamo at Intermediate at Hope Glen as planned, and then we'll do his first Advanced the next month at Sunshine State Winter One. I figure he knows the course so well, it'll make things easy for him."

I was awake now. "It's weird to hear you make plans for my horse," I said, because everyone was always saying honesty was so important in a relationship. "I don't know how I feel about it."

He smiled at me as if he'd been waiting for this opportunity. "I'm going to make you proud, Jules. You're not going to regret this. I really like him. I think this is going to be an exciting winter for all of us."

An exciting winter for *him*, maybe. Well, at least I was getting Mickey ramped up to go Modified, and then Preliminary in the new year. He was ready to step up; all that was left was proving it to his owners with a few more Training runs. Jim Dear was ready to move up to Training, too. I'd been on the fence about moving him up this fall, but he'd been jumping his eyeballs out all week, so it was time to put that scope to work. "I'm going to take Jim Dear Training at Hope Glen," I said. "In the horse trials, not the three-day division. And then I'm bumping up Mickey to Modified at the Sunshine State Winter One. Who else are you taking to Hope Glen?"

"Barsuk for Prelim like we discussed, Novice for Mayfair . . ." Pete paused, thinking. "I could take Rorschach around Novice in the horse trials . . ."

"Why bother? He wants to be a hunter. Sell him to Amanda's people already."

"I haven't seen Amanda out here in a week," Pete said, turning back to the laptop.

"I thought it was quiet and didn't smell like perfume around here," I said.

Pete snorted.

"So where is she? She doesn't like Rorschach all of a sudden? She was super high on him before."

"I think she doesn't like our living situation."

I tried to imagine how our living in a tack room could possibly affect Amanda. "Is this still about the apartment?"

"It doesn't look good that we live in a barn."

"No one knows," I said, suddenly remembering that *Eventing Chicks* hadn't mentioned our racing jobs, either. Huh. Maybe no one was interested in us anymore. The idea annoyed me. I didn't want to be gossiped about, but I didn't want to be no one, either.

"No one knows, yet. When it gets out, people are going to have questions. I don't blame her for distancing herself."

"And that means not selling a horse for us? What does she care? It's not *that* crazy to live in the barn. It means you're investing everything in your horses. It should be a badge of honor. Everyone should live in their barn at some point." I inspected the bottoms of my feet. "Although the sawdust in the rug is getting out of hand."

Pete ran his hands through his hair and leaned back in the chair, which groaned alarmingly. All of the barn furniture was on its last legs. I watched the chair tipping back slowly and wondered if he'd get the clue before he landed on the floor. Probably not. Pete wasn't used to old, broken things. That was *my* area of expertise.

"You better be careful with that chair," I told him.

He sat forward and it made a crack against the floor. I winced. Pete ignored me. "Amanda isn't going to bring a buyer or a student out here if there's a chance they might see we've got a bed in the tack room. She's not even wild about them seeing this barn. She wanted to know if I could hang on to any stalls in the training barn, if only to stick the horse in for a sales visit. Of course I had to say no, we had to rent out the whole barn. And that was the last time we talked about a client. So I don't know. Maybe it's over."

"We're better off without her and her money," I said. "Not that we were seeing her money, anyway."

"Our bank account isn't better off. Remember how much she expected to get for Rorschach?"

I did remember. All the zeros. I pulled out a Diet Coke and cracked it open, rather than give him the satisfaction of a reply. I sighed loudly after a long gulp, as if I was in a TV commercial, perched upon craggy Italian cliffs and gazing at the Mediterranean, quenching the thirst that came only of being a model sharing a sailboat with dark-eyed men all day.

"We needed that cash. Kind of desperately."

"Fine," I said. "So maybe I'll call her."

Pete looked as if I'd suggested dancing naked in the barn aisle. "*You'll* call her?"

"What?" I asked innocently. "You think it's a bad idea?"

"It depends on what you call her."

"Lovely Amanda whom we haven't seen in forever? She should respond well to that."

He laughed. "Christ. Why not. I mean, if you can't scare her into coming over, nothing will."

Amanda answered her phone on the first ring, which sucked for me because I hated talking on the phone and I wasn't actually prepared to be the instigator of the conversation. I'd been hoping for voicemail. She could call me back and then I would feel less awkward about the whole thing.

"What's up, Jules?" Amanda sounded busy. I realized she had my number programmed into her phone.

Why would she have my number? We never spoke. She was Pete's contact.

"Nothing," I answered, like I was a teenager calling a friend for absolutely no reason.

"Nothing? There must be something."

Like she was a friend's mom.

"We were just wondering when you were bringing out that

buyer to look at Rorschach," I blurted, going with the why-bother-trying-to-be-casual angle. Smooth as always.

"Rorschach?" Amanda paused, as if she was trying to recall which horse Rorschach was. Now that was smooth. Why couldn't I be smooth like that? "Oh . . . the paint cross?"

Ouch. When she was hanging around the barn, being the benevolent bringer-of-buyers, she called Rorschach a *draft* cross. It made a difference in this business. You put the least Western-sounding breed in front of "cross," always.

"The draft cross," I said now, my voice taking on more familiar sharp patterns. "You know, the Clyde-Thoroughbred with the amazing square knees and the daisy-cutter trot? That you previously wanted to see in action every other day? He's still here, waiting for his new mama."

"Hang on a second, will you? I have to dismount." I heard her speaking in flawless Spanish, presumably to a groom waiting to take her reins. "Okay, sorry about that! That was my last horse of the day. Now I have lessons until six thirty, so gross." She laughed. "Okay. Rorschach. I *might* be able to find someone to look at him, but I don't think he's going to show well over there. Maybe you could bring him here."

"Did the other buyer fall through?" I asked innocently. "The one you kept telling Pete was going to love him?"

There was a pause. "That buyer?" she asked after a moment, stalling for time. "Oh, they went with another trainer. In Miami. They moved. To Miami."

Wow, hell of a stumble there, Amanda. I felt more confident. "It's too bad you didn't tell Pete. He had a lot of faith in you." I emphasized "had" ever so slightly.

"Oh, I didn't realize . . ."

"Yeah, he was always saying what a super trainer you were, and how he was looking forward to teaching with you because your students were so dedicated. And then all of a sudden I noticed he wasn't mentioning you anymore, and you weren't around the farm anymore. And no students for Pete, even though you'd said you wanted him to teach. And I thought that was totally weird, so I thought I'd just call and ask . . ."

"Well it was because of the client . . . moving to Miami. I didn't know, they didn't really give me any warning."

"Of course, that all makes sense now, now that you've told me," I said comfortingly. "But I guess you have others who might be looking for a big eq horse."

"Sure. I mean, of course I do, I have tons of clients looking, I just have to go through my list and see who might work for him."

"Because Pete always likes having you around . . ."

"Yeah?" Her voice lifted, hopeful.

"He does," I confirmed, crossing my eyes at Pete. He stared at me, confused.

"I'll come by tomorrow," Amanda decided. "And take you guys to lunch. Is a late lunch okay, around two? Sound good?"

No, it actually sounded awful. But she was right, two was the perfect time. We'd be done with horses until dinner. I cleared my throat to sound genuine. "That sounds amazing. We would love to go to lunch."

Pete's eyebrows went up.

"I'll bring my client list," Amanda said. "We can find matches for your sales horses and work it all out."

"That's great. See you tomorrow."

Amanda made promises to text us with lunch plans and said to tell Pete to bring his negotiating hat, because we were going to make hard decisions about Rorschach tomorrow. *Hard decisions, my ass.* The only hard decision would be how much of her commission I was going to make Pete withhold to punish her for making us keep the horse an extra few weeks while she went through whatever games she was playing in her head, trying to decide if poor Pete was still worth chasing the way rich Pete had been.

The thing was, Pete had always been poor. He just looked rich before, because he was playing with someone else's toys.

Hard to blame her for that mistake, though. I'd been taken by the same false impression when I first met the guy. A big farm and a nice trailer can do a lot for your imaginary credit score.

Well, now we had to deal with Amanda again. I had to wonder what the hell was going on with my year. First, it starts going really well. Nice farm! Nice guy! Nice horses! Then I start giving everything away. My time. My horse. My pride.

I remembered back in May when we got the sponsorship news from Rockwell Brothers. How bright everything had looked for one exciting moment. And then the bad news started dropping, like great big file folders of awful from the sky.

Pete's going to England without you. *Wham!* You're going to a dressage apprenticeship. *Wham!* You've pissed off Pete to the point where he's ready to break up. *Wham!* Pete's grandmother has died. *Wham!* Regina's torn her leg up. *Wham!* That was the sound of everything going to hell, and no one could hear it but me.

18

THE BABY DAYS of jogging around the pasture were already coming to an end, as golden October mornings dawned later and later over the Ocala hillsides. I was mildly disappointed and slightly apprehensive the next morning, when Alexander announced that our first set would be going to the track instead of the pasture.

I'd been riding the same four or five horses each morning, and we'd gotten into a pleasant rhythm. I'd been amazed at my uncustomary good luck in coming to Cotswold, and getting paid for what were essentially daily trail rides around a dew-glazed meadow. It wasn't exactly what I'd imagined when I was told I had to go out and get a tough racehorse-training job in order to pay the bills. I supposed it was inevitable the happy mornings had to end. Reality was always stalking me from down the shed row.

The barn was short on grooms for the morning, and Alex had put Lovely Lily's stall number next to my name first, so I went down to the chestnut filly's stall to tack her up. A groom had already clipped her by the halter to the short tie hanging in one back corner of the stall, and she was standing with her head turned around, looking like an inquisitive young owl, watching the action pass by in the shed row. She nickered when I ducked under the stall webbing with a hoof pick in one hand and a dandy brush in the other.

"Morning, princess," I told her, giving her a quick rub on the stripe between her eyes before I knocked the shavings off her back and cleaned her hooves.

That was all the grooming she'd get—she was still a yearling, and her winter coat was starting to sprout, so there was no reason to polish her up too much. She'd go back outside for the day after work, anyway.

By the time I had the saddle towel folded over the thick foam pad and was slipping the saddle on her back, I'd forgotten all the drama waiting at home—Amanda's lunch today and the renters moving into the house and a late-day phone call from the lawyer yesterday that had essentially boiled down to "no progress, need more money." Trouble has a way of drifting away when you're grooming a horse.

Instead, I was thinking about the filly—the way she felt through my seat and hands when she jogged and galloped, the way she put up her nose and gaped her mouth when I asked her to slow down or halt, which might be a problem out on the racetrack, with no one's hindquarters in front to run her into—and I was thinking about the tasks of grooming and tacking. Some people might have thought an equestrian performed these rituals like a machine. But tacking a horse took on a meditative quality as our fingers ran through the familiar buckles and straps in their beautiful, unchanging order. I took a subtle comfort in knowing I could be dropped into any stable with English saddles in the tack room for the past five hundred years, and I would know exactly what to do. As equestrians, we are all brought together by our love of tradition and order.

Lily shifted her weight as I tightened the girth, and lifted one hind leg to let me know how deeply offensive she found the leather cinching around her svelte little belly, but this was part of her particular routine and I ignored the gesture.

One thing I'd learned about working with the babies in the training barn: you never escalated the conversation about manners until it was absolutely necessary. There just wasn't time to fix things if you accidentally blew something like a raised hind leg out of proportion. If she wasn't violently kicking at my skull, it wasn't a real problem.

We were working with kindergartners here. As trainers, we shouldn't be asking for cotillion manners when these baby horses were just figuring out how to play nicely at recess.

The familiar morning rhythm didn't change immediately. We took our usual turns around the shed row, walking and jogging, the babies gazing wide-eyed over the railing and into the foggy Ocala morning. The sun was starting to lighten the eastern sky, which was capped here by a hill with a small barn on top—the stallion barn, Alex had told us, although I'd never been up there and didn't know who her stallions were. There were wreaths of fog around the blackboard fences of the paddocks circling the barn, and when we turned onto the gravel pathway leading out to the training track, moisture beaded on my bare arms and made me shiver with a sudden chill—the first time I'd felt cool outside since April.

It's fall, I thought, and shivered again. Being from southwest Florida, which could skip fall entirely some years, Ocala could feel strange to me sometimes.

Lily felt my shudder and bounced a little, darting forward for a second until her nose ran into the dark gray colt in front of us. He squealed and threatened to kick, setting her back on her heels. "What an adventure," I told her, reining back just a touch. "Wasn't that exciting?"

"Forward march!" Alex called back from her spot at the head of the line. "We're going to walk them up to the gate and let them look at it, then we're going to stand up at the railing for a minute. Follow me."

The gate! I got another shiver that had nothing to do with the fog. I'd seen the small starting gate parked off to the side of the track, nestled under a copse of oak trees, but we were heading for something more crude near the horse path, a set of wooden poles standing upright with crossbars over the top, meant to mock-up a gate without being too confining. They were for just this purpose: walking the babies through so they wouldn't feel panicked when they were confronted with the real thing.

Even though I knew it wasn't the real gate we were headed for, I still got a tremor of nerves in my stomach. I was as claustrophobic as any one of the horses—trailers made me nervous and keyhole jumps made me positively sick—so the thought of going into the starting gate with a horse someday was unpleasant, to say the least. I wondered if I'd be able to get out of that particular job when the time came. Then I realized I was getting way ahead of myself. Who knew what I'd be doing in six months, or however long it would be until these babies were ready for gate training? I might be long gone from the galloping world, snug in my bed at five o'clock instead of getting up to ride horses through the darkness.

The gray colt in front of Lily startled as a mockingbird darted in front of his head, and she jumped again, this time to the left, taking me straight into the low-hanging branch of an oak tree.

When we came out of the leaves, I was wet with dew and had Spanish moss dangling from my hard hat. Luis, the rider behind me, rode up and plucked it from my hat—he held it up, laughing, right before *his* filly caught sight of the training gate, looming up in the mist like a silent giant, and spun around a full 180 degrees, ready to go straight back to the barn and put all this racing nonsense to bed immediately.

He dropped the moss and the grin and got busy paying attention to his own damn horse. I choked up the reins on Lily instinctively, but she wasn't too concerned by the gate—she'd somehow managed to get a mouthful of grass and was working her way through it, chewing around her loose-ring snaffle.

"Alex, your horse needed extra breakfast," I called.

Alex laughed and pointed at the poles off to our right. "Walk her up there and see if she'll put her nose on the training gate," she called, nudging her own ducking, rooting filly with her heels as if there was nothing unusual going on. I admired her quiet seat and unruffled demeanor—the filly was saying no, but Alex wasn't demanding a yes. She wasn't saying anything, she was just sitting there nudging the filly as if to say, *Aren't I annoying? Wouldn't you like me to be less annoying? There's a way, you know.*

The ability of the racehorse trainer to be unruffled by the extra stuff, to ignore the acting out as long as it wasn't hurting anybody . . . *that* I found fascinating. I'd been raised to be a stickler for good manners, to insist on horses who behaved like princes and princesses at all times, respecting my bubble of personal space, but here they seemed to think it was crazy to believe they could get perfect-pony behavior out of a yearling or even a three-year-old who was trained to the pinnacle of fitness, and so they just didn't even try.

It explained why racehorses came off the track with such poor manners, but it also explained why they *didn't* come off the track cowering with fear the way some privately owned horses did. Most racehorses weren't beaten or punished when they were silly—they were just ignored.

Now Alex ignored her filly's antics and just kept nudging her forward, kick-kick-kick on the ribs, like she was riding a thirty-year-old school pony, and finally the filly went up and touched her nose to the gate softly, tremulously, but with her ears focused back on Alex instead of trained on the scary poles. That was an important lesson, I thought. An effective trainer can simply be annoying instead of forceful. Look for *that* in the textbooks.

It took a while for everyone to circle up to the gate, but eventually all six horses had done their job and walked up to the mock gate without too much trouble, and it was time to head to the track. Lily jigged sideways as her hooves hit the soft loam. She knew, I thought. She knew what this was all about. It was in her blood.

Alex had us line up in pairs, with me alongside her, and we walked up the center of the track a few paces and then turned to face the inner rail. "Everyone touch their nose to the rail!" she shouted, and no one made any jokes about leaning forward and touching their own nose to the rail, which I found admirable. This was a pretty goofy bunch most of the time, but now that we were introducing babies to the track, I could see things were tightening up. We were putting on our game faces, to help our horses learn to do the same.

Slowly, with gentle nudges, I convinced Lily to walk up to the rail and she stretched out her nose to touch the white PVC, nostrils flaring. I looked to the right and left, proud of my professional baby racehorse team, and saw—

—Juan leaning nearly out of his saddle, over his colt's shoulder, straining to touch his nose to the rail. His horse was bowing his neck to try and get away from him, looking deeply disturbed by his human.

The professional racehorse team dissolved into laughter and babies started hopping around, Lily included, remembering they weren't racehorses after all, just eighteen-month-old Thoroughbreds being ridden by a bunch of goofballs.

"You can't do it, Juan," Alex was shouting, laughing hysterically. "You try every time and you can't do it!"

"I can do it!" Juan insisted, reins sliding through his hands as his colt plunged through the center of the track, momentarily out of control. He laughed uproariously. "You know I can do it!"

"Maybe next time. Come on. We jog around the track now."

"Sí, we *yog*!" Juan hollered back, kicking his colt straight. They went careening down the middle of the track, going "the wrong way" as I knew to call it now, and Alex followed, her filly straining to catch up, trotting with monstrously long strides like a Standardbred.

"In pairs!" she called over her shoulder. "Right down the middle!"

I found myself paired up with Stacy, a pale-haired, pale-lashed, brown-skinned Oklahoman who was tougher than her girly name implied. She was built like a six-foot-tall bull, and bent over her little bay filly with a jockey's curl to her spine. Something told me she'd been riding racehorses for a long, hard time.

Stacy grinned at me as we posted trot, our stirrups nearly clinking together when one of our fillies jigged at a haunt in the writhing fog. "You're an English girl," she said after a while.

I pondered her Southern accent. Was Oklahoma part of the

south? Or was it a country accent? When did a country accent end and a Southern accent begin?

"If you mean I ride English," I said. "But I'm *from* Florida."

She laughed. "Yeah, that's what I mean." She looked down at her knuckles, pressed into the filly's brown withers. "You came over to the dark side—you like it?"

I looked around us, at the cool dim morning, the pink streaks in the east, the soundtrack of hoofbeats rhythmically striking the conditioned ground, the jingle of tack, the soft curses and laughter of the riders as they muttered to one another, to their horses, to themselves. I preferred to be in bed at this hour, with Marcus somewhere around my head dreaming quiet dog dreams, and the horses out in the pasture but slowly grazing their way up toward the gate, always hoping someone would rise early and decide to feed breakfast a few minutes ahead of schedule.

I liked my bed and I liked my old mornings at the farm, but I liked this too.

I liked the camaraderie, even if I didn't really talk too much, and I liked watching everyone ride their horses with that interesting blend of stillness and activity, so much more going on in the saddle than I usually noticed when someone was just trotting a sport horse around an arena. I liked the horses. I liked the freeform nature of pasture and racetrack, the lack of square boxes to ride in, the way we just kept going in a relatively straight line, as if there was no ending. I liked the purposeful nature of building up a horse for the sole intention of getting there first.

"I do like it," I said, and I surprised even myself.

19

IT WOULD BE nice to say the good feelings lasted throughout the day, but of course that would be asking for too much. I got back in the truck and drove home ready to tell Pete how much fun it had been taking the babies to the track for the first time, but found myself racing a dark cloud with ragged white edges, lightning flashing beneath. The wind was picking up, too, trees thrashing in the gusts. The midmorning sun shone on bravely, but there was clearly a cold front on the way—the first of the season, right on time.

I hoped it wouldn't interrupt the afternoon's riding. We had an event this weekend. My mind was on training schedules as I drove beneath the oak trees of Briar Hill's long driveway, but when I saw the crowd outside the house, I forgot all about the coming storm.

I'd seen him when he came to look at the farm, so I knew it was Blixden standing there, Blixden in a Margaritaville T-shirt and flowered shorts, looking every bit the Northern businessman who had found his way out of the frozen north and into his own tequila-fueled version of eternal spring break. He stood on the front yard in a cluster of beautiful people in bikinis and board shorts, all clutching sweating Corona bottles. No one seemed to realize there was a storm bearing down on the farm from the northwest, or even that there wasn't a pool for this bathing suit party.

I threw the truck into Park and stormed out of the cab.

Blixden waved his bottle. "Jules, Jules, good morning. Look, we finally got here! And we're already living that Florida lifestyle!"

"This is *not* how we live in Florida," I snapped. "And I am sure the lease rules out parties."

"Not a party," he said, his smile unwavering. "These are just friends who came up to help us move in." He turned and gave the girls a little wave. A few waved back; most stuck to their conversations. "Friends from West Palm. They have horses down there. You guys have a lot in common!"

I looked at the crowd, who were studiously ignoring the dirty, sweaty woman in riding clothes who had come to break up their party. "I doubt it," I told him.

Blixden's smile turned into a smirk. "They said that the Wellington-Ocala feud was real! Now, now, no fighting over who has the best equestrian town. We're all friends here."

"Why are they wearing swimsuits?" I asked. "We don't have a pool."

"Maybe we should. There's room behind the house."

I didn't like that he was already scoping out the property for the changes he'd make if he were in charge. "Don't be loud out here," I said, retreating behind an aloof property manager mask. "We're going to be working horses in the arena shortly."

"Oh, that's great," Blixden said, still hearty. "Alejandro and the team arrive tomorrow. They'll be working out their training calendar with you, I suppose."

"That's your trainer?"

"Alejandro is the best in the business," Blixden said. "And his brothers are just like him. They're going to get those horses jumping like kangaroos for my daughters."

"That should make your daughters feel really accomplished."

Blixden nodded, like he wasn't even listening—I supposed that was just as well. Pete would freak if he heard me being rude to this guy.

"This year just keeps getting better," I muttered, as the oak trees and fence boards slid by.

Pete was on Barsuk by the annex barn, and Becky was standing out front, holding Mickey by the reins. He was tacked up and ready to go. "Pete thought you might want to ride before the storm," she called.

Pete waved. "Hop on, quick, and we can fit in fifteen minutes or so!"

"Good thing I'm dressed for the job," I said, almost forgetting about Blixden and his stupid party. I mounted Mickey from the ground, gathering up my reins as he sidestepped toward Barsuk.

"You kids have fun," Becky said. "Come back before it rains."

Thunder growled in the distance, and a cool wind whistled through the barn. But the sun was still shining, yellow autumn light streaming through the live oaks, and the cloud, as dangerous as it looked, didn't seem to be making much progress toward us. "Want to trot up around the cross-country field?" I asked. "We'll be close enough to canter home if we need to."

I couldn't help but canter Mickey once we were out on the

202 | Natalie Keller Reinert

sloping cross-country field. Up here we could see the storm front stretching across the northwestern sky, and the cool breeze kept puffing in hard, uneven gusts. Lightning flashed like a strobe light in the opaque dark sky beneath the cloud's white front lines.

"That looks extremely nasty," Pete observed as I circled Mickey around Barsuk, lifting my hands so that my silly horse couldn't buck.

"It's gorgeous," I said.

Just then, a small tree branch flew past our faces, and Mickey jumped backward, his head in the air and his ears pricked. I pressed my hands into his withers to stay centered. His fluffy white forelock blew between his ears.

Next to me, Pete steadied Barsuk and gave me a look. "Are you ready to go back yet?"

"Not yet, please—"

"I honestly think there might be something tornadic about this storm," Pete said.

Just then, a smooth white roll of cloud rushed forward from the storm complex and bore down on us, wiping out the sunlight as it rushed over the hill.

Suddenly, I felt very small and exposed.

"The light's going green," Pete observed, sounding like a scientist. "Look at Mickey."

The horse's gray coat had a tinge of emerald to it, as if I'd dyed him for St. Patrick's Day and it hadn't all washed out yet.

Realization tingled up my spine, just as both our phones began that familiar squeal of a tornado warning. Another branch went past my head while I fumbled to shut off my phone, Mickey dancing beneath me and tugging at the reins, and the nearest pasture gate began rattling, snapping back and forth on its chain in the stiff, cold wind. A half-grown turkey oak bent over in the gusts. Mickey backed up apprehensively, his head high and neck bent backward. I felt like I had his gray ears in my face.

Pete pointed toward a coop between the fields and cantered Barsuk up and over it. Mickey reached for the bit and I loosened the rein, letting him follow.

We trotted back into the dark barn just as the first burst of rain rattled over the metal roof. Becky poked her head out of the tack room. "I have Marcus and Barn Kitty in here!"

"You're in charge of them!" I shouted back, sliding out of the saddle. The wind cast sand from the aisle in our faces, and I led Mickey into his stall, barely staying ahead of his rushing hooves. Outside the window, a solid sheet of water came down, and it blew through the barn aisle, soaking everything in its path. Hail followed, little stones splashing down in the puddles and pinging off the windows' steel frames. The roar on the metal roof was deafening. Mickey shied and bucked as I pulled his tack off. The power blinked out, leaving us in the greenish darkness, lit only by lightning slamming down all around us.

Tack stripped and horse bouncing around but safely shut into his box behind me, I took everything in one big armload into the tack room, blinking away the raindrops once I was inside. Marcus looked up from the bed, where he was sitting with his head in the notch of Becky's elbow. She was stroking his ears.

"Barn Kitty's under the bed," she reported. "We might want to join her."

Fortified by his battery backup, Igor the robot meteorologist, who lived in my weather radio, was still droning to his unseen audience: *"This is a dangerous storm. Take precautions to secure life and property now."* There was a brief pause, as if Igor was

204 | Natalie Keller Reinert

gathering the papers on his desk, and then he started his spiel over again. *"At twelve forty-two P.M., the National Weather Service in Melbourne issued a tornado warning for Marion County, Florida. Locations affected include: Ocala, Reddick . . ."*

Another lightning bolt crashed outside; I heard muffled rumbling after the accompanying explosion of sound, which made me wonder if we'd just lost a tree. "Thanks for the update, Igor," I told the radio. "This oughta scare the Virginian."

Pete came in, dripping wet. I pulled a cooler out of one of the remaining tack trunks in the corner and wrapped it around him. He smiled at me, and if the window hadn't started rattling in its frame, I might have felt warm and fuzzy inside. Instead, I turned around to watch the air conditioner wobbling in the window. Something went past the rain-streaked glass, something large and dark.

"What's happening?" I said to no one in particular.

Marcus got off the bed and crept under it.

My ears very subtly popped.

Igor paused, began again as if he'd had to catch his breath. He had a new spiel now. *"At twelve fifty-five P.M., spotters reported a tornado on the ground near Reddick, moving southeast at forty miles per hour . . ."*

The wind took on a new, ominous depth, and I felt something primal within telling me to seek cover, an instinct that everyone else seemed to share. Pete pushed me onto the bed alongside Becky and pulled the pillows over our heads just as the barn began to shake. There were a few sizable crashes, and some bangs I knew had to be hooves hitting walls, and then nearly as soon as the noise began, it ended. Nothing like my hurricane experience, which had been a marathon of terror. I pulled the pillows away and looked around. Everything looked the same.

Pete's gaze met mine. "Are you okay?"

Surprisingly, yes. "I guess I don't have hurricane PTSD after all."

Becky grinned. "When I tell you it would take more than a hurricane to faze you, please take it as both compliment and insult, okay?"

"Sure," I said.

The rain was pattering on the air conditioner with something like its regular roar. It was a comforting sound: just a Floridian thing, I guess. Pete slipped off the bed and stuck his head under the mattress. "It's okay, Marcus. You can come out." He looked up at me. "Marcus says he'd like your assurance."

I jumped down and knelt on the rug, poking my head under the bed. Marcus thumped his tail on the concrete floor and licked my hand when I extended it. But he ignored my suggestion to come out. "I think he's good there right now," I decided. "He's fine. Marcus has been through a lot of bad weather."

Pete stared at me in disbelief. "Bad weather? I had to drag him out from under your demolished house last year."

"Well, that's why he's staying under the bed now. I'm certainly not going to change his mind." I pushed Marcus's favorite chew toy, a large plush frog well on its way toward disembowelment, under the bed. A moment later we heard a satisfied squeak. "See? He has his frog. He'll be out for dinner. Let's go check on the horses."

The horses were all in one piece, all in their stalls; everything in the barn was fine, if wet. I went to the end of the aisle and peered out into the pouring rain. It was difficult to see more than fifty feet or so, but I could make out a hulking shape lying across the barn lane. "Whoops," I said. "We lost a tree."

"That will have been the crashing noise." Pete sighed. "I'm guessing we can't get around it, either."

"Oh, of course not," I said, shrugging. "Stuck at the barn . . . what else could go wrong?"

"Well, we're supposed to have lunch with Amanda in half an hour."

I laughed. "Looks like I got us out of that one."

20

RAMON BROUGHT HIS chain saw from home that evening, and while the horses were eating dinner, he and Pete went out to chop up the oak tree blocking our drive. Becky and I started mucking stalls around the horses, not ready to take them out while the miniature lumberjack show was taking place just past the pasture gates. I was dying to ask Ramon if he'd seen any destruction around the rest of the property on the way in, but his set jaw and drawn-together eyebrows dissuaded me. It would seem he hadn't gotten out of bed that morning bursting with a keen interest in woodworking, and he was taking it all out on the poor tree. I left the boys to their crashing and smashing, and set out to gather up all the smaller branches that carpeted the ground around the barn, tiny versions of trees quivering in an apologetically gentle breeze, studded with halos of half-shredded green leaves. The horses shoved their heads out of their windows and watched me with interest, occasionally nickering encouragement as the hours ticked on past turnout time.

Becky was already gone for the night when Ramon and Pete finished and came back into the barn through a fiery sunset, both of them drenched with sweat and coated with an interesting mixture of wood shavings and mud. "You look like horses," I observed. "You rolled in your stall *and* out in the pasture."

Ramon grinned through his mask of dirt, his good humor restored now that his tree-trimming duties were complete for the evening. "You got a road again. Gotta get to work in the morning, right?"

I groaned. "You're killing my imaginary tornado day. I kept telling myself I could sleep in tomorrow."

"We have to work Dynamo on the track tomorrow," Pete reminded me. He smiled. "I thought you might like to bring Mickey."

Now I was back in the swing of things. "Hell yeah, I want to bring Mickey! He's ready for a good gallop work." My mind raced with possibilities. What would the ex-racehorse do on the training track? His racing days were a lot more recent than Dynamo's. He might freak out, or he might be a ton of fun. I was excited to find out.

"You might wanna call and ask first," Ramon suggested, picking up a lead shank in preparation for turnout. "Lotta trees down on the way over here."

"Ugh," I sighed. "Florida."

"Oh, and tree down on the training barn."

"What?" Pete and I gasped at the same time.

"At the east end by the jumping ring. That big tree came down. Broke the railings, maybe roof, but the stalls are fine."

"That should've been your lead story, Ramon," I said sharply.

Ramon gave me a shrug. "I forgot. Too busy taking care of your driveway."

His subtle emphasis on the word "your" reminded me again that chopping up trees was not in his job description, and was probably worth a lot more per hour than what we paid him to muck stalls and feed horses. "Sorry," I said contritely. "I was just upset about the barn."

"Yeah, that's okay." Ramon opened Dynamo's stall door. "Mister up there, he's pretty upset too. I'm surprised he didn't call you."

I exchanged a glance with Pete. "Did I ever mention I don't think I'm cut out to be a landlord?" I asked him.

"Nice try," he said. "But you're coming with me."

B lixden was pissed. I supposed anyone would be, but I didn't like the way he swaggered up to us in the twilight before we even turned off to the barn, full of accusations about poor planning and rotten trees. He was dressed more appropriately than he had been earlier this morning, having changed out of his cruise attire in favor of a sensible polo shirt and cargo shorts, with bare feet shoved into loafers. He looked like every middle-aged man who moves to Florida but isn't comfortable with flip-flops and T-shirts in October yet. The sunburn blooming on his cheeks and half-bald scalp only added to the look.

Pete tried to get a couple words in but Blixden just went on blustering, so we turned away and kept walking, letting him chase after us. I looked down, watching the scarred toes of my boots as I stepped around puddles and larger branches, concentrating hard on the hazards of the road so I wouldn't accidentally turn around and tell Blixden if he didn't like a little crazy weather, he could take his ass straight back to Virginia.

At the pathway between the arenas Blixden called a halt. We were nearly to the barn at this point; I could see the great old oak tree leaning against the nearest end. "You go on down there and look," he snapped. "I'm going back to the house. I have the pictures to send my lawyer."

"Lawyer" was becoming Pete's trigger word, with every penny we earned going toward the attorneys in town. He held up his hands. "I don't think we'll need to get any lawyers involved, Mr. Blixden. I assure you we're fully insured and we'll handle the situation."

"You'd better, and I don't want to see one hair out of place on my horses. You sit down there in that barn built like a bunker and we're in this ridiculous open-air shenanigan—I don't even know what I was thinking letting you lease me this barn—"

"Are you proposing a trade?" I asked coolly, still looking at my boots. For some reason they hadn't stopped me from opening my mouth. *Come on now, boots.*

"Excuse me? What was that?"

"Mr. Blixden, we better go see the barn," Pete interrupted, pulling at my arm. "Come on, Jules—"

"Anytime you want to trade barns, you just let me know," I said over my shoulder, finally making eye contact with him. I twisted my lips into a mocking smile Pete couldn't see. "I'll be happy to take this shenanigan off your hands. We *like* a little breeze."

"A little breeze!" Pete muttered as we left Blixden behind. "Why would you say that? It sounds like you're trying to stir up another tornado."

Why did I say anything? Because people pissed me off and I wanted them to know it. "He doesn't deserve your nice barn and I don't want to hear him running it down," I said stoutly. "And if he really wants to trade barns, well, I'm not about to tell him no. He can sweat it out down in my barn any day."

"Where will we live, again?"

I shrugged. "This barn has a tack room, doesn't it?"

Pete shook his head. "You're a mess."

"A mess of *good ideas*," I told him.

We heard a door slam behind us in the distance, and didn't have to turn around to know it was the front door of our former home. We passed the jumping arena and approached the barn, my toes curling in apprehension.

What if it was really bad?

The horses who were stalled inside for the night lifted their heads and watched us walk along the shed row, while the ones turned out in the neighboring paddocks barely lifted their faces from the grass they were snarfing up as quickly as possible. I had a feeling the October grass in Virginia wasn't as green and lush as the Ocala variety. Overhead, clouds were scudding rapidly away, their tails glowing orange in a lush, apologetic sunset. The horses in the paddocks had a reddish tinge to their coats as the fiery rays of sunlight bounced around the farm, picking out individual blades of grass and fallen tree limbs. The beautiful old oak tree leaning on the roof of the training barn looked like a fallen god, still glowing as the last bit of immortality seeped from its branches.

Pete sighed. "It's only on the roof. It could be worse."

The training barn was built like a covered arena, with formidable steel struts holding up the roof, and the stalls resting on a concrete pad underneath. Thank goodness, because if a tree this size had landed on *my* barn, we'd be looking for a new place to live. And new horses. I stood as near to the tree as I dared and looked up at the darkening struts. It didn't look like the barn was damaged at all, actually. Pretty rich of Blixden to complain about his open-air barn, when the design was what saved his horses.

"The barn just broke the tree's fall," I remarked. "All we have to do is get the tree removed—"

"Ramon can't do it. We'll need a crane to get that tree down."

"And convince the insurance company to pay for it," I finished.

"I'll call it in right now." Pete pulled out his phone and started flicking through his contacts list until he found the insurance company, and put the phone to his ear as he tramped away, continuing his walkabout.

I leaned against the shed-row rail and looked down the aisle. There was a light on in the tack room, down the middle of the barn, and I decided to go say hello to whoever was there. Like a nice landlady, of course. Not because I was awfully nosey and didn't feel like listening to Pete wrestle yet again with the insurance company, who already weren't our biggest fans thanks to our chronically late payments.

As I grew closer to the tack room, I heard Spanish words spilling into the aisle, and I slowed my steps. I didn't speak much Spanish, and I didn't want anyone to think I was snooping around if I couldn't defend myself. I was on the verge of turning around when a horse shoved his head over his stall grill and whinnied at me, which naturally set off every other horse in the barn. Well, I should've seen that coming. It was a little like walking into a kennel and hoping no one would bark, I supposed.

I was glaring at the horse with exasperation, noticing how different he looked in the stall that had once been occupied by Pete's svelte Thoroughbreds: this was a huge Roman-nosed warmblood, with a thick neck and jaw, and he was braying in my face like some kind of deranged donkey.

"Uh, hi," I said to the horse.

He neighed back at me, then kicked his door.

"You're quite a looker," I said.

I was still gazing at him, bewildered by such an un-athletic-looking specimen in our repurposed racing barn, when a trio of men came out of the tack room.

They were horsemen, and alike enough to make me sure these were the brothers Blixden had told me about, each of them built slender, with sinewy biceps popping from tight polo shirts. In the light from the tack room I could see their curious faces—they looked young, but in the backhanded way young horse people often do, with enough deep lines cutting through their faces to mark them with middle age.

The man in the middle seemed to be in charge. He was the shortest—none of them were very tall—but he had a commanding air, like he was Brother Number One. Alejandro, I thought.

"You are other trainer?" he asked in accented English. "From other barn?"

"That's right." I was really hoping they *did* mean the other barn on the property and not some other barn, with some other trainer, who was about to pop up in our lives and steal away another chunk of the farm. Because the way things had been going, that wouldn't have been surprising at all. "From the barn down the lane," I clarified. I pointed over my shoulder and down the aisle, where Pete could be spotted walking in slow circles, his head bowed to the phone at his cheek as if he was leaning over a desk in an office somewhere back in the '90s. "This is our farm."

It wasn't really our farm, was it? We just treated it that way. But weren't you supposed to put the things you wanted out into the universe, and then the universe was supposed to be a peach and give them to you? I was pretty sure that was the gist of that one Oprah book people had liked so much. Say it and it becomes true. *This is our farm.* I should repeat it ten times before bed every night, a prayer to the eventing gods and the probate gods and anyone else who felt like listening in.

"Oh! That is—Pete," Alejandro said, looking pleased that he knew the name. "Mr. Blixden told us of Pete. And you?"

Of course Mr. Blixden didn't mention me. Why mention a girl? "I'm Jules."

"*Joules.*" He laughed as if it meant something hilarious in Spanish. "I'm Alejandro. This is Miguel"—he gestured to the man on his right, who could've been his twin—"and this is Guillermo." The man on his left wasn't quite a twin, but he was close, with a darker, older version of Alejandro's bright smiling face.

"And you're all brothers, right?"

They all smiled, even Guillermo.

"That's right," Miguel said. "We are brothers. From Argentina. We grow up riding together, we come to America to keep riding together but make some money at it, you know?"

I knew. The impossible dream of making money with horses. "And these are the horses you're training this winter?" I turned back to the warmblood I was mentally calling a cart horse, who was watching me while he pulled at the scraps of hay in his hay net. He was actually a really nice horse, he just had a hammer-head.

Alejandro put his hand on the horse's neck. "This one is Copper. He has long show name, it's no matter to us. He is our favorite. He jumps like—" Alejandro waved his hand in the yawning space over our heads. "To the moon. Champion jumper. He will be a big stud someday."

"Oh, a stallion." I guessed he did have the jowls of a stallion.

It just seemed lost in all the bigness of the whole horse, overall. He was built like a Clydesdale compared to the slim horses I was around all day.

"Sí, a stallion," Miguel agreed. "Big balls!" He laughed, and Alejandro and I joined in. In the background, Guillermo lifted his eyebrows, his smile long gone.

The laughter attracted Pete, who came down the aisle as he slipped his phone into his pocket. "What's so funny?" he called.

"Copper's balls," I explained helpfully, and then introduced him to the three brothers. Pete was more polite than I was and said it was nice to meet them and asked how they were enjoying Florida, instead of being distracted by their horses. Alejandro, the spokesman of the group, said they had been enjoying Florida fine until it tried to blow them away, and now they weren't so sure.

"That's what Florida does," I interjected. "Once a year or so, it tries to kill you."

Pete put his arm around my shoulders. "This one has been dodging the weather pretty nimbly," he said. "She'll have to tell you about it sometime."

"It's a good story?"

"It's a real war story."

There was a chorus of insistence. Beer was produced. We found ourselves sitting on folding chairs in the shed row as the clouds cleared and the stars came out, and everyone listened to "The Tale of Jules and the Hurricane."

And I thought maybe things with the Argentine show jumpers wouldn't be so bad, after all.

21

THE YEARLINGS' HOOVES beat a regular rhythm on the harrowed surface of the training track, and the huffing little breaths of the colt beneath me puffed like a steam train. He was getting good at this, cantering along the long sides, trotting along the short sides. We were getting ready to start teaching flying lead changes, which absolutely astonished me. Didn't that seem like advanced work for a horse who wasn't yet two years old?

But of course racehorses did flying lead changes on their own all the time; all you had to do was watch a race a little more closely than the average Joe Public and you'd see it. It was funny how something that caused such anxiety in the show ring was such an everyday part of life for the racehorses.

I was finding that about a lot of things, though. In many ways, the racetrack life felt like a simplified version of horse life, with a lot of the hand-wringing left by the wayside and nothing left but the most basic facets of horsemanship: keep the horse clean, keep the horse fed, keep the horse fit.

This life needed more jumps, though. Alex told me I'd like steeplechasing, but it wasn't really done in Florida.

"Too bad." I'd sighed. "We don't do anything fun here."

She looked at me from the back of her little chestnut colt. "We're literally sitting on baby racehorses as the sun rises over the fog and you're telling me we don't do anything fun?"

"Well, if we're not going to jump . . ."

Alex laughed. "You have a one-track mind, Jules."

The sun was already up, but it was barely piercing the films of cloud as they wrapped around the live oaks and trailed across the training track. The second week of October had brought a sudden chill to the dewy morning air.

The afternoon thunderstorms were letting up, and we'd had a few dry days since the little tornado tore up the trees, as if Florida had just been saying so long to summer with a theatrical bang.

We'd started calling it "the little tornado" to differentiate a lot of twigs on the ground and two fallen trees from something more serious, like a world-ending hurricane, and while the Argentinians had liked the designation, Blixden had been hopping mad over the way we kept saying it yesterday afternoon while the tree crew was out taking down the damaged oak tree. Pete came back from the vet clinic, where he'd been checking in on Regina—still stall-bound, still miserable, and losing weight, he'd reported—and told me to stop teasing the poor man.

"I'm not teasing him, I'm trying to scare him out of Florida."

"Who's going to pay the rent then?"

I'd shrugged. "Someone else. It's almost the winter season, Pete! Ocala's a hot ticket in winter."

"You think we're the only ones broke and trying to make some money renting out barns, Jules?"

He was right. Being broke and trying to make it in Ocala was like the horseman's version of trying to be a musician in New York City.

The little tornado had done some damage at Cotswold Farm as well: I saw the white hearts of broken branches hanging from some of the grand old live oaks in the broodmare pasture, and a section of fence in one of the training barn paddocks had apparently just blown right over, no tree limb required. But overall the storm had just been a bit of a scare, a little reminder of what Florida could do when Florida felt like it. Pete insisted I'd brought it on with my own personal voodoo because I'd been so mad at Blixden for his swimsuit party, and I couldn't confidently say he was wrong. I felt like Florida and I had an understanding these days. I'd been through a lot and still hadn't abandoned the state of my birth. There had to be points for survival and loyalty in there somewhere for a native daughter among all these transplants.

Another hour, another set. The fog burned off and the sun glinted yellow above the trees, its light weaker than it had been when I started working here a month ago. I wondered if I'd be riding here in spring when the sun slowly inched in the other direction, back toward its summer brilliance. I rode out on a bay colt with a splash of white on his forehead and a yawning void where his brain was supposed to be. He jogged sideways, as if this was somehow more efficient than moving in a straight line. I had given up trying to straighten him out; at some point he'd get tired and start moving like a normal horse.

Alex was sitting out this set, because only four riders had shown up this morning and she liked the horses in pairs. As we cantered around the final turn and returned to the backstretch, slowly slipping into a jog, I could see her waiting near the gap. Her pony, Parker, snoozed with his chin pressed against the white railing. She'd told me she'd bought Parker from a riding academy in New York City, which felt like the unlikeliest of places to find an off-track Thoroughbred to be one's favorite track pony, especially with the wealth of free Thoroughbreds dotting the paddocks of central Florida. But Parker was one in a million; anyone could see that. He was just one of those special horses who earned your trust with a glance at his half-mast ears and his lazy lower lip.

I was in the lead, alongside Alex's top rider, Juan; somehow I'd found my way to the front of the pack on these rides, superseding the more experienced riders who had been jogging yearlings since before I was born. He grinned at me now when I glanced over at him, checking my speed against his. "You *yog* that colt good," he said. "Maybe tomorrow we gallop all the way around, yeah?"

"I'm up for it," I said brightly, and remembered how scared I'd been when I'd first shown up here. Yeah, things change in a hurry around horses. You don't have time for a lot of extra emotion.

We pulled up the horses near the gap and turned them toward the infield, walking them up to the rail and asking them to touch it with their noses. A few complied at once, a few decided to be punks, my colt included, and hop back from the railing as if it was a new and disturbing replacement for the one they'd touched just yesterday. I got busy with my heels and my elbows and drove him forward until he was slobbering all over that scary railing, and then I gave him a generous pat. I looked at the nameplate shining dully through his thick rough of black mane, the neck strap he wore his only identification from the other plain bays in the bunch: COTS-WOLD RAMBLE—OH LAWD. "I'll bet you take after your mother," I told him. "Something tells me she earned that name."

After a few minutes of quiet reflection/quivering indignation (depending on which colt we were talking about), we backed the babies up a few steps, pulling on the neck strap as we drew back on the reins and pressed our legs. They reversed in a ragged line, responding more to the pressure on their chests than any other cue, and then we turned them to the gap, pairing up again. Alex picked up her reins, waking Parker, who begrudgingly blinked his eyes against the orange sunlight cascading through the thinning fog, and shifted his weight from one hind leg to the other to prove he was awake already.

Alex put Parker alongside Oh Lawd as we walked back to the barn, the oak trees raining condensation down on us. "You coming this afternoon with Dynamo and your gray horse?"

"We sure are." I was excited to gallop Mickey on the track. He was doing fast gallop sets in the pasture already, in preparation of the higher cross-country speeds awaiting us at Preliminary, so I knew what a pleasure he was to let out into full stride. Playing on the track was just a little bit of fun I hadn't anticipated. "Mickey's an off-track horse too, so I'm really excited for his reaction."

"Can you stay for a few minutes after and take a look at Tiger with me? I think the weather's finally at a place where we can make afternoon plans without expecting a rain delay. Tornadoes excluded." She grinned. "And I'd really like to get your opinion."

"Of course!" I loved that Alex wanted my opinion on something. It was kind of like that giddy, unexplainable high school feeling when a senior buddied up with a freshman. I'd been waiting for that feeling a long time. People didn't often seek me out for advice and conversation. I felt like I'd been invited to sit at the cool kids' table.

Plus, I was sure her horse was incredibly nice, so it wasn't as if I had to be afraid she'd present me with some clodhopper and I'd have to break the news that the two of them weren't going anywhere, let alone eventing. Alex knew horses. There was no reason she couldn't produce a nice event horse if she wanted to. All a person had to do was look at the easy way she sat Parker, with her gentle hands following his mouth with every move, to know she would be a star horsewoman in any discipline. She was so naturally talented, I was almost annoyed by it. Old Jules would have gone nuts over it. But I liked Alex enough to forgive her for being as good as, if not better than, me.

"That's great," Alex said happily. "I'll get him tacked up while you're cooling out your guys, and then you can throw them in a stall or a paddock and we'll just ride him in the open. We're schooling Training level dressage movements but I really want to start jumping him again, and I'm just not sure where to begin. We goofed around with it a little during the Thoroughbred Makeover, but we weren't being very scientific about it and I'd like to be sure we're doing everything right. I just don't remember the best way to go about teaching jumping. It feels like a million years ago."

"Teaching jumping can sound intimidating," I agreed. "But really if he likes you and he likes to work, he'll probably just want to jump, and it'll be more a matter of learning to rate him before the fence."

"Well, I'm used to rating horses," Alex laughed. "Still, finding strides and spots and everything? I'm afraid I'll screw everything up and we'll crash. I'd just feel better with a little help."

"You got it," I assured her warmly. This was the person who'd given me a chance when everyone else in Ocala turned me away.

She was basically feeding my horses right now, thanks to this job. I owed her. "This is going to be fun."

Back at Briar Hill, things were feeling a little . . . *crowded,* shall we say?

Pete had stopped to pick up Regina this morning, and after settling the convalescent mare into her stall, we got a late start to riding. We took out Jim Dear and Barsuk together.

"Think there'll be anyone riding?" I asked as we set out.

Pete swung his legs along Barsuk's sides, stretching his ankles. "They just came in yesterday. I doubt it."

"You're probably right."

We were wrong.

Before we'd even reached the arenas, we could see the chaos awaiting us.

Alejandro was riding an admirably well-mannered horse in the dressage arena, but Guillermo and Miguel were crashing around the jumping ring with abandon. There didn't seem to be much worry about left-rein/left-rein traffic protocols for passing horses, or even shouting out what jump they were planning to leap over.

"Great," I said. "It's a schooling show warm-up arena now."

Alejandro hailed us from the dressage ring, trotting his horse over to the fence. It was the big red warmblood we'd seen last night, the stallion he'd called their barn champion. What was his name? *Copper.* The horse blew his nostrils at Barsuk and Jim Dear, but didn't say anything. I was happy Pete wasn't on Mayfair. I knew show stallions were supposed to be able to deal with the excitement of meeting mares, but this stallion had a wildness to his eyes I didn't quite like—as if he was used to being a holy terror, and getting away with it. I'd known a few of these horses, and I was meeting more of them as I dealt with racehorses. They made me nervous.

"Is a beautiful morning to ride, eh?" Alejandro called, an ear-to-ear grin splitting his face in two. He waved at the cloudless blue sky overhead. The fog had melted away and left the day sparkling and clear. "Not so hot, no rain, this is why we spend winter in Florida. Summer, it's a mess."

"I can't deny that." Pete chuckled. "It's nice to have the barn right here on those hot days. Just ride straight back into the shade."

"Our barn is very convenient," Alejandro agreed.

Our barn! It *was* their barn, but I still hated hearing it. I stiffened, and Jim Dear, who had grown nervy with fitness, skittered away from the fence, backing straight through the in-gate of the jumping ring.

"Heads *up*!" Guillermo shouted, as his horse thundered past, dangerously close to Jim Dear's hindquarters. Jim Dear danced nervously, spinning me around, and I watched as Guillermo rode the horse right up to a series of bounces set across the center of the ring. Our full course was gone, replaced by gymnastics. The horse leaped through the closely set jumps like a bullfrog.

"Bueno, Guillermo! Again, just like that!" Alejandro sat his horse in the center of the ring and clapped as his brother circled his horse at the end of the arena.

I looked at Pete, who shook his head slightly at me.

I shrugged in reply, although there was a *lot* I wanted to say.

Trying to keep Jim Dear around the outskirts of the jumpers, I managed to get the high-strung little Thoroughbred to settle in his warm-up, and trot nicely over a few small fences along one side of the arena. He was a talented jumper, but he tended to rush fences and take off with his head held high afterward, out of a combination of nerves and lack of confidence. I liked Jim Dear a lot, although he had become mine in the casual way inexpensive horses often changed ownership, simply by default, when his owner stopped paying her board and disappeared. I thought he'd make a nice amateur horse someday, if I could ever get a handle on his self-esteem problems.

After he'd settled into a quiet tempo over a few easy jumps, I decided since the gymnastics were set up and just sitting there, we might as well tackle them. None of the jumps were higher than two-six, and gymnastics with a lot of bouncing encouraged a rushing horse to settle into his stride, exactly the exercise Jim needed. I took in my surroundings, making sure the coast was clear to approach the fences without getting in anyone's way. Alejandro had apparently finished work; he sat on his horse in the center of the arena, his posture erect and his lower legs slightly forward like a polo player, watching the action like a ringleader. Guillermo had changed horses and was warming up a flashy gray warmblood who had to be at least seventeen-two, most of it leg. Miguel was walking the big stallion, Copper, in lazy loops. And Pete was cantering Barsuk in a tidy twenty-meter circle, jumping a low square oxer with every revolution. Everyone had found a place to work or cool out without getting in someone else's way.

We were humming along nicely, I thought. We were managing this awful arena-sharing thing. Everything was going to be fine!

I picked up the reins, squeezed Jim Dear into a rolling canter, and circled near the bounce, watching for an opportunity. The series of five fences had been built right through the center of the arena, on a diagonal, so I had to be sure there was no one crossing either end of it, or between the fences, when I made my run.

An opening appeared between circling horses and I called out, "Jumping bounce!" as I sent Jim Dear toward the fences.

He pulled at me as soon as he saw the jumps in front of him, seeking to get out of the nice round frame he'd been cantering in, but I sat deep and half halted, squeezing the reins and my core muscles as if to whoa, and then driving forward with seat and leg. His power bubbled up from his hindquarters into my hands and his weight rocked back, lifting his forehand until he was balanced, his mouth light for just a moment. "Good boy," I murmured. His ears swept around to listen, then pricked again, and his nerves took back over. Jim Dear tugged at the reins; I half halted, we did it all over again. All this happened six, then five, four, three strides before the first jump. We were reaching the fence in a series of mini corrections.

I half halted again right at the base of the first jump. Jim Dear rose up for the initial leap, and I went with him, my hands pushing forward and my seat rising from the saddle. I kept my lower leg tight around his girth, pushing him on so he didn't lose momentum as we hopped through the fences. A bounce taught precision, but it required a balanced, forward-moving horse or rails would rattle to the ground in our passing.

Guillermo suddenly appeared in my field of vision, the chestnut stallion flashing onto the scene like a fireball as he trotted right past the far end of the bounce formation. *We'll have time, she'll be out of the way,* I thought, but Jim Dear disagreed.

He threw on the brakes mid-jump, a move that requires a lot of talent and imagination from a horse, and we came down in the middle of the third fence, the poles rolling from their cups and sliding around his hooves. Jim Dear leaped to the right, trying to get away from the scary poles, and my leg slammed into the jump standard and brought it along for a few strides, the pretty latticework caught on my knee and stirrup. Then the standard dropped to one side as Jim Dear twisted away from it, pulling us to the left, where Alejandro was still sitting like a bored king atop his dozing horse.

There was a moment of surprised awakening, his eyes widening even as his horse's blinked wide open, and then Jim Dear collided with the dozing horse, nearly knocking him over, and my *other* knee slammed into Alejandro's before his horse jumped away and bolted through the arena, looking for a safe space where a horse could just take a nap without another horse running up and crashing straight into him like some sort of psychopath.

Jim Dear, to his credit, just stopped and stood still, his ears swiveling and his head swinging back and forth, as if he couldn't believe what had just happened.

I resisted the urge to drop the reins and clap both hands to my aching knees. I felt as if both legs were on fire.

"Are you okay?" Pete was cantering toward us. Barsuk's head was high and his eyes rolling with agitation. He snatched at the bit as Pete brought him to a halt and threw a rebellious little crowhop. Pete ignored him. "What the hell was that?"

I just shook my head. "I think I ruined *both* my knees in one accident. How's that for talent?"

Unfortunately, there wasn't time for sarcasm. An angry buzz was already rising up from the other people on horseback, and they were all converging on the spot where Jim Dear stood shakily, huffing hard breaths and trying to figure out what the hell had just happened. I could practically hear his thoughts. He'd been jumping fences and then this maniac had come out of nowhere! What was a horse supposed to do? His rapid heartbeats thumped through the leather of my saddle. I rubbed my hand under his mane and murmured for him to settle, but the mob was upon us.

"What is this, hey?" Guillermo was angry, his hands tight on his reins, his horse's mouth gaping open. I winced for him; the elevator bit was pulling at the corners of his mouth and pinching his poll with every yank. "You going to run us all over, this is how you ride in arena? You eventers are all crazy!"

Pete's eyebrows came together in an angry line. "This wasn't her fault, sir. You watch how you talk to Jules. We own this property."

My heart leaped at the way he used "we," the way it always did. His inclusion emboldened me to speak up. "If you behaved like that at one of the big shows, you'd be dead or kicked out or both. You can't just cut in front of a jumping horse."

"Ah, but what about my horse?" Alejandro interjected. "You run him right into us!"

"He panicked! What were you doing just sitting in the ring, taking up space, anyway?" I rounded on him, ready for a fight.

"That's enough." Pete's voice cut across mine. "If we're sharing these arenas we have to be careful and respectful of one another's space. All of us will work harder at that."

I glowered at him.

Alejandro continued to glare at me like *I* was the one at fault here. "The accusations I am hearing from you people is unacceptable. I thought you were our hosts. Yet we come to this farm and almost right away we have a tree hanging on our roof, we have this problem with using the arenas—this is not what Mr. Blixden promised us for our winter quarters. I will be telling him we should be in Wellington. Ocala was a mistake."

I heard Pete make a choking noise next to me and I reached out and grasped his hand tightly. He couldn't speak; well, that was fine, I would speak, I would be the adult and I would contain my emotions and I would make sure these awful people stayed and

kept paying our bills. They couldn't leave. I couldn't let them leave.
I had to deal with them like an adult.

Shit.

"Alejandro," I said slowly, hoping I could keep the tension out
of my voice if I just paced myself, "I want to apologize if it seems
like we're being inhospitable. You are our guests. A few unfortunate
things have happened. We are working on them. The barn is re-
paired. We will all work on better ring etiquette." My throat closed
and I had to pause and swallow to get the anger down. The cycle
never ended; there would always be spoiled horse people who had
never had to do things the right way, the hard way. And we would
always have to kiss their asses. "We can make things work out for
you. Don't put your horses through the stress of another move."

Alejandro nodded, pleased, and I knew I'd said everything
he'd wanted to hear. Then he asked for more. "We need more paddocks," he said.

"I didn't know there was a problem with the paddocks." There
were six paddocks up here, each big enough for two horses. They
had twelve horses. The math worked for me.

"Our horses go out individually. We have space only for six
horses."

"Well, I'm very sorry, but those are all the paddocks we have."

Alejandro shrugged. "We see a large pasture there with no one
in it."

He nodded toward something behind me.

I didn't have to look around. Behind us, on the other side of
the training barn, was the gate to the cross-country fields. Oh, no,
no, no, Alejandro. Those fields were not a pasture option. If there
were horses out there, we'd have to go out and catch them before
every schooling, and since we used the field nearly every day for

hacking, galloping, and jumping . . . no. Not possible. "That's the cross-country field," I said, since Pete still seemed to have something lodged in his throat. "Not a pasture."

Alejandro's dark eyes, so recently angry, seemed to twinkle. "I see grass and fences?"

I bit the inside of my cheek. He could not have the cross-country field, and yet if he was going to make this a do-or-die issue before he took his tale to Blixden and told him he wanted the horses to go to Wellington . . . what the hell would I do then?

Finally Pete came back to life. He smiled, but his eyebrow was arching as if he couldn't stop it. I hoped Alejandro didn't notice and assume he was being laughed at behind Pete's smooth facade. "The cross-country field is for riding," he said matter-of-factly. "And unfortunately, it can't solve your turnout problem because it's going to solve your arena problem—that's where Jules and I will be schooling our horses from now on."

I looked at him, eyes wide. *Are you kidding me?*

He gave me a cheerful shrug.

Alejandro looked surprised. It was clear he'd been looking forward to a big fight before Pete backed down and gave him what he wanted. But Pete just went on with that blank smile, spreading his hands to show what a generous and understanding guy he was. Barsuk, bless him, stood still as a statue. "It's obvious these arenas weren't built for half a dozen riders at one time. This is a private training center, not a public riding school. We'll move some schooling standards out to the cross-country field and use that space for our horses. That way there's enough room for all of you in the arenas. You're clearly much busier than we anticipated, and we're sorry for the trouble."

Now I thought Alejandro looked just a little disappointed.

Maybe he really wanted to go to Wellington. Maybe he just liked to cause trouble. "That is gracious of you," he said loftily. "But the extra paddocks—"

"We simply don't have," Pete said firmly. "You knew the specs of the place before you moved the horses here. Six paddocks. That's what there is. You might want to string electric tape down the middle of a couple of them, split them into two pens." Then he turned to me, and his face was wiped clean of good humor, exhausted lines filling in for the smiling curves he'd shown Alejandro.

Pete's wiped out, I realized. I pushed my horse closer to him with one nudge of my leg, until our stirrups clinked and our boots brushed together.

"Let's go," he murmured. "Before I murder him."

We turned our horses as one and rode boot-to-boot from the arena, feeling the suspicious stares of the trainers and the teenagers on our backs. I waited until we were walking along the gravel lane, a good distance from the jumping arena, to speak.

"Well, this is a pile of shit."

"I'm sorry." Pete's shoulders slumped and he was sagging in the saddle. I thought that kind of sloppiness took real effort from a horseman as precise as Pete. It worried me.

"Why are you apologizing? We went into this together," I reminded him. "*I'm* sorry I raised my voice at them. Oh, wait. No I'm not."

"Oh, you screaming at them was inevitable." Pete chuckled.

"It's what I do," I agreed, cautiously optimistic. If he could laugh at me, he wasn't mad at me.

"So now we are banned from our own arenas—I did that by myself."

"I don't want to ride in there with them, anyway. They're reckless. Look at poor Jim Dear—he's got a scratch from hitting Guillermo's stirrup irons." I ran my hand down his shoulder, past the big V-shaped scar left behind by flying debris in the hurricane. "It's not like the poor guy hasn't gotten beat up enough in the past year."

"More than a year," Pete said.

"Hmm?"

"It's been more than a year. You've been here over a year, Jules. Think about that. We've been a team for a whole year now."

"Not quite," I mumbled, not ready to give in to any sentimentality, and well aware I'd done things that made me anything but a team player—as he was. But deep down I was pleased he was choosing to see us as a team. Maybe the summer was fading in more ways than one. Maybe we'd gotten past the drama of the past few months.

As if he'd been listening to my thoughts, Pete went on. "I wish things were more stable a year on than they were a year ago but . . . I think we're going to come out on top, Jules." He paused. "I'm glad you're here."

I squeezed Jim Dear closer to him, and the gelding cheerfully rubbed up against Barsuk's dappled side as if he hadn't just crashed into another horse about fifteen minutes before.

"I'm glad I'm here, too," I told him. "Even though half of it's been shit and the other half has been a pain in my ass."

He grinned at me and leaned over to give me a smacking kiss on the cheek.

The motion startled Jim Dear, who jumped ahead, and I had to grab at the reins to keep him in check. "My eloquent love," Pete chortled. "My poetic princess."

I let him laugh at me, partially because he was right, and partially because it finally felt like we were moving on from summer.

22

THERE WASN'T TIME to sit around and lick our wounds from the arena battle, or even discuss the new terms of our riding life, because there were still horses to train before we took Dynamo and Mickey over to Cotswold for their gallop.

Since we were staying after to help Alex with her horse, we had to have everyone ridden, cooled out, and stalled with fresh hay and water. By the time we got back, the sun would be sinking and it would be time to feed dinner.

"Do we have any idea what sort of help she wants?" Pete asked as we slammed the trailer doors shut behind my horses' gray and chestnut hindquarters. "I mean, is this a riding lesson?"

"I really don't know. I think it's more of an evaluation, to see how she's doing. I mean, she's a perfectly capable rider. She could probably get on anything in this barn and get it around a course. She's just nervous she's been making mistakes without a trainer around."

"Well, whatever she wants is fine. It's not like we couldn't use some time away from this place anyway."

He was right, and it made me sad. We shouldn't have to go looking for escape from our own farm. I watched the black-board fences slide by and hoped the worst was over. Every day for the past month had brought some new, awful drama.

I glanced at Pete, studying the lines settling around his mouth and along his forehead, and wondered if they were permanent. If just one season could wear a person down so much, how could those scars ever heal? Was all of life going to be like this, requiring as much courage to get up in the morning and face the day's problems as it took to kick toward a looming drop on a cross-country course?

We pulled into the lane at Cotswold and Pete punched in the gate code we'd been given to speed up access. We'd found midafternoon was generally quiet here, given over to busywork like pulling manes or cleaning out the feed rooms.

Once we'd looked up into the broodmare barn as we drove past and seen the grooms lounging in the aisle for an afternoon break, two-liter soda bottles by the side of their folding chairs.

Something was definitely up today, though. As we passed the turn for the broodmare barn, we could hear Latin music spilling down the hillside. When I squinted up the driveway, I could see people dancing in the barn's dark interior.

"Hell of a day around here," I observed, and Pete nodded, his eyebrow notching up.

At the training barn's loading dock, no one came out to meet us, and we could hear whoops and shouting from the office in the middle of the barn. We took down the horses and led them to the open stalls on the end, then went in search of humans.

We found everyone—Alex and the grooms, that is—in the

234 | Natalie Keller Reinert

office, engaged in some kind of awkwardly excited dancing. We stood in the doorway, feeling like we'd stumbled onto some kind of secret ritual, until Alex caught sight of us and dragged us into the room. She pointed at a TV on a low dresser in the corner. "Shearwater just won the All Out Stakes! We're all kind of freaking out."

On the screen, a dark bay horse was being led from the racetrack to the winner's circle. Dirt coated his face and chest, and I could see the red flare of his nostrils. "He's one of yours?" I asked inanely.

"One of our homebreds! We shouldn't be so surprised he won, but he was out of commission most of the year after he hurt himself at Gulfstream over the winter, and it just feels *so* good to know he's still got it."

"Well, that's awesome!" The energy of the room was spilling over and I was getting genuinely excited. So this was what it was like to win a race. "And there's Alexander!" The tall Englishman, his pale golden hair covered by a light fedora, stepped forward to take the horse's reins from the groom. He looked even more imposing in his suit and standing in his natural element than he did here at the farm. "Why aren't you there?"

Alex smiled at me. "Usually, I would be. But I really wanted to ride Tiger with you today. Alexander said he'd handle things."

I knew Alex well enough by now to realize this was a big statement for her. She very clearly wanted to be at the track—I could see it in the way she watched Alexander and her horse. Her gaze was hungry, flicking to his every movement, eating up each step Shearwater took. She was analyzing the way he moved, reassuring herself he was just as sound as he had been five minutes before, when the horses were first stepping up to the starting gate.

A groom came bursting into the room holding up big glass

bottles of neon-colored Mexican soda. "Alex, where you hide the champagne?" he shouted. "We have only Jarritos to celebrate this big win?"

She laughed, holding out a hand. "Jarritos is fine." He deposited a soda bottle in her palm and passed out the rest around the room. It was electric orange, like a biotech experiment gone mad. "Jarritos now, champagne later. I have to go out and ride with my guests. You finish feeding early, we'll toast Shearwater then."

The grooms seemed content with this proclamation and we all popped the lids off our bottles.

Ten minutes later, feeling bloated with orange soda, I finished tacking up Mickey. He crab-walked back and forth in the stall, tied "on the wall" instead of crosstied in the aisle, and something told me he associated his surroundings with his childhood as a racehorse. How much had Mickey enjoyed being a racehorse? I had a feeling I was about to find out.

He was dancing underneath me as I mounted up. Beside us, Dynamo was alert and ready to go, nothing more. He'd gotten used to the gallop sessions already, my good level-headed Dynamo.

Pete smiled at my jigging gray horse. "Looks like somebody woke up."

I decided there were two ways I could handle Mickey's high spirits: I could embrace his happiness, or I could be a mean mom about it and try to tamp him down. I chose to go with the former.

So I grinned at Pete like I didn't even mind the bouncing pony underneath me. "I think he's finally fit enough for Prelim," I said. "All that dressage has him moving right."

It was true: even with his over-the-top action, I could feel the positive effects of our summer of dressage. He hadn't felt this good in spring, even when he'd been performing well, but not amazingly,

236 | Natalie Keller Reinert

at Novice level. Once again, I had a good feeling we wouldn't be spending too long at Training or Modified. And Preliminary was where the real fun began, quite honestly.

So out we bounced, Mickey jigging sideways and holding himself in a bubble of restrained energy like a Roman equestrian statue, and Dynamo stepping nobly forward with his mouth on the bit and his ears pricked, looking as if he'd decided to exemplify good manners for his goofy little brother. Alex and Parker were the picture of trail-horse calm; Parker probably hadn't gotten excited about anything besides dinnertime in a decade, and Alex had on her game face, ready to jump into action if either of us novice gallopers got ourselves into trouble out on her track.

We trotted around the oval one time; the Florida sky alternating between sunshine and shadow as fluffy cumulus marched across the afternoon sky. Here we were in early October and the days were growing shorter, I thought regretfully. Even though Florida was a thousand times more comfortable between October and March, something in me felt hopelessly melancholy at the onset of autumn. When the bright white sunlight of summer began to darken into shifting golden rays, I could get into moods where I barely cared about the eventing season ramping back up. There was an inexplicable sorrow at the back of my mind, even while my body rejoiced as the temperature and relative humidity both slowly slipped below ninety degrees. Maybe it was just that I'd hated school.

Pete glanced over at me and saw my downturned mouth. "What's wrong?" he called. "Mickey looks great!"

He was right, of course. I knew Mickey looked great, just from the way he felt. He was not as professional as Dynamo, nearly yanking my arms out of the socket at every striped quarter pole, ducking his head down and trying to bolt into a gallop, but all in all he felt fit and ready for whatever the season threw at him. "Summer is over," I replied, shrugging. "It feels sad."

"This summer was brutal," Pete pointed out. "I would think we're both glad it's over."

I smiled and nodded, unable to reply. Dynamo trotted smooth as silk beneath him, and I wondered if Pete didn't realize this fall promised to be brutal for me, too.

We got around the first lap of the track and pulled up near the gap. Alex looked at Mickey, all bunched muscles and foaming sweat and rolling eyes. "Do you want me to pony you, or maybe just hang out with you guys for a little bit? Parker's up to a gallop."

I gave Mickey a pat on the neck and he used the loose rein as an invitation to jump sideways, nearly running over Dynamo, who stared at Mickey as if he couldn't believe what an asshole his stablemate was. "That's okay," I decided. "He'd probably just get revved up more with a horse right against him. I'll pace him alongside Dynamo, like we would do in the field."

Alex nodded. "Okay. Don't get killed—I really want your opinion on Tiger later." With those comforting words she turned Parker with a flick of the reins, retreating back to the shade of the oak trees along the gap.

I looked at Pete. "Well? You ready?"

"Let's do this." Pete wrapped up his reins as if he was going to exercise a racehorse, and it suddenly struck me as funny that we did the same job every morning at different farms, but never together. He didn't know what I looked like on a baby, and I didn't know what he looked like on the older horses he had started galloping and breezing. Now, as he pushed his hands down onto Dynamo's withers and stood up in the stirrups, clucking to the horse to head out, I could see he was born to do this, despite his height. Pete was a talented horseman in every respect.

God, he was so damn annoying.

I lifted myself into my own imperfect galloping position and sent Mickey alongside Dynamo. At least when we did this I was able to admire my chestnut horse. When I was on his back, I couldn't see how perfect every inch of him was. He was driving down on the bit now, just as Alex had predicted. Changing his surroundings had worked, and he was learning to differentiate between dressage and cross-country work.

Things were getting better, I thought.

Fall, despite my misgivings, had brought silver linings to my dark summer clouds. We raced around the track in an arrow-shaped formation, Dynamo just ahead of Mickey, and the horses were so workmanlike, so focused on their strides, that everything else in life slipped away. Nothing mattered but these galloping horses, and their joy.

After we finally brought them back to the barn for a shower and some time with hay nets in a few spare stalls, Alex took out her retired racehorse. Tiger was beautiful. We watched Alex ride him around the small paddock in front of the training barn and I practically salivated over him. Dark bay with lean muscles, a slim frame, long heron's legs—he was one of those incredibly slender Thoroughbreds who looked like they might snap under pressure, but was in fact tough as nails and twice as hard.

He didn't make riding easy for her, though. She kept him going in a decent Training level dressage frame but it took a lot of leg and wiggling fingers. He bobbled his head every six or seven strides and I could see her push him through another half halt, rebalancing him over and over and over. Well, that was dressage, in a nutshell. They would just learn to do it more quietly.

Beside me, Pete leaned on the fence and watched Tiger with the same hunger I felt. "That's a really nice horse," he said after a while, like he just couldn't help saying it aloud.

"Too bad she isn't shopping for a buyer."

"We couldn't afford him."

I smiled. "Maybe she'd let me work him off."

Alex cantered Tiger around the paddock, showing off a little with a skipping flying lead change as she crossed the diagonal, and then brought him down to a walk and over to the fence. Her face was flushed with heat. "He jumps a little, too, but I had to take the fences down for the mowing crew and haven't had time to set them up again."

Pete rubbed his chin thoughtfully. "Where have I seen this horse before?"

"He won the Thoroughbred Makeover down in south Florida this past spring." Alex grinned as if she couldn't believe it had happened. "It wasn't a big show, but you might have seen something online."

"Wait," Pete said. "That was you? I knew you looked familiar!"

"I missed that," I said. "Sorry."

She laughed. "It wasn't a big deal, not like the one in Kentucky."

"It was a big deal," Pete insisted. "You were up against some very nice horses!"

"Well, thanks."

We all paused while Tiger turned in an energetic circle. His muscle tone still looked racy and streamlined. I guessed if he'd raced until he was a mature adult horse, the movements had become ingrained into his physique and mindset permanently. This probably made him much tougher to ride than our horses, who had all retired before the age of four. Finally, I asked, "So what do you want to do with him?"

"And how can we help you do it?" Pete added.

Alex looked a little sheepish, as if she'd been keeping her true ask from us. "I need a home base for him. I tried keeping him here, but it's just no good trying to train on my own. It's a little boring riding alone, to be honest. My friend Lucy has space now, but she's too far away to go riding every day. I know you're right down the road, so I was wondering . . . can I board him with you and train with you? I really want to event."

My mouth dropped open. Alex had the most beautiful farm I'd ever seen, and she wanted to come board with us? If only things weren't so insane at the farm, this would have been wonderful news. As things stood, I wasn't sure if she'd really want to come once she found out we had no riding arenas and tenants hell-bent on making our lives miserable. She'd be walking right into a turf war. "Alex, we'd love to have you, but . . ." I trailed off, not sure how much Pete wanted out in the open.

"But?" She tilted her head. "I promise I'm an easy keeper. I only look high maintenance because my husband likes fancy barns. I'm really just a suburban Florida girl like you."

Pete spoke up. "But we've rented out our training barn and arenas," he said. "And we're only riding in the cross-country field now. We have jumps, and we're going to mark out a dressage space with cones, but there's not much fencing. It's really not as professional as what you're looking for."

"But you guys are there," Alex said. "And that's what I'm really looking for. I want a trainer. Trainers. If you have a stall open, and you're interested in taking on a really dedicated student, you think about your fee and get back to me. Because I can tell you like this horse." She grinned knowingly. "I see you looking at him, Jules!"

I blushed.

Alex laughed. "I want to be on Team Briar Hill. I'm tired of just fumbling around by myself and looking at different boarding stables and never finding anyone that I like. I like you guys. Let's make something great out of it."

"Wow, Alex." I didn't know what to say; I wasn't used to people pouring out their hearts to me. Or saying they liked me. Or saying they wanted to spend time with me. With the exception of Lacey, of course, and even Lacey had left me in the end and gone home to Pennsylvania. It would be really nice to have a friend at the barn in the afternoons, hanging out, riding with us, getting in the way, singing along to the radio, doing barn-girl stuff.

Plus she made really good coffee. I wasn't sure how she did it, but the girl was a whiz with a cheap barn coffeepot. That sort of talent shouldn't be overlooked.

"Pete," I said softly, "I'm game if you are."

He nodded, his eyes crinkled against the glare of the half-mast sun, sinking in a yellow bulge toward the horizon. "Alex, we'd love to have you at Briar Hill."

Alex grinned and leaned down from Tiger, who danced from side to side beneath her. She ignored his antics and reached out a hand. We both shook. "Team Briar Hill," she said, eyes glinting.

"Team Briar Hill," we both said back, and I wondered if Alex knew she was changing everything with those words, a tagline no one had ever spoken before, drawing us together in the best possible way.

23

TEAM BRIAR HILL, galloping their horses in the fields. Team Briar Hill, sleeping in a tack room and cooking in a horse trailer galley kitchen. Team Briar Hill, slowly waking up to reality.

The day after our gallop and the formation of our new superhero eventing team, we'd come home from another disappointing meeting with the attorneys to find Amanda sitting in her truck, parked by the annex barn, flicking her thumb up and down her phone. We'd never had that lunch with her, thanks to the tornado, but Pete had somehow brought her around to the idea of selling Rorschach again.

She hopped out when she saw us. I got out of the truck more slowly than Pete, still feeling sick from the meeting, in which we'd been told nothing had happened and it was going to cost twice as much and could we please send them a new credit card for billing. I decided to hang back as Pete went over to see what she wanted.

"My client wants to come out tomorrow," she began, "and if

she likes Rorschach we can take him for a two-week trial at my place. She'll be boarding with me if she buys him anyway, so can you have him ready to show at nine o'clock? She has a Monday-through-Friday job so it's got to be a weekend."

"Can it be later? I have work in the morning."

Amanda appeared confused. "Oh, I forgot you were galloping in the morning. Still? You're not done with that yet? I was hoping the lessons at my place could replace those for you, Pete!"

"Not yet." Pete's smile was thin.

"Well, um . . . do you have a groom here in the morning?"

"Ramon's here, why?"

"Can he just tack the horse up and I'll show him? Because it's got to be early. She has to take her kids to some karate thing, I don't know what. And she's ready to buy right now. She's in the sweet spot. I have her *drooling* for this horse. She'll bring her checkbook and we can just grab his things and load him up. Believe me, the less her husband knows about this before he's in my barn, the better."

Pete looked at me questioningly and I glared back at him. Why was he even considering this? There was no way I'd let Amanda show up here and ride one of our horses without us around, and when you added in the situation with the arena, the new trainers in town—did we really want Amanda stepping into that mess?

Pete shook his head at me a little, and I took it to mean he was going to tell her to reschedule the showing. I relaxed.

"That's fine, Amanda," Pete said instead. "Did you see where the jumps are set up over here? We're using the cross-country field instead of the arena. It's more convenient to this barn."

"Oh, I was wondering what was up with that. Yeah! Right there—no problem. You're right, it is convenient. A little rustic, but . . . she'll see how well he behaves in the open, so that's fine.

Thank you, Pete. Sorry it's last-minute. You know how these people are." She made a show of checking the time on her phone. "Well, gotta go, lessons to teach! I'll call you tomorrow and let you know how it went."

I headed into the barn and started rubbing noses as they appeared over the stall guards. Mickey shoved his face against my side, nearly knocking me over.

Pete followed me after Amanda's truck rumbled out of the yard. "She's ridden the horse plenty of times before," he said to the back of my head.

"She's going to take him up to the arena." I dug my fingers into Mickey's fluffy forelock and scratched his poll. Mickey swooned.

"No, she just said she'll use these jumps right here."

"She's never going to show one of her fancy clients a hunter prospect in a pasture. She's going to go to the arena and cause problems." I knew Amanda. I'd been watching her all these months while Pete had been talking to her and putting her on his horses and ignoring the obvious. "Also, that could have been a phone call. Or a text. Why did she drive over here?"

Pete sighed. "Don't start about her, please."

"I'm not *starting* anything, I'm just saying, there was no need for her to drive over here and sit around waiting for us." *For you.*

"Why worry about it? You heard her. Checkbook-ready. I'll fix whatever mess she makes once I have that money in the bank. It can't cost us any more than what we've lost already." He started down the aisle. "I'm going to get shavings into the stall next to Regina's. We can put Tiger in there."

I looked over at Regina, hanging her head over the stall wall. We'd brought her home from the vet clinic and she'd expected to go straight out to the mare pasture to restore order, but instead, she was on stall rest. She glared at me before turning her head to chew at the wall. The doorpost was already showing signs of her boredom; it looked like a very large beaver had been running very large beaver teeth down the wood, carving out deep scars. She took a whole chunk out of the corner now, a good inch long, and spit the wood onto the ground, shaking her head to get the splinters off her tongue. "You need a toy," I told her. "Maybe having a horse next door will give you something besides the barn to rage at."

In the tack room, Marcus stretched luxuriously on my pillow and thumped his tail against the mattress when he saw me. I noted the mud on his paws as I dug around in a trunk for something Regina could chew on. "So nice to see you've been playing in the puddles," I remarked. He put out his tongue and panted at me, the picture of a good dog, such a good dog, and waved his muddy paws in the air.

I found a crusty old horse ball in the trunk and took it down to Regina. She eyed the ball with its rubber handle like it was some kind of monster. I stuck it in her stall near her hay anyway. "It's fun," I assured her, while she gazed at me skeptically. "You'll like it." None of my other horses had ever cared for it, but there was a market for those things, so sooner or later I'd find its target audience.

Pete came into the barn with a wheelbarrow full of shavings, still wearing slacks and one of his few nice polo shirts with the farm logo embroidered on the chest. "You didn't change?" I chided, unable to stop myself from nagging. "You're going to get grease or something on those pants."

"I just wanted to get to work," he said tersely. "Why waste time?" The skin beneath his eyes was puffy from worry and insomnia.

"This doesn't have to be done right now. Let's go sit down. Have some coffee."

"When else is it going to get done, Jules?" His voice took on a steely edge, but I could hear the brittle fragility underneath. "I'm not going to stop now. I'm not going to stop until it's finished."

I backed off. This was not about shavings.

Pete was not reacting well to the attorney meeting, and who could blame him? They'd basically told him it was going to cost a fortune in legal fees to get the one thing he'd been killing himself for: his grandmother's farm. After nearly two months of living with this, after nearly two months of paying their fees, we'd thought we'd hear something else. Not *We need more money*. Not *We need more time*. Not *It doesn't look good*.

I wandered outside to give him a little breathing room. The afternoon was waning, the big blue October sky touched with yellow as the sun began to sink toward the hills. We had passed over into the dry season, and I could feel the moisture pulling away from the air. The sunlight was still hot, but the breeze wafting through the oaks and brushing my face was cool. *A little taste of winter*, I thought, and then laughed at myself. Winter was two months away, and even then it might get into the eighties during the day. Last Christmas had been nearly ninety degrees. Still, the nights would be cool. It was almost time to start turning the horses out during the day.

I ran through the calendar ahead day by day, mentally checking off the big days to come. Tomorrow Amanda would come and ride Rorschach, and hopefully leave us a check and an empty stall. In a few days we'd be taking the weekend off from our galloping jobs and trailering the event horses to Sun Valley Horse Trials for their fall opener, a nice chance to stretch their legs and get them ready for a long winter of eventing. Two weeks after that, Sunshine State Fall Trials. In six weeks we'd be taking them to Hope Glen, the first serious event of the season. It was all on, whether we were ready for it or not.

Time to hit the road and jump some fences.

I looked around at the farm, at this sweep of green grass and black fence we'd been fighting so hard to keep. I could feel the final credits waiting to roll, somewhere in the wings. At the end of the day, Briar Hill was beautiful, but it was just another farm in a sea of farms, and I was tired of fighting. My horses were my lifeblood, not the earth they galloped over.

Maybe this fight didn't matter to me so much anymore. I was growing resigned to my status as a nomad. A journeyman-horsewoman, so to speak.

Would that be so bad? I could make my peace with leaving. It would be harder for Pete. He thought of Briar Hill as the home he'd been trying to secure for his entire adult life. What he didn't know was this: he was the home I wanted to cling to, despite his new moods and darkened spirit. I wanted to keep him happy, safe, and complete, because I thought he could do the same for me. If that meant we continued to throw money into saving Briar Hill, well, then that's what we would do until he was done.

And when it all fell apart, I'd pick up the pieces.

I rode babies all the next morning in a state of panic, hoping I could get done early and get back to Briar Hill before Amanda showed up and caused trouble with Rorschach. I just knew she was going to take that horse straight to the jumping arena. I was willing to bet she wouldn't even let the buyer down to our barn, but would tell her to wait at the arena while Amanda brought the horse up.

We were galloping the last set along the back turn when a couple of wild-eyed young horses under two crouching riders went galloping by on the other side of the hedge. My colt jumped about six feet to the left and then went on galloping with admirable dedication to his job. Stacy from Oklahoma, riding on my right, was less lucky and had to contend with a bolt-and-buck combo which, while remarkable, could do nothing to unseat her stout frame, or wipe the implacable expression from her face. Stacy always gave the impression of having endured much worse, even when she was spitting out dirt after a fall.

"That was weird," I said as we backed our horses off a few minutes later, getting them ready to turn back to the barn.

"Mary Archer's pieces of shit," Stacy grumbled. "She comes and goes. She never has horses for more than a few weeks."

"Oh, Mary Archer." I remembered the weed-filled track, the rider galloping away from me at full tilt, the grim-faced woman telling me not to mention her name to the trainers next door. "What's her deal, anyway?"

"She's a trainer who gets in all kinds of claiming schemes. Brings horses up here when they get vet-scratched, turns them out for a while, gallops them until they look fit, and takes them back down to whatever track will give her stalls. She has it in for Alex, between you and me. That's why that hedge got put in back in June. Used to just be a wooden fence between the two farms." Stacy rubbed at her chin, leaving a streak of dirt behind. "You heard of her?"

"Not really," I said. "Just curious." No one needed to know I'd ridden one horse for her. That job was so brief, it barely happened.

Ahead at the gap, Alex was waiting for us on Parker, and I hoped Stacy would let the conversation die before we reached the boss. She did, but she still glanced at me significantly, which told me there was a lot more to say about Mary Archer.

Everyone was watching Rorschach cantering through the jumping arena by the time I got back to Briar Hill, and I mean everybody:

the buyer and her daughter, Alejandro and his brothers, even Mr. Blixden. Turns out just about anyone can be a sucker for a draft cross who moves nice and has a flashy color pattern, and I had to admit Amanda really knew how to get a horse around a hunter course.

The big-boned horse had no problem getting perfectly spaced strides between each fence, and executed effortless flying lead changes at each end of the arena.

I would have been more impressed if watching a hunter round didn't bore me after two or three jumps. Still, I hopped out of the truck and slipped over to stand near the buyer, a pace or two away from Alejandro and company.

Alejandro turned his head and waved me over. "This your horse?" he stage-whispered.

"Pete's," I said.

"I never see this horse before."

That's because you guys were jerks and now we ride in a pasture like peasants. "Well, hopefully you'll never see him again, because we want him sold today."

"Daisy Blixden really likes these spotted horses." He raised his voice just a little, and I saw the buyer, a middle-aged woman in dark breeches and a stretchy tech riding top, the kind of thing Amanda was always wearing, turn her head. She pushed dark brown hair behind an ear and looked at us curiously.

"Look away," Alejandro whispered. "Look at me." Louder, he said, "When the girls come down to show this winter, I know they're wanting one more horse, for the equitation."

I couldn't believe he was being so helpful. "If Daisy's interested, you should've said so. I mean, you're right here on the farm. We'd be happy to schedule a test ride, if this one doesn't work out."

Alejandro sighed theatrically. "What are the chances of that? This horse is perfect."

From the corner of my eye, I saw the buyer shift her weight from side to side. She was holding her daughter's helmet by the harness, and suddenly she thrust it at the girl. "I want Bella to try him now, Amanda!" she called. "Bring him over to the mounting block!"

As the girl mounted a patient Rorschach, her clucking mother glancing fearfully over her shoulder toward us, I looked over at Alejandro and caught the twinkle in his eye. "Thank you," I mouthed. I didn't know what possessed him to help us sell a horse, but there was no doubt he'd put the fear of missing out into that poor woman's head.

Alejandro shrugged and grinned, then looked back into the arena, like everyone else, the happy peanut gallery enjoying the spectacle of a test ride as only horsemen can.

By the time Pete returned from his morning's galloping, little Bella had taken Rorschach around two courses of fences, and was beaming at her mother from the saddle. It looked like a match. Luckily, tweens were easy to buy horses for. They loved them all.

Alejandro continued to make eyes at Rorschach whenever he thought appropriate, and even walked over and whispered in Guillermo's ear at one point, pointing at the horse. The buyer narrowed her eyes at him and tugged Amanda's elbow. Pete walked over and Amanda introduced the two of them.

I watched until there was a handshake, then I turned to Alejandro. "You're a star," I told him.

He shrugged, but he was smiling. "Maybe you'll do the same for us someday."

As promised, the buyer brought her trailer, and after a quick shower in the crossties while Amanda produced paperwork for

Pete and Rorschach's new owner (pending that two-week trial) to sign, the horse hopped in for the short ride to Amanda's barn.

His colorful nose pushed against the screen in his window as the trailer started to move, and he whinnied plaintively to the horses left behind. Everyone called back, a barnful of hollering horses calling their goodbyes and good lucks. I leaned against Pete, so breathlessly grateful for his arm wrapped around me I could barely speak. I wasn't entirely struck dumb, though.

"We can't even tell them they'll see each other at shows, because he's off to hunter-land," I joked. "Poor spotty horse, I hope the warmbloods aren't too snobby to him."

Pete laughed. "You're so awful."

"I know," I said. "But this all worked out a lot better than I expected. I still can't believe Alejandro helped out like that."

The trailer disappeared around the curve, its high roof brushing the allée of oak trees. Pete pulled out the bank check from his wallet and held it up for inspection once again. "Why do you think he did it?"

"Maybe he felt bad for kicking us out of the arenas."

"Not bad enough to apologize and tell us to come back?"

"Oh God no," I said. "I'd never expect that."

"I need you to interpret mean people for me," Pete said. "I'm just realizing your real purpose in my life."

"I'm your guardian demon," I agreed. "Much more useful than an angel when you're in the horse business."

24

PACKING FOR EVENTS was always chaotic, even in the simplest of times.

Having our trunks and supplies scattered between the tack room, the spare stalls, and the horse trailer made things even worse. Trying to track down everything we needed was making both of us crazy. Ramon knelt with sopping-wet jeans in the wash rack, scrubbing Mickey with purple shampoo and shaking his head with disgust at the green manure stains the gray horse had managed to acquire just that morning, while Pete and I ran back and forth with wheelbarrows, trying to condense our lives into a couple of neat trunks.

Think living out of a suitcase on a business trip is hard? Try doing it with a horse.

Dressage saddles, cross-country saddles, jumping saddles. The realization you've been switching your stirrup leathers between your cross-country and your jumping saddle all summer instead of buying new ones—because the ones you like are two hundred dollars and Rockwell promised he'd send you a pair but he hasn't yet—and agonizing over whether you want to continue switching them at the event, or if that's going to be an extra level of stress no one needs, especially when you don't have a working student to pile all of these chores and frustrations upon. The realization that the constant knot you've been tying in the reins of your bridle, because you got so used to doing it at the training track in the mornings, has left a permanent and unsightly kink now it's been untied, something that will catch the eye of the dressage judge in a most unfavorable manner. The realization your favorite white dressage pad didn't get put back into the tack trunk after the last show, and has instead been serving as an unofficial cat bed for a certain Barn Kitty for the past week . . .

I dropped the last load of laundry, or so I prayed, into the washing machine and leaned against it as the machine went to work, humming and vibrating its way through the saddle pads and polo wraps. The washer and dryer sat on an uneven deck of pallets in the stall we used for tools and wheelbarrows and whatever else needed a home. The floor was pitted in the middle, remnants of the broodmares who had lived here, pawed here, paced here, even had their foals here. I wondered if any champion racehorses had been born in this stall. Was my laundry room built on the birthplace of a Triple Crown legend?

Anything was possible in Ocala. That's why we loved it here.

Pete went by with a wheelbarrow full of hay bales. Ramon went the other way with a now-spotless Mickey, a new stable sheet flung over his coat to keep him as white as possible. I admired the sheet for a moment—navy blue and embroidered with silver thread at the hip: BRIAR HILL FARM. It was another piece of the Rockwell sponsorship: new rugs, quarter sheets, stable sheets, rain sheets . . . we were overwhelmed and flooded and buried under horse clothing, although I was still feeling a little overlooked in the riding outfit department. My Instagram #ROOTD game was seriously lacking right now, although my new innovation, #horseselfies, was killing it. I had nearly six hundred likes on this morning's mugshot with Dynamo alone. The comments were kind of nice, too. I was starting to love *Ponymama626,* who always took it upon herself to post something like "great to see you and Dynamo looking so happy!"

She had no idea. Dynamo was loving his life for sure. Now that Pete was his rider, he had *two* humans in the palm of his hand.

Alex, who made it out nearly every day to ride Tiger now that he'd joined the annex barn herd, came wandering into the storage stall with a travel mug gripped in each hand. I held out my hands and she placed one of the mugs into my possession like a beloved child. "Sweets for my sweetheart," she said with a grin. "How you guys holding it together?"

"Like we ran out of glue," I admitted. "We've never packed together. We were always in separate barns. And I had a working student doing most of this for me before. Now there's no routine."

Alex nodded sagely. A lack of routine in a stable was the most desperate situation, the darkest timeline. "You'll get used to it. I guess you're planning on staying this way for a while, right? So it will get natural."

A while. Yes. The foreseeable future of Briar Hill Farm: the Blixden party reigning over the front three-quarters of the farm like kings, the arena lights on late into the night while they jumped their horses endlessly, prepping for the winter season as if their lives depended on it. All the while, the deposed owners moldered in the old barn out back. Very natural.

Our story might be made into a romance novel someday, I reflected. Or a cautionary tale.

"I can't see any end point," I admitted. "No one wants to make a move. We can't afford the latest round of fees from the attorney. Looks like we live here until the farm actually gets sold and they kick us out." I'd never said the words out loud, I'd just thought them, usually in the middle of the night. Now that they were voiced, they felt real, and hopelessly insurmountable, as if I had just constructed a mountain and sat it down in front of us.

Something in me itched to climb that mountain immediately; I didn't like waiting. But I had to hold back, waiting for Pete to figure it all out for himself.

Alex's eyes widened. "That *sucks*. I didn't realize it was that bad," she said. "I'm really sorry. But hey, these things can take years. So even if it looks bad now, or next year, things could change before you actually end up having to leave. It might turn out okay in the end."

Oh, I liked Alex so much! She was optimistic without being chipper. I couldn't deal with chipper. Lacey had been chipper but in a totally adorable way. Alex knew how to dole out just the right amount of rain with her sunshine. It was truly a gift.

"I think it will," I said cautiously. "It just depends on your definition of 'okay.' Like, at this point? I'd just like an end. I don't care if it means we leave Briar Hill. I'd leave tomorrow, if it just meant an end to all this . . ." I wound my finger in the air. "Round and round, never getting anywhere bullshit. I don't think I have years to give to this mess."

"It's a beautiful farm, though! You'll never get another place like this. Isn't that worth a little trouble?"

"We won't be able to afford it even if we win the court case. We can't afford it now, and we're living in the tack room. A property like this costs a fortune, *you* know that."

Alex had the courtesy to look a little embarrassed. "I guess Alexander was already in a good position when I moved in."

"That's fair," I told her, even though it really wasn't. I wasn't going to resent Alex's good fortune in meeting a guy with a nice farm and the money to run it. "We never were. And frankly? I don't think we ever will be. I think Briar Hill is a dream. Just a pretty dream."

"So what are you going to do?"

I shrugged. "Wait it out. Wait for Pete to wake up, or money to fall from the sky. It won't . . . but, you know. It could."

A wheelbarrow's metal feet clanked on the aisle a few stalls down, and I realized I'd better keep my mouth shut and my thoughts unspoken with Pete somewhere in the barn. Alex caught my suddenly guarded expression and tilted her head out the stall door. She shook her head slightly. I let out a breath.

"It's not really that bad," I said loudly. "Sometimes it just feels nice to complain."

"Oh, I completely agree," Alex said, matching my tone. "Just ask Alexander sometime."

We grinned at each other, conspiratorial to the end.

"Okay," I said, pushing off from the washing machine. "Let's go see if Pete needs help."

Pete didn't need help.

That was what he said to us, and we listened to him and went back to getting my pile of tack into the trailer, but I'd noticed the toneless quality to his voice, and the way he'd avoided my glance. He'd stepped away, over a line of tack trunks, when I'd moved to touch his hand. Then he'd acted as if he hadn't realized he'd avoided me, and apologized.

This had to end, and soon. Even if I was the one to push him into realization. He'd only hate me for a minute or two.

As we shoved my trunk into the trailer's storage compartment, I made nervous eye contact with Alex. She gave me a frown of concern.

"He definitely heard me," I whispered. "Now he's going to hold a grudge for a day."

"It's going to be okay," she replied gently. "All of it."

"How do you know?" I was genuinely curious. She seemed very sure.

The trunk slid into place against the wall with a gentle thud. "After a while, it always is," she explained. "Because you both want it badly enough."

Wanting it badly enough was the currency I tried to use on everything, with mixed results. As for Pete, well—"What if he doesn't want the same thing as me?"

"He'll come around," Alex said. "You two are good together."

In the middle of the night, Pete stirred from the bed and I sensed him moving through the dark tack room like a ghost, trying not to wake me. The air conditioner had been turned off for the first time all season, and without its green light glowing into every corner of the room, I couldn't see a thing. But I knew he was there.

"Pete," I whispered. "What's up?"

"Me," he joked, and came back to sit on the bed. Marcus, who had already been angling for his pillow, wiggled back toward my feet, aggrieved. "I'm just restless. I didn't want to toss and turn in bed and wake you up, so I was going to go for a walk."

"Oh." A walk at—I looked at my phone—3:23 in the morning. That made perfect sense. "Stay here. It's fine."

"I'll just be a little while. Go back to sleep." He leaned down and pressed a soft kiss to my lips.

The kiss was unexpected; it sent blood rushing to my lips and my cheeks, and I lifted my hand to catch him, arrest him there, but he was already slipping away, moving through the door and into the barn aisle silently. The door closed behind him. *If we both want it enough.* I wondered if I should follow him, and knew instantly I shouldn't. If he wanted me, he would come back for me. Instead I wrapped my empty arms around Marcus, who sighed long-sufferingly and snuggled his long hound-nose along my neck.

I heard Regina rumble a welcoming nicker as he went down the aisle. I pictured him stopping to visit with her. Beautiful Regina, with her elegant legs in bandages and a growing hay belly. Pete now paused on stallion ads while flipping through magazines, his eyes lingering on their show stats and conformation shots, mentally matching them up with Regina and picturing the foal they might make together.

That was the good thing about mares, I thought idly. If they broke, you could put them to work making babies. When geldings broke, they were only good for eating grass, and I didn't know anyone who had an excess of grass.

I rolled over, restless, as Marcus wriggled from my grasp. Satisfied Pete was gone, he crept back up to Pete's pillow and stretched out alongside me, heaving a wet doggy sigh in my direction as he settled into feathery comfort. I ran my hand along his short coat, digging my fingers into the folds of skin around his neck.

When all else failed, there were always dogs.

"If he asked me, I'd tell him," I murmured to Marcus. "If he wanted to know what it was like to lose his home, he could just ask me. He was there."

He was there the night the storm took it all and left only our lives. He came and scooped us up from the literal eye of the hurricane, and brought us back to Briar Hill. I felt like we'd met for the first time that night, after all the chance meetings at events. He'd contrived to see me again and again, and I'd pushed him away again and again, but that night, we'd finally, truly met each other.

If I went back, would I do it differently? Or would it still take that night, with all its terror, to bring us together?

"He went under the house to find you," I whispered in Marcus's ear.

Marcus sighed. *I'm asleep.*

I wished I could save Pete, the way he'd saved me. The way he'd saved us. But there wasn't a storm to rush into. This called for a different kind of courage.

All I could do was wait. He was going to nurse this hurt, walk it around the farm he loved and show it all his favorite spots, and let the grieving nestle where his happiness should be. That was his choice. I would let him, and I'd wait for him.

In the meantime, there was Marcus.

I lay awake, missing the glow of the air-conditioner light, the healthy rattle and roar of its motor; I was uncomfortable with autumn, and change, and the uncertain winter marching rapidly up to meet us.

25

WE LOOKED GOOD at horse shows and trials these days, there was no doubt about that. I looked at the lacquered new tack trunks emblazoned with ROCKWELL BROTHERS SADDLERY and BRIAR HILL FARM in shining golden letters and knew I'd come a long way from discounted plastic tubs from Walmart.

If we'd been in the hunter/jumper circuit we would have been hanging fringed curtains on the stall fronts. When Amanda went to shows, her grooms laid out Persian carpets and potted palms, with wicker tables and chairs. Her show setup made it appear her horses had crashed a Victorian beach resort. The only things missing were parasols and a silver tea service.

We were eventers. We put our trunks in front of our stalls, clipped up our vinyl stall guards (more Rockwell Brothers/Briar Hill Farm branding here as well) and made sure all of our buckets and bandages were blue. And we left it at that.

The barns at Sun Valley were fresh and still relatively new, with big open shed rows. This venue had only provided temporary stabling in years past, the horses blinking at one another through white vinyl half walls, with bars on top. You had to be careful who was stabled next to who, or wars would break out along the flimsy dividers.

Now we were in the real barns, with wooden walls and high ceilings. I bungee-corded box fans to the bars along each stall's front wall, and plugged them into actual, convenient plugs that did not spark or pop even one single time, like we were in some sort of civilized country and not at a horse trials. It was going to be a hot weekend. Only October, and we were looking at a ninety-degree day. The horses from up north were freshly clipped, looking dull in the sunlight, sharp vees of winter fur at their tailbones and pockets of dark, lush hair at their elbows and cheeks, where the angles were difficult to maneuver a heavy clipper head. Their breath came hard and fast in the humidity, but they'd adjust in a few weeks. I wiped sweat from my face with the front of my shirt. Oh, Florida!

Mickey poked his head over his stall guard and whinnied a hello to every horse within earshot. He got back about a dozen replies and looked pleased with the response. Dynamo swept back his ears as a competitor walked a tall black warmblood past, and retreated into his stall. "Crotchety old man," I told him, leaning over the guard to rub at his ears, just inside the stall. He pulled at his hay and blew hot, grass-scented breath at me, telling me what he thought of me and my name-calling.

Pete had gone to get numbers and packets; we both had dressage and show jumping today, and cross-country early the next morning. Becky would be out shortly to help us get through the day. With six horses, we could have used a second person. Lacey joked that if I sent her a round-trip plane ticket, she'd be here in a second. I counteroffered with a one-way ticket, and she lived in the horse trailer, and never left me again.

Lacey's reply was a bunch of skull emojis followed by one laughing-face emoji, so I guessed she wasn't coming.

I sat down for a moment on one of the blue tack trunks, careful not to press my boot heels against it and scuff the paint, and watched the circus of the eventing life around us. Everywhere there were horses, horses, horses, and wasn't it glorious? I felt so at home here, among my people.

Wasn't all this worth the struggle?

I closed my eyes and let the sun soak into my bones. I imagined winning my divisions, pictured one of the *Eventing Chicks* bloggers taking my picture and writing up something very flattering and nice about me. *We misjudged Jules Thornton,* they might write. *This woman is the queen of eventing!*

When I opened my eyes again, Pete was sitting next to me, manila envelopes in hand. He smiled at me as I came back to the world. "Hey, sleepyhead, maybe you better take a nap before dressage."

"I think I just did." I rubbed my eyes, and then the back of my head; leaning your head against a hard wooden stall wall isn't the most refreshing thing you can do for your body, let me tell you.

"I was only gone about fifteen minutes. I don't know if you could even consider that a catnap. Anyway here's the numbers and the ride times if you care. I'm not here to see anybody so I didn't even look." We had always had a ritual of flipping through the ride time printout to see who else had shown up; unlike me, Pete knew lots of people in the industry and liked to pop around the other barns to say hello and catch up. I probably should start doing the same, but at the moment the only news I could share with people included exciting and uplifting details on losing the battle to keep our farm, and Pete's big horse damaging herself possibly beyond repair, and so I'd given Pete my big horse to ride, and also we were living in our tack room and had been kicked out of our own arenas, wasn't that something?

It didn't feel like the kind of thing I wanted to share with the world.

Something told me Pete was feeling the same way.

"At least we have the sponsorship," I said into the silence.

Pete looked at me with a smile, and I knew we'd been thinking the same things. "If nothing else, we look fantastic."

"I think Amanda would say that's the most important part."

"Am I dreaming or did you just quote Amanda?"

I elbowed him. "Tease me again and you can find your own tack trunk to sit on."

Pete laughed and wrapped an arm around me.

Riding Mickey around the dressage arena while the preceding rider wrapped up her test, I reveled in the way his hindquarters reached underneath his body and propelled him forward with such surety. I couldn't help but smile.

Three months of dressage boot camp and this is what I had: a young horse who moved with the confidence and power of a much more mature horse, and gave me everything I asked for without a moment's hesitation. He wasn't perfect, of course—he was a horse, for goodness' sake, and we'd always have arguments and disagreements and misunderstandings—but for right here, right now, performing this lower-level dressage test, he was everything I needed.

I sat and closed my fingers on the reins, and Mickey shifted down to a walk, then a halt. We paused as the former rider, a bronze-tanned older woman riding a shimmering bay warmblood, rode out of the arena.

She gave the horse a stiff pat on the neck as they passed the white cone at A, as if she couldn't quite let go of the formal dressage pose, even after the final salute to the judge. I myself was guilty of some pretty serious neck-hugging after a good test, but to each her own. As soon as she passed the sandy warm-up area I lifted my seat and hands and Mickey effortlessly sprang back into a trot, his ears pricked at the crowd of Pony Clubbers, volunteers, trainers, and parents who made up the spectators at a typical eventing dressage test.

"Good boy," I told him clearly, since I'd have to be silent during the test. "Very nice."

We took one more round of the arena, the bell ringing, as usual, while we were as far away as possible. The judge's gazebo hid the annoyed twist of my mouth when I heard the *ding!* Why did every ring steward ever, since the beginning of humankind, ring the goddamn bell when I was at the opposite end of the ring? Could they ever ring it when I was at E, the perfect spot to gather my thoughts and prepare to trot my horse down the center line? No, they had to do it at C, and make me feel like I had to rush. Well, as usual, I would try not to rush Mickey into anything. We had sixty seconds. It didn't take sixty seconds to trot sixty meters.

Did it? I trotted him faster without being able to help myself.

I was a self-fulfilling prophecy.

The sharp final turn into the dressage arena is always a nerve-wringing one for me. Trotting down the center line straight as a die is next to impossible, but of course it's the ideal. And it's an ideal you're trying to reach as the judge is getting their very first impression of you and your horse. There's no second chance to put an idea into your judge's head: you want the judge to think, *My God, what a collected and put-together team we have here!* and let that impression color the next five to six minutes as you walk, trot, canter, and perform lateral movements in front of them and they scribble their comments next to the number score they've given your movement. Dressage is the least objective thing you can do with a horse. There are guidelines, and there are judges, and your score lies within their personal interpretation of the guidelines.

I gave Mickey a half halt, pushing his impulsion into the bridle, just before the gap in the arena chains came up to meet us. Seconds before the A cone marked the gap, I shifted my inside leg to his girth and my outside leg back to keep his hindquarters from swinging out. I didn't want him to turn like a steamship; I wanted him to turn like a sea serpent, bending around the corner sinuously and gracefully. I turned my shoulders into the arena, my seat bones shifting with the bend, and Mickey's mouth and neck and spine and tail followed the curve, flowing into the arena and finding the center line like a stream seeking its bed.

We had done it. I resisted the urge to run my hand up his neck in a quick pat of thankfulness. Praise was for the end of the test. Right now we were being judged.

I squared away all of my joints and bones and muscles and pressed Mickey forward toward the gazebo. His head came up a little because he wanted to look at the lacy white structure, and I squeezed first my left fingers, then my right fingers—*Hello, pay attention to me please*—and he mouthed the bit and dipped his nose again, rounding his neck in a beautiful curve. I kept the pressure on with my legs just behind the girth, so far back it nearly hurt my hip, the way Grace had shown me, and my heels touched the sweet spot on his abdomen where I could twitch the muscles that lifted his entire back.

The center of the arena, the imaginary marker called X, was rushing up to us now, and I began to prep Mickey for the halt. Half halt, half halt, half halt, closed fingers, closed seat, closed leg, pushing his energy into the bridle, pulling his hindquarters beneath him, telling him to bunch it all up, and then everything was closed, I shut the door I had been opening, soft fingers alternating with hard; and he came to a halt as I wanted, his forehand high and light before me, his hindquarters right underneath him, square and military, a leg at each corner.

I wanted to burst into tears at his loveliness, but that wasn't considered good form in dressage, so instead I put my right hand at my thigh and gave the judges a martial nod. I had never quite gotten the hang of saluting the judge—was it a graceful dip that included the shoulders, was it a short nod of hello, as if we were acquaintances passing on the street? What I gave was a little more severe than some riders, and a little less than others. There were as many ways to salute the judge as there were horsemen in black dressage saddles, and for all I knew everyone was doing it slightly wrong. Then I picked up the right rein again, half halted again, and sent him forward once more, trotting like a force of nature, like a warhorse marching to battle, like a horse and rider team who knew exactly what they were doing, and wasn't that the most unlikely thing of all, when you really thought about the past year, and what we'd all been through together?

It was a good test. It was a *good* test. I came out of the arena fairly dignified, Mickey's reins slipping through my fingers as he dipped his head to stretch his back and relax after five minutes of rigorous self-carriage and collection, but as soon as we got past A and I could see the impressed smiles and nods of the spectators, I leaned down and wrapped my arms around his sticky-wet neck. The smell of hairspray in his braids and Show Sheen on his coat mixed with the good earthy smell of horse, and I breathed him in. "Oh my God, Mickey, I love you, boy," I told him, my lips against his coat, short white hairs tickling my cheek. "You're such a fucking fantastic horse."

There were a few nods and even a few claps as I straightened up and walked Mickey back toward the stable area. I waved at the people who had been nice enough to stand around while we trotted and cantered in circles through the sandbox. They were the real MVPs, to make us feel like we weren't alone out there, riding in a vacuum.

A girl of maybe ten, clad in jodhpurs and a pink polo shirt, shouted, "We love you, Mickey!" and I didn't even know how to react to that. The only appropriate thing seemed to be to burst into tears of thankfulness that some literal girl was in love with my big goofy unicorn of an event horse, but instead I waved and grinned at her. Her mother smiled at me reservedly; I could see in her clean capris and neat blouse that she was a classic horse show mom, out of her element, up early on weekends, and totally confused as to why her daughter hadn't just picked dance like all of her friends. I had one of those moms back home, probably still asleep now that her horse-crazy daughter had moved out and stopped requiring her chauffeur services for events.

Then I looked up and saw Pete walking up, horse-free and on the ground.

"Did I miss your test?" he called.

"Yes," I said. "It's fine." It really was. Maybe I'd done better without him there. I still thought he judged my dressage harder than necessary.

"How did it go?"

"It was great, actually." I reined back Mickey and he put his hand on my boot and smiled at me. "I think we really nailed it."

"After this summer, I can't see how you could miss," Pete said. He looked past me to the arena, where the other horse was cantering in a smooth circle.

"Wait until they're done and we'll hear the score."

"We can hear it on the way back to the barn."

"Let's just wait and hear it right here," he insisted. "They'll say it in like two minutes."

I shrugged and loosened Mickey's reins, letting the horse drop his head to nose at the stubs of grass on the dusty ground. "Fine."

Pete smiled at a few acquaintances, shouted a few hellos, and was basically Mr. Cool while we stood in the milling crowd of people. Everyone at an event was going in all directions—riders heading for arenas, grooms taking sweaty horses back to barns, kids dragging their parents all over the place, tweens running around in giggling, bedazzled little packs, their knee socks mismatched rainbows over their staid beige breeches. Then a familiar figure appeared, making a beeline for us. The trademark suit had been traded in for something vaguely country—khaki pants and a pink-checked shirt, adorable—and the boater on his head was pure frat-boy preppy, but at least it covered his shiny scalp from the Florida sun.

"Mr. Rockwell," I said, smiling through my teeth. "You came."

"I try to make it to the local events, to check in on my team," he said genteelly. "That was an excellent dressage round, Jules. It's nice to see how well the summer's investment worked out."

I couldn't deny the technical truth of that statement. "Thank you," I said. "Mickey was really great. I'm proud of him."

"You rode him," Rockwell said, rocking back on his heels. His penny loafers were dusty with the red clay from the horse paths. "Take some credit for yourself. Dressage is about strong riding."

Well, no, it wasn't, I was pretty sure, but that was fine. Rockwell was no rider. He was an investor, and I happened to be what he'd invested in. For whatever reason. "We're just waiting for the score," I said.

On cue, the horse in the arena walked out, his rider patting his neck, and the loudspeakers crackled to life. "In the Training Horse division, number 112, Danger Mouse ridden by Juliet Thornton, has a score of twenty-five point five."

"Holy shit," Pete said, and squeezed my knee.

I couldn't say anything at all. *Twenty-five point five.* That was blue ribbon territory right there, without even having to hope the leaders ended up with time penalties or a refusal. I'd never gotten anywhere near that kind of score. I'd never gotten within ten points of that kind of score.

Mr. Rockwell smiled and nodded. "That's why, Jules," he said. "I'll see you all later for the stadium jumping. I probably won't be up early enough for the cross-country." He turned and walked away, while I still sat dumb and in shock.

Twenty-five point fucking five.

Then I turned back to Pete. "What did he mean, *that's why*?"

Pete grinned. "I think it's pretty obvious he meant the summer with Grace, babe."

Oh, that. "Did he just tell me 'I told you so'?"

"Jules, he's got the big bucks. He *can* tell you that. And anyway," Pete said mischievously as we started walking back toward the barns, acknowledging the nods of congratulations from the obviously impressed crowd. "With a score like that, he's damn right. That's why we did it."

I smiled, but it was a smile full of half regrets. Was a perfect dressage score worth this awful year? "Would you do it all over again?"

"Me?" Pete looked up at me, a little surprised I had to ask. "Of course I would. And I hope you would too."

I thought about it as the event unfolded around us. I knew I'd do it all over again, although hopefully I'd do it a bit differently. But even if the outcomes were the same, even if I couldn't change a damn thing about the way I'd behaved and the way Pete and I had nearly fallen apart, I knew I'd have to do it again. This was our lives. There was no tearing the eventing out of it. We were stuck this way.

"I'd do it again," I admitted, and Pete smiled up at me, his hand on my knee, a familiarity I had missed for so many months now.

"Of course you would."

26

A DAY LATER, Sun Valley Horse Trials was in the books and we were loading up to go home. I was so proud of our horses and us, I could hardly stand myself. According to Pete, that meant no one could stand me, either, but he seemed to be managing.

Pete closed the ramp behind Barsuk's gray-dappled hindquarters and I double-checked the hitch with my usual obsessive-compulsiveness. Then we climbed into the truck cab and admired the splash of color on the seat between us: our five big rosettes from our five big wins. My eye caught Pete's and he flashed me a smile that was still largely surprised at the way the weekend had turned out.

"I can't believe we won all our divisions," he said for the tenth time.

The fact *Pete* was amazed made it all the more astonishing to me. I wasn't used to blue ribbons. I was used to red ribbons, and yellow ones, and white ones—God I had so many snow-white fourth-place ribbons, it was like I was trying for some kind of purity championship—but as we'd gotten to the upper levels, where it was more about finishing the event in one piece than bringing home the top prize, I'd resigned myself to being a bit of a lady-in-waiting for the first-place spot. I figured it would come with time and experience, but it wasn't my moment yet.

And now all of a sudden, I'd won two divisions.

Okay, it wasn't a big event. *Okay,* it was for Training Horse and Novice Horse. *Still.* Pete's blue ribbons were for Open Intermediate, Open Prelim, and Open Novice. We'd swept our divisions. That was crazy, and it was bound to get us a little buzz. Team Briar Hill was officially on the map for the winter season.

Now all we had to do was kick ass at Hope Glen in six weeks, against actual competition. Sun Valley Horse Trials was nice, but it wasn't a three-day event in the middle of Florida's winter season, when the world descended on our cross-country courses for a piece of our good-weather pie.

The sun was in our eyes as we drove west on the county road toward the interstate, the fence lines on either side of us dipping with the rolling hills of south Marion County. I looked out the window, counting the horses, thinking about coffee. "Let's get off at 200 and stop at Starbucks," I suggested.

"It'll add a half an hour to the drive home," Pete protested. "And the stoplights there are such a pain with the trailer."

I pointed at our blue ribbons flooding the dashboard—there'd been too many to hang from the traditional spot on the rearview mirror without impeding Pete's view of the road. "We deserve espresso. And cookies. Maybe pound cake."

Pete nodded—there was no assailing that logic, I thought

triumphantly—and I wiggled in my seat a little, anticipating the bite of coffee on my tongue. It was four o'clock, with a full day behind us and a full evening ahead of us. A girl could use some caffeine to get through it all.

My phone buzzed on my lap and I grinned at the name on the screen. "Alex wants to know how the event went."

"Tell her we bombed and we're closing the farm."

"Too close to the realm of possibility," I said snidely. I texted back *all blue baby*.

Yes!!!! Next time Im coming.

As a groom

Of course!!

"Alex wants to be our groom at Hope Glen."

"Isn't she your boss?"

"Yes. I could see where this could get weird."

"Is this like, horse-girl inception?"

"I didn't understand *Inception*."

"I didn't think so."

"Whatever." *It'll be fun*, I texted her.

An hour later, coffee in hand, cake crumbs on shirt, I walked Mickey to his stall, threw the lead rope over his back, and let him walk into his stall without my assistance. He dug his nose into the feed bucket Ramon had left waiting there, the sweet feed covered with a light handful of hay to keep the flies off. I snapped up one of his stall guard's ends and went back to get Jim Dear. Pete walked by with Dynamo and I managed to stop myself from gazing longingly at my chestnut horse's profile as he went past me, apparently utterly content with whatever human was going to direct him to his stall and his dinner. It hurt, but what part of the Pete/Dynamo arrangement didn't hurt? He'd just won Intermediate on his first time out on my horse. That in itself was a wound I would need plenty of alone time to lick.

Jim Dear, on the other hand, greeted me with quivering love, whinnying uproariously as I walked up the ramp to get him. He was the last one in the trailer and didn't know how to react to this sort of tragedy. "Did you think we were leaving you out here for the night? Silly. Only humans have to sleep in horse trailers." He pulled at my grip as I walked him down the ramp, but I let him slip alongside me without letting him bother me too much. I'd spent so much time at Alex's barn, I was starting to ignore antics just like a racetracker.

Horses got silly sometimes, so what?

It was a huge turnaround from my entire life of demanding perfect manners from my horses, but right now I didn't have time to think about the life-changing philosophy of it all. I just needed to get shit done.

Jim charged into his stall and started digging into his feed before he'd even gotten his hindquarters all the way in. I smacked him on the butt. "Can we please enter the stall before we eat our dinner, dude?" He shoved the rest of the way in, rubbing his tail on the wall as he scooted his hindquarters around without bothering to pull his nose from his bucket. "You're a dork," I told him, but he ignored me.

Across the aisle, Regina eyed me darkly. She had her horse ball at her hooves, as if she'd been pushing it in front of her as she shuffled around her stall, dribbling the ball like a kid playing soccer, and shavings clung to her burgundy bandages and her short dark mane. She'd been down while we'd been out horse-showing. Her boredom was a palpable presence in the barn, like an angry spirit hovering in the rafters, eyes watching us wherever we went.

I walked over to say hello and her nostrils flared at my Starbucks cup. I remembered seeing Pete give her little handfuls of coffee sometimes, and the way she'd lapped it from his palm like a dog. "I can't give you any caffeine now, princess," I told her regretfully. "You're already too keyed up as it is."

She snuffled at my hair and my shirt, then swept her ears back and pulled her lips up, showing her teeth. I stepped away quickly. She was getting nastier as the days of stall rest went crawling by. By the time she was allowed turnout again, she'd be a dragon.

A shadow appeared in the barn aisle, and I looked up, expecting Pete. But it wasn't him—Pete was pulling the trailer around behind the barn. I saw who it was and jumped, back into biting distance of Regina, whose teeth clicked dangerously near my ear. I jumped again, and Alejandro laughed.

"Your horses are so crazy! She almost take off your ear!"

"She's on stall rest," I said. "We just got back from an event. What's up? Did you need something up at the training barn?" I wasn't sure what terms we were on after Alejandro helped us sell Rorschach the other day. I still felt like there was a lot of bad blood between us, even if it was all on my side because I missed my arenas.

"No, just came down to say hello." Alejandro came into the barn and rubbed at Mickey's face as the horse poked his head out inquisitively. "This white horse is pretty."

"That's Mickey," I said reflexively. "My big horse." Maybe it was kind of sad my big horse was only at Training level, but that would be remedied. I ticked over the weeks in my head again. Six weeks to Glen Hill. Then we'd make the jump to Modified, run around a few times, and go Preliminary. So soon, yet not soon enough. I missed the big jumps.

"Ah. Big horse." Alejandro nodded. "We want to tell you how much we like the farm. Mr. Blixden say when this barn come available, he rent it too. Rent whole place. Now he wants to breed. Racehorses!" Alejandro laughed, as if this was the most insane thing he'd ever heard. "Everybody in Ocala wants a racehorse. There is something in the air."

I started to take a step back, then remembered Regina and moved to the center of the aisle. Anything to put a little space between me and Alejandro, who was still slowly moving closer and closer, with a stealthiness that reminded me of a coyote flitting through the morning mist, tracking a foal. "This end of the farm won't be for rent, though. We're not leaving."

"Not now." He smiled a toothy smile. "Maybe later. Maybe the trustees get tired of waiting."

"The trustees?" I was halfway down the barn aisle and my constant backing away was getting obvious. Where was Pete? Cleaning out the trailer, probably. I wondered if it would be too obvious if I shouted for him. "The trustee is working with us to take care of the estate while it's in probate." I used a lot of words I only half understood, hoping Alejandro didn't know the first thing about real estate law either. "Everything is moving along at the correct pace."

"Really?" Alejandro took two quick strides and he was right in front of me, so close I could smell the leather and horse on him. "Because what I hear is you cannot pay, and the attorney is no longer going to represent you. What I hear is you are going to get a letter very, very soon. And then Mr. Blixden is going to buy some broodmares for my brother to manage. Guillermo is good with breeding. He has several big winners in Argentina. He would prefer to be breeding horses rather than jumping with me. He's crazy, but what can you do? Ocala makes a man insane, only thinking about fast horses and money."

"I thought you were better than this," I said bitterly. "The other day, with the horse for sale? You were on our side."

"A favor," he said. "It was good fun." Alejandro reached out a calloused brown hand and touched my shoulder. I jerked backward, but his fingers closed around my arm. His dark eyes bored into mine. "I am sorry you will lose the farm," he said softly, "but you need more money to play this game."

I wrenched away from him, clenching my fists almost automatically, and he had the presence of mind to take half a step back, as if he hadn't expected me to have any fight.

What did he think, I'd spent my life wrestling with horses and dealing with gross men like him just so he could come into my barn and put his hands on me and offer softly spoken threats?

"You can get the fuck out of here," I snapped, as vicious as Regina, who fed off my anger and kicked her stall wall in outrage. "You can get the fuck out of my barn and don't you dare ever come down here again. You put a toe past the training barn lane and you're on *my* property, and I call that trespassing. And if you have a problem with that I can call the sheriff's department and tell him you've threatened me and I am in fear of my safety. And we'll see what he thinks about that. Get. The. Fuck. Out."

Alejandro didn't get the fuck out, which *really* pissed me off— and kind of scared me, too.

"I'm thinking you'll regret all that," he said. "Maybe someone should teach you a lesson."

Instead of leaving, Alejandro got closer. A lot closer. Suddenly, I was against the wall and although my fists were still clenched, I was aware that he was bigger than me. My lip curled. I wondered where exactly I should hit him. It had never come to this before. I had ideas, though.

A half a breath later, my hand *hurt* and Alejandro was backing away with his own hand to his face and Pete was coming into the barn shouting and Regina was kicking the wall again and Alejandro started screaming and Pete actually *picked up a pitchfork and ran after him* and I didn't know what was happening anymore. I went into the tack room and shut the door and sat on the bed, and Marcus climbed up onto my lap, and when I eventually started to cry, he licked away my tears as a disgusting, darling beagle will do, and I let him do it.

27

PETE CAME IN after a few minutes.

He sat on the bed next to me, annoying Marcus deeply, who wiggled away and curled around my other side, his tail thumping on the bed. Pete ignored Marcus; he was used to the beagle's maneuverings to be my one-and-only. "Did he touch you?"

"No." I leaned my head against him. "I punched him."

"Of course you did." Pete sounded amused. "Why would I think he would get to hurt you? Of course you'd throw the first punch."

"The *only* punch," I said, proud despite myself. Who's afraid of the big bad trainer? Then I sobered again. "He basically admitted that they're plotting to kick us off the farm. I didn't realize it was going this far. He said Blixden wants the whole place. Got a bug in his brain about breeding racehorses now."

"I had a feeling it was something like that. Should we be surprised? Isn't this just par for the course? Isn't this just how horse people are? Everyone's all acting like we're in the same boat, blah blah blah, and then you get stabbed in the back and they take your horses, they take your students, they take your farm." Pete rubbed his face.

"That's exactly what this business is like." It was a jungle out there. Too many crazy people, too many rich people, too many long days and sleepless nights for too little money—it drove the semi-normal to acts of insanity, and the genuinely insane to heinous conspiracies. Like conspiring to get a struggling couple kicked off their family farm. Little things like that.

I felt like this was an in, though. A moment to help Pete come to the only rational realization. If I could cut a few weeks or months off this cycle, I was going to go for it.

"How far are you willing to fight this?" I asked. "Because we can keep going as long as you want. But—"

"But?"

But we're going to lose. But in my head I've already moved on. But we can work our asses off and throw money on this bonfire for the next six months and the final result will still be the same: too much farm, too many players, not enough cash from the two smallest competitors in the room.

I wanted to say all of it, but I knew that if Pete hadn't already begun coming to this conclusion himself, he'd resent me like hell for saying it.

I backed down.

"Nothing," I said softly. "I'll do whatever you want. It's your farm."

He tightened his arm around me. "It was going to be *our* farm."

I closed my eyes, but the tears were long gone. "Maybe it wasn't."

We turned out the horses in the glowing embers of an October sunset, the sky fiery orange and red, as if it was trying to make up for the lack of fall colors in our still-verdant trees. I walked Dynamo and Mickey out together, a lead rope in each hand, and they trailed behind me, nibbling at each other's noses and nickering deeply to each other. They'd become friends through all the trailering and time spent in different stables, pushing their noses through the bars and looking for familiarity in a place full of strange horses. When I turned them out and closed the gate behind them, no one went running off to act silly—the weekend had taken too much out of them. They just ambled a few strides away and then stopped to groom one another, grinding their teeth against each other's withers in a show of brotherly affection. Barsuk and Jim Dear watched with pricked ears and astonished expressions, as if they couldn't imagine that level of love between two competitors—but I'd bet they'd be doing the very same thing after the coming season.

Pete was resetting Regina's bandages when I went back in, the aisle's fluorescent lights flipped on to pick out all the chipping paint and sagging wood of the old stalls. She tipped her hind leg and hung her head from the crossties, barely bothering to prick her ears when I walked into the barn. Sixty days of stall rest wasn't easy on any horse, but do it to a top event horse at the literal peak of fitness, and you saw full-scale depression kick in. We'd have to spend time with her, cheer her up. Maybe buy her a goat for a friend? Or would a goat just piss her off?

I crept over and leaned over the leg for a look, careful to stay out of Pete's light. He was dabbing the wound site with cotton soaked in Betadine. New flesh was creeping up to meet over the long gash that ran around the back of her heel and fetlock.

"Almost patched," Pete said hoarsely, putting aside the spent cotton. He rubbed a flat cotton pad with antiseptic and wrapped it around the wound, then carefully held it in place while he took a fresh pillow wrap and covered Regina's leg from knee to fetlock. It was insanely hard to get the pillow wrap to hold the cotton pad in place, but after doing it daily, Pete had become a master. He could teach college-level classes in wrapping now.

I handed him the roll of wine-colored standing wrap to go over it and he slowly unwound the length of nylon into place, until the white pillow wrap was almost completely covered. He pressed his finger under the top layer, by her knee, to be sure it wasn't too tight, nor so loose it would slide down. Wrapping complete. He groaned as he stood upright and I thought of offering to reset the bandages on her other leg, but decided to let him do it. It would be better to have the same hands and muscles handling the wraps—that would keep the pressure the same and help her feel balanced and comfortable.

Regina flattened her ears and showed me her teeth when I ducked under the crossties to look at her from the front. I took a respectful step back. Pete was able to walk around her with impunity, but then again, she'd always regarded Pete as her personal property. If she hurt him, she would probably only do it out of some sense that it was for his own good. One thing I'd learned about mares from watching Regina (and listening to Pete wax poetic about mares): they thought they were in charge of keeping their humans safe. They were the heads of their herd, no matter whether it was a herd of mares and foals or a foolish two-legged rider. Boss mares were tough to convince that anyone was in charge but them.

"Do you want to do stalls tonight?" Pete asked when Regina was finally wrapped. "I'm going to pick out hers. But I'm kind of tempted to just eat something and go to bed early tonight. It's been a long weekend."

"We can get up early and do stalls in the morning." I sighed. "I'm tired too."

"Or just get up when we feel like it and do stalls."

Neither of us were working in the morning. We could sleep in. Still, I looked over at him skeptically, but Pete was already in Regina's stall. A forkful of dirty hay came out of the stall door and sailed into the wheelbarrow parked out front.

"Whenever we feel like it?" I asked.

It felt like Pete was living extremely dangerously. A dirty barn? *Overnight?*

But then again, what difference did it make, at this point? Who was going to see it? Who was going to question us? We were alone out here, at the back of the farm. We'd looked good in public this weekend, and maybe that was really all that mattered. Maybe the scrutiny Carl Rockwell and Amanda feared wasn't going to come. Maybe no one cared what our barn looked like, as long as we won divisions. "What the hell. Let's do it. I'll help you finish up here."

As I went down the aisle to grab him some shavings, I wondered, with a curiosity that was almost clinical, if this was where it all began to end.

28

SUNRISE CAME LATER and later as autumn marched on, and the small window, half obscured by the air conditioner, didn't let in much morning light.

Which meant we slept luxuriously, the air conditioner droning in our ears like a giant white noise machine, until just past seven thirty.

That might not sound like a lazy morning to everyone, but for Pete and me, after six weeks of getting up at five most mornings to gallop, and six on Mondays, it was incredibly decadent. I stretched and looked with awe at the faint light in the window, and Marcus wiggled at my feet, hoping I'd just stay in bed all day with him.

Too bad, puppy-dog—once I was awake, I was awake, my senses alive to the thousands of things on my to-do list. The very first thing, of course, was getting the barn ready to bring the horses in. I climbed out of bed, leaving a drowsy Pete to protest behind me, and pulled on a pair of shorts and a sports bra. There was leftover coffee from the night before waiting in the fridge; I took a deep drink from the icy cup and waited for the caffeine to hit my veins. "I'm going out," I said unnecessarily, a throwback to the days when we lived in an actual house with separate rooms, and one of us could be momentarily unaware of where the other person might be. I'd nearly forgotten what a luxury that had been.

Regina stretched out her neck and whinnied at me, a demanding *Where the hell is my breakfast, wench?* kind of whinny. I blinked at her for a moment, trying to decide if I should give her grain or hay first, and then I realized there was someone in the barn.

"Oh!" I said stupidly. "Mr. Blixden!"

There was absolutely no good reason for our tenant to be in the barn right now, or ever, actually. Then I dimly remembered the events of last night. Had I actually hit Alejandro in the face?

I flexed my fingers and felt the soreness in my knuckles. Yes. Yes, I had.

Well, shit.

Blixden was looking around the dirty barn with disgust. We hadn't even raked last night, so the place really was a mess. Regina whinnied again and I realized what a mess she was, too; covered with shavings and hay in her mane, her bandages rumpled and stained with manure from lying down last night.

Really it was just general, overnight dishevelment, but for a man like this, who had probably never seen a horse who wasn't sparkling and ready for the show ring, it had to look like plain old bad horsekeeping.

"Jules," he barked. "I came down to see what you have to say for yourself."

"I—" It was too early for this. I needed more coffee and possibly some coaching from an attorney. "What?"

"You attacked my trainer last night! This is absolutely unacceptable. We're going to be pressing charges, of course—"

"Wait, stop there." I was awake now. "Pressing charges? Your hotshot show-jumping champion is going to press charges against a woman he was attacking in her own barn? Even in Marion County I don't think that's going to get very far."

"Attacking, Jules? Can you cut the drama?" The phrase was very teenage girl but that was exactly who Blixden liked to surround himself with, so I guessed it made sense. "We both know that Alejandro wasn't going to touch you—you took things too far by hitting him. We're not going to tolerate this kind of behavior. You've been difficult from the start. We're doing you a favor by renting this place and—"

"No, no, no." Lack of caffeine or not, no one bullshitted Jules Thornton. I straightened up and walked down the aisle, taking heart from the way Blixden stepped back a little as I approached. "You can yammer about your idiot brigade down there at *your* barn and that's fine, I'll let you. But you're not going to stand here and lie to me. You're not going to tell me you're renting my barn and my house and my fields like some sort of act of charity. You're here because the price is right and the location is right, and you still try to bully me around constantly. I haven't ridden in my own arenas in weeks. That's right, *mine*," I growled when he tried to protest. "We stopped using the arenas because your little band of bullies wouldn't give us enough room, despite the contract that says we all have to share the arenas. You have been taking up far more of what's mine than any dollar amount you've been able to pay us, and sending your trainer down here last night to try and scare me is just the icing on the cake. You know what? I think we're going to evict you."

Blixden stared at me. He didn't know we couldn't evict him for months, did he? He wasn't a real estate mogul or anything. He'd never been on the receiving end of thin white letters from landlords. He was just a rich asshole. "Eviction sounds a little crazy . . ." He started to chuckle, as if we were just joking around here.

"No, I think it's the right answer," I said thoughtfully, index finger to chin. "I think it's for the best if you just start packing up. We'll have no problem finding someone else. I mean, it's less than two months until the winter hunter/jumper circuit begins, and we're five minutes away from the showgrounds. Renting this place out to the highest bidder is probably the best strategy now. We're bound to get twice what you agreed to pay."

"What's going on here?" Pete came out of the tack room at last.

"Oh, just letting our tenant here know that we're about to kick him out. You have anything you want to add?"

Pete, bless him, played along. "I'm sure you covered everything. Mr. Blixden, did she cover everything?"

Blixden spluttered like a wet cat.

"Excellent. Jules, ready to get started?"

"Of course. Mr. Blixden, I apologize but we have work to do. So could you just . . . move along?"

And I turned my back on him, heading for the storage stall to get a fork and wheelbarrow. There were nine stalls to clean before we could even feed. It was going to be a long morning.

But at least we'd gotten some sleep, and I'd finally gotten to bitch out Blixden. I was focusing on the little triumphs right now.

Over post-chores coffee, watching the horses snarf through their grain, Pete asked me the big question.

"Where are we going to go next?"

I looked at him over the rim of my mug. Pete was ready to take the next step, at last? This was the push I hadn't wanted to give him last night—the violence, Blixden's bluster, the knowledge that we just couldn't afford to play this game anymore, and it wasn't doing us any good to pretend.

I swallowed something; coffee, the lump in my throat. Finally, Pete was ready to admit what I'd been thinking for weeks. We had to go.

I took a moment to probe my heart for regrets, but I was ready for what came next. The main feeling, right now, was relief that Pete was going to be okay with the next step.

Finding a new home.

"Do you want to stay in Ocala?" I asked him, after clearing my throat.

"I think so—I mean, our contacts are here. Amanda is here—don't make that face! She got the price for Rorschach, didn't she? Plus we have Alex, and I know you don't love teaching but Alex could be the start of something good in that department. Plus, this is where the events are. We'd have to drive back constantly—it would be crazy to try and head somewhere else. We have to stay through the winter, if nothing else. There won't be anything going on anywhere else until spring." Pete paused for breath, then laughed. "That's my laundry list. What about you, though? Where do you want to go?"

I thought about the whole wide equestrian world as if it was mine to play with. Aiken, South Carolina. Hunt Valley, Maryland. Lexington, Kentucky. Or someplace off the beaten path, where we could probably make some money training, where we'd be big fish in a small pond. I imagined riding in Texas, in Arizona, in Washington State, in Ohio . . .

"I'm a Floridian," I said eventually. None of those other places sounded appealing to me. Maybe for a summer home. I'd always kind of dreamed of going to upstate New York and competing on the Area One circuit some improbable summer. But year-round, to give up this crazy place with its palm trees and its gentle hills and its big animated sky that lit up in a million colors every night at sunset? "This is my home. I'd like to stay here."

Pete nodded. "I don't blame you. And anyway it seems like half the world is moving here. If we left, we'd be giving up a lot. And just driving here constantly regardless."

"Things are probably more expensive outside Ocala," I added. "Feed and hay and bedding."

"Exactly. We'd be pushing our expenses up, and we can't do that. So the next question—where in Ocala?"

That part, I couldn't answer. I'd come here with just enough money at just the right time, and bought my own little farm without ever having to rent stalls or board my horses. From my farm, I'd moved straight to Briar Hill. What would we have to pay for something decidedly less high-end, that still gave us access to training facilities? I imagined life without our cross-country course and nearly choked on my coffee.

Pete whacked me on the back. "You choking?"

"I'm fine," I coughed. "We're just going to have to shop around, I guess. Consider someplace not so convenient, like Romeo or Bronson." Way out west or northwest, in the sandy hills beyond Ocala, close to where my old farm had been. Desirable only by proximity, not by actual quality of grazing. Or passable roads.

"Good idea." Pete got up to refill his coffee, leaving me to gape after him.

Seriously, how was he so calm right now?

290 | Natalie Keller Reinert

"Pete, are you really ready for this?"

He shrugged. "I don't know. I guess I want to be ready."

"It's just talk," I said, trying to be reassuring. "Nothing's definite."

"You've got that right." He laughed, and the sound was brittle.

I reached for him, and he let me take his hand.

We stood still for a moment, watching the horses across the aisle shove at their feed buckets, slamming them against the walls as they got down to the last few precious bites of sweet feed. Regina took her bucket and shoved it into the wall. She'd break the snap off this one soon; she broke at least one snap a week, and then she'd throw the bucket into the center of the aisle and glare at it. She'd blame that bucket for all her troubles. I could almost hear her raging mare-thoughts.

What is going on? Why am I stuck in a box? Where the hell will I be tomorrow, in two weeks, in six months? Who is making the rules in this game?

29

I STOPPED BY Amanda's after work the next morning.

I didn't really mean to; that wasn't my trajectory when I got back into my truck at Alex's barn. But I hadn't yet told Alex that we were looking for a new place; since she had a horse with us, she'd be full of questions that I couldn't answer right away. Still, I was bubbling over with nervous energy, and I had no one to help me use it up. Pete was still working. Lacey was busy, and all my texts were left on *delivered*. Becky wasn't generally the kind of person I could go to for advice or support; we were on good working terms, but I didn't want to push my luck.

So I had all these ideas, and one big, silly, possible idea that kept floating to the top of my mind, and there was no one to tell me if it was really good or really bad.

When the turnoff for Amanda's came up, I just flicked on the turn signal and took it.

She wasn't my first choice for our rescuer, but I knew deep

down Amanda was naturally sweet, something I was not, and wouldn't hold my previous coldness against me. She wasn't a frenemy type of person. Amanda was just *nice*. I didn't like it, because I didn't understand it. But right now, I thought she might be exactly what I needed. What Pete and I both needed, perhaps.

Her farm was down a long driveway lined with oak trees, which opened up to a center-aisle barn with cream paint, green shutters, and a trotting-horse wind vane on the cupola. Palm trees danced around a bubbling fountain. There were a couple nice cars parked out front, BMWs and Mercedes and a Subaru wagon, students or boarders or buyers I guessed, and there was a striped tabby cat lying in front of the aisle, soaking up the sun and watching a couple of long-legged ibis poke their red beaks around in the grass lawn.

Next to the barn was a tidy red-clay arena with a hunter course set up. The jumps were so boring, I could cry, all brown and gray and green, set up in prim and proper straight lines. *Give me a show-jumping course any day,* I thought, and then decided to try not being so judgmental for just ten damn minutes. Resolved to behave myself, I went into the barn.

A shining chestnut horse whinnied at me from the first stall, peering through the bars, and farther down I recognized the dark head and white blaze of Rorschach, leaning over a plaid-patterned canvas stall guard so he could eat his hay in the aisle, like a cretin. Even though the barn was paved with immaculate horse-friendly paving stones, and evidently swept and dusted to a sheen of almost alarming cleanliness, I could see that Rorschach was up to his usual habit of making a total mess, and it brightened my spirits. Even a perfect barn was still just a place to keep horses.

In the center of the barn, about six stalls down, there was the usual office/tack room/restroom arrangement, and above these three doors a staircase led up above the stalls. My eyes followed it to its second-floor landing, and settled on the size of the apartment at the top. It extended above the offices and tack room, but not much more, which likely meant it was a twelve-by-twenty-four-foot box. Basically, a foaling stall.

I considered it for a moment, and the point of my visit.

We lived in a twelve-by-twelve box with optional horse trailer right now. Doubling the size would be pure luxury.

I heard Amanda speaking in the office and poked my head in. The oak-paneled room with its satin ribbons hanging from wooden rails and framed photos of jumping horses had been lifted directly from an equestrian lifestyle magazine. Or maybe I'd seen this room in a magazine at some point. Jesus Christ, how rich was Amanda? I'd known she had a nice farm and nice horses, but this place was the last word in hunter/jumper luxury.

Amanda was leaning back in her chair, deep in conversation with . . . a phone. I backed out of the office as soon as I realized she was on FaceTime with someone. I gave the wall a little knock to announce my arrival.

"Hold one sec—" Amanda peeped around the doorframe and saw me, Little Orphan Annie in skinny jeans and a stained polo shirt and two-hundred-dollar paddock boots from my rich benefactor, and smiled in confusion. "Jules? What's up? Is Pete—" She looked up and down the aisle and then back at me, her eyes widening. "Is Pete okay?"

"He's fine, he's fine, he's probably just getting home from work by now," I said quickly, holding up a hand to slow her racing thoughts. It hadn't occurred to me she might jump to the worst reason why I showed up alone. Although it was interesting she'd think I'd come to her doorstep if anything happened to Pete.

Whose doorstep *would* I come to?

Enough of that for now. No time for introspection. Time for action. "I came to talk to you about the apartment."

Her eyes softened, her lips turned up. "I was wondering when you'd come to your senses," she said. "Come right in." She went back into the office and picked up her phone. "Diane? I'll call you back later."

I caught sight of the face on the phone's screen just before it went dark. "Was that Diane *Meyer*?"

"Mm-hmm! She's a really good friend. We were just talking about a horse of mine that'd be perfect for one of her students."

Diane Meyer was an elder stateswoman of the eventing world. I'd never even met her, just seen her from afar at events and wondered how someone got so . . . so awesome. So confident and wise, gray-brown hair pulled back in an eternal bun, lines grooved into her tan skin that came from galloping strong horses over big jumps in bright sun all goddamn day . . . I wanted to *be* Diane Meyer someday, and Amanda was chatting with her on FaceTime about a hunter?

"I didn't know she did hunters," I said cautiously, settling into one of the green-padded leather chairs before the desk, which would have been well suited to a Manhattan gentleman's club.

"Oh, she doesn't. But you know I just find horses the right homes. And I have a really nice client horse out there who was bought to be a jumper and is just dying to be an eventer. So I called Diane and she's into it. We work together a lot."

"What about Pete?" I blurted, because this seemed dishonest, telling Pete they were partners on all these sale horses but then calling someone else the moment she had a *really* nice horse for sale.

"Well, Pete can't afford this horse," Amanda said bluntly, softening the blow with a friendly smile. "And Diane has students who can afford it, too. I'm on the lookout for him, of course. And when he does have a student with the cash, well, I'll call him. The same goes for you, by the way. Especially with the goofball Thoroughbreds. You're so good with them. I'd call you in a heartbeat if I got one in."

She was laying the flattery on pretty thick, but that didn't mean I couldn't enjoy it, just a little. "Thanks. I guess I see your point." Pete used to have students, but with the loss of the arenas the last of them had disappeared. I hadn't paid too much attention; I didn't like teaching and avoided it whenever possible.

Except for Alex, but that was different. Alex was a horsewoman who just needed help with a young Thoroughbred. I'd probably have helped her out for free. If there were more people like her, maybe I'd have more students. "How often do you get Thoroughbreds?" I asked suddenly.

"Not that much," Amanda confessed. "It's a shame, because there are so many nice ones and most of them are next to free, but a lot of people just can't ride them or they need too much work to get to the point where your average ammie *can* ride them. I mean, there's plenty who would try, but they just need constant help and A, I don't have time and B, they're not my area of expertise. Not like you and Pete."

"Amanda, what if . . ." I paused, because what I was about to say was crazy, but then went on because everything was crazy now. "Amanda, what if we partnered up with the students you have that might want a Thoroughbred, but aren't sure they can school it on their own?"

She lifted her eyebrows. "You mean like, you come over here and teach the student? I haven't had outside trainers before."

"No," I said. "I mean we take the student on together. You

work on their form, I work on their horse. When I have questions I come to you, and when you have questions you come to me. We tag-team. We teach together."

"That's interesting. I never heard of anyone doing that . . . Wait. Is that why you came over? I thought it was about the apartment, and I gotta be honest, I would love you guys to stay here, I would love to help out in any way possible, of course, but—"

"It's about the apartment, I admit, but I think this could be good for you, too. How many cheap Thoroughbreds have you passed up because you didn't have time to prep them for a client? And how much could you have sold them for in six months if you'd taken them?"

"Oh, God, dozens in the past year alone. They're like apples hanging off trees, you just reach out and choose." Amanda grinned. "Jules, I think you're really onto something!"

I settled back in the club chair and let Amanda think aloud, writing down notes, making the project her own. And I thought about the phone call I'd make to Grace later, letting her know I'd finally figured it out, I'd finally found a way to make money that wasn't like everyone else's model, the way she'd told me to all summer long.

"And you'll move into the apartment?" she asked, her eyes bright on mine.

"I think we can work something out," I said. I almost believed we could.

I stopped to get bagels on the way home, and the guy's price was so good on alfalfa I had him throw a couple of bales from the semitrailer behind the deli into the back of the truck, too. Typical Ocala transaction: grab breakfast for yourself *and* your horses in one stop. That was why it would be so hard to leave this town, where everything was built for the convenience of horse owners. I didn't know if there was anywhere else in the world like it. Was Lexington this convenient?

Well, it snowed in Kentucky, so that was an automatic DQ, either way.

Alejandro and the rest of the boys were riding in the jumping arena as I passed by. I guessed his face was okay after I punched him, because he didn't have any problem sending me a menacing glare. I got the message—stay far away from my own arenas. No problem, asshole. I was in the process of putting Briar Hill behind me. There wasn't going to be any more time to mourn. We'd lost. Again. So what? As long as we kept winning at events, I'd take it.

Pete was already mounted when I pulled up to our barn, sitting on Dynamo but not actually going anywhere. He just paused there, face lit up by the late-morning sunlight, as if he'd been waiting for me all this time.

"Where were you?" he asked when I got out of the truck. His eyes fell on the white paper bag I was brandishing in one hand. "Is that breakfast?"

"It is, but since you decided to go riding without me, I'll put it in the fridge for you."

"That's okay, I'm sure Dynamo wouldn't mind hanging out in his stall for a few minutes while I share breakfast with his lovely mother." Pete swung down from Dynamo so fast I had to wonder if he'd been planning on riding at all. I peered at his face, trying to read his mood, but he turned away from me, leading Dynamo back into the dim barn aisle.

"Everything go okay this morning at Ridge?" Pete had started riding grown-up racehorses at Ridge Thoroughbreds, a gargantuan operation about twenty minutes away. I'd driven past the place and found the sheer size of it intimidating—it looked like an actual working racetrack, minus only the grandstand. There had to be fifty or sixty stalls in the training barn alone.

"It was fine. I got to ride a few breezes for horses about to head to the races, so that's some extra money. We'll be able to pay the vet bill this month."

"That's awesome!" The vet bill for Regina had been added to the list of imaginary payments we'd be able to finish someday, like my Visa bill. And my MasterCard bill. But Ridge paid really well, and breezing a racehorse paid extra. It wasn't something I'd ever done, and I wasn't sure Alex was planning on teaching me, so I had to be content with the less lucrative work of training the yearlings and taking a few older horses for long, "slow" gallops that still felt incredibly fast when they weren't broken up by rolling terrain and jumps.

"And I got an offer on Barsuk that would help us out a lot with the attorneys."

I stopped dead. Pete went on walking, taking Dynamo into his stall. He slipped off the bridle and left my chestnut horse to browse at the hay pile in the corner.

"What?" he asked, looking back at me.

"Pete, you can't sell Barsuk."

"Why not? We need the money."

"Why not? Because he's a good horse and he has a lot of potential and you two could go places together!"

"That's why he's a good buy for somebody," Pete said patiently. He hung up the bridle and walked over to me, taking the paper bag from my hands. Marcus appeared like magic from wherever he'd been snoozing and nosed the bag, his tail beating against Pete's boots.

"But if you sell him, you're losing your best horse—with Regina out of commission. And who knows—"

I stopped myself. Pete looked at me. Regina looked at me.

Marcus looked at the bag.

I swallowed and went on. "Who knows when Regina will come back? What if she doesn't? Then you have a bunch of novices and show jumpers. What about your next upper-level horse? That's got to be Barsuk. Or you're going to have to buy something. You have to have a three-day horse of your own next winter and that's going to be Barsuk. Obviously. Or—"

Pete's jaw tensed and he looked away.

"No," I said.

His hand tightened on the paper bag. "Of course not."

"I'm sorry."

"No." Pete looked back at me. His eyes were red, his cheeks were flushed, and I could see his jawline trembling. Just a little, just a tiny tremor, but it told me all I needed to know—this was the breaking point. This was as far as casual, easy-breezy Pete was going to make it. This was when the reality was going to take over. His voice was wooden when he spoke at last. "I'm sorry. It was awful of me to even think it. He's your horse. This was always temporary."

We both looked at Dynamo at the same time, pulling at hay from behind his stall guard. And I had to admit, he didn't look like something that should cause so much conflict we couldn't even voice it out loud. He was a nice horse, he was an athletic horse, he was a beautiful horse, but he was still, if you had to say it in so many words, just a horse. And this was Pete, and we loved each other, and we'd been through so much together, I'd thought I'd let nothing come between us ever again.

But he couldn't keep Dynamo forever.

My sacrifices could only go so far.

"I'm sorry," I said again, and Pete started to reach out a hand to touch me, then pulled back, as if he didn't know if he should be mad, or sad, for both of us.

30

WE DIDN'T TALK about the ending, not at first. We just ate our bagels (because no matter how sad you are, when you work this hard, you have an appetite), and I tacked up Mickey and we rode out to the cross-country field together. We jumped some fences and galloped some sets, because we both felt too aggressive and miserable to think about anything more precise than a hand gallop and some big fucking fences, and then we walked the horses with a loose rein along the top of the ridge and looked at Ocala beneath us. It was nearly noon already, and the main work of the day was done at the breeding farms and the training centers. Only the sport horse people slogged through the entire day, riding and riding and riding and riding. Everyone else got naps built into their schedule. We'd picked the wrong discipline. I yawned.

"These mornings are killing us," Pete said eventually.

I nodded absently. We'd been working six mornings a week for at least six weeks, an equation for exhaustion squared. But bills had to be paid.

"We can't keep doing it through the eventing season," he went on.

"It's not just talk anymore."

He looked at me questioningly.

"Yesterday?" I reminded him. "Yesterday it felt like it was just talk. Today, we have to make up our minds for real."

About home, about horses, about us, I thought. But two of those decisions were already made. I looked at him, and knew he felt the same way.

Pete ran his hand through Dynamo's mane. "Wherever we can go and make this work, I'm in. Are you?"

I looked at him. He gazed out across the farms, his hands resting gently on Dynamo's burnished copper mane. "Pete," I said, "as long as we're together, this works."

He closed his eyes. I nudged Mickey closer, until our stirrups clanked together, and leaned into him. I wrapped an arm around his shoulders and pulled him closer to me. I felt his shoulders sag, I felt his face crumple, I felt the hot tears touching my cheek, and then my own eyes were burning and my tears joined his. We cried for Briar Hill Farm, and Pete cried for his grandmother, and probably his grandfather, too, and I cried because seasons end and horses get older and our time together is so short. "I'm sorry," I whispered. "I'm sorry, I'm sorry."

The horses shifted beneath us, but kept in one place; they were used to being close to one another. At events, in the paddock, in the barn, in training, Dynamo and Mickey were my two children, siblings bound by their mother's love. They knew, with a keen and arguably bizarre instinct, when their humans needed them to just be still and behave themselves.

We cried until a cloud drifted in front of the sun and a cool breeze, perhaps the first truly chilly air of fall, brought up goose bumps on our bare arms. Then we laughed, a little hysterically to be sure, and compared our bumpy flesh, holding our arms together. "It's winter," I said, giggling. "Winter is here."

"We have to find someplace warm for winter," Pete said solemnly, and then he grinned. "Do you have a plan for us?"

I remembered the morning that had been a thousand years ago. "Almost. I'm going into business with Amanda, so maybe we should just move there."

Pete pulled back far enough to stare at me, to lift his eyebrows, to let me know that he was completely and utterly floored. "With *Amanda the Hunter Princess*?"

"Yes, so? Shut up. You can keep Barsuk now. We'll have a place to live and extra money coming in, and next winter you'll have Barsuk ready to go . . . it all works out."

"I'm just thinking that you really, really love Dynamo," Pete said, his smile rueful. "That you'd pick working with Amanda over giving me your horse."

"The fact that I could let you ride him at all—" I began soberly, but Pete put a hand on mine, cupping my palm against Mickey's warm neck, and I waited for him.

"I know," he said softly. "And I'll never, ever forget it. But I'll try and make it up to you."

Alex came over to ride in the afternoon, and I told her we would probably be leaving Briar Hill before the year ended. As soon as possible, really. I hated waiting around.

"You can't do that," she said confusedly. "No."

"Well, it's kind of like . . . we have to?"

"Well, what about me?" She looked very agitated, pushing loose strands of hair behind her ears.

"There'll be stalls wherever we go. You can come with."

She sighed and pressed a hand against Tiger's neck. The dark bay leaned back into her, as if he was happy to offer comfort, but then his demon apparently won out over his angel, and he whipped his head around to nip at her. The crosstie stopped him and he pulled back, startled. We had a fun couple of moments convincing him not to flip over in the crossties, during which time I thought about the way he tried to bite her without ever pinning his ears. It was like he thought she was just a buddy horse. I'd never had a horse who had raced for as many years as Tiger had, and clearly it adjusted their behavior and the way they related to humans in interesting ways.

Alex came back to his head once there was finally some slack in the crossties and Tiger was standing quietly again, pretending he hadn't just scared himself half to death. "It would've been easier to just keep tacking him in his stall," she panted. "What a dummy. It's just crossties, Tiger! For God's sake. Let's put him on the wall and forget this. He needs something behind him."

"What if you go to a schooling show without stalls and there's nowhere to tack him but at the trailer?"

She gave me an *Oh you just have an answer for everything* glare. "Fine. But how long is this going to take? He's gone back against the ties every day for a week."

"But he only reared up and broke them once," I reminded her. "And he hasn't flipped over at all."

"You have weird benchmarks for success," Alex informed me.

I shrugged and grinned. I didn't have to tell her that as a racehorse trainer, she had a lot of weirdness going on in her brain, too. We were birds of a feather.

I slipped into the tack room, where Becky had made an appearance and was sorting through bits, tossing the ones that didn't meet her specifications into a bucket of warm water. She'd put a newspaper on the carpet to keep it from getting splashed.

"Where did you get a newspaper?" I asked.

"Where did you get a carpet for a tack room?" she countered, raising her pale eyebrows at me. She tossed a seldom-used elevator bit into the bucket. *Sploosh.*

"Hey," I protested. "This is my home. I didn't invite you into my home to make fun of it."

Becky took a long, appraising look around the tack room's comforts: the queen-size bed with the dog prominently sprawled in the middle, the jumble of boots and sneakers by the door, the pile of breeches and T-shirts teetering on top of the antique dresser, the mini fridge humming beneath the silent window air conditioner. "It's actually really nice," she said. "I'd live here."

I felt a warm feeling spread in my chest. It wasn't often Becky said something approving to me. My homemaker skills were definitely questionable, but I thought I'd done a nice job turning the tack room into a studio apartment. And we'd managed to live here for nearly two months without even thinking about killing each other, which, considering the state of our relationship at the end of the summer, was pretty impressive. "It's worked out better than I thought," I admitted. "It was spur-of-the-moment, but I think we've managed okay. The kitchen situation can suck, like you said it would."

Becky started unbuckling the straps on one of Pete's show bridles. "Are you going to stay like this all winter? Remember how cold this barn gets?"

Pete hadn't told Becky we were going to leave? He probably hadn't said anything to anyone, now that I thought about it. "I don't know," I said finally, not sure where we stood.

She looked at me in that piercing way she had. Becky knew we'd already made plans. "Where will you go?" she asked.

"Amanda's," I said honestly.

"Oh," Becky said. That made me nervous, the way she said "oh."

"It's for the best," I said.

Becky put down the bridle in her lap, ready for a *let's get real* talk.

"Don't go to Amanda's," she said.

"What? Why?"

"Because Amanda is obsessed with Pete, for starters. Did you not know that?"

I blinked. "I didn't . . . I mean, I know she likes him, but she seems like she's getting over that. She's hardly ever over here anymore. Ever since we moved to the annex barn she's been pretty much MIA. She barely wanted to show one of Pete's horses to a buyer, we basically had to force her—"

"Because someone told her to keep her distance from Pete or there was going to be a problem. But I bet the minute you suggested moving into her barn she was all over it, right?"

"Someone—who?"

Becky gave me a more familiar look, the one that said, *Oh Jules, how do you remember to breathe all day long?* "Who do you think? I ran into her at the tack shop one day. I was behind some blankets when I heard her talking to one of the clerks about Pete. She said it was basically a done deal. She said he was the hottest guy she'd ever seen and . . . a lot of ridiculous teenager stuff, basically. The clerk was all over it because she was *actually* a teenager, but Amanda had no excuse for talking like that. So I came around the corner, the clerk ran for it, and I told Amanda that unless she wanted everyone in Ocala to know she was a homewrecker and that she injected horse tails, she'd better keep her distance from you two. And so she did."

Becky finished her story and went right back to wrangling with Pete's bridle buckles as if this was not the most astonishing thing she'd ever said to me in my entire life.

I sat down on the bed, cradling Marcus as he crawled into my lap, and stared at her. "I can't believe you said . . . and wait, injecting horse tails?"

Becky shook her head. "That's what you took away from that story? You never change."

"Why would you ever inject a horse tail?"

"So they won't swish it in the hunter ring. You numb the tailbone and they keep it still through their class."

My jaw fell open. "That's the most insane thing I've ever heard." I suddenly felt bad we'd sent Rorschach to that world. "And they say eventers are insane?"

"You jump piles of logs bolted together," Becky pointed out.

"But our horses *like* it."

"Well, that's true." She pulled the now-sparkling bit out of the water, triumphant, and held it up for a moment as if to let it know who was boss. "So anyway, back to the human drama, I just really don't think you should go to Amanda's. I'm not saying that you have anything to worry about with Pete, but I do think she's going to make your life a living hell. And, not that it matters to you, but I think it's going to make her life a living hell too. She just doesn't care because she thinks she can win this one. Like she wins every-thing else. Basically, things are going to get very ugly, and I know you don't like drama, so I thought you should be aware."

"Well, shit, Becky." I pulled at Marcus's ears. "I don't know what to do, then."

Becky shrugged. "There's always the horse trailer."

I glanced out the window at the trailer, parked behind the barn. Our mobile kitchen. The living quarters weren't exactly five-star. Or two-star. The thin mattress rested over the gooseneck in a claustrophobic cubby, and there was a couch facing the galley kitchen, a closet, a tiny bath, and . . . that was it. It seemed like the same amount of space as the tack room, really. Just with more stuff crammed into it. At least the tack room had a concrete floor and concrete walls and stayed in one place during storms.

I didn't want to live in the trailer. Plus, we'd still need someplace to park it. It was a nonstarter. Terrible idea. Perish the thought. "The trailer could solve our problems, but not the horses'," I heard myself say thoughtfully, as if from a distance. Why did I say that?

"You could find a pasture to rent." Becky put her hands into the bucket and started rubbing the bits, pulling out the leftover morsels of grass and hay that had caked into the joints despite a daily dip in the water bucket. "It would cost way less than trying to find a place with a house, too. Maybe you could throw the extra money back at the legal case. I'd think about it."

A *pasture* to rent, after having all of this! I thanked Becky ab-sently and walked back down the aisle of the annex barn, looking at the horses as I passed each stall. The barn had its faults, sure, but it was part of one of the most wonderful eventing facilities in Ocala. And it was still a barn. At least at Amanda's farm we'd still have arenas to ride in, an elegant barn to welcome clients to, a solid home base where we'd look professional to students and owners and buyers.

If we were living next to a pasture in a horse trailer, who would ever take us seriously?

A rock and a hard place, sure. But there really wasn't a choice to be made. I could fend off Amanda. I couldn't change the perceptions that owners would have of us if we were living like hobos alongside a rented field.

I wasn't even sure the owners would be wrong.

And so we waited, unable to decide. Blixden, possibly choosing to believe we could evict him, kept his distance—probably waiting for the legal system to evict *us*. I didn't tell Pete about Amanda, although I began to dislike it when he drove over to her farm to teach. She hadn't found any students to share with me yet, and I was glad. We just rode our horses, planned our winter season, and waited.

October turned into November in a series of cool nights and warm days. It didn't rain, although the humidity remained, creeping up at night and washing every surface with dew. Every morning, I watched the slow roll of gray fog twisting in the oak trees, hiding the turns one by one as we galloped the maturing babies around the racetrack.

The green pastures started to brown just a bit, left wan by the shrinking sun above and the dry sand below. We fed the horses dinner in the dark, and led them out to the pastures by the orange glow of the streetlight outside the barn. We watched TV on our laptops and talked about horses all the time, as if we hadn't just spent our entire day with them. We ate so much ramen Pete got fed up and bought a grill on a credit card he'd been saving for emergencies, and started making hot dogs and burgers and chicken every night until it ran out of propane.

Then we ate some more ramen. I didn't really mind. I found the warm noodles and salty broth comforting in the early darkness.

Sunshine State's November Horse Trials came and went so quickly I scarcely noticed it. We went, we competed, we got some ribbons, we came home. Carrie Donnelly, Mickey's half owner, emailed to congratulate me on Mickey's Training level win, and asked when he was going to move up. I pulled out the new wall calendar I had lying in wait for January first and double-circled the mid-January event at Sunshine State I'd already noted there, and wrote *Mickey— Open Modified!!!!!* underneath it, with a couple of smiley faces for additional effect.

Pete watched me with a smile. "I thought you'd already decided to take him Modified there?"

"Sure, but I really had to wait for the owners to green-light it," I admitted. "He's not my horse."

"You'd never know it," Pete said mildly. "You treat him like he's your infant son."

"Wouldn't you? Mickey's perfect."

Pete shook his head at me and went back to his phone. I rolled my eyes at him—he was one to talk about adoring his horse, with the Million-Dollar Mare pulling at her hay net a few feet away.

The day after Thanksgiving, we took advantage of a Black Friday sale and bought some electric tape and posts to make a little paddock for Regina just outside the barn. With her leg out of danger but her hoof still damaged from the wire, we were allowed to turn her out with the hoof wrapped up tight to keep the cracked wall secure. She went limping around the little pen with her head held high, swiveling her gaze this way and that, whinnying over and over until the entire farm was in an uproar. I could hear neighs from up the barn lane—even the Blixden horses were getting in on the action. A top farrier was being summoned as soon as he arrived in Florida for the winter, to lace up her cracked hoof with some special technique he'd pioneered, and the price quoted had made me feel faint.

Still, we waited.

We were waiting to know for sure—would the lawyers ask for more money and make no promises, or would they have good news for once? As December arrived with warm sunny days and crisping dry grass, we went once more to Gainesville and sat uncomfortably in office chairs for thirty endless minutes while a sharply dressed woman told us all the reasons Briar Hill would probably end up going to the college Pete's grandmother had willed it to years ago, despite our best efforts and all our cash.

"And they'll sell it," Pete said flatly.

"Probably," she admitted. "If you think you can raise the money, our real estate associates can assist you with—"

I thought fleetingly of Mickey's owners, who both had money of their own, but it wouldn't be enough. Not for a Millionaire's Row estate farm like Briar Hill.

Pete had looked just as lost. "We'll let you know, of course," he said finally.

"We look forward to it," she said.

We drove home in silence. In my head, I heard everything Becky had said to me in the tack room a few weeks ago. The Amanda problem wasn't going to go away—it would only get worse when we moved to her farm. She'd hang all over Pete until something happened—either Pete would fall for it, or we'd be so uncomfortable we'd have to leave, possibly in the middle of the night, following in the footsteps of so many horse trainers who fall out with their crazy landlords.

I looked out the window as the exit signs flashed past, testing each one of them for suitability as a future address. Archer Road—too built up, too many college students. Micanopy—too many expensive rolling hills and centurion oaks, just like Reddick. Highway 318—that new international equestrian center was going in here, driving up prices. We were going to have to wander farther afield than Ocala's suburbs to find a farm to replace Briar Hill.

Not that anything ever could.

"Let's get through the three-day," Pete said eventually. "Let's not decide anything until after that."

We had two weeks.

"That's fine," I agreed. Still, I knew neither of us would think of much else.

31

GLEN HILL THREE-DAY Event. Three days, three ways, as they used to say.

Dressage on Friday, cross-country on Saturday, show jumping on Sunday, Epsom salts soak on Monday. The fourth day just wasn't as publicized as the rest.

I wished my life still had a bathtub in it. Unfortunately, horse trailer living quarters were usually light on luxury amenities like that.

The weekend would be a nice trial run for Becky's idea of living in the horse trailer, anyway.

We were parked in a field full of other eventers living in their horse trailers, all of them varying degrees of fancy, some of them with elaborate setups out front for competitor parties, or just to look prestigious. A three-day event was a cause for breaking out the fancy outfits and scrubbing up the nice rigs. This was Big Name Trainer country, like a double-A-rated hunter/jumper horse show.

I loved it.

Sure it was intimidating to walk through the showgrounds amid all this so-called glamour. Eventing was still a muddy, dirty sport but it was getting fancier every year, trying to catch up with the champagne and silver watches of show jumping. I would have preferred it if we'd stayed the scrappy underdogs of the equestrian world, but a lot of people seemed to think eventing would be better if sponsors threw tons of money at it, and while admittedly it was nice to have actual prize money at these big events, rather than a gift certificate for a framed copy of your favorite photo from the show photographer, I still looked around at the big-name trainers' tents and stall curtains with a wary eye. The more money in the sport, the less room for people like me.

Of course, I *did* have a big horse with big owners, and he was hanging out back in the stable, waiting to see what this was all about.

Meanwhile, Pete would be riding Dynamo.

Dynamo's first run over an Intermediate three-day course. He was a little late for it as a teenager, but he could handle it. My red machine of a jumper could handle anything. Even going out into the toughest competition of his life without me on his back.

Could I handle it? That was another question, one I wasn't willing to answer on record, which was going to be a legitimate problem if Pete and Dynamo won, because the *Chronicle* reporters were definitely going to want to know how I felt about it. I was resolved, though; if there were tears, I'd keep them private.

There was a food truck parked by the vendor village with a small crowd around it, waiting on orders. I felt in my breeches pocket for cash, came up with a twenty, and rolled on over. I had twenty minutes before Pete was meeting me for our cross-country walks. Time for a snack.

The food truck seemed to specialize in grilled cheese, which was not the most healthy food for a crowd of so-called athletes, but probably the most logical offering since we were all facing a bloody terrifying cross-country course in a few days. I joined the queue, trying to decide between the gorgonzola and bacon, or the cheddar and apple. The one with apple was at least *pretending* to be healthy. If I had that and a bottle of water, I wouldn't be the worst person in the world.

"Jules! Hey, Jules!"

I spun around. Alex ran up, face bright like a kid's. I heard a few people nearby murmur my name to one another.

"Alex! I thought you'd be here tomorrow."

She slid into line next to me. "I'm buying. Put your money away. And surprise! I wanted to course-walk with you, if that's okay. If not, I can babysit the horses. It'll be like the old days in the quarantine barn."

"The what?"

We shuffled forward in line. "Some tracks keep the day's racing horses in a special fenced-off stable with security. It's to prevent drugging and foul play. I once spent six hours just sitting in a folding chair in front of my horse's stall, because we were in the last race and rain delayed the card halfway through."

"That sounds . . . boring."

"You'd be surprised what we get up to at the track," Alex said. "One of the other assistant trainers gave everyone who wanted one a free haircut."

I eyed Alex's shoulder-length tresses. "Did you take her up on it?"

"Free haircut? You better believe it." She ran a hand over her hair. "Was it the best haircut in the world? No."

I laughed. "Well, you can walk with us or you can hang out with the horses—it's up to you. We have to do a couple courses so it's going to take an hour or two to go over everything."

Alex grinned. "I'm here to learn, boss!"

Around us, I heard whispers intensify. I bit my lip to stop myself from smirking. People wondered who the woman with Jules Thornton was. They wondered who Jules was competing this weekend. They were probably wondering what kind of show I'd give them, either on horseback or off.

It didn't matter where we lived, I thought. It mattered where we showed up, and how fantastic we looked and rode when we got there.

T here's not a question on this course that Mickey hasn't answered already, and looked good doing it." Pete put his hand on a casual pile of logs that happened to be a Novice level obstacle and gazed back across the field we'd just traversed. "He'll come flying up to this log, though, because this galloping lane is going to have his blood up. So you'll really have to whoa him before that."

We were paying more attention to Novice fences than I ever had in my life, and that definitely included my first time out at Novice, when I was a bloodthirsty and fearless tween. I needed everything to go right for Mickey today. Even though his division was unrecognized by the United States Eventing Association— three-day events didn't technically become a thing until Preliminary level—they were high profile, loved by competitors and fans alike. There would be press coverage at every level, even Novice.

Alex stood nearby, arms across her chest while she studied the jump. "Why do all the jumps look so much bigger now than they did when I was sixteen?" she asked, head tilted.

I grinned. "Never take a break, first rule of fearless eventing."

Pete walked a few strides away and looked at the logs. "Whoa him *here*," he said. "Half halt, half halt, leg—"

"I'm aware of how to get him over a log jump," I said dryly. Pete the Trainer was in full effect, which brought out my automatic response to authority: scorn. "This is nothing. It's *that*—" I pointed to a fairly unnerving setup around the water complex, down the hillside from us. The jump into the water was tricky enough, over a small upended boat and down several feet before splashing into the water. Then we had to canter through the water and jump out over a skinny angle set against an oak tree. Everything was within Novice height and width parameters, but the questions were much tougher than anything I'd asked Mickey before—or anyone else had asked their Novice horses this year. We could end up a lot of places we didn't really want to if our landing into the water was anything other than perfectly straight. We could have a run-out to the left, around the skinny. Or we could accidentally run right into the oak tree to its left. Anything was possible, really.

Pete eyeballed the water complex. His targets weren't much better. The Intermediate boat was sized up so significantly it looked more like a yacht, and his skinny obstacle, on the other side of the tree, was actually a pair of skinnies a stride apart. Oh, and there was a fence in the middle of the water to jump too. *Another* damn boat. Had there been a sale on boats the day the course designer was picking out new fences for the year? "We better go down there and walk some distances," he said.

Well, that was why we wore Wellingtons.

A few other riders and trainers were splashing around in the water when we got down there, some pale-faced Young Riders stepping up for the first time, with a lined and grave-looking coach watching them count their strides and lean on the top poles of the skinnies, checking to see how forgiving their bolts were.

That some horses were going to hang a leg over one of these fences wasn't just a possibility, it was a certainty—a lot of horses were going to lack the impulsion they needed, coming out of the dragging water, to get over both of the skinny fences with style.

I felt a momentary pleasure that I was riding the lower levels this time around.

Sure, Advanced was my goal, but why borrow trouble from someone else's course? It wasn't my battle to fight today. I just had to show Mickey a good time so he wanted to step up in the next event.

"If you land slightly to the right, you'll be set up good for the middle jump," I told Pete, pointing out the line. "It's not dead even."

He sloshed over and squinted at the drop into the water. "You're right. It's a broken line. What fun."

"Dynamo will have a lot of power through the water so you're going to have to land facing this fence or he's going to drag you right past it before you even know what's happening."

He nodded and climbed out of the complex to examine the footing and approach to the drop a second time. I smiled. Who was the trainer now?

I went over to wobble my own skinny, noting the wooden branch across the top was pretty flexible and probably wouldn't cause any problems for our forward momentum if Mickey hit it. I paced out the complex again in my head, deciding on the speed we'd need for it, and then I watched Pete muttering to himself at the drop. He was going to ride my horse out here in two days. He was going to take my advice and ride it the way I would ride it. We'd come a long way, hadn't we?

Still, sometimes he looked blank when I glanced over at him, after I'd made a stupid joke and didn't get a reaction. He was far away a lot these days, off in his head, inaccessible to me. There was no denying he was different than he'd been last year.

He was putting on his competition face long before we departed for the shows, because it was the one that came with blinders, the one that allowed him to shut out everything else in the world. It made him a better competitor, but it took him away from me at the same time.

He started splashing through the water again, scattering Pony Clubbers with the determined set of his chin, marching through the strides he'd ask Dynamo to canter on Saturday. I felt a kind of longing as he walked through, his focus so far away from me I missed him as if he'd been gone for days, for weeks, for months. I was going to have to bring him back, I realized suddenly. I wasn't going to be able to wait him out. Pete was the most determined competitor I'd ever met, even more so than me, though he'd never admit it. What I accomplished with bluster and ambition, he accomplished with quiet determination and an inability to be shaken from his chosen path.

He'd disappear into that terrifying dedication if I let him.

I pushed off from the hanging log and made my way around the massive oak tree dividing our two fences, meeting him as he came out of the water for a second time. Only he didn't see me.

"Pete," I said as he walked past, his chin jutting and his eyes fixed on the next cluster of obstacles. I reached out and caught his arm.

He nearly pulled away from me and my stomach dropped; then he stopped himself and blinked at me. His eyes were the color of his royal-blue jacket.

"Wait for me, huh?"

"I'm sorry," he said, looking confused. "I guess I got distracted."

"The opposite," I said, pulling his arm so we pressed together. "I had to distract you."

Pete looked at me for a moment, opened his mouth as if he was going to say something, and then pressed his lips closed. He gave my arm a gentle tug. *Time to move on, time to finish walking the course.* I beckoned to Alex, who tripped after us, staying a little behind to give us room.

We needed the space, I thought. A quiet place where we could just be together, thinking only about our horses—not what came after this weekend, the big question we couldn't answer yet: Where were we going to go next?

Hoofbeats. The rhythm of Mickey's breath. His nostrils made a purposeful little snort every time his front hooves hit the ground, the force of his gallop making his exhalations more efficient. A Thoroughbred, molded by rich Englishmen to turn oats and oxygen into miles and speed, nature's most perfect machine. My hands were pressed close to his mane, his hot neck, the sweat soaking my gloves; my breath huffed with his.

The world cupped around us like a bowl of blue on a pale green saucer, winter fields and live oaks draped with Spanish moss, a flock of ibis that strayed into our path and flew away in a white cloud, and Mickey galloped on, ears latched onto that log pile leading down to the water complex.

I lifted my hands as we neared the fence, bringing my weight back slightly. He shifted his balance in response, raising his head and shortening his stride to collect—then he changed his mind and dug down against the bit, anxious to get at the fence as quickly as possible.

"Nope," I scolded in my trainer voice, my mom voice. "Come back, mister, we aren't going to land on your nose!" I was a little more insistent with my hands, pushing my heels against his sides as I reined back.

His head came up again, and this time he stayed with me, bouncing in stride right to the base of the log pile. Up, my hands sliding forward along his neck, keeping a contact with his mouth, connected to his thoughts, but giving him room to maneuver.

Mickey saw the water ahead mid-leap. I felt the surprise in his body, a sudden stiffening, but by the time he landed he was charging forward again. *Water, that's not so scary,* he seemed to be telling himself. *We've done water.*

"We've done water," I agreed aloud, guiding him toward the jump that would take us into the water. "We've done it all, buddy."

The water splashed all around us, creating sparkles in the sunlight, landing in cold drops on my thighs and arms. Mickey threw up his head, his gaze latched onto the skinny jump beyond the water complex. We wouldn't miss it. We couldn't miss it. We were unstoppable.

32

ALEX MADE US stand posed with our rosettes and our horses, fully tacked, the sweat wiped clean from our faces. "You deserve a win photo, you guys," she insisted. "I don't understand why that isn't a thing in eventing."

"We didn't win?" I pointed at Mickey's red ribbon. "There's not a show photo in racing, don't lie."

"Or a place photo," Pete said, sighing. "Yellow is not a great color for you, Dynamo."

"How dare you," I countered. "All colors are good on Dynamo. He is a red rose who makes everything better."

"Maybe not a professional photo, but it's fun to take a pic with the barn crew after a successful race," Alex said patiently. "Hey, hey buddy!" She waved down a passing horse show dad, who looked at her, startled, and then accepted the phone she pressed into his hands. "Just a real quick photo for us please. *Landscape,* not portrait." She righted the phone in his hands. "Unless your daughter is around?"

"She's off somewhere with her horse," he said, holding up the phone. "I've been looking for her for two hours."

"Horse-girl life," I said approvingly, as Alex wedged herself up against Mickey and clung to his bridle. Pete and I stood next to each other, reins in our hands, hard hats on our heads.

The horse show dad tapped the phone a few times, evidently already aware of his photographer duties thanks to his daughter. "Anything else?"

We inspected the phone's camera roll.

"I like Mickey's face in this one," Alex announced. She patted Horse Show Dad on the back. "Check the picnic tables by the food truck. There's like two dozen teenagers over there grazing their horses. I guarantee your daughter is one of them."

"Thank you," he said gratefully, making his escape.

"Good weekend, guys!" Alex said, snatching the rosettes off the bridles. She was a startlingly efficient groom, probably because in real life she was a training barn manager, and this was just a fun weekend off for her. "Let's get your ponies untacked and showered. I'll go fill some buckets."

"Where's Becky?" I asked, looking around.

"Finishing up packing the trailer," Alex said. "We have a plan in place to get out of here in two hours. You're welcome."

The horses were back in their stalls for some hay and relaxation before we headed home, and Alex had already festooned the stall bars with their red and yellow rosettes before she'd gone off to have a beer and watch the end of the show-jumping competition. The efficiency of the weekend had been dizzying.

I wasn't sure I wanted to go back to life before Alex started volunteering for us.

Even Becky had been nicer than usual.

I flicked a mosquito off Mickey's second-place ribbon. "This was a good weekend."

Pete leaned against the stall wall. "Too bad it's over, right?"

I laughed. "Exactly. Are we ready for this talk?"

"No time like the present."

"Okay." The deadline was here. Glen Hill was over. We had to make up our minds. "I don't think we should move to Amanda's. I think we should rent a place for ourselves. Even if we still train with her." The last part was half-hearted; I would rather cut ties with Amanda altogether, knowing what Becky had told me, but there was still the question of how to pay rent on another property.

Pete crossed his arms. "Seriously? Still against Amanda?"

I sighed. "I don't want to argue about this, Pete, not here—"

"Look at what we got this weekend." Pete gestured to the rosettes. "We're on a roll right now. We have a sponsor. We have momentum. We have to run with this. If we go to Amanda's, we'll have exclusivity. We'll be able to charge a premium for stalls and training. It's a really sound business move—maybe even better than having our own place."

I held up my hands, the universal symbol of surrender. *I give up. I won't stand in your way, please do whatever you think is best.* "I already told you I was willing to work with Amanda. It's fine. But I think you should know she's into you."

"What?" Pete shook his head. "Let's not do this again—"

"No, Pete, this isn't me being weird. Becky told me. She said we shouldn't even go over there, it was so bad."

"Well? You want us to pass this chance up because our landlady has a crush on me?" Pete's voice was so harsh and cutting, it hardly sounded like the man I knew. The man I loved. The man who could get away with a lot more than anyone else with me—but he better watch it.

"Of course not," I said. "It's just an FYI. If things do get weird with her—"

"Things won't get weird," he said brusquely. "We're all professionals."

Were we, though? We might be professional horsemen, but we were still humans. With . . . hearts, and things. The emotions I had always tried to avoid, but which Pete stirred up in me so effortlessly. He wasn't just my first boyfriend in the shacking-up department; he was my first boyfriend in the *holding hands omg he likes me* department. Maybe I was the emotionally stunted one here, but moving into Amanda's space with our relationship in recovery mode and her eyes firmly on the prize didn't sound like the best move for our future.

Still, I could only say that so many times.

Becky rolled up with a wheelbarrow full of water buckets, pushed so delicately by her precise efforts that hardly any of them spilled, and we, along with a few barn neighbors, gathered around her to exclaim at her extreme bucket-transportation prowess, leaving behind the conversation about our future.

Becky didn't seek the center of attention, but she did enjoy being told she was a genius groom, so she basked in the praise and laughed at the stories of bucket-lugging gone wrong—"My boots were soaked for the rest of the weekend, there was water dripping from my heels in the show jumping"—while I stood on the outskirts and laughed along, trying to shake off Pete's refusal to listen to me. I scanned the showground absently, taking in the constant press of horses and humans and dogs.

I caught my breath when I saw her, and then my fists tightened at my sides.

Amanda was here. On *my* turf, dammit.

She was walking between the barns, looking around with avid curiosity. I knew what she was looking for. I thought about raising my hand to wave her over to us, get it over with, but then I stopped. I didn't want to be found. Not yet.

This was Pete's problem now. I'd tried to get him to listen to me. Maybe if I gave her a few minutes of alone time, Amanda would give herself away.

I crept down the shed row a few stalls and slipped behind a fat steel support.

I peeped around it like a child playing spy, and saw Amanda's face the moment her gaze landed on Pete.

She looked at Pete with an adoration I knew she couldn't help, and my heart broke for her, and for myself, and for Pete, because I knew this was going to end badly. For her, more than anyone else. I'd end her before she'd get her claws in Pete.

Then he slipped away from the crowd, retreated into the barn aisle, and she stayed with the rest of the eventers. I watched her until I realized Pete had emerged from a breezeway and sidled up behind me. I jumped at his touch on my shoulder. "What the hell are you doing?" I hissed. "You *scared* me."

"Are you okay?" he asked softly, not answering. "You wandered off. I'm sorry if—"

"Watch her," I interrupted, and pulled him behind me.

Amanda was looking around with naked longing plain on her face, wondering where her man had gone. A blind person could see it. A heartless person could feel it. This had gone from fun crush to true love. This was why she'd stopped coming to the farm, where we heedlessly entertained company and clients in our bedroom. This was why moving to her farm would be a complete disaster. Would Pete see it?

"Oh, Jesus," he whispered, probably more disappointed I was right than anything.

I tugged him back into the breezeway he'd popped out of a moment before.

A lop-eared gray horse leaned over his stall webbing and watched us curiously, chewing slowly at his mouthful of hay. I pulled Pete behind the horse's hay net and the horse ducked back into his stall, surprised. "We can't do it, Pete. Not with her feeling like this about you."

"Jules, I would never . . . There's nothing to worry about from her. You don't have to keep us apart, I swear."

"Pete, I won't do that to *her*."

He looked at me from lowered lashes, like a guilty child. "We can't let this stand in the way of our plans."

"We can't do this to her. You saw the look on her face. She's in love with you. I'm not going to parade around like a happy couple in front of her, even if—" I stopped.

"Even if?"

I set my jaw. I wasn't going to say it.

"Even *if*?"

Why bother now? I was in too deep. "Even if you haven't decided to forgive me for the summer yet."

"Oh, Jesus," he said again. "This?"

"I haven't been able to do *anything* that makes you happy yet," I plunged on recklessly. "But it's fine, Pete, that's not what this is about. This is about being the bigger person and respecting some-one's feelings."

"You've never been about that," he said. "That's not the Jules I know."

"Well, it's the Jules I'm trying to be. It's the Jules you always said you wanted to see."

His hand gripped my wrist and he pulled me to him. "I only want the Jules in front of me right now," he whispered.

Holy shit, what was it about men? I tiptoed around him and his hurt feelings for two months and he gave me nothing. I scolded him in a barn aisle and he looked like he wanted to throw me into a stall and rip my clothes off.

His face was so close to mine, his eyes boring into mine, that I would've let him do it, too.

He was moving in to kiss me, and I decided not to wait and leaped up to meet him, bumping our noses. It spoiled his grand romantic gesture, but part of me wanted that—he didn't deserve to get all the credit here, he didn't deserve to be the hero. After all, I'd been the one putting in all the time, waiting him out, edging around him with a sensitivity I hadn't known I'd possessed. I denied him his win even while I took mine.

Every now and then, the old Jules came out.

It didn't matter; if he wanted the win, he conceded to me grace-fully anyway.

He saw this as an ending to the hostilities, a truce, a return to our old treaties, and that much I could give him. I wanted the same thing.

At last we pulled back, breathless, and we gazed at each other with starry-eyed delight. As if after all the comfort and steady hab-its of living together, the heady excitement of *this person is so hot and this person is into me too* comes flooding back. It's like finding out your crush likes you back, even though you've been with your crush for ages already. It's all the fun of that first kiss without all the agony leading up to it.

Well, in this case there was a lot of agony, but it was mostly of the waiting-around variety, not the *will he or won't he* variety.

There was a rustle in the grass outside the barn, and then we both turned to see Amanda peeking around the corner. There was a lot of spying going on today, I reflected. Her pale face flushed red, and she stepped back, her expression clouding. I saw her unhappiness and for once my heart went out to her. She just wanted the same feeling I had, and no one could blame her for trying to make that happen, because it was the best feeling in the world.

"I'm sorry," she whispered. "I'm intruding."

Pete didn't say anything, and I couldn't think of what to say that wouldn't be a lie. And in a moment she was gone, lost in the sea of eventers and trainers and grooms and spectators wandering the grounds.

Pete sighed. "At least I think it's done. She's not going to come back after that."

No, she wasn't. You didn't walk in on your crush entwined with his girlfriend and then come back for more punishment later. Goodbye, business partnership. Goodbye, Pete's hunter broker. Goodbye, for real, barn apartment and stalls.

"Goodbye, Amanda the Hunter Princess," I whispered.

Pete put his arm around my shoulders and gave me a squeeze. "We'll figure this out."

I leaned into him. "We always do."

When we meandered back to our stalls, Rockwell had arrived and was introducing a well-dressed couple to Becky, who was holding out her hand gingerly. "I've been mucking out, and I'd hate to get manure on you," she was saying with the same measure of gentility she would use if she was explaining that she'd just taken her puff pastries out of the oven and might be a little sticky.

The woman refrained from shaking her hand and smiled gratefully, one of the few people who seemed to genuinely appreciate Becky's candor. She was in her fifties, dressed in that beige-y, linen-y, accent necklace-y kind of fashion wealthy women in Florida tended to affect, with the requisite capri pants and horse-show-friendly thick-heeled sandals. A straw sun hat was perched atop pale gold curls. Her husband, dressed for a Jimmy Buffet concert in a palm-tree-sprinkled Tommy Bahama shirt, made a big show of shaking Becky's hand and then wiping it on his khaki shorts. When he laughed, his tan face deepened into the kind of lines you got from squinting at the water. A fisherman, or a boater, anyway.

Rockwell looked anxiously over Becky's shoulder as we walked up, and I wondered how long he'd been looking for us. *He could've texted,* I thought, and then I felt the pocket of my breeches begin vibrating with the urgency of a series of aftershocks. I slipped the phone out and looked: text notifications filled the screen. I guess we'd been in a dead area down in the barn breezeway. *Whoops.*

"Pete and Jules," Rockwell called. "I've brought some friends to meet you. Mr. and Mrs. Delannoy."

"Please," Mrs. Delannoy said. "Call me Louise."

"And I'm Rick," Mr. Delannoy added. He held out his hand to Pete, but hauled me in for a hug and a kiss on the cheek. He smelled of sweat and cologne. I grimaced against his shoulder.

"The Delannoys drove up from the east coast for the event," Rockwell went on. "Melbourne, right Rick?"

"Melbourne *Beach*," Louise corrected. "The quiet side," she added to me, as if we shared a secret knowledge of Melbourne Beach. The only thing I actually knew was Kennedy Space Center was somewhere nearby.

"We'll make this short, because they have a long drive ahead of them," Rockwell said. "The Delannoys want to syndicate an event horse. And after today's performance, they know they want you to ride it."

He was looking at Pete. I sank against his side, overwhelmed with both the bad news and the good.

Pete seemed to be shocked into silence. He was thinking the same thing, I thought. He was thinking that he'd just won an event, but not on his horse.

"That's incredible," he said after a moment. "I don't know what to say."

"Say you're up for it." Rick laughed. "Or else we're going to have to shop for another rider! But we were looking for a Florida boy and you fit the bill."

My mouth fell open. I couldn't help it, I *couldn't*. Pete wasn't even *from* Florida. *I* was from Florida. I was Florida-born and bred. Pete lived in Florida because that's where his grandfather had moved and built his farm. His family was from up north. If Rick knew that, he'd have called him a Yankee and moved on.

Louise caught my look and smiled sympathetically. "Rick just said 'boy' out of habit. We thought you looked wonderful out there. Maybe when you have an upper-level horse we can talk more. That gray is really beautiful, isn't he?"

I almost died right there on the spot. *Maybe when I had an upper-level horse?* Who the hell did they think had trained Dynamo to Intermediate? Who made this all possible? Who had saved the damn day by letting Pete ride her big horse to keep the sponsors happy?

Me! Me! Me!

"Mr.—Rick, I think you need to consider—" Pete's voice was strained. "I think you need to understand—Dynamo is Jules's horse. She just gave me the ride while my upper-level horse is out of commission. Jules *does* have an Intermediate horse. It's Dynamo."

Louise raised her eyebrows. Rick looked from Pete to me and back to Pete.

"That so?"

Pete nodded.

"Well, that's pretty impressive," Rick drawled.

I stopped breathing and waited, heart thudding.

"That's a devoted woman and that's the kind of thing we like to see. And you sure did an impressive job winning with a horse you just started riding. Carl, you were right about this guy—he's the one, all right!"

There was a lot of backslapping and laughter and self-congratulating while I felt myself falling into a deep pool and Pete did an impressive job of holding me upright, his arm like steel around my shoulders while he accepted their hearty praise and agreed to send them a list of potential horses by the end of the month.

I hardly noticed when they left, although I'm sure I shook Louise's hand again and endured another kiss from Rick. I just knew the afternoon finally grew quiet and I sank onto a straw bale outside of Mickey's stall, letting the horse lip at my hair when he grew bored of his hay net.

Pete sat next to me and took my free hand, the one that wasn't playing with Mickey's mane. "I don't know what to say," he murmured after a few minutes of silence ticked by. "That wasn't expected."

I choked back a bitter laugh. "Pete, that's what I'm starting to expect all the time."

"You should have been riding Dynamo, though. This is my fault."

"This is no one's fault," I said, and I knew it was true. "This was the way the stars aligned. The sponsorship terms, Regina, the farm . . . neither of us could help any of it. It happened *to* us. We didn't do it."

"I always thought we had more control than that in life. They tell you, you can do anything if you just work hard enough. Remember? I don't remember a teacher of mine ever saying, shit just happens and you can't control a damn thing."

"They didn't want to scare us away from reality." My mouth twisted in a wry smile. "How hard would *you* have worked if you'd known life would be ninety-nine percent just surviving crazy quirks of fate that happen without rhyme or reason? A horse is fine one minute and dead lame the next. A farm has kind-of-annoying tenants one day and tenants blackmailing us with legal action the next. All the bio homework in the world couldn't prep me for real life. Those teachers just lied to keep their jobs."

Mickey chewed thoughtfully on my hair, and I pulled gently at his whiskers to tickle him. The scent of his warm breath on my cheek was comforting, and so was Pete's hand tightly clenching mine, grinding my fingers against his. Skin to skin, bones to bones, we were forged tightly now, a partnership baptized by one wildfire after another.

"I'll help you find a horse," I said after a while.

"I don't want you to be my *helper*," Pete said. "It's not like that guy said, it's not like you're here to help your big brave boyfriend succeed—"

"I want you to get a new horse so I can have my horse back, stupid." I laughed, and kissed him to make up for calling him a name.

Becky walked into the barn looking businesslike. "Off that straw bale. I need it. Also, if you're looking for a pasture to rent with arenas nearby, High Springs Equestrian Center has some open. There's a flyer down by the manure pile."

Pete and I looked at each other. High Springs was at least an hour northwest of Ocala, maybe farther. It was a long way from our snug central location along Millionaire's Row. But it was rolling and green, and not total exile.

"Let's take a walk to the manure pile," I said, extracting a chunk of hair from Mickey's teeth.

"I knew you were a romantic at heart." Pete offered me his elbow.

33

"WELL DONE, ALEX!" I shouted. "Bring him down to a walk and let's call it a day."

Alex sat down in the saddle and imperceptibly brought Tiger from a canter to a walk. He rolled the bit in his mouth and held his neck in an impossibly beautiful arch for a moment before she let the reins slip through her fingers, and he stretched his nose to the ground. "That was amazing," she said. "I should have come here a year ago."

"You've done plenty on your own," I said, waving away her compliments. "I'm literally just an extra pair of eyes for you."

"Much-needed extra eyes. I can't believe I'm going to drive all the way to High Springs to take lessons with you."

"I can't either."

Alex laughed and I waved to her as I started back to the barn. The clear patch of ground where we'd been riding for the past few months was slowly turning to hard-packed dirt, as our horses' hooves wore away the grass. In spring, the grass would return, because we would be gone.

Alex wasn't letting go of Team Briar Hill, though. She'd insisted we keep the name, and to seal the deal she'd literally stolen my truck one afternoon while I was riding in the cross-country field and had a vinyl decal with BRIAR HILL FARM—EVENTING and my phone number applied to the doors. I couldn't believe she'd do something so audacious, but she just laughed and said life with Alexander was teaching her to do whatever she wanted, because he wasn't going to approve of her either way. "Now I just apply that philosophy to everyday life," she went on. "Because the entire horse industry disapproves of me for something or another. Tell me you love the truck."

"I love the truck," I'd admitted.

The next week, she'd done the same thing to Pete's truck.

So we were stuck with the name, for at least as long as we had these trucks. I liked the gesture; it made our leaving less final. As if maybe, someday, we'd get back here.

Pete was in the tack room, which was nearly all packed up. Our little studio was just a bed, a bin of saddle pads and another of wraps, and the couple of saddles and bridles we absolutely needed. Everything extra, even my desk, had been moved to a storage unit. There wouldn't be room for it in the horse trailer, although I was considering turning my smaller trailer's horse-space into an office once we were moved and settled. It wouldn't be climate-controlled, but it would be a shady place to keep my desk and files.

The plan was up in the air, though, until we saw what life would be like at the new farm. Everything, except for the eventing schedule, was up in the air.

Pete was sitting on the bed, teasing Marcus with a piece of

hoof. When he saw me, he tossed the hoof into the aisle and Marcus launched after it like an Olympic long-jumper. "You done with Alex?"

"She's all set. She's taking Tiger home tomorrow."

"I still feel bad about that."

"She's trailering up once a week, and I'm coming down once a week. Two lessons a week should be plenty. She's got someone working on jumps; I guess she finally just took a paddock out of commission and told her husband it was her riding arena now."

"What a life."

"What a life," I agreed. "Anything else going to storage, or are you all set?"

"There's just one more thing," Pete said. "And I thought you should see it first."

"Oh? What's that?" It wasn't like Pete to be mysterious. I looked at him questioningly, and he quirked his eyebrow at me, the way he always had, since the day we'd first met in an airless barn aisle just a few miles away, waiting for our futures to begin.

"Come on."

His grandfather's tack trunk was in the farthest corner of the storage stall, and until we'd started pulling things out to send into true storage, I'd forgotten it was there, buried underneath a show cooler. Pete pulled the cooler away, and there it was. The leaping horses carved into the wood glowed, as the afternoon sunlight pouring into the stall seemed to bring them to life.

"What's in here, Pete, the Ark of the Covenant?" I joked nervously, and he shrugged, grinning up at me as he flicked open the latches and lifted the lid.

"Oh," I sighed, catching sight of the treasures within, and knelt down beside him.

He lifted out the saddle first, the chocolate-colored leather so buttery-rich with life I had to touch it for myself. This was an antique jumping saddle, yet it still bore all the marks of loving care. I touched the brass nameplate on the back, with his grandfather's name engraved in classic Roman letters.

"Pete, this is heavenly." The rich aroma of the leather wafted from the trunk and my contentment was complete. There was no perfume on earth so heady as the scent of a good saddle.

"I learned to jump in this saddle," Pete said fondly. "He left it in his will to me. This and his boots, but they don't fit my calves. He was so slim."

I glanced past the saddle cradled in his arms and saw the boots resting on the floor of the trunk. I pulled them out—they were hunt tops, stuffed with wooden boot trees and polished to a high sheen. I slipped out the boot tree of one to read the bootmaker's signature inside. "Vogels! Pete, these are exquisite. You should have them altered to fit you. They'll last forever the way you've kept them up."

"I didn't want to see anyone cut into them but Vogel." Pete sighed. "I'd hate for anyone to ruin them."

"Sounds like a trip to New York is necessary." I slipped the boot tree back into place. "We'll put it on the list. So is this going to the storage unit?"

"I was thinking . . . we don't have the room, but . . ." He put the saddle back into the trunk with all the care of a mother with an infant. "They're kind of my good luck. Like my grandfather is with me."

We didn't have any good luck, I thought, but there was no reason to point that out. And for all I knew, everything we had was due to our own peculiar version of luck. Maybe without it, we would have been forced out of the game a long time ago. Maybe we'd be working in offices somewhere. Maybe none of this ever would have happened.

What a nightmare that would be.

"We'll find the room."

Pete closed the trunk and leaned against me. I leaned back into him, letting the January sunshine wash over us for a few moments of quiet. In a minute Alex would bring Tiger back in, and the afternoon would start up again: horses to bring in, evening feed, the usual tumult of whinnies and kicks and snorts. That was all I wanted, I thought. That was all we needed.

ABOUT THE AUTHOR

Natalie Keller Reinert is the award-winning author of more than twenty books, including the Eventing and Briar Hill Farm series. Drawing on her professional experience in three-day eventing, working with Thoroughbred racehorses, mounted patrol horses, therapeutic riding, and many other equine pursuits, Natalie brings her love of equestrian life into each of her titles. She also cohosts the award-winning equestrian humor podcast *Adulting with Horses*. Natalie lives in north Florida with her family, horses, and cat.

www.nataliekreinert.com